THI

The Bid

A novel by
Alec McGivan and Hugh Roderick

YOUCAXTON
PUBLICATIONS

FOREWORD

This book has its origins in discussions at my hospital bedside five years ago. I had suffered a serious stroke, recovery from which was to keep me in the Oxford Centre for Enablement for the best part of three months.

This came on top of having been diagnosed with Parkinson's disease five years before that. Although there is no cure for Parkinson's at the moment, and each case is different, it is generally agreed that regular exercise can often slow the disease down.

I knew as I lay in hospital that in addition to exercise I needed to set myself some challenges and targets in the years that lay ahead, things that would keep me motivated and active. One ambition that I put on my list was to write a novel, something I had wanted to do for a long time.

I felt reasonably confident that I could write something worth reading. However, given the physical and mental effort that I knew would be involved, I concluded there was a lot to be said for finding a coauthor to share the load. One of my visitors was long standing friend Hugh Roderick, and the rest as they say is history – or in this case fiction.

Alec McGivan

ACKNOWLEDGEMENTS

I want to record my gratitude to all those who have given their time to read manuscripts of *The Bid* and to offer advice, especially Nick Barron, Mark Brown, John Burdass, Michael Drury, Nick Edwards, Rob Gargett, Gill Green, Tony Halmos, Bob Howarth, Stephen Navin, Keir Radnedge, Sybil Ruscoe, Ben Stoneham, Frank Wheeler, Jack Woolley, and Ian (not the footballer) Wright.

A lifelong thanks to my brother Malcolm for all his companionship watching Bristol City at The Gate over nearly sixty years, and to Andy Lewis whose personal friendship and support is beyond the call.

A massive 'thank you' as well to Hazel Ruscoe whose energy, professionalism and sheer enthusiasm has made such a difference. The added benefit of Hazel's involvement is that she has brought back happy memories of working together on Euro 96. Finally, my personal thanks to Hugh Roderick who agreed to join me in writing this story and claims to have no regrets.

Alec McGivan

ABOUT THE AUTHORS

Alec McGivan

Alec was born and brought up in Bristol, the son of Welsh parents. From his first day at university he became involved in politics, joining the Labour Party and subsequently playing a lead role in mobilizing the student vote to win back the marginal seat of Oxford in the October 1974 general election.

In 1981 he was appointed National Organiser of the Social Democratic Party (SDP), the new party's first member of staff. He quickly established a reputation as a formidable campaigner in a series of high-profile parliamentary by-election victories.

A decade or so later Alec was recruited by The Football Association to be part of its management team, set up to plan and stage-manage the highly acclaimed Euro 96 tournament. He then became Director of a bid to stage the World Cup in 2006. Following the bid, Alec joined the BBC, working first on the project to renew the BBC's Charter and then as Head of BBC Outreach.

Hugh Roderick

By a strange coincidence, Hugh Roderick was also born in Bristol to Welsh parents. But the authors first met much later, while living in the same village in Oxfordshire.

After university Hugh became a journalist, specialising in education. He went on to write speeches for Government Ministers (including Shirley Williams... coincidentally one of the SDP 'Gang of Four' that Alec was working with shortly afterwards) and IBM UK's chairman and CEO. Hugh later headed marketing and communications at the Science Museum, and then became director of a corporate marketing agency.

To Liz, Tom and Flora

Power tends to corrupt and absolute power corrupts absolutely.

First Baron Acton (1834–1902)

Contents

Requiem

It was the eyes that held her attention. Despite the cruel disfiguring of the rest of his face, the eyes still spoke to her with deep emotion.

Puzzled, she thought of Rudy, all those years ago when the local farmer carried him back in his arms to the family home. A face just as disfigured, she remembered, but the dog's eyes had borne no expression.

She had never seen a dead man before. Is this what always happens, she wondered. The human eyes living on when the rest of the body is broken. Or was this the special reflection of a tormented mind, frozen at the moment of a bloody death. She shivered as she stroked his cheek.

Two men at the door were whispering. She glared at them and they left the room.

'*Oh, mein armer Liebling*,' she said when all was quiet again, and softly kissed the dead man's forehead.

She sat on the side of the bed for a few moments with her back to the man's body, struggling to control her feelings. Then she rose steadily and decisively.

She peered down at him, took a tissue from a bedside box, wiped away a little smear of lipstick, and snapped the used tissue into her evening bag.

She stood and looked at him again. Then she took a deep breath, smoothed down her dress, and left the room.

In seconds she returned, unfastened the '*Ne pas déranger*' sign from the inside handle and hooked it to the outside of the door as she closed it for the last time.

Chapter 1

Safe hands

July 1995...two years earlier...
'Gentlemen, we are more powerful than kings and queens and presidents. We have more countries affiliated to our Global Football Organisation than belong to the United Nations. We are rulers of the greatest game in the world....'

The twenty-four men around the boardroom table nodded and muttered in agreement, and some applauded politely. The meeting was underway. World football was in safe hands.

Less than a month had passed since the 1995 GFO World Cup in Australia. It had been a triumph. Record numbers had watched the matches on television. Sponsorship had soared above the levels of World Cup 1991. The GFO's decision to allow an emerging football nation to host its flagship event had been justified.

But even while basking in World Cup success, President Larsen liked to remind the Global Football Organisation's Board members how heavy their responsibilities were. As he welcomed them to the Ritz Hotel in Paris that morning, his beaming face turned into a well-rehearsed, more serious expression.

'Gentlemen, we must never forget that football is more than just a game,' he said as he looked meaningfully around their meeting room. 'Football is a business. Beyond our national and local organisations, and our clubs, millions of people are employed in the business of football, making billions of dollars every year. And football business relies on us – all of us – for its worldwide success.'

The Napoleon Lounge on the first floor of the Ritz Paris was more opulent than the Imperial, the Windsor, the Ernest Hemingway, or any of the hotel's other iconic suites.

Furnished – anachronistically, perhaps, given its name – with original Louis Quartorze tables and chairs, chests and cabinets, chandeliers and mirror frames, the lounge sparkled with lapis lazuli, agate, marble, silver, gold, tortoiseshell, and ivory. The heavy terracotta curtain fabrics framed the floor-to-ceiling paintings and tapestries with effortless elegance. The room was a simple but spectacular statement. This was a meeting place for special people. Men who expected to be surrounded by the finest things, but who didn't expect to marvel at them.

The meeting in the Napoleon Lounge that day carried a full agenda, weighty with policies and decisions to be made. But it ended promptly at 4:30 pm – as Board meetings always did – to allow plenty of time for drinks with the ladies before dinner. These 'ladies' were the first ladies of football. They travelled the world with their husbands. And President Larsen made sure they were treated with respect and generosity by the Organisation.

The ladies didn't involve themselves in the politics, but they did engage in the shopping.

'I do so love Paris,' Giselle Schneider confided to Vice President Juan Gutierrez as she sipped her third glass of Krug Clos d'Ambonnay before dinner. 'I have a clear understanding with Helmut. He gives me his allowance and I am content. Of course, I spend the lot every time but he doesn't care. He doesn't need it!'

She snorted a naughty giggle, and her glass trembled in her grasp. Juan found her girlishness endearing. It distinguished her from some of the other GFO wives, who seemed to take the benefits of their men's positions entirely for granted. Juan was proud of the Organisation and its generosity, and he puffed out his chest as he delivered news he knew would delight Giselle. 'My dear, perhaps you haven't heard that the allowance threshold was raised again today. "For the wives" the President said... and he is right of course.

The "most important decision of the day" the President said,' Juan smiled. 'A bit of an exaggeration perhaps, but not much of one. We must keep the ladies happy mustn't we?' His smile broadened as he read the pleasure in Giselle's face.

'HOW exciting!' she purred. 'Helmut didn't mention it to me, but then I've hardly seen him since the meeting finished.' She sipped from her glass and took a furtive glance over Juan's shoulder. If she had noticed that Juan was attempting a mild flirtation, she had no intention of acknowledging it.

'He's probably fixing something,' Juan continued. 'Your husband is very good fixer. He's so clever at doing deals. I imagine you have very little time to talk together...'

Juan was suddenly aware that the citrus fragrance of Dolce & Gabbana perfume was no longer wafting under his nose. Giselle had caught the eye of Chiara Moretti and was lip-brushing her cheeks before Juan had finished his sentence. 'Chiara darling!'... 'Darling Giselle!'

Christian Larsen understood the value of the GFO women who supported their Board-member husbands. He always made a fuss of them.

'Tonight it is my pleasure,' he said as the guests relaxed after dinner that evening, 'to propose a toast to our wonderful ladies.'

He held his glass high above his head and beamed at the women around the dinner table one by one, silently mouthing each of their names in turn as he gestured his glass towards them.

'Ladies, we know how much you love Paris. Tomorrow, please enjoy the sights of the city.' He paused. 'We know of course you will enjoy the shopping.' His pale blue eyes twinkled as he paused again, waiting to deliver the little joke he had carefully prepared.

'Just don't bankrupt us please!'

The men of the GFO Board responded at once, the women took their cue, and the laughter around the room grew more certain. Some of the men banged the table with the flat of their hands. Some of the women exchanged winks and stage whispered little pleasantries between each other. The President knew his teasing joke would be well received, but he was pleased to hear it confirmed. He waited, grinning, until he could be heard again above the laughter.

'Ladies... your good health!'

President Larsen sat down briefly to allow the waiters to refill glasses. After a few words with Vice President Juan Gutierrez, sitting two chairs away, he smoothed back his thick white hair and again got to his feet.

'The second important duty I have to discharge tonight,' he said as the room grew respectfully silent, 'is to welcome our very, very good friends Albert and Monica Lewis from the English Football Organisation to their first GFO Board meeting. Albert,' he inclined his head towards the English man in a baggy dinner jacket, sitting midway down the table. His voice became serious once again. 'Albert, you represent the home of football.' There were murmurings of agreement across the room. 'England gave birth to our wonderful game, and we are proud you have taken your rightful place within our football family, at the decision-making table for the whole of world football.'

As he listened to the applause, Albert, who had never met Larsen before that morning in the hotel lobby, was struck by how imposing the President was – more impressive than newspaper images suggested, he thought. He might be seventy-one years of age, ten years older than the Englishman, but he was still youthfully slim, tall and commanding with words. Supremely confident, too, thought Albert enviously. The President used no notes.

Albert guessed that Monica would tell him later that Larsen had a 'way with women' despite his years, and Albert didn't doubt that she was right.

The President might have appeared to speak spontaneously, but he had of course thought very carefully about how to address the new Board member and his wife. He had a deliberate purpose: to win their enduring loyalty.

Christian Larsen preferred that members of the Board never disagreed with his or the Organisation's decisions in public. Unquestioning allegiance and total confidentiality were the standards he expected. That commitment tended to happen naturally as new men joined the GFO Board, particularly once members realised how much they had to lose if they broke the unspoken rules. But the President never left anything to chance. He knew that his charming welcome to new arrivals was an important first-strike weapon in fostering uncritical devotion.

At tonight's dinner, the English – not always the easiest allies – must be made to feel valued. And it must also be made clear to Albert Lewis that his presence amongst football's elite owed much – perhaps everything – to President Larsen's personal influence.

'As you know, Albert, I made England's case quite forcibly to your Prime Minister only last year when I visited him at Downing Street,' the President continued with a casual wave of his hand.

'To have little Wales as the UK flag bearer on our GFO Board never seemed quite right to me. Indeed,' he smiled, 'it was rather absurd.' There were chuckles at this daringly undiplomatic aside.

'So I am so pleased that your Prime Minister acted on my advice. England has been absent from football's top table for too long. And how right it is that you, Albert, should be our English delegate. How pleased we are that, after all your dedicated service in Cornwall, you have finally reached the highest echelons of the game.'

Albert glanced at Monica, sitting on the President's immediate right, but she didn't meet his eyes. Perhaps she was worried he would blush and seem foolish. Yes of course, and she was right to be worried, he thought, as the President peered at him down the table.

'Your achievements are so impressive Albert...'

He turned away from Lewis as if to share his information confidentially with the others. 'Ladies and gentlemen, did you know that Albert does not even have any professional football clubs in the area where he works?'

There was a murmur of surprise. Larsen drank from his champagne glass and wiped his mouth with his napkin. The delay was perfectly timed for a change of pace and a final salute. Now he spoke more slowly, addressing himself directly to the Englishman.

'But, Albert,' he said solemnly, 'it's long-serving, dutiful men like you who we treasure most in our Organisation. You're the lifeblood of football. You're the heart and soul of our great game.'

Albert stared resolutely at the plate in front of him, desperate to avoid the President's gaze.

'So, congratulations, my dear friend,' the President concluded, as he turned to Monica beside him. 'My warmest welcome to you, Albert, and to Monica, your lovely wife.'

The President took his seat and the applause slowly died away. As diners began to talk and push their chairs from the table, he suddenly rose once again, as if something had slipped his mind.

'Oh, ladies and gentlemen, my sincere apologies. I have one other small thing to say to you. Perhaps I should have made this announcement in the Board meeting this afternoon, but I prefer to share it with all of you, ladies and gentlemen.'

The room went silent.

'Well it's only this,' and his voice was quiet, bashful perhaps. 'I've told the world's Press that I will not be standing as President again next year. After all, as you know, I've served the GFO for two terms, and I honestly believed that my football family would have had quite enough of me.'

The President took time to view the friendly faces around the room.

'It seems I was wrong,' he said. 'You see I've been overwhelmed, ladies and gentlemen...' his voice cracked slightly, and he wiped the corner of his eye with a napkin. 'Overwhelmed that so many people have come to plead with me to stand again in 1996.'

'Of course, dear friends, I have to remember I represent every member of the GFO, not just you, who are, may I say, the select members of our world-wide team. And unless I support the wishes of the smallest and most humble countries of the world, I feel here,' and he punched his chest hard, 'here...I'll be letting down the democratic spirit of our great Organisation.'

He listened to the sounds of approval around the table.

'And so, after much pressure from our members, I've decided that I'll stand for President once more – in all humility – to serve the interests of all our people everywhere.'

As he sat down, a huge cheer broke out. The President rose for the last time, raised his hand in acknowledgement, and nodded his gratitude.

At the other end of the table, there was a gleam in the eye of Joe Kumpa, representative of one of the poorer West African nations and President of AAFO, the Alliance of African Football Organisations. Joe was close to the President, and nothing would please him more than for their relationship to prosper for another four years.

Almost unnoticed as the men and women began to leave their chairs and chatter in groups, and as the waiters cleared away plates and glasses, Joe got to his feet and strode towards Larsen. The President smiled warmly as he saw him approach, and extracting himself from conversation with one of the wives, he motioned him to his side. Joe leant his big head close to the President.

'So.... good news for everyone,' Joe whispered, and his face broke into a wide grin. 'Tell me, Christian, just how many of our very special GFO members pleaded for you to stand again?'

The President's smile was inscrutable, but he was silent. 'I see,' said Joe, 'nobody.'

The President put his finger to his lips. Joe slapped him hard on the back, and emitted a guffaw.

'Very clever,' Joe said to himself, laughing loudly as he made his way back to his seat. Yes it was great news all round. The President would be standing for re-election, and the arrival of Albert Lewis was a bonus.

'Let's hope,' Joe whispered to Greg Turner, a Board member from Canada sitting beside him, 'that the Englishman's brought his cheque-book with him. All that money they spend on their Premier League needs redistributing to the rest of us,' he chuckled. 'And I'm first in line. I'm having lunch with our new friend Albert tomorrow, and I'll be making it quite clear, in the most friendly way of course, where his priorities lie.'

'Joe, you're never slow in coming forward,' Turner whispered back. He patted his colleague's arm. 'Let me know how you get on.'

Chapter 2

A gentleman's agreement

'So,' said Albert as he turned the key in the door of the Maréchal Foch Suite. 'I fancy a bit of telly before bed. D'you think they've got Sky?'

Monica looked at him severely. 'What d'you mean "before bed" Albert? You've got to go back down and talk to people. Didn't that German bloke ask you for drinks? And a few of the other men at dinner said they wanted to meet you. It's all very well having all this lovely food and champagne and luxury, but you're here to work.'

She broke off in amazement. 'Albert! What are you doing...?'

Albert was sitting on the four-poster bed. He had taken off his dinner jacket, unlaced and slipped off one shoe, and was rubbing his foot vigorously. He turned a world-weary face to his wife. It was a familiar look. Their daughter Angela called it his English sheepdog expression. Albert knew it would count for nothing that evening.

'Lovely food?' he grumbled. 'I couldn't tell you what half of it was, love. And that fizz always makes me burp anyhow. Oh, come on Monica, it's been a long day and these shoes are giving me terrible gyp. Tell you what. I'll leave a message with Helmut and say I'll meet him for coffee in the morning. I'm not seeing that Kumpa chap 'til lunchtime.'

'Albert! No! You'll get back downstairs and represent England.'

Monica was only 5'2". She had a lovely smile when she felt like using it and her round face could be cherubic when the light was right, but she could also be fearsome when she needed to be.

She was devoted to Albert, but although her love for him was unconditional, so was her determination to control his foolish behaviour.

Albert never took long to heed Monica's instructions. 'Alright love,' he said wearily, 'but just let me go and have a soak in the bath. It's only... what is it... nine o'clock? I'll just let the old joints relax for a bit.'

Monica smiled and kissed the top of Albert's balding head as he stretched out on the bed. Then her jaw dropped in horror. 'Albert! You've got your other shoe on the duvet now. Take it off, you silly man. Has all this high living made you forget your manners?'

Albert chuckled as he got to his feet and took off the rest of his clothes. Monica had disappeared into the bathroom. 'What are you going to do while I'm downstairs love?' he called to her as he put on a hotel bathrobe. 'Have you made a date with your new pal Christian?'

'That's not a bad idea,' she said as she opened the bathroom door. 'D'you think he'd like my negligee?' They both laughed. Monica was dressed from head to toe in pink pyjamas. 'No, I've done my bit, dear. Now I'm just going to lie on that comfy-looking settee over there and read my book,' she said. 'Go on, hurry up and have your bath Albert, or you'll miss out on your meetings.'

Albert hummed cheerfully to himself as he waited for the gushing water to fill the giant bathtub. He paced the room, measuring it by the length of his bare feet, and laughed out loud. Good grief, this bathroom was bigger than his dining room at home! He found a bottle of pink liquid, which he assumed to be bubble bath. He wondered for a moment whether to confirm its contents with Monica, but he felt reckless, and tipped half of it into the bath anyway.

He lay in the deep bubbling water, pondering the extraordinary events of the last twenty-four hours. Well, well, well, so here he was, Albert Lewis from Truro, staying in the fanciest hotel in fancy Paris. What was it that woman next to him had said at dinner?

'Not only the best bars, restaurants and spa. The Ritz is within easy ride of the most fashionable shops and finest museums and galleries in Europe'!

He shut his eyes for a moment. 'It's just unbelievable,' he mouthed to himself, and then he mouthed it again to make sure he wasn't asleep.

Albert's rise five years earlier to the EFO council had been remarkable enough, he thought to himself. Remarkable... but not without logical explanation.

There'd been reasons for his promotion from a football backwater to national headquarters. Finding good men from unfashionable regions – the 'grass-roots of the game' – was a big thing for the EFO. And his modest style, soft Cornish voice, and inexperience in football politics meant he was perceived to be no threat to the EFO hierarchy.

Anyway, he saw his EFO job as a fair reward for long and loyal service to football, and it made him proud. He wasn't vain, but he did like to impress his wife, family, and friends. But when last July EFO Chairman Sir Sidney Lovat suggested he might represent England on the GFO Board, it was altogether different.

He was, of course, deeply flattered by the idea of serving world football, but he was also seriously troubled by what it all meant. Why had he been nominated? Why not one of the other men? More articulate, more youthful, more representative of England's dominant football cities... Manchester... Liverpool... London? Why not the kind of man who regularly attended Downing Street receptions, and spoke at party-conference fringe meetings on football hooliganism?

Was he a compromise candidate, chosen because EFO decision makers couldn't agree on a favourite? Would he be controlled by his more powerful English colleagues, forced to follow their voting orders, and fight their battles on foreign fields? Or was it worse? Was he to be a patsy, expected to fail on the world stage as part of some devious plan he would never understand?

Some people in the EFO saw things more simply. 'Buggin's turn,' was the verdict from Alan Adams of the EFO Council. 'Old Lewis doesn't know what a lucky sod he is,' Adams had told a well-known English club manager.

'What a gravy train he'll get his snout into à *la* GFO! You know his missus has hardly been out of Cornwall? She'll be glad-handing it all round the world. First class this, first class that. She'll be like a pig in muck!'

But there was something that worried Albert even more than his nomination: as soon as he imagined himself sitting beside the world's great football administrators, he felt a horrible tightening of the muscles across his chest. It was a familiar feeling: he had doubted his own abilities for many years.

As a young man, at his first meeting of the Truro and District Football Organisation, he had heard sheer terror in his own voice. As time went by, being with his own people – football lovers first and amateur committee men second – he gained more confidence. As he rose to become County Committee Chairman, he taught himself how to get his arguments across more effectively, and how to quieten big mouths and empty heads.

When he joined the EFO Council, the presence of so many other older English men with similar education and social backgrounds soon assured him he could cope in London. But as he began to think about the global football stage, his fragile confidence began to desert him. Working alongside his fellow countrymen was one thing, but the GFO was abroad.

Albert and Monica Lewis hadn't travelled much in their long lives together. Monica had been a part-time health visitor before she retired. Outside work, her two children had been her main concern, and holidays had usually been to local seaside resorts. When she and Albert did plan their only family holiday overseas, they drove the 250 miles to London Heathrow and back the weekend before as a practice run. They also rehearsed several times what to say at the check-in desk.

Albert got more experience of international travel on the EFO Council. He certainly loved watching football in the great European capitals, but although he never admitted it to his fellow committee men, he hated flying.

And worst of all about 'abroad' were the football people he met in other countries. Those big tournament matches seemed to attract the most powerful GFO men and their wives, and Albert found them terrifying.

These people conversed confidently in languages other than their own, and many spoke English better than him. There were Middle Eastern sheikhs and Italian counts and African chiefs among them. There were men who owned islands and ships and oil companies.

As always happened when facing a crisis in his career, he had sought Monica's advice to get over this problem. He needed her help to explain to Sir Sidney why he couldn't accept the offer to join the GFO Board without embarrassing himself. And he had to have it quickly, because men like Alan Adams were leaking information, and the Press guys were speculating.

Albert had opened his soul to Monica about his doubts on a rainy Friday evening, as he drove her home from Bodmin station after her visit to the family in Bristol. Listening beside him, she was silent throughout the journey. Nor did she say a word about the matter as she re-heated left-over shepherd's pie for their dinner. Albert was confused and concerned. These silences usually presaged disagreement with whatever he had in mind.

'Well, Albert,' Monica said at last as they sat down at the table, looking deep into his eyes.

'So you think these men are better than you, do you? You think that all their money, and all their expensive schools count for more in the world of football than the years you've spent helping ordinary youngsters get better coaching, better pitches, better refs and better equipment?'

She paused, and her voice had a chill that Albert had only remembered once or twice in their married life. 'Well I'm surprised, Albert.' She spat out her words. 'No, I'm shocked by your lack of courage and respect for all you've done in your life.'

She got up from the table and handed Albert the phone. 'But if that's your decision, go ahead. You should phone the Chairman now and tell him.'

Nothing more was said. He did phone Sir Sidney, and agreed to his proposal with enthusiasm.

'Albert, it's nearly ten o'clock! Have you fallen asleep? Come on love, quickly, get out of that bath.'

Oh lord. Albert opened his eyes, and with a rush of water over the sides, he grabbed a towel and pulled himself out.

As he left the lift ten minutes later, Albert looked at the men and women sitting in groups in the Napoleon Lounge. He had changed into slacks and a tweed jacket, and his face was ruddy after his long bath. Most other guests were still dressed for dinner, and many were noisier and more unsteady than they had been an hour or so before.

He smiled to himself. He was glad he had chosen to drink British beer all evening rather than the champagne the others were drinking. Some of the ladies had thought that was rather sweet, Monica had told him, but he didn't mind. He didn't want to be tipsy and say the wrong things.

He sat down by the giant fireplace, but he couldn't see any of the men he had talked to earlier that day. Ten minutes passed. A waiter asked him if he would like a drink, but Albert declined. He rather fancied stepping out of the hotel and finding a little bar for a nightcap before slipping quietly up to bed. Monica would never know.

At just that moment, he noticed Helmut Schneider walking directly towards him and rose to greet him. The German nodded curtly. 'Albert,' he said. 'We'll meet upstairs in about ten minutes.

It's the Louis Pasteur Suite on the fifth floor.' It wasn't a question. 'I will call Alexei now.'

Albert made his way to Helmut's room reluctantly. His plan for a quiet drink on his own was scuppered. He didn't know why he was being summoned, but Albert knew it was sensible to agree to the German's invitation. Albert didn't know much about Alexei Baskin, or why he was coming to the meeting with Helmut. A little unnerved by Helmut's formality in the lounge, Albert just hoped the meeting would be congenial. He needn't have worried.

'Come in Albert, my friend.' Helmut gave Albert a fraternal bear hug, the customary greeting between GFO members, as he was quickly learning.

'Delighted to meet you at last,' Helmut beamed. 'Now what will you have to drink?' He waved his hand at a collection of bottles on a tray on the cabinet. Albert chose the first he recognised. 'Oh... a brandy I think. That would be nice.'

'Of course, of course. Now, Albert, we'll be joined in a minute by Alexei Baskin, our excellent colleague from Russia.' Helmut poured generously into Albert's Cognac glass. As if planned in advance, there was a loud knock at the door.

'Albert, it's my pleasure,' Alexei greeted him, giving him another warm hug.

'Now do sit down, both of you,' Helmut urged. He handed Albert his brandy, and, without asking, poured Alexei a Scotch.

'How are things in England, Albert?' Alexei began. 'No more violence at England matches?'

'No, no, no,' said Albert warily. 'I think we've put all that behind us now.' He thought about enlarging on the topic, describing the benefits of all-seater stadiums and how they were changing fans' behaviour and encouraging more families to watch football, but Helmut gave him no time.

'And Wembley?' asked Helmut. 'All well now? You've got your planning permission sorted out?'

'Oh yes,' said Alexei with a guffaw, 'that was funny. Your big new national stadium, and a lot of local politicians trying to stop it going ahead! What's been done about that?'

'Oh I think we've fixed that too,' said Albert cheerfully. He decided this was no time to be defensive about these jokes at England's expense. 'We've worked out how to persuade the local councils now!'

The three men laughed and Albert was pleased. This was going well. Alexei raised his glass. 'Well, here's to the new Wembley. We look forward to playing there.'

Helmut had taken a flat-backed chair beside Alexei's plush armchair. He rose a little higher in his seat, indicating he now wanted discussions to become more serious. Albert began to feel a little tense.

'Well Albert,' Helmut Schneider began, with authority. 'There is one matter we particularly want to talk to you about tonight.'

'You see,' Helmut continued, picking up a cigar box from the coffee table in front of them, and handing it to Alexei, 'there's the question of the World Cup in 2003.' He paused and looked carefully at Albert. 'Of course, we all agree in Europe that it is our turn again in eight years' time.'

'Oh yes,' Albert replied, relieved that this was a subject he understood well enough. 'Absolutely right. Of course, it must be Europe after Argentina.'

'I'm glad we agree.' Helmut paused and glanced at Alexei. 'Well, Albert, the thing is this. As Europe's elder statesmen on the Board, the others in the European group will look to us for a lead. And we think it should be one of our countries that stages the tournament. We're not expecting any other European country to get involved.'

'I see,' said Albert, privately delighted to be viewed already as an elder statesman, and consulted on such an important decision. He took a large sip from his glass. 'Makes sense to me,' he said with a growing sense of authority.

'I'm glad you see it that way Albert,' Alexei said, as he drew slowly on his cigar. 'You see one or two people have mentioned that England might have ideas of its own. That would be rather inconvenient to say the least. So we're looking for reassurance from you, Albert, as a new member of the club, and one of the other big beasts in Europe shall we say, that you'll stick to the party line and not get involved in the bidding.'

Albert slowly realised he had been mistaken. The two men weren't talking about him as an elder statesman. Before he had time to react, however, Alexei had moved the conversation on.

'Helmut and I will sort out which of us will bid, but we would like to be sure that England doesn't get in the way... if you don't mind me being blunt.'

Through the brandy fumes, Albert heard himself reassuring Alexei. 'Oh no, I think I can safely say we'll go along with your plans,' he said, raising his glass to his lips.

In truth, Albert hadn't given the staging of World Cups a moment's thought since his appointment to the GFO. It seemed a long time off to be thinking about 2003, just a month after Australia 95, and he had certainly heard no discussion at the EFO. Anyway, Helmut and Alexei seemed to have a good plan in place to bring the World Cup to Europe, and he felt it was important that he showed solidarity with his European colleagues at his first Board meeting.

'Of course we'd like to host it again someday,' Albert added, in case he'd sounded too unambitious. 'But we can wait. Don't worry about it at all,' he said with a shy smile.

'That's good, that's very good.' Helmut and Alexei beamed at each other, and at Albert. Helmut rose to fill the glasses

'You're a very good chap Albert,' Helmut added, with what seemed to Albert to be genuine warmth. 'Very gentlemanly. Just like the English!'

'So, how exactly are you going to decide who bids between you?' Albert asked. He felt that this warm moment offered a wonderful opportunity to learn more about how these matters were handled at the top levels of world football.

'Oh don't worry about that my dear fellow,' said Helmut. 'We'll sort it out, won't we, Alexei? I think you would call it a "gentleman's agreement" Albert.'

He chuckled, and Alexei nodded and smiled. The Russian wasn't familiar with the term 'gentleman's agreement' but he was confident that Helmut's choice of words fitted their arrangement.

'Yes, we'll have a plan Albert,' Alexei said. 'It's the way Helmut and I like to do business. There'll be competition from outside Europe of course. Africa will want to have a go perhaps.'

'Yes, I can see that,' said Albert thoughtfully, and ventured a personal view. 'And surely the Asians will want to try, won't they?'

'Yes they will,' said Helmut quickly, 'but if we get enough support from South America and the USA, as well as Europe of course, we should be ok.'

The men chatted on for a while, although Albert sensed that the other two were not really interested in his views or his questions. Albert didn't like Alexei's cigar smoke, but he was certainly enjoying Helmut's brandy.

He sank deep into his chair and let the conversation wash over him. This was a long way from Cornwall or London, he thought. Meetings there were tame compared to this. Here he was discussing with two of the most powerful men in world football where the World Cup should be staged in eight years' time! He had information that would dominate the front page of every major newspaper if he disclosed it, he smiled to himself. He felt slightly giddy.

'Of course,' said Helmut, 'we must also talk to you about the next GFO Presidential election now that President Larsen has declared his plans, but we'll do that another time.'

Raising his glass, he added: 'So, welcome to the world's most exclusive club Albert. Now you'd better get back to your lovely wife I think. And if you don't mind, Alexei and I have other business to discuss.'

Albert took a moment to realise that the meeting was now at an end. Getting up unsteadily, he shook Alexei and Helmut by the hand, gave them a big, conspiratorial smile, and tried to remember which direction to turn to for the lifts as the two men closed the door behind him.

Albert eventually reached the Maréchal Foch rooms, found his key in his pocket, and unlocked the door. He was pleased that Monica was already in bed asleep. No need for explanations, then, and no give-away speech slurring either. He was quickly asleep as well, his loud snoring muffled by the thick walls of the room.

Chapter 3

Night fever

Not many other members of the GFO party were asleep when Albert closed his eyes that night. The Paris meeting was popular for more than just spectacular comfort and luxury shopping. There were also good casinos nearby, and darkened clubs where friendships and affairs could be nurtured.

Vice President Juan Gutierrez had guessed earlier in the day that Helmut would be in a late-night meeting, so he had invited Giselle Schneider to take a limousine with him to La Cave, the basement dance club he remembered well from past meetings in the city. Giselle had other plans, but a group of wives whose husbands were at the Antichambre casino party, or who had simply 'gone missing' that evening, were pleased to join him.

Juan's wife had been too unwell to travel from Chile, as was, sadly, often the case. He was a good-looking man, more Western than Andean in appearance, and at the right middle-age where women either convinced themselves they were safe in his company or were pleased that they weren't.

The Vice President's role might have been invented for Juan. It meant he was on the guest list at every major football event. He knew all the important GFO people, and those he didn't know worked hard to persuade him that he did. Mainly a courtesy post, Vice-Presidential duties rarely took him away from the social side. This lack of business involvement suited him well.

He had achieved his post because the GFO needed South American representation, not because of his abilities or ambitions. His standing in the organisation, his looks, easy charm, and wealth as heir to a successful timber merchant, all offered him pleasures enough.

Juan had a thing for Giselle. Unlike many of the other GFO ladies he admired, Giselle's appeal was subtly sexy. She had style, intelligence, and maturity. She was self-assured, reflecting her husband's power and influence but also her own success as a lawyer in Munich. Imagining this confident woman naked in his bed, giving herself to him, was exciting.

Juan also knew that Giselle was alone for much of her life because of Helmut's busy career, and he guessed that her marriage was not so secure that she wasn't averse to seeking a handsome lover. He was disappointed that she wasn't joining him this evening, but he could bide his time.

Meanwhile, another woman had caught his eye at drinks before dinner. Nina was thirty-two, one of the youngest GFO wives in Paris. Her husband, Tomislav Kovac, President of the Croatian Football Organisation, was seventy-eight, and one of the older men on the GFO Board. Juan hadn't met Nina before that evening. He had heard that Tomislav had remarried after his wife's death last year but assumed the new bride would be closer to the man's age.

There had been plenty of jokes before dinner about Nina's reasons for marrying a man nearly fifty years older than her. Chiara Moretti, an old friend of Juan's, had no doubts about her motives or her morals. Juan was little concerned with either.

Juan was intrigued by how quickly Nina had accepted his invitation to the nightclub. It wasn't difficult to notice Nina. Her golden Versace dress was slashed from the shoulder to the waist. He could hardly keep his eyes off her as she walked towards his party in the hotel lobby.

Nina had not made many friends amongst the other wives and she seemed genuinely grateful to Juan for his attention. They sat next to each other in the limousine, and as it pulled away at the traffic lights on Avenue George V, Juan felt the warmth of her thigh against his.

The other two ladies in the group, Julie Bresset and Luciana Garcia, knew each other well, and were happy to spend the car-ride talking together. They also knew Juan well enough, enjoyed his flirting, but had no intention of jeopardising their marriages by having affairs with him. They were confident that they would attract handsome young Parisian men that evening who would hold them closely on the dancefloor. That experience would be pleasant and reassuring enough.

Despite his growing interest in Nina, Juan was still careful to remember his manners. He had unfailing confidence in his ability to impress women of all ages.

'Julie, you are looking so gorgeous this evening,' he grinned across at her in the car. 'Just like a film star.' Wife of Belgium's Board member Serge Bresset, Julie was now in her late fifties, slim and elegant and quite able to handle Juan's thickly applied compliments. She smiled at him and blew a kiss.

'Ah, but I'm no competition for the lovely Nina.' Juan laughed and Nina's face was blank.

'And Luciana, is that a new hair style today? It really brings out the colour of your eyes. It makes you look so young, darling.'

The limousine drew noiselessly to a halt outside the entrance to La Cave. Julie Bresset stepped out first. Dazzled for a moment by the photographers' camera flashes, she peered in wonder at the giant floodlit pink elephant beside the door. She grinned at Luciana and started to say something but at that moment the door was opened and a rush of high-volume house music made talking impossible.

Juan led the way between two plastic lime green columns into the smoked glass lobby. Stopping to make sure his party was complete, he led on down three flights of stairs, following the music to the dance floor.

At the small table booked for Juan by the hotel concierge earlier in the evening, Juan and Nina sat closely together. The music was so loud that their heads needed to be almost touching to have any conversation. Juan made sure that his thigh was firmly pressed against hers. Nina made no attempt to move her leg away, and when she caught him glancing at her breast beneath her gaping dress, she smiled encouragingly. 'I suppose Tomislav is gambling away your fortune, Nina,' Juan said. Nina laughed. 'Tomislav? Oh no, he'll be in bed asleep now. He has so many pills he can't stay awake after 10 o'clock.'

Juan thought for a moment about this delightful news. 'Then you must be very careful not to be too late, Nina,' he twinkled. 'He will want to know you are safely in the room.'

Nina looked away and said nothing. Then she peered into Juan's black eyes, and put her lips close to his ear. Juan could only hear her breathing heavily at first, but suddenly she spoke. 'Perhaps you should know. Tom and I have an agreement. He knows I wouldn't have married him if I couldn't have my needs... satisfied... regularly ...'

'Now what do you think of that, Mr Vice President?' she said after a moment's pause. She didn't move her lips from his ear and ran the flat of her hand up Juan's thigh with practised skill. She smiled as she turned her head to look at him.

'And tell me. Are the rumours about you true?'

The Whistleblower writes...'
A' is for Avarice at the GFO bunfight
In the alphabet of world football, surely 'A' ought to stand for accountability. After all, millions follow the sport across the globe, as World Cup Australia has recently confirmed. The least that FANS can expect is that those who preside over the game are held to account for the way they run things, and how they spend the oodles of money that football now generates.

But when the GFO Board is in action, it's not hard to see why supporters everywhere feel so removed from the fat cats in charge of things.

Wherever they are in the world, GFO people always stay in the best five-star hotel in town. They sweep up to whatever grand events they are attending in chauffeur-driven limos. Expensive gifts are lavished by their hosts on wives as well as on the (exclusively male) members. And they strut about like Mafia bosses until they arrive at their destination: always the best seats in the metaphorical Royal Box.

When they meet together – as the GFO Board did a few days ago – the cities chosen are always favourites for shopping and night life. Paris is right up there. Of course Whistleblower cannot be sure what the GFO Board men and their wives actually get up to, because the meeting is private and security is impenetrable. But the number of gleaming German limousines leaving and arriving back at the hotel in the early hours suggest that GFO expense accounts took a bit of a battering last week. But who's to know or care?

It wouldn't be quite so bad if more of these people actually showed some interest in the game itself. Like the enthusiastic fans who regularly spend their hard-earned money on ridiculously expensive match tickets and travel arrangements at the international tournaments that the GFO men organise.

Chapter 4

Big beasts at sea

August 1995

'You might have lost the Cold War, Alexei, but you certainly won the peace.'

Alexei Baskin couldn't be sure whether Helmut's joshing comment hid bitterness, or whether it was a compliment for the fifty-five-metre yacht they were about to board at Cannes that warm Summer morning. Alexei had known the German football supremo since joining the Global Football Organisation's Board five years before, but their relationship had always been strictly business: football business. International affairs were the backdrop for the plans and policies of both men but they were not politicians, and Alexei had no wish to discuss his country's transformation since *glasnost* – particularly (he admitted to himself) with a German.

Anyway, he and Helmut were living proof of the new mood in Europe in the 1990s. Their countries might be historic enemies, but the two men could now work together to deliver a new goal for their people: domination in world football. Alexei knew all about the past, but he was delighted by the present. And if his cousin Stas had made enough money from property development to buy a yacht, he wasn't going to apologise to Schneider. He was pleased for Stas and grateful for the opportunities it provided Alexei and the new Russia.

'Sasha, come and take these cases,' Alexei called to the steward as his party reached the deck steps.

The day hadn't begun well. When Alexei drove Stas's car to meet Helmut at the Mouette Hotel on the Boulevard de la Croisette, he was cross and confused to find Giselle was also in the lobby, clearly ready to join them on *Bright Skies*. His invitation a month before had been directed only at Helmut. His purpose was to finalise bidding plans for the World Cup, not to enjoy a weekend of leisure with the women.

He liked Giselle, she was fun, and attractive, but he knew she wouldn't be happy to be left alone while the two men were in discussion. If he'd known that Giselle was to be there, he would have made sure there was another woman on board, he thought crossly to himself as he parked the Porsche in one of the old harbour private bays. He would have invited his girlfriend Malia.

Giselle and Malia would hardly be soul mates, of course. Malia was barely out of her teens, and her attractions were more physical than cerebral. Giselle was a forty-five-year-old lawyer with teenage children. But at least Malia would have occupied Giselle's attention while the two men talked.

Helmut appeared to be unaware of Alexei's irritation as the Russian directed the Schneiders towards their cabin suite, and this made Alexei even more annoyed. It was typical of Helmut to do just what suited him, Alexei thought, and as *Bright Skies* headed out from the harbour towards Théoule-sur-Mer, his conversation was stilted.

Like Helmut, Giselle seemed not to notice any coolness, and as she applied cream to her dozing husband's fair-skinned pate as they all lay on the sun deck enjoying the mid-morning warmth, she talked cheerily to Alexei.

Alexei was a small man of forty-one with a good head of light brown curly hair brushed back from his brow. He was not conventionally handsome, but his eyes sparkled mischievously and when each of his two marriages failed, he found no difficulty in attracting lovers. Younger women enjoyed his wealth and the treats he was able to provide. But he tired quickly of girls who offered no challenge to him.

Alexei was well aware of his appeal to women, and as Helmut dozed beside them, he found himself enjoying Giselle's attention. She was clearly impressed by *Bright Skies*, and Alexei felt a glow of pride that this urbane, intelligent and well-travelled woman was so interested in such a symbol of the Baskin family's success. She had stayed on yachts before of course, she told Alexei, but never one with its own helipad!

He hadn't seen Giselle in a bikini before that morning. She was tall and willowy, and as slim as any of his younger girlfriends, but her breasts were much larger than he had imagined from seeing her in formal dresses. As Sasha poured more champagne for them both, Alexei became increasingly spellbound. Giselle's flattering remarks about *Bright Skies* turned quickly into insistent questions about his marriages.

After twenty minutes or so, their conversation paused and Alexei wondered whether he was misreading the situation. Surely, he decided, Giselle was simply behaving as the attentive and charming wife of a business colleague, embarrassed perhaps that Alexei was alone, and wanting to ease any friction between the two men.

Besides, he thought, this was a dangerous game. He and Helmut were about to plan an important strategy for their football organisations, with huge revenue implications for their nations for many years ahead. Flirting with Helmut's wife was not a helpful step in their negotiations.

As if Giselle had read his mind, she suddenly looked at her watch, sat upright, and reached to her side for her wrap.

'Goodness! Sasha said that lunch is at 12:30, Alexei. I'd better freshen up. Do wake Helmut for me please.'

And with that, she walked elegantly along the deck and through the door down to her cabin below. Alexei watched her go and wondered to himself what their short time together had all meant.

He smiled to himself. Whatever its meaning, Giselle's company had certainly made this voyage more pleasurable than he had imagined an hour or so earlier.

At lunch, two bottles of chilled Sancerre enlivened conversation as the party took shade in the dining room on the main deck. Helmut now appeared to be genuinely interested in the boat, its manner of construction, its speed, where it was registered, the difficulties of maintaining an onboard crew, and how often Stas and his young family used it.

'Just imagine if we owned something like this,' mused Giselle.

'Our kids would be having parties on it the whole time,' Helmut responded with a loud laugh.

By mid-afternoon, *Bright Skies* was anchored off the Plage de l'Aiguille at Théoule-sur-Mer, where a tender transported them through the shallow water to the beach. Helmut decided he wanted to stroll along the sand to find a bar out of the sun for a beer. He asked Giselle, slightly half-heartedly, if she wanted to join him. When she refused, he nodded a brusque goodbye to them both.

Alexei stripped down to his shorts and laid three *Bright Skies* beach towels on the sand, with a respectful half a metre distance between them. He turned aside to light a cigarette away from the breeze, and when he turned back to Giselle he saw she was topless, lying on her back.

'I love the sun,' Giselle smiled as if by way of explanation, before closing her eyes.

They both slept until late afternoon and were woken by Helmut. 'Come on you two, you'll fry if you're not careful.'

It wasn't a serious concern. Helmut's skin was pink and sensitive to the sun, but the other two had bodies that were nut brown. Alexei woke groggily, stood up and waved to the tender offshore to collect them. Giselle covered herself with her wrap.

That evening, *Bright Skies* anchored off St Raphael. Dinner was to be served at 7:30, and Alexei was in the dining room at 7:15, sipping a gin and French Martini as he waited for his guests to arrive. Helmut appeared at 7:25, alone.

'My dear Alexei, I'm so sorry; Giselle has a dreadful headache. Too long in the sun, I'm afraid. She won't be joining us for dinner. Perhaps Sasha can organise some sandwiches for her?'

Alexei told Helmut how sad he was to hear that news and chided himself for letting her sleep for so long on the beach. He called Sasha, and they all agreed that an omelette would be best. The two men sat down to eat their dinner shortly afterwards.

'These coquilles are superb,' Helmut said, 'as good as any Paris restaurant, you know.'

Alexei nodded his agreement but was keen to talk business. He wanted to use this time with Helmut to good purpose.

'Well Helmut, I guess we have a clear understanding about our bidding plans,' he said, pushing his empty plate away. He lit a cigarette. 'Russia will bid for the 2003 GFO World Cup, leaving Germany clear to have the Euro Cup in 2005. I think with mutual support and a little help from our powerful friend above, we will make this happen, don't you?'

He took a long drag from his cigarette but continued without waiting for Helmut's response.

'It's Europe's turn, and we're the big beasts in the European jungle.' He liked this analogy: the big Russian bear. It recalled memories of the children's books he had read. He paused in thought before speaking again.

'I'm sure you have also heard that the English might bid after all, despite what Lewis told us in Paris only a few months ago. Shows what he knows. But they haven't a chance, don't you agree Helmut?'

Helmut smiled but said nothing. He also lit a cigarette. Alexei got to his feet and scanned the shore lights.

'As for the rest of the world,' Baskin continued, 'I hear China and Morocco are thinking about a bid. But they don't have any kind of support in the GFO do they? Have they ever lobbied the

Board in the past? I don't think so. And why would our... powerful friends... want them to win anyway?'

'Although the Argentinians are getting 1999, don't discount the South Americans altogether for 2003, my friend,' Helmut said. 'I think the new government might make the Brazilians bid – even though their biggest fear would be winning. It would break their banks!'

Sasha arrived at the table and cleared the dinner plates, filling the men's wine glasses on his return.

'Of course, Helmut, I can't stress how grateful my people are that you're not bidding against Russia for 2003,' Alexei beamed. 'It will make us feel very confident about our prospects for success, and our two countries will have a wonderful new relationship to take forward to the Euro Cup... and for the years ahead.'

Alexei lifted his glass. 'Za vashe zrodovye Helmut!'

But Helmut didn't raise his glass. His fingers were clenched together and his elbows were firmly planted on the table.

'Well sadly my friend, life may not be that simple.'

There was silence between them. Alexei was immediately alarmed. What did Helmut mean? This was a deal that the two men had discussed years ago. Was Helmut going to renege on it?

But the German didn't seem aware of any change in the atmosphere as he calmly explained the situation.

'You see, Alexei, my people will not accept that Germany isn't bidding for the 2003 World Cup.'

Alexei made no reply. He stared blankly at Schneider. Helmut hadn't wanted to make this conversation longer than it needed to be, but he knew he would have to expand on what he had said to reassure the Russian. Worst of all, he would have to frame his explanation apologetically.

'I am sorry,' he said with as much emotion as he could muster, 'but Alexei you have to understand that I'm under far more pressure to bid than I'd ever expected. That's the trouble with us Germans,' he said with an uncomfortable smile. 'If there's a contest going on, we have to be part of it. Even if winning is impossible, we have to be seen to be trying as hard as we can. It's the same on and off the pitch.' He wanted to say that was why German forces had continued to fight long after World War 2 was lost but thought better of it.

'So you see, Alexei, my people will just not accept that we aren't bidding for the 2003 World Cup. Certain powers in Germany... certain politicians... certain... business interests have made very clear to me that unless there's a Germany bid on the table, they'll withdraw their support from me... and my career will be over. And so,' he said slowly, 'will our plans for the future. Our plans for you and Russia to host World Cup 2003 and for us in Germany to host the Euro Cup in 2005.'

He looked straight at Alexei.

'Such carefully laid plans Alexei. Plans that will give you all the power and the influence you could dream of...'

Alexei cut Helmut short.

'But I thought we were buying "your people" off,' he said, controlling the frustration and anger in his voice as much as he could. 'I promised you enough money to deal with anyone standing in our way... in Germany or amongst your Board member friends, didn't I?'

'Yes, you did,' Helmut said quietly, averting his gaze from Alexei. 'And at first I tried everything to persuade them...'

There was a moment's delay as Alexei realized what Schneider was saying.

'At first?'

'Yes, of course.' The German sounded deeply hurt. 'Alexei... of course I tried like hell to argue that we shouldn't bid. And of course, if the money had made any difference... Alexei, we are business partners you and me... I'm your loyal friend...'

Alexei nodded slightly, as if to acknowledge the importance of their relationship.

'But you said "at first" you tried to convince your people... so what went wrong?'

Helmut smiled at Alexei, seemingly pleased at the way the conversation had developed. He lowered his voice dramatically.

'Yes, "at first", Alexei, but, you see, as I was trying to persuade them that Germany shouldn't bid, it suddenly occurred to me that for Germany to bid would serve our plan best of all. I don't know why we didn't think of it before.' His voice betrayed his excitement at the new idea he was about to share with Alex.

'You see, even though we had the World Cup last time in Europe... making it very difficult for us to host it again in 2003... it's always worried me that people would wonder why Germany hadn't bid. The Press is so suspicious. People might accuse us of working together – Russia and Germany. But if Germany bids, nobody can say that anymore. We're suddenly competitors!'

Alexei was confused. Sure, he could see that if Germany bid for World Cup 2003, nobody could say that there was any kind of deal going on with Russia. But if Helmut Schneider was running Germany's bid, how could Schneider help Alexei and his Russian campaign?

Helmut read the questions in the Russian's mind. He grinned.

'Yeah, you've got there before me, Alexei,' he said. 'Our minds work so well together. Of course, if I'm running Germany's bid I've got every reason to be visiting any country in the world. And I'll be there – on the ground – so I can influence the men we want to back your campaign, Alexei. They won't ask any questions, as you know. They won't ask why German representatives are inviting them to support Russia, not once they see your money, Alexei.'

Helmut poured himself another glass of wine and studied the Russian's face carefully.

'And when you win the bid, I will convince my people that the GFO Board has favoured Russia as the standard bearer for the new democracies, the great European nation that has never before hosted the World Cup. And as long as I can show how much effort

I have made... meeting Board members all over the world... my German colleagues will have to believe me – perhaps with a little help from your budget, my friend.'

He stood up, picked up his wicker chair, and moved it close to Alexei. He peered into the Russian's eyes.

'Trust me, Alexei,' he said. 'The end result hasn't changed. We're still the most powerful partners. It's Russia and Germany that will decide the future of football – together. Alexei, the 2003 World Cup will be in Russia. We have our gentleman's agreement, remember?'

Alexei said nothing as he absorbed what Helmut had been telling him. Eventually he nodded, smiled, and took the hand that Schneider was offering him. He called Sasha for two glasses, and a bottle of Domaine Boingnieres Armagnac.

Chapter 5

Spiritual home

February 1996

Some say that Ebenezer Cobb Morley has been badly treated by history. Some believe that global football owes as much to Morley as intercontinental aviation owes to Alcock and Brown, or satellite television to John Logie Baird.

After all, it was Ebenezer whose proposal in 1863 for 'an association of football clubs' and an agreed code of rules sorted out the chaos of Victorian football and spawned the playing framework for the world's biggest pastime for the future. It was Ebenezer's rules that governed the first international match between England and Scotland in 1872 – long before the game had been heard of in many parts of the world, even in many parts of Europe.

Sir Albert Lewis liked to look at Ebenezer's portrait in the EFO board room as he waited for his meetings to begin. What was it the President of the GFO had said as he welcomed him to the Board in Paris last year? 'You represent the home of football, Albert... England gave birth to the game.'

A burst of sunshine through the deep bay windows of the board room suddenly highlighted Ebenezer's whiskers against the dull green background of the painting. The mix of light and shade seemed to reflect Albert's thoughts as he sat alone in the cavernous room, sipping his coffee.

On the one hand, he was unquestionably proud of his achievements. After the previous EFO Chairman Sir Sidney Lovat's unexpected death last August, Albert had been approached to replace him by a number of friends on the EFO Council. He was surprised at their confidence in him.

Since becoming a member of the world's football leaders just six months ago, he had not tried to forge a reputation as a thought leader or even as an influencer. But he was from England, 'the home of football', and all the members knew it.

When he had been appointed Chairman of the EFO in November, he didn't mind that the English Press dismissed him as a 'naïve operator' on the world stage, who everyone liked. He felt he was a safe pair of hands in an increasingly turbulent football world, the latest mortal to wear Ebenezer's crown, with a knighthood in the New Year's Honours list to reassure him.

Albert was constantly grateful for the chances life had granted him. His aspirations had always been modest, and he knew it was circumstances that had helped him exceed them to an amazing degree. At the age of sixty-two, he was a happy man, happily married, with happy and healthy grandchildren. He was sharing with Monica unimaginable opportunities to enjoy life's luxuries and – despite his past suspicions about some of these foreign chaps – he really was meeting some remarkable people. But if a member of the EFO World Cup Campaign Committee had entered the board room early for the 10 o'clock meeting that day, Albert's frown would have been unmistakable.

The dark story it told was that Albert didn't like what was happening in the EFO these days. He didn't understand the type of young man and woman employed there. He didn't like the way they worked ridiculous hours, ate lunch at their desks, and talked and laughed about modern-day inventions he knew nothing about. They all seemed to carry their lives around in computers, he complained to Monica, and they talked to each other on... what did they call it... email.

And there was worse. Always driven by a passion for football that rivalled Ebenezer's, Albert wasn't sure that many of these young men and women actually loved the game itself. He had once been on a train to Manchester with young Luke Morrison from the 'Relationship Department', for a meeting whose purpose Albert did not entirely understand. There was no mobile phone signal as they left Euston Station, so Luke had no distractions. Albert put down his newspaper. This seemed an ideal opportunity to talk about the previous evening's European games.

'What did you think of Arsenal last night, Luke?' Albert noticed a look of confusion briefly cross Luke's face before he responded coolly. 'Oh, I didn't manage to watch it. I was prepping for our meeting,' he said.

Luke busied himself with a folder of papers but Albert wanted to talk. 'So, who's your favourite English player, Luke?' he asked genially. 'I don't mean right now – I mean when you were watching as a lad, ten years ago say.'

'Um,' Luke blurted. 'Um, I suppose, I like so many of them, um...', he paused for so long that Albert thought he had finished his answer. He watched Luke's face carefully, eyes darting between Albert and the train table as the young man searched his clever brain for information.

At last. 'Kenny Dalglish!' The cloud passed from Luke's face. Albert was too kind to mention Luke's error, but he didn't forget the moment.

But most difficult of all to deal with for Albert was the EFO's new Chief Executive.

Simon Carslake was forty-one years old. He had grown up in Surrey, where his comprehensive school reports regularly commented on his ambition and commitment to hard work but said little of his native ability or his popularity with classmates. After studying a business degree at a newly-created, north-eastern university in the 1970s, he had joined the marketing department of one of Britain's biggest retailers. His work rate and political skills were quickly recognised, and within five years he had become the company's director of marketing for fashion goods. After ten more years blooding himself in senior marketing posts, he was now looking for a bigger challenge.

It quickly became clear to them both that there was unlikely to be any close working relationship in the future. Albert, an easygoing man, would have been happy to offer advice to his young colleague, but Simon soon decided that there was little to be gained from collaboration with a Chairman who represented the very traditions that were holding back the EFO's progress.

Simon decided to put up with Albert's plodding management of those formal Board meetings needed to ratify Simon's executive-team decisions, but he made every effort to ensure those meetings were as infrequent and as swiftly concluded as possible. Albert, on the other hand, believed the Board was an important brake on the CEO's too-rushed decision making.

There were good reasons why both men were dreading the first meeting of the England World Cup Campaign Committee scheduled for 10 o'clock that morning.

Simon saw the EFO's bid to host the 2003 World Cup as the greatest opportunity of his career, and he had no intention of letting it slip away through the incompetence of the amateurish old guard. He was resentful at the Board's decree that Albert – the public head of the EFO, and member of the GFO Board that would decide the bid – should be at the forefront of the campaign and chair each team meeting.

It was an early reverse for Simon's campaign plan. He had wanted to streamline the meeting process, providing the kind of agile personal leadership he had learned in the commercial world. It was the best way the team could make fast, dynamic decisions fitted for a global campaign.

He was in no mood to make Albert's Chairmanship easy, and Albert feared the worst.

Chapter 6

Runners and riders

'Anybody at home?'

Greg Turner peered round the office door. Joe Kumpa got up from behind his desk and embraced the Canadian like a long-lost brother. They were both big men. President Larsen said they were like black-and-white prize fighters.

'Greg, Greg... so good you could spare us a few moments,' said Kumpa. 'I think you know our friend here.'

He indicated a man silhouetted in the window.

'Yes,' Greg Turner said carefully. 'Morning.'

The man nodded. Kumpa laughed. 'Don't worry about his manners, Greg. He's not paid to be polite.'

Greg Turner smiled. He understood. He perched his backside against Kumpa's desk as he waited to be told why he'd been summoned.

'Heard you were in Brussels today, Greg,' said Kumpa. He drained his coffee cup and exhaled with loud pleasure.

'So... what are you thinking about these bids?'

Greg Turner had been a Board member for nine years, even longer than Joe Kumpa. He had been involved in two bidding cycles for the GFO World Cup and was now something of an expert. As his Canada Football Organisation had never bid to host any GFO competition, he was a neutral party in any lobbying activity. But he loved the cut and thrust of campaigning, and he certainly enjoyed the fruits of each team's efforts to secure his support.

He was in the GFO Brussels headquarters that day partly to catch up with the bidding gossip. And when he arrived he wasn't surprised to find a message at reception from Joe Kumpa. Nobody could describe Greg as one of the President's men but he got on well with Larsen, and particularly with Joe. He knew that sharing his thoughts with Larsen's closest ally would pay good dividends for him in the end.

'You know, I often say to Christian: nobody knows more about what's happening with these fucking campaigns than Greg Turner,' said Kumpa with a wide grin. 'How the fuck you got the voting right round by round for the Aussie World Cup I'll never know. You weren't filling out the ballot papers yourself were you, you old bastard?'

'Not quite,' Greg chuckled, and his large backside jumped a little off the edge of the desk with pleasure at the compliment.

'Yeah, and wasn't Greg damn near hundred per cent right when the Argentinians got 1999?'

The man by the window nodded. 'He was,' he said.

'So come on Greg, let's hear what's happening this time. Let's hear your brain rattling away. Who's voting for who? Who's undecided and who's open to persuasion? Come on, Greg, sit down,' he said, tilting his head towards the green sofa facing his leather desk chair. 'There's nothing more important to us all for the next eighteen months, so take your time.'

Greg Turner eased his frame onto the sofa and crossed his legs.

'Ok, well I can only give you my best guess, Joe,' he said. 'Don't shoot me if I'm wrong.' He looked nervously at the man in the window. It wasn't entirely a joke, he thought to himself.

'The thing is, I reckon this is the weirdest contest I've known – because of the European situation. I mean, what the hell. Both Germany and Russia bidding? Two of the biggest players in Europe? Unprecedented.'

He took the cigar that Kumpa offered him and rolled it between his fingers as he thought for a moment.

'Then of course along come the English. Johnnie come lately. You ever see the Cagney film?' Greg was keen on movies. He liked to show off his knowledge, like a Classics tutor teasing students with references to ancient literary sources.

'Cagney? No.' said Joe.

The man by the window shook his head, slightly impatiently.

'Well, you've probably heard the phrase,' Greg said, rather wishing he hadn't started the puzzle. '*Johnny Come Lately* is a Cagney movie. He drives the bad guys out of town.'

Joe nodded politely.

'Anyway,' Greg continued quickly, 'if England thinks they're going to do any of that hero stuff, they've got it very wrong. For three reasons.' He looked at Joe Kumpa before expanding. Joe arched his eyebrows in encouragement.

'First, guys – and you'll know this better than me Joe – the English haven't done anything like enough to make friends around the world. Nothing like Germany's overseas football development work for example. There are plenty of Board members who feel England has to prove its generosity before they get rewarded with the first World Cup in the twenty-first century.'

Greg got up from the sofa to take a silver GFO-branded ashtray off the bookshelf, flicked his ash into it, and sat down again.

'Second, the EFO's only got a member onto the Board in the last year. And while old Albert Lewis is a nice enough guy, he's not the sharpest operator. Not exactly a wheeler-dealer is he? So they're a bit off the beat when it comes to GFO politics.'

He looked at the two men before continuing.

'And the other thing is, the timing of the vote might be a problem for the English. We haven't decided on a date for the Board decision meeting yet have we. If I was England, I'd be worried to hell if it takes place in September next year. That's just after next Summer's Euro Cup in France remember. Maybe the English will sort out their trouble-maker fans before then, but if those guys are rampaging though France next summer, who will want England to host our flagship competition? With the eyes of the world on it? Maybe it'll be a case of Johnny come too lately!'

Joe Kumpa nodded thoughtfully. He picked up his pen from the desk and wrote quickly on the GFO writing pad in front of him.

'But of course, that would be a very big decision, guys... that would look like the English were being deliberately screwed.'

Greg Turner had not been entirely serious about suggesting that the GFO Board voting date should be manipulated to cause the English bid campaign the most difficulty. He wanted no part in that kind of manoeuvre and was unnerved that his jokey suggestion had been noted by Joe Kumpa.

'Anyway,' Greg continued quickly, 'whatever happens with England, that still leaves two Europeans in the frame. The one thing we can be pretty sure about of course is that after last year's World Cup in Australia, and '99 in Argentina, 2003 is most likely to be in Europe.

'And I can't tell you right now, gentlemen, whether it will be Russia, Germany or even whether England will make it to the vote. Perhaps they'll all slug it out in public. Or perhaps there'll be some kind of deal... Russia and Germany most likely, knowing Baskin and Schneider as we do.'

'Interesting,' Joe said. 'Sure, Europe looks likely for 2003. But there's no rule that says the Cup's got to go back there. And if the stakes are high enough... who knows? So what about the others? What d'you reckon about China, Greg? They're gonna get it one day.'

'Yeah, one day,' Greg responded, 'but it won't be one day soon. I think China might have a go, but more to put down a marker for the future.' He drew on his cigar, as he continued to think.

'But if you're talking about non-Europeans, Morocco's more credible than some people think. They've bid before and done ok, and they're willing to invest a lot of money in infrastructure. Who knows? But of course, they don't have a power base. They'll have problems getting beyond a few votes from Africa and Asia. So it's credible, but I can't see them making the final round.

'And then I've heard maybe a country from the Gulf. Of course everyone says the Gulf is impossible because of the heat, but as we know, fellahs, money talks and it could happen if the price is right. And there's plenty of sheikhs to bankroll a Gulf bid. God knows who – but the betting's on Qatar.'

Joe Kumpa waved his hand regally for Greg to carry on.

'So who else...' Turner thought aloud. 'Well there's Brazil. Of course, Brazil always brings glamour and colour, carnivals and titties, Pele and Jairzinho... So you can never rule them out. But surely the Cup won't go back to South America so soon after Argentina.'

'Germany's got a problem too,' said the man by the window. His interruption surprised Greg Turner. 'Different problem sure. Of course we know it's Europe's turn, but Germany got it last time it was in Europe.'

Turner nodded to show that he understood. He chose his words carefully. He didn't want to sound argumentative.

'Technically, that doesn't break any rules. It's just a convention that the same country doesn't get it successive times in its own continent. But you're right. It's a well-established tradition, and some Board members will oppose Germany for that reason. And of course, the European Alliance might have something to say about it.'

He thought for a moment and smiled ruefully. 'But I doubt it. We all know what the Germans are like. If anyone's going to carry off that little trick, it'll be them.'

Greg looked at the man by the window. He interpreted the man's stony expression and silence as acceptance of his analysis. Joe Kumpa broke the silence.

'I don't class Morocco as Africa. What about the real African continent? Or rather the countries that can afford a World Cup. Will South Africa bid this time? Plenty of speculation Greg...'

Greg Turner stubbed out his cigar, picked up the ashtray and put it back on the shelf. 'Well, word is that they won't try this time, too many internal problems.'

'Yeah... plenty of crime to frighten the sensitive Europeans too,' chuckled Kumpa. 'It's what we Africans are best at, Greg.' He let out a deep roar of laughter. Greg couldn't help joining him. Joe Kumpa's humour was usually infectious.

'So,' Greg said as their laughter subsided. 'That's pretty much how I see it right now. It looks like Africa – Morocco that is, Europe, South America, and Asia will have candidates but not North and Central America. But by the end I reckon it will be a European-only contest. Other teams... Morocco, Brazil, China and the rest will be out of the race.

'Oh – and of course we mustn't forget the influence of our beloved President. Who's Larsen going to support? We all know the Board members who take their lead from him. And the President's casting vote could be very significant this time – voting could be close... Presumably you guys will be talking to him.'

Greg paused for a moment, but quickly understood that Kumpa and the other man were not going to tell him anything about their discussions with President Larsen. Greg Turner was a good friend, but he wasn't in the inner circle. Greg smiled to himself and continued his analysis. He knew his place.

'Then of course we have second preference votes to think about. Who will African members support after Morocco? Who will Asia support after China? Who will the South Americans support after Brazil?

'Guessing the first preference votes is the easy part. More difficult is working out what people do with their second and third preferences. As we know, some alliances vote as a bloc, while some members do their own thing. Your Africans usually stick together, Joe. You know better than me what your guys will do once Morocco goes out. Likewise the South Americans usually act as a bloc, don't they – in terms of supporting Brazil and what they do afterwards?

'My guess is the Europeans will give a lot of attention to the South Americans. The Latins are pretty flexible, and hungry – or greedy, depending on your point of view.'

Greg looked at the two men for a response. There wasn't one. He knew what they wanted to know. He took a deep breath.

'Of course, I can't be sure about all our Board member colleagues and their motives, Joe... but if you ask me, and I'm sure you will, we can be pretty clear whose votes will be up for grabs. And from what I know, there'll be plenty around for the bidders with the biggest wallets.'

The man by the window walked up to Greg and handed him a piece of paper with a short, handwritten list on it. Greg looked at the list, and quickly understood what it was.

'Yes,' he said firmly. 'I think you've got them dead right. Those are the guys with votes up for sale.'

Kumpa grinned.

'Ok Greg, we've taken too much of your time. You must be a busy man. And I've got a big lunch.' He slapped Greg heartily on the back, grabbing his arm to take him through the office door. Then he stopped, as if remembering the other man.

'You use the office if you want. I won't be back this afternoon.'

The man nodded and slung his briefcase onto the desk as the door closed behind Kumpa and Turner. He reached for the phone.

'Gerald,' he said quietly. 'Need to see you. Now.' An hour later, there was a knock at the door. 'Sit down over there.' The visitor took the seat that Greg had vacated.

'We got what we want. No surprises, but Greg Turner says the names are right.'

Gerald copied the handwritten list of names into a notebook he took from his inside jacket pocket. When he had finished writing, he nodded. He got up from his seat, ready to go. He didn't expect any chitchat with the other man, but the man suddenly spoke.

'Just one more thing,' he said. 'What do you know about an Englishman called Simon Carslake? Someone told me we could do business with him. Heard of him?'

'I've heard his name,' Gerald said.

'See if you can check him out. I've heard he's an ambitious bastard. Out for himself too. Kumpa will be meeting him when the English go to Yora. So make sure you see him soon.'

Gerald nodded and left the office.

Chapter 7

Secret rendezvous

Albert's worries about the first meeting of the EFO World Cup Campaign Committee were well founded. Simon Carslake had successfully recruited a young team of marketing and PR experts from companies bearing some of Britain's biggest brand names, and Albert quickly felt out of his depth amongst them.

After Albert, as Chairman, had opened the meeting and welcomed the team (so new that he didn't recognise any of them apart from Carslake), Simon immediately took charge. He gave his own welcome – warmer, and slightly conspiratorial, as if he was reassuring the younger members of his campaign family that they didn't need to worry about the presence of an embarrassing old uncle. Albert thought he spied a surreptitious wink.

Simon continued at length and without pause, addressing the first three items on the agenda. He began by reviewing the EFO's past bidding record, outlined the likely approach of each of England's probable competitors, and detailed the GFO's voting process.

The team nodded their appreciation. Albert said nothing.

Then Simon introduced Sara Thurlow. She had a double first from Oxford, he said as she blushed slightly, an MSc in Marketing from Manchester University, and had been seconded to the team from BZH, the world's third largest advertising agency. He didn't need to explain that she was in her twenties, tall, blonde, and exuded an impressive mix of capability and sensitivity.

Sara described her analysis of each GFO Board member's current intentions in casting a vote for the 2003 World Cup hosts.

She supported each statement with video, image and documentary evidence projected on the screen behind her.

She identified those countries where the government decided who to vote for, and where the GFO member was told what to do. She also indicated where big corporate interests were involved and were expected to have a major influence on voting decisions.

It was a thoroughly researched and brilliantly executed presentation, and Albert couldn't help but marvel. Such a young thing. If it wasn't for the black business suit and patent leather shoes, he'd have seen a good bit of his bright granddaughter Joanne in this girl.

When Sara finished, she turned towards Albert and Simon, waiting for guidance about what should happen next. Questions? General debate? Simon jumped in quickly.

'Great, Sara! OK, Will, so why don't you hit us with the campaign plan.'

Albert thought he saw Sara smile shyly at him as she sat down, embarrassed perhaps at her momentary confusion over whether he was running this meeting, and uncomfortable at Simon's presumption.

Will Taylor unfolded his legs and rose to his gangly height. His voice was clear and commanding, but Albert's concentration was failing him. Afterwards, he remembered little of Will's masterly presentation, the campaign plan, or the 'action timeline' that Will changed mysteriously with that mouse-gadget thing he used.

In fact, Albert's presence seemed to be increasingly pointless. It was Simon who went on controlling discussion, managing decision making, and setting tasks for the team. This growing sense of detachment made Albert angry and frustrated – with himself as much as with Simon. He was letting that cocky bastard take over. But what else could he do? He wasn't a marketing man. He couldn't judge the decisions being made. And if he felt like saying anything at all, the overpowering presence of those bright young men and women sapped his confidence.

Just once, when it was suggested that a member of the Royal Family should meet the GFO delegation when it came to England to inspect stadium facilities, did he make clear how important it was that he, as Chairman, should play a major role. Simon seemed to agree. 'Of course, Albert, if we manage to get Prince Charles, you must certainly be there with him.'

Albert was pleased. Encouraged, he suggested he should write to the Palace on behalf of the EFO. There was an awkward silence, and one or two amused expressions. 'Don't worry, we'll sort out all the arrangements. Nigel has all the contacts,' Simon said, gesturing to Nigel Petterton-Stuart, a former Blues and Royals Guards officer, and heir to the Brissenden Baronetcy.

Even the proud prospect of accompanying Royalty for a GFO visit seemed like a Pyrrhic victory for Albert. He knew he had been outwitted again.

Carslake understood well enough that the EFO Chairman would have to be wheeled out during the campaign from time-to-time, so agreeing to Albert's wish to accompany Prince Charles was a calculated concession. But by rejecting Albert's offer to write to the Palace, Carslake was sending a clear message. Albert and his every action and word would be carefully managed at any meetings in which he was involved.

And there was something else that worried him: Albert had a memory about a conversation he had had with the German and Russian GFO Board members less than twelve months ago in Paris. He'd been asked by the two men whether he thought England would bid to host the 2003 World Cup bid. Although his memory had been confused by an unusual intake of alcohol that evening, he was certain he had said something reassuring to them about how England had no plans to bid.

Since the EFO Board had first discussed the idea of bidding just after he had become Chairman, Albert had been increasingly concerned over his secret commitment. When the decision was made public at the end of February 1996 – just a week ago – he had spent sleepless nights waiting for a call from his GFO colleagues.

But nothing. Were they slowly and carefully planning an angry response...a public declaration to expose Albert's deception, and ruin his honour and career for ever?

Or was this how the GFO worked? Discussions and commitments soon forgotten as the political landscape changed, and men's words never assumed to be a bond? Oh Albert, he thought to himself, not for the first time, this is a strange old world.

'What's that?' Albert suddenly realised that people were talking and putting away their laptops. By the end of the meeting, everyone in the team had seemed to notice that the Chairman had been marginalised in discussions. So when Simon had to explain to him what was happening, there were more than a few poorly disguised smirks around the conference table.

'End of the meeting, Albert! That's it. We're done,' said Simon. 'Everything's under control. Shall I get Steph to arrange a car for you?'

Simon was delighted by the way things had gone. There were no issues to discuss with members of the team at the end of the meeting, so he walked quickly back to his office to get on with the never-ending stream of emails before he went home. He allowed himself a moment of contemplation, pushing back his plush leather desk chair for comfort.

Not bad, he thought as he stretched his arms behind his neck. We've got a clear set of messages. We're big on the history of the game. Fantastic facilities. Loads of government money to support us. We know we're the best. We just have to tell the world. Without sounding too cocky of course, he reminded himself.

He smiled, thinking how easy it had been to manage Sir Albert – much easier than he had imagined. Oh, dear, poor old Albert, he really was from a past era. That time had once been described as the 'age of the family business' at the EFO, he remembered being told by a friendly hack. When expenses were paid in cash from an actual war chest housed in the basement. How extraordinary were those old fossils on the Board, he thought to himself.

Well, he was proud of what he was doing to drag the organisation into the next century, and there was no stopping him now. Where would a successful World Cup campaign take him, he began to wonder.

Successful campaign! Ha! What were the chances of that happening if old Albert had been running the campaign – with the help of a couple of old soaks from the Press Office, and his secretary trying to run events!

Albert and his breed might not like him much (Simon had taken a strange pride when he had once overheard himself described by a Council member as 'a right little bastard') but they'd be grateful enough if he brought home the World Cup. And many other organisations would be impressed by his efforts as well.

It was past 9:00pm now, and Simon was surprised to hear Will Taylor's voice on the phone in the open-plan office. Well, it was a good opportunity to show what a supportive manager he was, and to share his sense of success with a key member of the team. So he went into the open office and leaned on Will's desk for a while.

It was nearly 9:30 when Simon and Will stopped chatting and Will had left the building. Back at his desk, Simon was just about to tackle some emails when the phone rang. Steph had gone of course. Oh I'm just going to ignore it, Simon thought. But hang on. Good image that he was still at his desk at this time. Pity to waste it. He picked up the phone.

'Carslake,' Simon had practised this response over the years – recorded and refined it - and was now very happy with it. Authoritative and busy, but not unfriendly, he had decided.

'Mr Craslake.' Who was this joker at this time of night, thought Simon.

'Carslake... Simon... Carslake,' he said coldly.

Silence at the end of the line. 'Look are you still there?' Silence. 'Who is this please?'

Simon was about to put down the phone, when he heard a low voice. 'Craslake. You are leader. Yes.'

Simon put the phone to his ear again. 'Yes I'm Simon Carslake. Do I know you Mr..?'

'You are leader for the English bid.' Again, a statement. The voice was guttural, but despite the man's lack of English fluency he was assured in his manner. 'You want to win this bid very much. But you need my help.'

Simon was intrigued. He was supremely confident about how the England bid campaign was progressing. But at the same time he was a modern manager. He was always ready to think outside the box. It was what made him different from the old guard after all. What could this man do to help his bid?

'Do I know you?' he started.

'Never mind that,' the man said. 'I cannot give you the details, but you just need to know I am representing... shall we say... important interests. I can help you get some very important support for your bid. But I need to know how valuable that support is to you.'

'Well, we think we've got a very good bid and have an excellent chance of success,' Simon said. There was no comment from the man, and Simon sensed he needed to be a little less pompous if he was to find out what was on offer. 'Of course,' he continued, 'we are always looking for support from wherever we can get it.'

'Oh yes, you certainly need help,' said the man, and his voice reflected a moment of amusement. 'You think you have a good chance, you say. Why do you think that? What solid commitments have you got to back your bid? You've got nothing, my friend.'

Simon quickly assessed what the man was saying. It was true, his team had no firm commitments of support from anyone yet.

They had heard soundings from around the world about GFO Board members offering good will to England's bid, and vague positive comments had appeared in the Press and Media, but how reliable were they? The stranger's comments stirred a sense of danger. Simon's future career plans were heavily bound up in the bid's success. Could he afford to ignore this detached voice, and dismiss anyone offering any kind of help?

He tried to buy time as he gathered his thoughts. 'Ok, well I don't know how you might be able to help my bid... perhaps you'd better spell it out.'

'I don't want to discuss this now. The phone. Not secure. We meet tomorrow evening – at the *Windows on the World* bar. You know it. Nine o'clock. I find you. I'm only in London for two days, so it's tomorrow or nothing. What do you English say? You don't want to 'miss the boat' my friend.' And with that, the line went dead.

Simon sat in silence, deep in thought. Then he remembered his last train, gathered his raincoat and briefcase, turned off the light, and closed the office door.

Overnight, and travelling to the EFO from his home in Barnes next day, Simon considered his conversation with the stranger on the phone. He knew he should be taking soundings from others about this bizarre exchange, and about the decision whether to attend the planned meeting that evening. But who could he talk to?

He dismissed Albert as a sounding board straight away, and other senior members of the EFO quickly afterwards. None of them had relevant experience. They would almost certainly advise against the meeting. They might even categorically forbid it.

He thought about members of his own team. Will was bright. He could assess the situation and express a view very quickly. So could Sara, and Nick, and Chris... He would value their opinions, but... the more he thought about it, the more convinced he was that this was something that only he could handle. His team was great, but it was only he who could provide the kind of new thinking that would drag this organisation out of its past. It was a test for him, and he would not fail it.

He shut himself in his office for much of the day, telling Steph not to disturb him except for emergencies. Team members wondered idly what it was all about, but they were too new, and too committed to their own tasks, to think about any possibilities. Maybe this happened a lot at the EFO.

As people trickled out of the open office from 6:30pm onwards, Simon found himself getting increasingly impatient, and nervy.

He loved the idea of being a risk-taker, but if he was honest, organisational risk-taking did not generally involve a *ménage* with a stranger at dead of night. Was this a scam? Supposing this man was from another country planning a bid campaign – a rogue Middle Eastern state for example, or Russia even – intent on uncovering an illegal activity or intention, or, more sinisterly, wanting to remove him from the bidding game entirely...

Removing him? What might that mean? he thought, horrified. Would he be followed out by a couple of heavies, and bundled into a car?

The thought made him jump as he heard his office door open. It was Michael Sutton, the EFO Deputy Chairman. Simon wondered if Sutton could hear his heart fluttering.

'You're late, Simon. You off to the match tonight?'

Match, match? Simon racked his brain. He knew how important it was to have good knowledge of football tournaments and who was playing whom – for his credibility before the Board and, even more importantly, before the ranks of informed Press and Media people. He didn't mind watching the game when he had to, but – unlike the Board members – he wasn't always aware who was playing whom every day.

Luckily for Simon, Michael Sutton didn't have time to watch him squirm with embarrassment, even though he would have enjoyed the prospect. 'London derby,' he offered. Simon breathed deeply with relief. 'Sadly not, Michael, too much work to do on the campaign. Should be a cracker though.'

Sutton waved absently in his direction and left the office. After a few minutes, Simon picked up the phone. 'Tony? I'll be down shortly, can you get the car ready. I need to make a call in Park Lane on the way home. Shouldn't add more than an hour.'

He unhooked his coat from behind the door and thought for a moment whether he needed anything more than his briefcase with him. No. Let's do it. He headed confidently for the lift that took him to the executive car park.

Tony was sitting in the big black Jaguar, glancing through a copy of *The Sun*. As he saw Simon's figure in his wing mirror, he jumped out to open the back door. Tony had heard and seen it all during his eighteen years with the EFO. Nothing surprised him anymore but nothing escaped his notice. Not that he was indiscreet. He kept most of what he heard in the back of the car to himself. He didn't think much of this Simon bloke. Fancied himself a bit. Wasn't really a man's man, like some of the old blokes on the Board. Tony could understand what they were all about; they liked football and pretty secretaries and making money. He respected many of them as self-made businessmen.

Not like this geezer Simon. Stop by the Hilton in Park Lane 'for an hour' he'd said. What's that all about? Is he having it off with some fancy bird? Tony smiled to himself. Nah, don't adam and eve it. He's married so he can't be gay, but I can't really see him as a ladies' man, Tony thought.

The traffic was ok and the journey was quick. Simon was pleased that the meeting was to be in a place he knew well. Quite a few football events were held in the Park Lane Hilton Hotel, many of them finished off with a private function in the '*Windows*' bar. As he took the lift to the 28th floor, he was relaxed enough to remember getting pinned against a wall by the wife of one of the Board members. Not getting her a seat in the Royal Box at Wembley, he recalled. What a pain some of these football wives were. Worse than their husbands.

Simon's lift arrived at the '*Windows*' floor, and he stepped out, making his way to the bar between the generously sized, crushed-velvet covered chairs. Like all visitors, no matter how regular,

Simon's eye was drawn through the picture window to the view across Mayfair, and east towards the rising buildings of the City.

He took a corner seat: always best to have your back to the wall, he remembered reading in some thriller or other. He was much more confident now, but still gulped at a double gin and tonic. The bar wasn't busy, and from the moment the man appeared in his line of vision, Simon was sure it was him.

He was smaller than Simon had imagined from the phone call. That deep voice and authoritative tone had suggested a burly figure. Along with the soothing effects of his gin and tonic, the man's build improved Simon's confidence. He was not a tall man himself and asserting himself would be easier, he thought.

He rose to greet the man, trying to balance his nervousness with a sense of his own importance. 'Mr...' he began, offering his hand. 'I didn't catch your name last night.'

The man ignored Simon's hand, holding him with an icy look from deep-set pale brown eyes. He wore his slight physique with assurance. He was dressed in a cream suit, over a crisp white open-necked shirt, and looked oddly out of place on a chilly winter's night in London. His small head was shaved bald, emphasising an over-sized gold ring in one ear.

Simon usually prided himself on assessing people's origins, but this man gave him no clues. On the telephone the night before, he had seemed unsophisticated at first, calling him 'Craslake' as if the combination of letters was unfamiliar and difficult for him to say. Forced to guess the man's background then, Simon would have said he was East European. But as they conversed, Simon had noticed the voice on the phone becoming more fluent in English.

Meeting him in the bar, the man's appearance gave no clearer picture. He could have passed for a creative director in a top advertising agency or a slave trader, Simon decided. Or anything else for that matter. When he spoke, Simon was offered no new clues. The man's style was relaxed and articulate, but there were enough inflexions to indicate that he was not a native speaker.

'You don't know my name because I didn't tell you,' the man said. His face showed no change of expression. He wasn't trying to be clever, Simon sensed. This was a man who simply stated facts. He looked at Simon in silence for what felt like painfully long minutes as the man assessed his next statement. 'You can call me Gerald,' he said.

'Well, let me get you a drink,' said Simon, desperate to avert his eyes from the man's unsettling gaze.

As Simon ordered a soda and ice from a waiter, the man picked up the chair opposite and moved it carefully to give him protection from the view of others, while allowing him to take wary looks across the bar. As Simon watched these furtive movements, he felt for a moment as if he was in a movie.

Then the man began to talk, quietly but deliberately, and brought Simon back to reality.

'So you want to host the World Cup.'

Simon thought he detected a faint German accent. He wasn't sure what to say, but the man continued as if answering his own question:

'I think you're right to make a bid. England can make a wonderful World Cup.' There was a long pause. 'Such a pity that you won't win your bid. At the moment.'

Simon could not help responding to the challenge. He began to speak passionately about the English bid, its strengths, and its benefits to the GFO. Carefully avoiding details of the campaign plan, he talked about England's history as the home of football, its magnificent stadia, and the iconic English clubs known throughout the world.

He talked about Britain, the stable country, founder of modern democratic government, with a Royal Family loved by people everywhere. He talked about the hotels, the restaurants, the West End musicals, the museums, the galleries. He knew they had the best bid and was not going to be undermined by a strange foreigner who knew nothing about it! As he finished his case, he noticed that the man had a slight look of amusement at the corners of his mouth. Simon stopped abruptly. The man was laughing at him.

'Oh yes – such a pity that all that enthusiasm and confidence doesn't count for much.' He fixed Simon carefully with his eyes, and the amused look subsided. 'But do you have the cards in your hand to win the deal? And do you have the money to win?' He paused. 'Yes I know, you're a wealthy organisation in a wealthy country. You're putting twenty million pounds into your bid, I hear. But does that buy you the support you need?'

Simon couldn't think what to say.

'Do you want me to be blunt Mister Craslake? Despite what some of your hysterical newspapers report, nobody thinks you can win. I know, you English believe in fair play. You think that it will be very 'unfair' if your bid doesn't win. Well listen to me. As my friends on the Board regularly tell me: there are no level playing fields in the World Cup bidding game. Fairness isn't a word in the GFO dictionary.'

A long pause.

'You look very sad,' the man said. 'Well don't be. If you listen to me, I can help you. The reason I'm here is I represent a group of men that will vote as one bloc if ... circumstances... are right. They are from two different GFO regions, so they have great power over the result.'

He paused again. He wanted to make sure that Carslake was understanding him.

'It's simple. Four votes from these men will go to the highest bidder. And I can deliver these four votes. In the bag.'

Simon stayed silent. Was this what he had meant when he had promised every job appointment board throughout his career that he was a 'risk-taker'? Was this risk... or madness?

'You're offering to sell these votes to me,' he said finally.

'Oh, I would certainly deny that allegation,' said the man coldly, fixing him with a dead-eyed stare once again. 'That's for you to draw your own conclusions. But if you would like me to, shall we say, act as your go-between with these gentlemen by making a serious offer, that might be possible.'

Simon could hardly believe his voice: 'I'm not exactly sure what you mean by a serious offer.'

'Eight million dollars,' said the stranger quickly.

'That's ridiculous!' said Simon without thinking. 'Where am I going to find eight million dollars? Chancellor of the bloody Exchequer?'

The man swallowed the contents of his glass. He pushed his chair back, signalling his intention to leave the meeting.

'That Mr Craslake is for you to decide. But I have to tell you there are plenty of countries where governments could easily offer that kind of... support... to their bid for such an important event.'

'But... but... I don't even know where these votes are from. How do I raise money for them without any proof?'

For a moment the man's face was distorted in contempt for the Englishman. His voice was an angry hiss.

'You are so... ignorant! You think I will tell you names and addresses and phone numbers for you to go to tell Interpol? Listen my friend this is a matter of trust. You want to win. Then you trust me.'

'Look,' he continued, more sympathetically as he gazed at Carslake's pallid face. 'I know such things are sensitive in your country. I understand this may take time. But I like that expression you English like to say. What is it...? "Where there's a will there's a way".'

He got to his feet, without offering his hand to Simon. 'I have to go now. I'll contact you again soon. Think about what I've said. And think about what a successful bid could mean for you, my friend.' He looked at him hard. 'And don't leave things too long. Other people would love to have this opportunity, and they will not have your difficulties.'

'Gerald' left without saying anything more.

Chapter 8

Three in a bed

March 1996

'Good morning gentlemen.'

President Larsen rose from the small table in the dark corner of his favourite Brussels bar to greet his GFO Board colleagues. They could have met in his office just four blocks away, but when his secretary took a call from Helmut Schneider the day before, requesting an urgent meeting, Larsen knew instinctively that their conversation needed to have no witnesses.

Schneider would have preferred to meet Larsen at a restaurant. He knew that this little Brussels bar was a favourite Larsen venue, and he never liked to concede advantage of any kind in any situation. But the President had insisted.

Le Chalet was not a particularly attractive bar. The beers and the wine were no better than any served in a dozen other establishments nearby. In fact, the service was sometimes surly, and the glasses less than sparkling clean. Yet *Le Chalet* had been popular with generations of drinkers since its foundation in 1932.

As well as the GFO President, current clients included EC officials, one or two TV stars and a number of representatives of the Brussels judiciary. There had also been a time when *Le Chalet* was popular with Wehrmacht officers, who particularly appreciated its intimate seating arrangements and discrete staff when entertaining a better class of city girl. And this was the key to *Le Chalet*'s success down the years. If you wanted to do private business in Brussels with people you didn't want to be seen with, *Le Chalet* would never let you down.

Larsen knew Schneider well. As head of the Deutscher Fußball-Organisation, Schneider had been a GFO Board member for twelve years. He had enjoyed unrivalled success in securing support for his objectives, matched only by the performance of the German team on the field. Neither success tended to win Schneider close friends, but his organisation's pockets were deep enough to make sure that it maintained plenty of support amongst its worldwide friends.

Larsen didn't like Schneider. There was an arrogance about his manner and a reluctance to respect the President's office. It was fortunate for Schneider that his wife Giselle was so charming and worked so hard to buttress the Schneider name.

The President knew the Russian less well. Alexei Baskin had been on the Board for five years, but unlike Schneider, Baskin had never seemed to be a dominant force in the Organisation. Part of the reason was that Larsen was never sure when Baskin's decisions were his, or when he had needed guidance from political masters.

Things had changed slowly after *glasnost*. Baskin owed his position as President of the Russian Football Organisation to his family's global business wealth and Western sophistication, but the apparatchiks in the RFO still fiercely guarded their rights to influence.

The waiter took their drinks order. The pleasantries between the three men were brief.

'So gentlemen, you have some news,' said the President.

Schneider raised an eyebrow towards Baskin, who nodded agreement that the German should lead.

'I do indeed, and I think you'll agree it is VERY good news.'

He paused, enjoying for a moment Larsen's silent irritation at his dramatic tone.

'You see, Alexei and I have been thinking carefully about what is the best possible arrangement for the 2003 World Cup.'

He looked carefully at Larsen's face for a reaction. It was like stone.

'And naturally, we feel that you should know our thoughts, Christian.'

Schneider knew how Larsen hated him using Larsen's first name. But he liked to remind Larsen that he had known him before he achieved high office.

'Germany of course hosted the World Cup in '91 – the last time it was in Europe,' he continued. 'As you know, we Germans are very sensitive to the needs of other nations, so we don't expect to host the tournament again in 2003. However,' he took a sip from his glass of Kir, 'Germany believes it's *very* important that another European nation should be host after the World Cup goes to South America in '99.'

Baskin was nodding vigorously and Larsen allowed himself a little smile of irony at Schneider's claims of thoughtfulness about other European nations. Not a sentiment he usually associated with the Germans.

Schneider continued:

'So... we believe the thing for Germany is to find the right European candidate. And we think it's time for the Russian people to enjoy this great honour in 2003. We would like to help them. We would like to use our influence with our friends across the world to encourage support for the Russian bid.'

Schneider peered into Larsen's blue eyes before continuing. He took a pack of slim cigars from his jacket pocket and lit one.

'Now let me say that in all honesty there is a *little* self interest in this decision,' Schneider's eyes twinkled as he spoke.

Larsen's ironic smile widened slightly.

'You see, in return for helping Russia to win the 2003 World Cup bid, Germany will have Russia's support to win our 2005 bid for the European Championships. A small return for us perhaps, but a great partnership between our two nations that will secure for ever Russia's place in the GFO family.'

Schneider raised his glass towards the other two men. 'Prost!'

Larsen nodded to show he understood Schneider's proposition.

'So,' he said quietly, 'I assume that you two bedfellows will also benefit personally from this happy arrangement.'

Schneider grinned.

'You're quick as ever, Christian.'

He looked up to the tobacco-stained ceiling and blew three smoke rings from his cigar.

'And of course, Christian, there is room in our bed for three...'

Larsen ignored the comment.

'So Germany will now withdraw its bid for 2003,' Larsen said with only a hint of enquiry in his voice.

Schneider laughed quietly and beckoned to the barman. He ordered a repeat of the first round of drinks.

'Not exactly,' he said when they were alone again. 'No, I have to keep the German bid on the table... for two very good reasons.

'First of all, I have to be in the bidding game. Of course – if I am to help Alexei.' He smiled at Baskin. 'How could I justify going to see our friends across the world unless I'm managing a bid of my own? Alexei knows that I am most valuable to him and the Russians if we Germans are strong, with plenty of support behind our own bid. I can then persuade a number of our colleagues to switch at the last moment... No doubt at a price.'

Schneider leant forward to whisper in Larsen's ear.

'But let me assure you, Christian. We have sufficient funds between us to make this happen.'

Larsen recoiled at Schneider's closeness.

'And secondly, Christian...' He paused for effect, and his voice became more serious.

'Secondly, I have to bid because I need to be very careful with my sponsors in Germany... my commercial and political supporters... You see, we're so used to winning in my country that they wouldn't understand how we can't host the World Cup in 2003 just because we also hosted it so successfully the last time it was in Europe.

'I'm afraid, Christian, that they would regard my... arrangement with the Russians... as an act of treachery. I must be seen to be working hard to win.'

'I see,' said Larsen. He turned to Baskin.

'And your people are all in agreement with this arrangement?'

'Oh yes,' said Alexei quickly. 'The Russian people wish to host the World Cup. But we are very inexperienced in world football matters such as this. We need our German friends in order to do it. We have a gentleman's agreement you see.'

Larsen nodded his understanding. He looked at Schneider.

'What sort of support from friends in high places, Helmut? What sort of rewards?'

Schneider glanced briefly around the bar and drew his chair closer up to the table.

'Well Christian, we're realistic. We know that Russia's chances of winning, and our ability to help them do it, will be immensely aided by your personal commitment.'

'As for rewards...' He leant across the table so that his lips were again within a breath of Larsen's right ear.

'This will mean a gratuity, shall we say, like never before, Christian, for all of us,' he whispered. 'Alexei can tell you about his Russian resources and the ways that payments will be made.'

He sat back in his chair, and grinned.

Larsen got to his feet.

'Thank you for coming gentlemen. I must get back to the office now. There are plenty of taxis on the street.'

He felt inside his breast pocket and brought out a card with contact details printed in plain black letters. There was no identifying logo or design.

'Alexei, please phone this number. My colleague will need to sort out details with you.'

When Larsen was sure the two men had left by taxi, he picked his coat off the rack behind the bar door and decided to walk back to the GFO building half a kilometre away. He wanted thinking time and welcomed the fresh air and the exercise.

He had been in meetings like this many times before, as footballing nations prepared for the World Cup bidding cycle. He was rarely surprised by the strategies disclosed to him in confidence. But there was something about the conversation he had just had with his two Board member colleagues that didn't add up. It was so unlike the Germans to make way for a rival that it was scarcely credible, he thought, as he strode purposefully along the Boulevard de Waterloo. Indeed, he couldn't recall Helmut Schneider ever behaving so generously in all the years he had known him.

Yes, he mused, the Germans were certainly right to consider that they were themselves unlikely to get another World Cup to host so soon after their last one. There was no actual rule preventing it, but GFO convention was certainly not in their favour.

Was it just that Schneider was a man addicted to dealing and winning? Perhaps he would gain some kind of vicarious pleasure from brokering success for the Russians.

Or maybe it all came down to money. A gratuity 'like never before' Schneider had said. He knew very well that the Russian Football Organisation and its business backers had almost limitless resources. So maybe Schneider just wanted to maximise his payday by forcing huge compensation out of the Russians.

And, of course, it was no secret that Schneider had designs on the Presidency when Larsen retired. Would the Russians' financial support be extended to help fund the German's personal ambitions in the years to come?

As he marched up the steps of the impressive glass-fronted GFO headquarters, Larsen waved to the woman at the front desk and allowed himself a little smile.

Of one thing he was certain. If there was money to be made from this curious arrangement, he wanted his fair share...

Chapter 9

Local heroes

May 1996

There was nothing Albert liked more than to chat to old football friends over a beer and a sandwich.

Sadly, it seemed that these days he didn't have time to do much of it. No doubt some old friends interpreted this as Albert preferring to socialise with his new international colleagues at the GFO. This simply wasn't true, but Albert found the story hard to shift.

So when Albert chaired the EFO Council, the non-executive gathering of football administrators from England's grassroots, he always made sure he spent an hour in the bar afterwards to show how little he had changed since he was one of them.

For the May 1996 Council, Albert had invited Simon Carslake to present on the EFO's World Cup campaign. Inevitably discussions after the meeting were focused on the World Cup bid and what it would mean at local level. Albert understood the motives behind the questions he faced. These men were looking after their own local interests, just as he had done throughout his time at Truro and District Football Organisation.

Albert had tried to explain this special bond between Council men and the EFO to Simon Carslake when Simon joined the EFO. It didn't work. In fact Albert sometimes felt it was the moment that Carslake stormed off muttering 'bunch of selfish old dinosaurs' that really signalled a serious breach between the new Chief Executive and the Chairman.

'Well Albert, how are things?' enquired Ron Newby from Yorkshire, clutching his arm affectionately. 'How's the international jet setter?'

'Oh, I could do without all the flying,' responded Albert with a grin, 'but it's a powerful organisation that GFO, and we've got to make sure we're properly represented at the top table, Ron.'

'I'm sure you're right, Albert lad,' said Ron. 'After all it's not a bad deal for them. They get the benefit of all our wisdom as founders of the game. I bet some of these foreigners think they know it all until you turn up and set them straight.'

'Well, I'm not sure I would put it quite like that,' smiled Albert, 'but I do try to give them the benefit of our experience.'

Reg Smart from Derbyshire had also taken a seat at Albert's table. Albert could see he wanted to get something off his chest.

'Albert,' he said, 'to be honest I'm a bit concerned about this World Cup business. Last time it was in England our family firm had a very nice position for advertising billboards inside the stadium at Wembley. The thing is my son Richard – you remember Richard – well he's running the firm now, and I've told him I'm sure we can have the same again in 2003. I'm relying on you Albert to arrange it.'

Albert's response was a combination of his natural patience and his genuine fondness for old pals. 'Reg, I think things may have changed since the 1960s. There are global companies now sponsoring all these tournaments. You're up against the big boys, I'm afraid. It might not be possible for Richard to get any advertising.'

'That doesn't seem very fair,' said Reg slowly. 'We've been supporting English football for over fifty years.' He looked at Albert with disappointed eyes. Albert started to reply but was interrupted by another Council member.

'Albert I'm very worried about the toilets at these new stadiums everywhere.' Albert recognised Cyril Townsend's broad Liverpudlian voice. 'You know what it's like as you get older.

Nobody's thinking about that. People are complaining they're spending all of half-time queueing for the facilities. Albert, I think you need to tell the GFO about it. We don't want them turning up here for a World Cup only to find they can't use the toilets, now do we? It doesn't do our reputation any good at all.'

'Oh, I can see the problem,' said Albert, 'but to be honest Cyril, I don't think me raising toilet facilities at the GFO Board will help us with our World Cup bid. It's not top of their priorities at the moment.'

'Well perhaps it should be,' Cyril replied peevishly. 'And maybe we need to make sure we've got the best toilets of anyone. That could be a trump card you know, Albert.'

Albert started to turn away, but Cyril's voice was too loud to escape. 'And there's another thing, Albert. What about our drivers and cars? Council members need to get to and from matches you know. We don't want to be pushed out by this GFO lot.' Albert heard murmurings of agreement nearby.

'Their VIPs will think they own the place,' Cyril Townsend continued, 'but it's our patch, and if we're hosting we must look after the needs of our own members.'

Albert noticed that Simon Carslake was sitting at the other side of the bar with some of the campaign team. At that moment Albert hoped to God that Carslake couldn't hear them.

He turned to Townsend. 'Don't worry about it for now, Cyril,' he said quickly, glancing in Carslake's direction again. 'There's plenty of time before the bid gets decided. Now gents I'm really sorry, I need to...'

'It's been great to see you, Albert lad,' said Ron Newby, 'but one final thing before you go.' Ron looked around him, put his arm around Albert's shoulders and lowered his voice. 'Albert, the thing is, I want you to put in a good word for Barnsley. We'd like to host a match, and I know you feel like me, you don't want everything going to the big boys. We need to think about the smaller clubs Albert.'

'Yes ok Ron,' sighed Albert, 'We'll see what we can do.' He got up to go. He was meeting Monica who had been shopping while the meeting was on, and she would now be fretting.

'Hello love,' Albert said as he spotted Monica waiting patiently at the bottom of the EFO's sweeping staircase.' I've just had a nice beef sandwich with the boys, but I'll come round the corner with you if you're hungry.'

'I am a little bit,' replied Monica. 'We needn't take long.'

'Fair enough,' said Albert, and soon they were sitting at their favourite corner table in the local Italian restaurant. 'We've been coming here a few years,' he smiled. 'I reckon I'll always be happier here than going to all these posh restaurants the GFO keep taking us to. Even if I always end up ordering English grub when I'm here!'

Monica laughed. 'You know some people say that sort of thing and don't really mean it, but I know you do.' She took a sip of water. 'But goodness me, that hotel in Barcelona was fabulous, wasn't it, and that lobster main course was as good as you'll get in Padstow.'

'You're the one enjoying all this high living, Monica,' chuckled Albert. 'What on earth would your mother have said!' As he spoke, Albert beckoned the waiter. 'I was just saying to Lady Lewis, Giuseppe, we've been coming here a good number of years. Every time I had to come up to London for a Council meeting.'

'Well, I'm quite sure you haven't been coming as long as I've been here,' Giuseppe beamed. 'I've been here for thirty years.'

'You're right Giuseppe,' said Monica. 'Old Bill Parsons introduced us when Sir Albert came up from Cornwall for his first Council meeting.' Monica handed back the menu without glancing at it. 'I'll just have the lasagne, please,' she said. 'Sir Albert has already had a sandwich, so will you just have a beer love?'

Albert nodded in agreement. 'Just a half please, Giuseppe.' And with that, the waiter scribbled on his pad and left the couple on their own. 'So,' said Monica after a brief pause, 'how did you get on with all the Council men? I saw Barbara Townsend earlier. How old is Cyril now? He must be getting on.'

'Oh, he must be in his 80s. He talks about going to see Dixie Dean at Goodison way back.'

He thought for a moment about the meeting.

'Oh well love, it was good to catch up with them all, but the problem is these old boys are a bit unrealistic about the World Cup. And they think just because I'm on the GFO Exec I can fix it for them to get everything they want.

'And of course Carslake doesn't help. I'm sure he's ear wigging every daft idea the Council chaps bring forward and storing it away to taunt me with.' He smiled as Giuseppe brought his beer.

'I'll tell you something for nothing,' Albert continued. 'I wouldn't trust that Carslake fellow as far as I could throw him. He's up to no good that one. He's only interested in what's in it for him.'

'Albert, I told you that the moment I set eyes on him,' said Monica with a shake of her head. 'I know there's nothing wrong with ambition, but he's so cocky with it. I don't doubt he's done well in these big companies he's worked in but they probably like people like him. He's not our type at all. But I've said all this to you before. The trouble is Albert, like most men you don't listen!'

'I know love. I should have taken more notice of what you said before we appointed him. Still, it's done now, and I'll have to deal with him as best I can.'

'Now Albert, you be careful,' said Monica. 'He's a dangerous man that Carslake. Don't let him turn you against your old friends and colleagues. Some of them may be a bit out of touch but they're loyal to you and you might need to call on that loyalty one day. Just you listen to me this time. Monica knows best, alright? Remember that.'

Albert chuckled and nodded his head as Giuseppe brought Monica's lasagne to the table.

Chapter 10

Our man in London

Stephen Green decided to walk across the park to his lunch engagement. He was no great lover of the underground.

It was a pleasant May morning with the sun breaking through the trees. It was a morning that reminded Stephen how much he had missed London when he'd been abroad for long periods of time. He had of course chosen the diplomatic life, and he had no complaints, but he had always been glad that the Foreign Office system brought its diplomats back to base every three years or so.

Governments worried that diplomats might go native. Bringing them home from time to time was thought to be the best control mechanism. For Stephen, it provided precious opportunities to see old friends and visit familiar haunts in his home city.

Hyde Park held particularly fond memories for him. It was here every Summer, from childhood, that he had delighted in the promenade concerts at the Royal Albert Hall. He had often queued for tickets outside the Hall for hours, first with school friends then with Oxford friends who loved to come to London and stay at his family home in St John's Wood.

He enjoyed nothing more than to share thoughts and ideas with other music enthusiasts as they waited in line outside London's Victorian cathedral of culture. Never competitive on the sporting field, he now vied intensely with other young experts for intellectual authority as they duelled over the symphony or concerto they were about to hear. Extra points were won by awareness of some obscure composer or piece of music that the proms director had tossed into the programme. When the doors opened, Stephen's heart had always pounded in the rush to get to the front of the promenaders.

Now aged sixty-five, other memories came flooding back as he made his way across the park. He had fallen in love here, not just with the proms, but with more than one girlfriend. He could still remember the picnic spots. He could hear the corks popping.

After coming down from Oxford, Stephen had gone straight to the Foreign Office. His early overseas postings had been interesting, even by his understated standards. For his second tour he had found himself in Moscow at the time of the Cuban missile crisis in 1962.

Stephen had captivated dinner parties over the years with his Cold War memories. He could provide a minute-by-minute account of the crucial day when the world almost ended. Young and inexperienced as he was, he had come face-to-face that day with Nikita Kruschev himself. 'It was like looking into the face of Armageddon,' he would tell his nephews and nieces, few of whom had any idea what he was talking about.

Remarkably, twelve months later Stephen Green had been appointed Third Secretary in Washington and was in the capital the day that Kennedy was assassinated in Dallas. He had loved Washington from the moment he arrived. He had fitted into the political scene quickly and easily, and soon had a vibrant group of American and British friends. The Americans particularly enjoyed his dry sense of humour, even if they were sometimes baffled by it.

Like many of his generation, he was charmed by the young US President who presided over the 'Camelot' fantasy and who looked destined for greatness. Kennedy's assassination had affected Stephen Green profoundly. When the time came to return to London three years later, he still felt a deep sense of loss.

There were not many diplomats who could boast such a high profile 'double' in his young years, and Stephen told his stories very well.

Thirty-five years later, and after a career topped by stints as an ambassador in Central America and the Middle East, he was on the point of retiring. He was reasonably comfortable with the notion, but he knew he would miss the service.

Deep in thought, he walked with a good pace through the West End from Hyde Park, and soon reached the door of The Ivy, his destination for lunch. After sharing a few pleasantries with the doorman, he handed over his coat at the cloakroom bar and was taken to a corner table on the far side of the dining room.

His partner for lunch rose immediately from his seat and shook his hand. 'Hello Stephen,' said Sir Graham Hood. 'How wonderful to see you looking so well.'

'Well, I can return the compliment with spades, Graham. Not missing Paris too much it seems,' beamed Stephen.

'No! Quite fun to be back in Whitehall with this crazy new Government. Exhausting though. They keep wanting to do things but don't really have a clue.' The two men laughed heartily.

'And Marjorie is loving getting the old Highgate house out of mothballs at last. And so nice to be able to see the girls so often of course.' His face became a little more serious. 'Now, pressing matters, Stephen. Tell me what you think of this claret before I order it.' He handed over the calfskin-covered wine menu, with his thumb marking an entry for Chateau Laungoa-Barton 1994.

'You have been busy in Paris, Graham, learning all about the very best that Bordeaux can offer.'

Hood grinned and called over the wine waiter. 'Well, coming from you, that's flattery. "Stephen the Nose"... they still call you that in the office!'

Stephen had known Sir Graham for years. Their careers had taken them to different parts of the world, but they had always kept in touch when their leave in London coincided. Then they would lunch together, put the world to rights, and gossip happily about the comings and goings of colleagues, family, and their political masters.

'But more like "on-me-'ead Stephen" now you're the Foreign Office's very own Mr Football,' Hood said with a loud laugh.

'How very interesting. Never heard you mention you were interested in the round ball game, Stephen. You fancy the idea of bringing the World Cup tournament back to these shores do you? I suppose it has the virtue of keeping all the England fans at home. Saves us apologising all the time.'

Sir Graham thought he detected a little defensiveness in Stephen's reply. 'Well, I thought it might amuse me for a while you know,' he said. 'And actually, yes, I used to watch Chelsea a bit in the late Fifties. Went to Stamford Bridge when I had the chance. Jimmy Greaves was a youngster there. Great times. Never mentioned it in the office though. I don't think it would have been a good career move, do you?'

'Quite!' said Sir Graham without comment. 'However,' he continued, 'the good news is that – as you well know of course – the PM is very keen on the opium of the masses, and particularly on English football's world domination. Number 10 is making that very clear to all government departments.'

He handed Stephen a copy of a memorandum issued to Whitehall Permanent Secretaries, dated the previous day. Stephen read the short but very clear note, instructing every department and government agency to offer whatever support was required by the EFO bidding team. Stephen had heard from the Minister of Sport that Number 10 was planning to do this, but he was grateful to see the memo had actually been sent. He folded it and put it in his inside pocket.

'That's clear enough,' Stephen said. 'I daresay it will be easier with some departments than others.'

'Certainly,' nodded Sir Graham. 'But of course this is where I come in. As I mentioned on the phone, our Perm Sec has asked me not only to ensure full support for you from within the Foreign Office and our overseas missions, but also from across Whitehall. That's a pretty exceptional mandate Stephen.'

For the first time, Stephen thought he heard a little resentment in Sir Graham's voice.

'I think the first thing you must do is to present to our staff in London. Tell them about the bidding process. What happens when, and what sort of help you're going to need.'

Stephen understood why Sir Graham was a little miffed to be running around after him and his new colleagues at the EFO. After heading Britain's diplomatic mission in Paris, he might well feel that this liaison role was a bit beneath him.

'Of course,' said Stephen, trying to make his formal response still sound friendly and grateful. 'I'll get the EFO's Chief Executive chap to come with me. He's quite bright. He's got a very good team and a well thought-through plan.'

Sir Graham nodded his agreement in silence as a waiter poured another glass each for the two men. Stephen took the opportunity to engage his friend's interest.

'D'you know, Graham, one of the fascinating things I've found out so far is how few people are actually involved in this decision to award the right to host the World Cup. It seems the power to decide between us and the Russians and whoever else is bidding simply rests in the hands of twenty-five men – the Board and its Chairman, the GFO President, Larsen. There's no accountability as you and I would understand the word. It's all pretty murky.'

Sir Graham was listening carefully to every word. Stephen knew that, even if he disapproved of the role he had been given, he would brief himself meticulously in order to carry out his duties with total professionalism. Stephen also knew well enough that a little global gossip went a long way with him.

'You know, these guys and the rest of the GFO members are sitting on huge piles of revenue, mostly income from the World Cup tournament, which is a real money-spinner what with sponsors and so on. I've no idea what the money amounts to – and nobody really does know apart from the GFO bods – but it dwarfs any other sporting event I believe.'

Stephen glanced at his old friend, who was still listening intently without offering a comment.

'You've probably heard, these guys fly first class everywhere, often with their wives, and stay in the very best suites in the very best hotels. They expect to be treated as royalty wherever they go. A few of them from the Middle East really are from royal families... and the rest think they are!'

'Graham, I've learnt that it's all something of a fantasy world and with so much finance involved there's great scope for corruption. Some of these Board members are very dodgy characters.'

'Oh dear,' Sir Graham said at last, smiling inscrutably. 'So we're going to have to get our hands a little dirty are we?'

'I'm afraid so,' smiled Stephen.

'Well let me know if you need a bit more information on these men. If Her Majesty's Government can't claim to have spies everywhere, I'm not sure who can.'

Chapter 11

Playing with fire

Giselle Schneider was curious. What was Alexei Baskin playing at, inviting her out to dinner? There could only be two reasons. Either he wanted to bed her, or he wanted information about her husband's plans.

She loved intrigue and she loved Turkish food. So she accepted his invitation to the best Turkish restaurant in Brussels without hesitation. Helmut had already returned to Munich from his meeting at the GFO. But she had arranged to fly to Paris next day to see their daughter Celestine at the Sorbonne and was staying an extra night in Brussels. Convenient, she thought.

Giselle hadn't seen Baskin since she and Helmut were visitors to his family yacht nine months before. She had found him attractive then, and she knew that he had liked her, but she hadn't thought much more about him since. God, she smiled to herself as her taxi headed for the Ixelles municipality where they were to meet in the restaurant. I can't jump into bed with every damn sexy man I meet!

Besides, there was a time and place for having fun. Giselle and Helmut had a relaxed relationship; she loved men and he loved his work. Neither wished to confuse the boundaries, and the arrangement suited them. They were also attentive and caring parents and delightful company together with friends.

People who knew Giselle well often said she had a much sharper mind than her husband. She certainly fell for lithe young bodies, but her meaningful affairs were only with interesting and intelligent men. A number of her suitors had been frustrated by this fact.

She had certainly found Helmut interesting when they first met as junior lawyers in Munich. But even before they were married, Giselle told him that although she was happy to give up her career to raise their children, she intended to maintain her 'wide interests' in future.

In return for her freedom, she never interfered with her husband's love of football politics. When Helmut had suggested that she might be 'unwell' on Baskin's yacht and take herself to her cabin so that the two men could talk, she didn't for a moment demur. She knew none of the details of her husband's dealings with the Russian and had no intention of finding anything out.

The morning after her dinner with Alexei, Giselle was the first to wake, and for a moment she cursed her lack of self-discipline. Alexei had been an extraordinary and fascinating dinner companion. He had regaled her with stories about his childhood in Minsk, his grandfather's escape from the Bolsheviks, the old man's romantic but futile escapades with the White Russian Army, his family's cruel fortunes under Stalin, and its remarkable transformation under Gorbachev.

She had been spellbound by the sheer guts with which Alexei and his cousins had strived to build and protect new businesses during *glasnost*, using treasure that his uncles were at last able to access from Western European bank accounts that had lain dormant for fifty years. Fortified by two shared bottles of champagne, she had listened to him as he talked about the two wives who had only ever been interested in his money. She had nodded understandingly as he blamed himself for only being interested in their bodies. If only, he had said, he could have found a connection with a woman who loved him for himself. Impassioned by emotion, Giselle had hushed his words with a lingering kiss, and from that moment the journey to his bed had been inevitable.

But now, the morning after, she pouted and sighed her displeasure as she pulled up the pillows behind her back. Alexei woke immediately. She looked at him. Handsome sure enough. Not a bad lover. But what the hell was she doing?

Alexei made no attempt to interpret Giselle's expression.

'Darling,' he said. 'We had better have breakfast in our room. I don't know who might be staying in this hotel.'

Giselle said nothing but smiled weakly. Sleeping with the Russian was certainly outside her agreement with Helmut. But all her experience taught her that extracting herself from a situation like this would require subtle moves. Antagonising Alexei now would only make things worse. She needed time to think. She pulled the covers across her naked body.

'Yes, that would be wonderful.'

Alexei looked at her curiously. He seemed about to say something else but telephoned to room service instead. Then he rose quickly from the bed.

'I'll take a shower before breakfast arrives. Are you ok?'

Giselle smiled as warmly as her troubled mind would allow. She dressed while Alexei was in the bathroom. Then they sat at the coffee table and ate breakfast in near total silence. As they finished their coffee, Alexei rose to his feet.

'Giselle. I need to say something. Last night... I think we had a beautiful connection.'

Oh God, thought Giselle, what do I say... She nodded.

'The thing is Giselle, there is of course your husband.'

Giselle heard herself say faintly: 'Yes, Alexei, there is.'

'You see, Giselle, I'm a weak man. I invited you to dinner because... I think you are a wonderful woman. And I have no wonderful woman in my life. But you're Helmut's wife. And I can't betray him with you any more. It's a terrible thing for me to do to my friend. And I'm sorry.'

Giselle looked at Alexei. She thought she had never seen a sadder face. She rose to her feet, put her arms around him, and squeezed him tightly. 'You're not a weak man, Alexei; you're a good man. We will never refer to this moment again.'

She kissed him on the cheek and left his room.

Chapter 12

Danny boy

After the EFO's World Cup 2003 campaign had been announced in February, Simon Carslake had spent as little time as possible seeking Albert's views on campaign plans. He had no expectation that Albert would offer useful insights: the only time for consulting him on anything was when he had to defer to his position.

Albert was EFO Chairman, and he was formally responsible for the campaign.

When he needed his support before the Board, Simon usually had a well prepared strategy for making Albert feel he was involved in the campaign. It was the same strategy he had used with senior managers as he had worked his way through his career. It meant presenting three options, and making sure his preferred solution was so carefully crafted and watertight that only a fool would reject it.

However, Simon had to admit that there were some – fortunately very rare – occasions when the Chairman's input to the campaign was not just necessary; it was valuable. One of these occasions was when a footballer had to be chosen as the figurehead for the campaign.

Simon had met enough of the men who had played football for England in the past thirty years to have some idea about who to choose for the role – and certainly who to reject. But he had to admit to himself that Albert, for all his inadequacies in other areas, possessed an uncanny depth of knowledge about footballers past and present.

It had taken a while for it to dawn on him that Albert's entire career was explained not by ambition but by a much simpler fact: Albert just adored football.

Love of the game was why Albert had put his muddy boots on at school and spent every Saturday afternoon hopelessly chasing fleetfooted young wingers. That was why he had run the touchline in Army matches, fully aware he wasn't good enough to play with the professional lads in his unit doing National Service, but desperately keen to be involved. And that was why he first stood for office on Cornwall's football committees, making the case for better pitches, coaches, and referees, in the vain but determined hope that he might pull the west country's footballing prospects up by its bootstraps.

Nowadays, Albert loved nothing more than to spend time with footballers. It was his way of sustaining his passion, of feeling the same thrills as he had felt as a boy. He was seriously in awe of them, of course, as any true fan always is. But as his developing career offered more and more privileged opportunities to meet his heroes, he had been able to overcome or at least shelve his shyness.

When he went to club matches, sometimes two a week in the season, he was always welcome in the board room. Club chairmen were sometimes EFO Council colleagues, and they knew that Albert loved to be taken down to the dressing rooms and introduced to the team after the game.

He wasn't only interested in the top players or the top teams. He still believed, as he had believed as a boy watching Bristol City on the odd occasion he could afford the fare for the long bus journey from Truro, playing professional football at any level bestowed some kind of stardust on any young man. He chuckled sometimes when he remembered approaching City's reserve left back in the club car park all those years ago, mumbling a request for an autograph, fearful that terror would strike him dumb at the critical moment.

He had nothing to fear from today's players. The club and international players that Albert met were usually warm to the EFO Chairman's childlike enthusiasm for the game. They joked about him when he'd gone... 'ooh that were a lovely goal you scored in the second 'arf Steve... Were that yer second of the season..?' But he was a good bloke. Pity more of that lot at the EFO weren't like him.

Simon wasn't in the least jealous of Albert's footballing connections. In fact, quite the opposite. Simon's starting point with human relationships was an assumed sense of superiority. He hadn't met any footballers with his intellect or interests, so he hardly expected to bond with them. It was only those few players who were able to turn their celebrity into tangible benefits that he grudgingly admired.

As for Albert's encyclopaedic knowledge of the English game, he was welcome to it. Simon could never be accused of loving football. He certainly enjoyed watching some games if there were plenty of goals, but he also enjoyed watching rugby, and his sport at school had been hockey.

He knew enough about the game and its history to research additional detail to help him at his EFO interview, and he was always skilled at feigning enthusiasm. But after getting the Chief Executive job, he saw little need to keep it up. Now he firmly believed that football knowledge was only useful if it could advance the EFO's cause and his own career. He knew how to use the resources around him, and with Albert there was always plenty of keen interest on tap.

'Good morning, Sir Albert,' Simon said brightly into his office phone handset. 'Simon here. Did you enjoy the match last night?'

Simon had a copy of *The Chronicle* opened at the back page. He wasn't sure which cup replay Albert had been to. There were two in London last evening, and he was ready to discuss them both with Albert.

'Simon? Yes?' Albert was too nice a man to show Simon his true feelings towards him, but he was damned if he was going to sound friendly on the phone.

Simon caught the mood. He folded the paper quietly and threw it in the bin. 'Sir Albert, can I have a few minutes to get your thoughts on something quite important?'

Albert breathed in and out as he thought for a moment. What was he wanting? 'Yes,' he said coldly.

'The thing is... Albert... we need to decide on our player for the campaign. You know them all so well. I would really appreciate your suggestions.'

'Suggestions?'

'Yes. I suppose the obvious ones are Bill Christie, Mike Potter, Bobby Williams... But I wonder if we ought to be looking at a more recent crop. You know. Darren Gilchrist – he seems to have a good TV profile, even if he does have trouble getting a sentence out without three 'you knows'...' As soon as Simon laughed at his own comment, he knew it was a mistake.

'These players haven't been to university, Simon,' Albert said quietly, 'and nor have most of the fans.'

Simon kept his counsel. He really wanted to remind Albert that many of the GFO members had themselves been to university and expected EFO representatives to talk English at least as well as they did – especially if their support for a World Cup hosting bid was required. But this was not the moment.

'No I know. Fair comment. So any thoughts on who else?'

'What about Gary Summers.'

Simon was flummoxed. Who was Gary Summers? He reached for his *Compendium of English players (1960 to 1990)*. Summers... Summers. Here we are. Played twice for England. 1973. Both times in *friendlies*. Hardly a national hero, thought Simon.

'I was thinking of someone with a high profile, Albert. How about Leroy Ryan?'

'Who?'

'Leroy Ryan, played 68 games, including two World Cups in...'

'Yes yes yes. I know who he is.' Albert was thinking as fast as he could. 'He's one of the first black boys to be capped isn't he?'

'That's right, Albert. He's also a great communicator. He's on all our access committees. Very keen to promote multi-culturalism. Encourage more ethnic minority coaches. Stamp out racism amongst fans. All that kind of thing.'

Simon paused. There was silence at the end of the phone.

'And Albert, I think Leroy Ryan could play very well with the African nations. Kumpa and his gang would like him. And he ticks a lot of boxes amongst the more far-sighted Europeans too.'

Simon waited.

'Simon, I don't want you to think I'm racist at all.'

'Of course not, Albert.'

'It's just that... surely we need an English player...'

'I think you'll find Leroy Ryan was born in Bermondsey, Albert. That's why he played for England.' Simon smiled to himself.

'Yes of course,' said Albert uncomfortably. 'Of course, I didn't mean in that way. I meant, you know, a traditional Englishman.'

'You mean a white man.'

The phone was silent again.

'The thing is, I'm not sure the EFO Council would like it very much. You know he's very critical of the EFO sometimes. What if he said something at the wrong time? Supposing he talked about the sort of racist chants he used to get in his early years.'

This time it was Simon who stayed silent as he thought about Albert's comment. He really liked the idea of Leroy Ryan in many ways. Great PR opportunity. He also took wicked pleasure, thinking about the red faces amongst Albert's EFO Council colleagues at the very prospect of this rather smooth and cultured black player representing them all over the world. How good it would be to hear their objections...

But in his calculating head, Simon knew that Albert was right. Maybe Leroy Ryan would provide a trump card amongst the nonwhite GFO nations. Just suppose he *did* find himself in a bar one night with a journalist, answering searching questions about his career and the challenges he had faced as a young black player in England. It was a risk. No doubt. Too much of one.

'Yes, yes I see what you mean, Albert.'

Simon heard Albert exhale, seemingly with relief.

'So... you don't think he's the right man, Simon?' Albert heard Simon's muttered agreement. 'A great pity of course... but you're always telling me what a cut-throat business all this bidding is... it really wouldn't be fair to him.'

Simon caught Albert's conciliatory manner, and naturally exploited it.

'Ok, so if not Ryan, who else? Someone from the last ten years. Who's made a big impact on the world stage, popular, charismatic... easy to manage? Who would world leaders like to meet?'

'Well, there is Danny Creighton,' said Albert. 'European Cup winner. GFO World Footballer of the Year.'

'Danny Creighton,' repeated Simon. He had a vague memory of the name. 'Yes that's interesting. No skeletons in his cupboard? No wife beating?'

'Really Simon,' said Albert, genuinely disgusted by Simon's comments. 'You do always think the worst of people. Danny is a fine young man, and so is Chrissie his wife. Three lovely children. In fact young Daniel is in the England Under 15 squad.'

'Good, good,' said Simon. He liked the sound of this. Good family man. He needed a supportive wife. 'Attractive???' he wrote on his note pad. Perhaps they could do something with the boy, too...

'Oh and Simon...' said Albert. 'Danny is half-caste.'

'You mean he's mixed-race Albert,' Simon corrected him as he shook his head in despair. 'And you think the EFO Council won't mind that?' he said, unable to betray a note of cynicism in his voice.

'Well no, I don't think so. He's never been involved in any of that racism business... I think he sees himself as white.' Albert thought for a moment. 'Anyway, Chrissie's white.'

Simon looked to the ceiling before gathering himself to respond.

'Albert, I'm so grateful to you. I KNEW you'd have the answer. Will you check what the EFO Council thinks, and I'll get Creighton in to meet us straight away. Goodbye.'

Chapter 13

With the generals

The President loved New York. It was his favourite city, period. It gave him a buzz from the moment he stepped off the plane. It became irresistible as the limousine took him closer to Manhattan. He didn't know why New York had that effect. Perhaps its aura reflected on those who had done well in life.

President Larsen never doubted that he had done well. He was the man that kings and premiers had to meet. All over the world, football was the people's game, and he was in charge of it.

Larsen hadn't achieved greatness by chance. His Presidential elections were built on painstaking analysis of GFO members in each country, and a promise of rewards to the doubters.

For two terms in office, he had made managing enemies his priority. There were men who envied his power and wanted it for themselves. He could do nothing about that, but he could find out who they were and stop them before they were dangerous. His judgement was unerring, his patronage precise, and his support network robust. It was said that every GFO man in the world was somewhere on the President's radar, listed according to value or threat.

Larsen's personal style was part of his strategy. He was effortlessly friendly and listened carefully to the most trivial concern. His memory for names was legendary. He would show it off at GFO events, going walkabout with his aides through the cafes and bars where his colleagues were relaxing. Smiling broadly, he could switch with ease between seven languages, convincing everyone he met that they had individual access to their President.

It was a simple way to win support and frustrate enemies, and it made the smallest nations in the GFO family feel they really counted. 'Your vote is just as important to me as those of the Europeans,' he would declare to a man from a South Sea island. And so it was. All countries' votes did indeed score equally in Presidential elections.

At seventy-two, President Larsen had no intention of loosening his grip on power. But he was a realist. He understood change. He needed help from tomorrow's men to stay supreme today.

His close allies found those men of tomorrow for him in each region of the world and helped him monitor their progress. He gave each of them his attention as required: a chat over drinks in the Presidential Suite, perhaps, or even a full-scale Presidential visit. A sound man might find his country suddenly eligible for a 'development' grant, decided by a subcommittee chaired until recently by Larsen himself, and now by his friend and ally Joe Kumpa.

The President could power an ambitious man's career, and that usually resulted in lasting loyalty. His support was regularly renewed, and the future was secure.

From time to time President Larsen liked to take stock of his football empire, or 'meet up with the generals' as Joe Kumpa liked to put it. New York was a good place to do it.

Joe Kumpa was one of the President's most loyal supporters. He had served on the GFO Board for the same seven years Larsen had been President. There had been a time when Joe had himself thought about standing as President, but although he was not the kind of man to analyse deeply or question his own abilities, instinct told him it wasn't the job for him. Loyal and influential, Joe was the main conduit to the President for GFO people, and as his value had grown over the years so had his rewards.

New York was as much of a favourite for Kumpa as it was for Larsen. As well as the restaurants and comfortable hotel rooms,

Joe and his travelling secretary Maggie liked the city's late-night jazz spots.

The President had arranged dinner at one of New York's finest restaurants, *Osteria Morini*. He liked to arrive early at the table to gather his thoughts and enjoy an Alabama Slammer cocktail alone. He knew Carlos well and liked the way the headwaiter recognised him without overfamiliarity.

The President and Kumpa would be joined at the table on that spring evening by a guest who inspired little of their affection but had been critical to their success over the years. Neither Larsen nor Kumpa ever used the man's real name. Neither could remember who had first started to call him 'the Laundryman' as a joke, but it had stuck because it described him well. He was a man with many skills, and his stock in trade was clearing up the kind of business where Larsen's or Kumpa's involvement would be inappropriate.

The Laundryman had no formal role within the GFO. There was no need for it. People who met him, like Greg Turner when he had briefed Joe on World Cup bidding scenarios a few months earlier, knew better than to ask his name or his job title.

At the President's insistence, Joe Kumpa arrived after Larsen but before their guest. Larsen liked to prepare for every meeting, with allies as much as with foes. The Laundryman was certainly an ally, but the relationship with him was more complicated than between the two football men.

They knew the Laundryman was always punctual, and after planning the agenda with Larsen, Joe had time for two cocktails before he arrived. With his tongue loosened a little, Joe teased the President. His special relationship allowed it.

'Do you ever wonder what would happen if your empire fell apart?' Joe began with a grin. 'Just suppose one morning you were sitting in your grand office, and the Belgian police battered at the door with a search warrant?' Kumpa laughed heartily. 'Just imagine! Watching all your Board member friends and all your staff being arrested, one by one, and taken away in police vans.'

He paused, and his grin slowly disappeared. He asked the question again, more seriously, as if to reassure them both. 'But Christian, do you ever think about something like that actually happening?'

There was silence for a moment before the President muttered a chilly response. 'Don't be ridiculous, Joe.' A bottle of his selected Amarone 1988 had just been planted on the table, and he moved it carefully away from Kumpa before continuing in a more indulgent tone.

'You are being melodramatic, my old friend. We're not fool proof of course, but it would take a hell of a lot to break open my... what we have built up. We're in control Joe, don't worry about that.' Then he added portentously: 'And I intend things will stay that way.'

But Kumpa persisted.

'Just suppose, Christian... just suppose that the Laundryman turned on us. He knows everything. About the money. How you run the organisation. He's a dangerous man. Suppose somebody offered him more than we pay him.' He grinned. 'What if he sings – like a canary...'

Larsen smiled, and patted Kumpa's arm. 'And who's going to pay him more than we do?'

Their dinner guest arrived, and the two men rose to greet him politely but without warmth.

To diners at other tables, the man would not have seemed out of place as a member of the President's party. Although in his mid-forties – younger than both the other men – he wore an expensively tailored suit with highly polished black brogue shoes. He could have been a corporate executive, or a GFO man. But a discerning observer might also have noticed a link to another life: the insignia of a parachute regiment - entwined angels - tattooed on the back of his right hand.

The three men had plenty to discuss that evening. The emerging bids for hosting the 2003 World Cup needed careful management.

So too did the next Presidential election, due to be held in only six months' time at the October 1996 GFO Congress. These were separate events, run with different voting processes, but lobbying for one could have a big effect on the other.

Only Greg Turner understood the politics of GFO elections as well as these three men, but his expertise was theoretical. For the men at dinner in New York, the results of both elections were critical to their careers.

On the face of it, voting for who should stage the World Cup appeared to be a relatively simple affair, resting with an electorate of twenty-five Board members (the President's casting vote had never been used, but his influence on other Board members was immeasurable). The small number of votes meant the stakes were high for securing the support of each Board member, and competition between the bidding teams was intense. The chances of a tie between candidates were also high, so getting commitment to second and even third voting preferences could be crucial to the result. Lobbying was complicated and expensive, and the potential for double dealing was real.

The Presidential election had different challenges. Each national football organisation affiliated to the GFO – 204 in all – cast one vote for the President. Naturally, bigger nations opposed this form of democracy, but President Larsen did not support their view. Democracy suited his style, and his electoral calculations.

It was the Presidential election that the three men discussed first.

'Well Mr President... Mr Kumpa... I bring you good news,' the Laundryman said. He spoke English well. 'Yes, our friend Lelei Fiso is up to his neck in shit with the FDA here in New York.' He looked over his wine glass to see the reaction. Larsen smiled encouragingly.

'It seems his people don't like all the bad publicity he got for his financial affairs. They aren't sure they want him re-elected as Asia

Alliance President. And that won't do his challenge to you much good will it?'

The President smiled again and nodded. It was good news. Kumpa poured himself another glass of Amarone. 'Poor old Fiso,' he said. 'If he'd kept his drug business going, his gangsters could have put the shits up them Asia Alliance guys.' He guffawed loudly.

Larsen spoke in soft and measured tones. 'I agree. This is very helpful.' He smiled. 'Poor Fiso, it couldn't have happened to a nicer chap.' The three men enjoyed the joke.

Then Larsen's face darkened a little.

'But I don't think it's over with the Asians. These people never quite forgave me for standing in their way when they wanted more places on the GFO Board. They'll find somebody else to challenge me, that's for sure. Or they'll join up with the Europeans and encourage them to find another candidate.'

'You're right,' Joe Kumpa said thoughtfully. 'When I last saw that old boy Albert Lewis he said he'd been told by his colleagues in Europe to expect another candidate for your Presidency.' He laughed.

'These English – do they really know what's going on? Anyway I told him straight: they better be careful who they vote for or they might as well kiss goodbye to their precious World Cup bid right now.'

'What did he say to that?' the President asked.

'Well, he looked like a crocodile bit his arse. Like he never thought about that,' grinned Joe. 'They gotta learn, life is not so easy for the great English EFO. They been dozing on the sidelines too long. Now they want the world to jump into line and give them the World Cup for free! They gotta think again.'

Kumpa warmed to his theme.

'They just don't get that the little countries need some help to grow up big and strong like them. They so stupid these English. The Germans been doing football aid for years, but not them. They don't see how clever the Germans are – using corporate sponsors' money to make them look good. Using it to line a few pockets as well.'

The President nodded again with a slight acknowledging smile. 'Yes, sure, but as we know, the Germans are very smart operators.'

'Anyway,' Joe continued, 'they English coming to see me soon – in the dark, scary continent. Don't worry Mr President. Big Joe'll frighten them off - but not before we get their money first.' He roared with laughter.

'The English had another shock recently,' added the Laundryman. 'My sources say they had a financial proposition put before them. Let's just say a price tag on a block of four votes. My guy says this Carslake Chief Executive fella was like a rabbit in the headlights. Didn't seem to understand that if they want to win, English money might actually have to change hands.'

The President looked at the Laundryman with an icy stare, and the Laundryman's smirk quickly evaporated. 'I knew nothing of this,' Larsen said. 'Who authorised this approach to the English?'

The Laundryman looked down at the table and tapped an unused fork gently on the tablecloth.

'Boss, aren't my orders to get what we can? These votes could be worth three million bucks to us.' He paused. 'But don't worry. They won't help the English to win. Anyway, they haven't got the balls to find the money.'

'Then why bother trying,' Larsen muttered, as he put his knife and fork down. He looked down at his plate for a moment as he thought about what to say next.

'Gentlemen, I know the English, and I don't trust them. Yes, yes, yes, they look so amateurish and out of touch with the real world. But be sure of one thing: they're determined to win. There's a lot at stake for these guys. The government. The Press. The public. Their pride. They've wasted years in World Cup football, that's how they think. We can't always be sure they won't find the money somehow. And if they find money for four votes, that might just give them the confidence to tough it out and get over the line.'

'Well,' said Joe, unconvinced. 'How I see it, the English think it's all about the best bid will win.' He looked at Larsen, and shook with laughter, thrusting all his weight backwards on his chair. 'They're so stupid.'

Larsen smiled. He enjoyed Joe's rough and irreverent humour, and he could easily lighten the President's mood. He was so different from the smooth Europeans he was used to dealing with.

'Ok,' Larsen said. 'But listen,' he addressed the Laundryman. 'Let's see what the English do with the offer, but no more deals from your guys. Let Joe work on them to get money out of them for Africa. But no more selling votes. We know the horse we're backing. I don't want to risk the votes our friends need.'

Larsen rubbed his chin.

'And Joe, I hear this guy Carslake is a different type from the rest of the old men at the EFO. Keep an eye on him in Yora.'

The President allowed himself a wry smile.

'Here's something to amuse us. I've been invited to Number 10 Downing Street to meet the new English Prime Minister. I shall have to go of course,' he said, absently, brushing crumbs from his suit front. 'You know, whenever I come away from one of these meetings with a head of state, I talk in glowing terms about their excellent bid and their beautiful country. The newspapers and TV people always think I'm backing the local bid. They're so gullible, it works every time.' He laughed, and his blue eyes glistened with pleasure.

The men shared his laughter, and the President poured dessert wine into three unused glasses. After a moment, he continued:

'Oh gentlemen, something else.'

Larsen pushed back his chair for comfort.

'I've been thinking about the English World Cup bid,' he said slowly. 'You know, we must of course be completely fair to all parties in the bidding process... but we could make life quite difficult for England if we put back the date of the Board's World Cup vote until after the Euro tournament next year. The English fans are bound to cause trouble during the Euro Cup. And if they do, who will want England to host our beautiful World Cup? It will spell the end for their bid.'

He looked at them both. Joe chuckled, and there was a hint of a smile on the Laundryman's stony expression. Neither man was concerned that President Larsen was claiming this idea as his own. He had clearly forgotten the phone call from Joe suggesting just such an action on the very day that Greg Turner had proposed it in jest two months earlier.

'As you say, Mr President, of course we must be very careful that we're fair to everyone,' said Joe, seemingly in deep thought. 'Of course, some people might think we had deliberately chosen the date of the vote to ruin England's chances...'

His face broke into a grin. 'Let's do it.'

The men clinked their glasses together. 'Poor old England,' Kumpa chuckled again. 'No wonder they want to host the World Cup. It's the only way they can control their violent fans and protect their precious old image.'

'So gentlemen,' the President said at last, 'enough of England and their World Cup ambitions. Now let's talk about how we get ME re-elected.'

Chapter 14

A little local difficulty

The Laundryman rarely used his real name on GFO business. He flew to Moscow with a Dutch passport as Andres van Biesen, aged forty-two, born in Eindhoven, married with three children. He liked to be Dutch. He could converse in the language a little, but everybody knew that the Dutch spoke good English so it was an easy disguise.

He didn't enjoy travelling to post-*glasnost* Russia. He preferred the certainty of the Soviet state. Since its dissolution five years earlier, he couldn't be sure who was working for whom. He had lost close contact with many of his old friends in the KGB. As for the men he still knew in Moscow, he couldn't trust them as he did in the old days. Where did their power lie, and how long would it last under the Yeltsin regime?

He had no plans to hang around in Moscow anyway. His Aeroflot Ilyushin landed at midday, and he would catch the afternoon flight to St Petersburg. Both he and Alexei Baskin preferred meetings in the second city. Although the Russian Football Organisaton's Director General had his main office in Moscow, St Petersburg attracted many more tourists, and the Laundryman felt anonymous and secure there. Its museums and galleries also provided plenty of quiet places to talk, and the leafy Alexander Garden was ideal for an evening stroll and private conversation.

On this occasion, Baskin would not be present. The meeting was with a man called Vasin. Baskin had identified the venue and time: the Eastern exit gate from the Lower Gardens of the Peterhof Palace at 7pm. The gate would be busy as people left before the

Gardens closed. The Laundryman had never met Vasin but he had carefully studied the photograph Baskin had sent and was skilled at remembering a man's features.

The Laundryman arrived at 6:40pm. He was early enough to find an empty bench seat before the crowds built up and had time to check that the venue was not under surveillance. He also didn't need to wait so long that his presence would arouse suspicion with the uniformed woman in the exit kiosk ten metres away.

He recognised Vasin as he walked along the path. The Russian was closely following a talkative group of camera-toting Eastern European men, and his large briefcase didn't look out of place among the camera bags. That was good. So Vasin wasn't a fool. But the Laundryman noted that Vasin hadn't spotted him as quickly as he had identified the Russian even though the Laundryman was more exposed, sitting alone on the bench. That was good too. The Laundryman liked to feel professionally superior to friend or foe.

Vasin sat down beside him with the briefcase at his feet. Neither man said anything. Good, thought the Laundryman again, Vasin understood the rules. After a few moments, the Laundryman broke the silence in English: 'These gardens are beautiful today.'

'Yes,' nodded Vasin, looking ahead. 'The flowers are welcoming spring.'

People were now crowding the footpath and beginning to queue around the gate. The woman at the kiosk could not see either of them anymore. The Laundryman glanced slowly to left and right. He got to his feet and turned ninety degrees as he stretched his arms extravagantly. He was happy that nobody was watching. Without looking at Vasin, he picked up the briefcase from in front of them and joined the crowd at the gate.

Like his GFO masters, the Laundryman stayed in the best hotels if he could. When he got to his suite at the Belmond Grand, it was nearly 8pm and he was feeling the effects of a long day.

He wanted a sauna and a soak in the giant bath before dinner, but he couldn't relax properly until he opened the briefcase. It was locked and he had to use a carbon tool on his keyring to force the brass clasp. The case was brimming with notes. He counted 35,000 roubles... $600,000. Good. A useful down payment subject to results. He opened the safe and deposited the money. After dinner he walked along Nevsky Prospekt towards the Embankment. He climbed down the dark steps beneath Troitskiy Bridge and threw the briefcase into the river.

The Laundryman slept well that night, and his taxi got him to the airport in good time to catch his flight to Beirut. The money was secure in the cavity of his suitcase. He was confident that the bag's specially treated material would render the contents opaque to the scanning technology at both ends of his flight. It had been proven at much better equipped airports in London and New York after all.

The two-stop Turkish Airlines flight took more than ten hours. His meeting with Galeb Roda was scheduled for next evening, so he had time to relax in his hotel in downtown and watch a movie. Roda was an old friend, who had taken care of money transfers for the Laundryman for many years. There was no need for too much security: Roda would ensure their privacy at the Em Sherif restaurant.

Perhaps that was why he was rather more relaxed than he should have been as he walked down Rue Victor Hugo towards the restaurant, carrying a holdall full of roubles. He certainly didn't see the figure that emerged from a doorway and pulled him into a dark hall. He couldn't make out the fists that hit him from two directions, and his efforts at fighting back were futile.

After what seemed like long minutes of sharpening pain all over his body, he felt a crack on his head from some kind of pipe and tasted the warm blood that quickly flowed from his scalp into his mouth. He collapsed with a wheeze of despair and passed out.

When the Laundryman woke, the light from his prison-cell window indicated the arrival of dawn. As he tried to raise his head, he felt a dull ache. He put his hand to his cranium and winced as he touched a crust of dried blood. He groped groggily and hopelessly around his bunk. There was no bag. He cursed noiselessly and fell asleep once more.

Galeb Roda woke him later in the day, accompanied by a policeman. 'Come on, let's get out of here,' Roda said. 'Here, put these clothes on.' The Laundryman noticed for the first time that his linen shirt was torn and his trousers were filthy. He put on the Lacoste polo shirt that Roda had brought, together with a pair of navy blue shorts.

The two men said nothing as they got into Roda's Land Cruiser and drove out of Beirut into the Wadi Hills. Roda stopped the car on a deserted track and waited for the Laundryman to speak.

'Find those bastards,' he said. 'Get the money. Make them suffer. And then rub them out. Do you understand? I don't want witnesses. It doesn't matter what it costs. Nobody does this to me.'

Roda nodded and drove the Laundryman back to his hotel.

Chapter 15

The white imperialists are coming

Joe Kumpa's office was rather more modest than the building next door. But it amused Joe that as President of the Alliance of African Football Organisations he wielded more influence than his neighbour at the Mboge State House, the President of the West African nation of Yora.

Joe's office was at the front of a single-story building with a corrugated tin roof. It was down a dusty track beside the State House, off the main road that boasted most of the country's major attractions and connected the island capital to the Yoran mainland. The only clues to the building's importance were two flags, one each side of the entrance, one for the Alliance of African Football Organisations, and the other for its parent body, the Global Football Organisation.

Inside, the facilities were sparse. Joe's big oak desk and chair, with a view to the front of the building through a metal framed window, had been sourced from the Governor's house – vacated when the country was made independent in 1962. Joe found the big desk comfortable for his heavy frame, and the wide top easily accommodated his collection of African football memorabilia. (He had given up displaying photographs of Yora politicians lest they caused offence to each new regime.)

Adjacent to Joe's desk was a smaller 1980s desk acquired from IBM where his secretary Maggie sat. She had the office computer and the only phone, together with a printer and fax machine. The fax was gathering red dust.

'We don't need that old fax since emails,' Maggie used to tell Joe, but it stayed where it was.

On the wall by the door, there was a ceiling-to-floor mirror that both Joe and Maggie used when appearances were important. Other than a scramble of cables poking through the ceiling and running to the skirting board, the walls were bare. Some of the cables went to Maggie's computer and others to the big screen television in the corner, but some were hanging loose. Mboge Technology kept promising to sort out the cables, but Maggie had given up chasing them.

Next door was Joe's meeting room, with a conference table and twelve leatherette chairs. In the corner was an old drinks cabinet, with an assortment of glasses. Next to it was a Coca Cola-branded chest fridge, mainly stocked with beer.

A single lavatory was enough for Joe and Maggie and any visitors. Maggie used a daily burst of fragrance from an aerosol to keep it welcoming.

The offices and the location were deliberately chosen: ideal when representatives from the wealthy footballing nations of the world came to visit. The building made a good backdrop for photographers, and sent a clear message that Joe's country and Joe's African football region needed a massive injection of financial aid to keep the global game healthy.

It was the morning of the day that Joe's latest visitors were due to arrive. Joe stood at the window, watching the small oil truck spewing out its diesel fumes and laterite dust as it disappeared up the track. He was impatient for news that the GFO World Cup bid campaign team from England had landed at Mboge Airport, and when he heard the phone ring and Maggie pick up the receiver, he felt a little frisson of anticipation.

'Well Mr K, that was George,' said Maggie as she hung up. 'The white imperialists have arrived. They're on the bus now with the High Commissioner. Are you ready for them – or shall I send them away?'

Joe roared with laughter. 'White imperialists! Yeah, that's right. Come to pay homage to the king eh Maggie? Ohhhh... I'll be ready for them colonial fuckers with their fuckin' High Commissioner – you be sure darlin'.'

He stopped laughing, and his voice slowed to become more menacing. 'They'll find out today who's boss alright. I'm gonna screw them for every penny they got. If they want that World Cup they're gonna have to pay for it, Maggie.'

Maggie put her arms round Joe's chest. 'Now don't go getting overheated Joe Kumpa. You just save a little energy for me.'

She stroked his cheek and reached up to wipe a bead of sweat from his temple. She knew how lucky she was, and she didn't plan to lose her big Joe Kumpa golden ticket through any lack of personal attention. Not many people knew about her and Joe. And those that guessed had little idea why the man who had a wife who'd been crowned Miss Yora 1992 should choose plump and matronly Maggie as his mistress.

Joe didn't care what anyone thought. If anyone had dared to ask, he wouldn't have denied or confirmed that Maggie was anything more than his secretary. He certainly wouldn't have tried to explain the skills that made her a very special secretary for a man with his appetites.

'Don't you worry, Maggie,' Joe beamed, revealing three gold teeth in his upper jaw. 'I'll always have plenty of energy for you.' He kissed her hard on the lips and held her close in his arms, pressing himself against her, hurting her rib cage with his diamond studded trouser belt.

Maggie drew away. Now was not the time for love. But she liked Joe's attention, so she resumed her playful talk. Maggie knew how much Joe loved teasing – almost as much as he loved holding her so tightly she could hardly breathe.

'Ohhhh yes, you treat me good NOW Joe Kumpa. But what will happen when you get your hands on that GFO Presidency? I'd like to know.' Maggie buttoned her blouse to the top in a show of mock rejection. 'You and Mrs K gonna be living it up in Europe, eh. And Maggie will be like one of those old bitch dogs in the street. No use to no-one.'

Standing before the mirror, Joe undid his suit trousers and folded in his sparkling white shirt tail. He tugged the knot of his tie under his collar. He chuckled at Maggie's nonsense.

'You know very well, my girl, I got no ambitions to be President. And I don't wanna deal with those fuckers in GFO day in, day out. Hey, remember – I'm the boss's right-handman. The whole idea is get him re-elected while all this World Cup bidding is going on. We got a good President.' He smiled. 'He's good for both of us.'

Joe stared long at his image in the mirror, and his face creased into a broad smile. 'Anyway, forget all that President stuff, we got a BIG meeting to think about TODAY, Maggie.'

Joe loved hosting these football administrators from the West. These guys were from England. He knew Albert Lewis, a fellow member of the GFO Board for the past couple of years. He had visited him in London a couple of times. What did some of his English colleagues call him after drinks at the Ritz? 'Old buffer,' that's it, Joe remembered. He chuckled. 'Old buffer Albert.'

And who were these other chaps? Carslake. He'd met him once in London a few months back. Flashy business type. And the rest of them would be the same. A few old men like Albert, full of England's 'great football traditions'. It didn't really matter to Joe who they were. He didn't care about pompous claims for their country or clever talk from the likes of Carslake. As for the British High Commissioner, he'd met Butler many times, and he knew he was afraid of Kumpa. Joe laughed to himself. How like the English to think they could influence him with an old colonial title like that.

But whatever country these football administrators were from, Joe would have prepared carefully for them in exactly the same way.

Two weeks before any visit, Maggie would book the old Toyota eight-seater from Joe's cousin George at the airport. When the passengers got in, George was always careful to turn off the air con. He always followed the same non-tourist route to Mboge, too, taking in the old port area along a network of potholed dirt roads. As the internal van temperature soared, the passengers could almost breathe the squalor of Joe's people between the narrow strips of tin shacks and breeze-block houses.

If the van was waved to a halt at one of the army check points every mile or two, some of the more faint-hearted passengers even feared for their lives. Sullen soldiers sitting on broken chairs in the middle of the road, armed and drinking... they unnerved the most experienced of football's world travellers, Joe had discovered.

Joe particularly enjoyed seeing the visitors as they arrived. He could usually smell the fear. He could see discolouring under the armpits of expensive linen jackets. He could feel the clamminess of hands as he grasped them in his giant fist. It was a simple but effective introduction to his world, and it gave Joe all the advantages he needed.

As the minibus drew up outside the office in a cloud of dust that afternoon, Joe Kumpa was the perfect host.

'Ah! Hello my friends. Ohhhh dear you've had such a long journey. I hope George has shown you all the sights of our beautiful country.' He laughed uproariously. Some of the party tried to laugh back, but weren't sure whether the joke was on them or not.

Philip Butler stepped forward and offered his hand. High Commissioner in the country for four years, Butler knew Joe Kumpa and his reputation. He knew that the whole minibus tour was a charade, but he was powerless to object. Any attempt to interfere with Joe's arrangements would have backfired. It would have been grotesquely rude, just the behaviour that diplomats with titles like 'High Commissioner' wished to avoid in developing countries.

Butler dared not tell the English party that the tour was deliberately designed for their discomfort. That Carslake fellow wouldn't have understood the difficulties of the Diplomatic Service. Arrogant man, he would have expected Butler to challenge the arrangements and make new ones. Sod him, Butler had reasoned. He had his own problems and these football types had theirs. Just leave them to Kumpa, Butler had decided.

'Ah! Mr Lord High Executioner,' laughed Joe. 'How wonderful to see you again.' But he didn't allow Butler time for a diplomatic response before rushing towards the Organisation's Chairman as he stepped gingerly out of the van. 'Albert! Greetings my old friend...How you liking the dark continent?'

One by one, the English party were shown into the offices by Maggie. Most of the group's members visited the single bathroom and reassembled in the meeting room where Maggie had opened bottles of local beer straight from the fridge. Simon Carslake took the chair next to Joe at the head of the table and tried to introduce his party. Kumpa put his hand on Carslake's arm.

'Let's wait until we're all here shall we,' he said brusquely, grinning beneficently at anyone who came into the room until all the group's members were seated. Then, ignoring Carslake, Joe stood up.

'My friends... I hope I can call you that.' There was nervous laughter in the room. 'I'm delighted to meet you as you embark on your bid to stage the GFO World Cup. Albert has told me about your ideas, and I'm impressed!' He grinned at Albert, who smiled back weakly. Albert was feeling a little fragile after the journey and didn't welcome any encouragement to speak at present.

'But today,' Joe took on a sterner expression. 'Today I think I should talk to you all as – shall we say – a critical friend.'

Joe looked slowly around the room. Simon Carslake thought this might be the moment to speak, but Joe's manner was clear. This was Joe's show. Nobody else's.

'Yes, I'm gonna give you some advice today, and perhaps you should take it,' Joe paused again, gazing intently at each member of the group to make sure his audience was listening carefully. 'You see, you've done the right thing by coming to see Joe Kumpa first. I'm your fairy godfather.' He held his arms out wide and laughed heartily. Then again, his mood changed.

'I know what some of you guys are thinking. Why is this Godforsaken fucking country so important to winning our bid? And what's this big ugly mug Joe Kumpa got to offer us?'

Joe stood silent, his eyes settling on each of the visitors in turn. The group waited with apprehension.

'Well, my English friends, the answer is simple. You ain't gonna win no World Cup bid without Joe Kumpa's help. And Joe Kumpa ain't gonna help you without a LOT of persuasion.'

'Maybe,' he continued, 'you think Africa is the shit-hole of the world.' He paused for a moment. 'Well, you're right.' Joe roared with laughter. Silence again.

'Ever wondered why?' His face hardened. 'You ever wondered why those little boys you seen from the bus are dressed in rags? When your little boys are dressed in Eton collars and top hats? You think African little boys don't love football just as much as your little boys?

'You ever thought your 'English home of football' might have helped my people just a little bit more? You ever thought your fathers and your grandads might have left just a little more money when they screwed my people?'

He stared at his audience, long and hard. And then once again he broke into a grin.

'Don't look so worried,' he laughed. He lowered his huge face to the level of Sara Thurlow, the youngest member of the team, and the grin changed quickly into a menacing leer.

'Don't worry darlin'. I ain't going to EAT you.' The menacing leer changed once more to a hearty laugh as Sara jumped.

Joe spied Maggie through the open door and gave her a huge wink. None of the English team noticed. They were all too busy staring at their notepads on the table, desperately avoiding Joe Kumpa's attention.

Maggie smiled to herself. Nobody could match what she called Joe's ju-ju man act. There was a time when she'd get cross with him for teasing visitors with his silly pidgin English curses and talk of eating people. She felt it was shameful for a proud and successful African man to behave like that. But then she realised that these educated Westerners fell for it all. They were either ignorant or racist, she decided. She stopped worrying about them, and she stopped nagging Joe.

But Joe knew that his powers were best used sparingly. When Maggie had closed the door, he stopped laughing, got to his feet, and addressed the whole team with a serious expression.

'No, my friends... I need you, just like you need me.' Joe slowed his delivery right down. 'My... people... need... your... help. You get it?'

Joe took a long swig at his beer bottle before continuing. A few of the group nervously did the same.

'We need your money to build pitches for our little boys, to buy footballs, to pay coaches, to pay for buses to take our teams around, to stay in hotels when they represent their countries. You, my friends... you pay your famous Premier League players more in a week than our best footballers make in their lives!'

'We gotta change all that, MISTER Carslake.' He looked Simon straight in the eyes.

'So... You've come to the right place at the right time. But I gotta say this to you all,' Joe held his stare. 'Why so long, uh? Why weren't you here ten years ago – like them bloody Germans? Where you been all my life?'

And as if he found the line hilarious, Joe leant down to Simon again, roared with laughter, and lifted him out of his chair with a huge bear hug.

'Yeah,' he repeated as he pulled himself upright, but this time with even more feeling. 'Yeah, where you been all my life? Why you treated me and my people with such hate? Why should the poor people of Africa help you, the wealthy founders of football?'

He left the question hanging in the air as he made a dramatic show of removing his suit jacket, and rolling up his white shirt sleeves. Sara noticed the glint of rings on his fingers.

'Well, English. You got some catching up to do,' he said at last. 'And tomorrow I show you what I mean.'

'And my friends,' he continued. 'This isn't just Joe Kumpa talking. I know how the other members of the GFO Board feel. Them from Asia and them from South America. You ignore us for all these years then suddenly you come to see us cos you want the World Cup. Well listen, some of my colleagues are gonna say: Too Late!'

He lowered his voice. 'But I tell you this for nothing. If you can show Joe Kumpa how serious you are to mend your ways, I can help change a few minds in the GFO Board.'

Joe walked to the fridge and pulled out some beers. He took one and left the rest at the centre of the table. Nobody made a move, though. Joe's command of the room was too frightening.

'But hey, let's not get ahead of ourselves. Let's think about my votes first.' He looked at Butler with a rueful smile. 'I'm sorry, Mr Commissionaire. I'm very blunt, I know. I talk like an African, not like a diplomat. So I tell you now, and I don't want no misunderstanding. If you English look after my people right, the three votes that I control will come your way.'

Joe looked around the room, and locked eyes on Sara again.

'Hey, pretty woman, you think bidding for the World Cup is like playing cricket?' Sara trembled but looked straight back at him. 'Well let me tell you: it's not all about fair play. Every one of them GFO Board members will want something for their votes. Money for themselves... maybe. Or they want to go and meet your

Queenie or something. Or they want some girls laid on at their hotels. Oh yeah, pretty, what d'you think of that?'

Sara still looked at him, hoping he didn't notice her rising blushes.

'Me, I just want my people to have some little, little improvements in their lives. To play football with a proper ball not rags and tin cans. To play in competitions outside their towns, and get home on safe transport, not beaten up by criminals. Is that too much for me to ask, my friends?'

Joe stood silent for four minutes. The group could hear Maggie tapping at her keyboard.

'Ok,' Joe said at last. 'Let's seal our deal. Maggie got a photographer coming at 5pm. Ladies, you want to go to the lavvie before he arrives?'

The English campaign team gathered in the lobby of Mboge's Sunshine Hotel that evening, waiting for their transport to the reception at the British High Commissioner's residence. Nobody said much. They were tired. But they were also in a collective state of shock. Not one of them had endured an attack on the senses to compare with the experience in Kumpa's office, and nobody wanted to talk about it.

Simon Carslake was angry and frustrated. The day's events seemed like a judgement on the chances of an English-hosted World Cup. He had prepared meticulously for a triumphant visit to the headquarters of one of the GFO's most important leaders, but he had been fatally wounded in front of his own people. He was deeply ashamed of his failure.

Why, he asked himself, did he not insist to that fool Butler that he take control of the transport arrangements? Why didn't he stand up to Kumpa, and get across his powerful campaign messages before the rogue bullied his team into silent submission? And why didn't that old bastard Albert Lewis use his one bit of leverage, shared membership with Joe Kumpa of the GFO Board, and insist on a fair hearing for the English EFO?

Most frustratingly of all perhaps for a man of Carslake's self-confidence, he could see no way to turn around this disaster. This evening's reception would be a gathering of the country's government and tribal officials, UK diplomats and advisers, businessmen with an interest in Western trade, a handful of local football administrators, and perhaps some African players and managers. (Simon had asked for a list of attendees and their profiles from the High Commissioner, but a terse letter had told him two weeks ago that this kind of detail would simply not be available 'for security reasons').

Then for tomorrow, Kumpa had promised a tour of the country's football facilities, and a chance to meet some of the clubs and players that so badly required the injection of funds he was demanding. Even if he could get the EFO to commit massive amounts of money to Africa, it might already be too late to save the English bid, Carslake thought miserably, and the end of his EFO career.

The hotel concierge walked towards the English party. 'Mister, missus,' he said, addressing anyone who would listen. 'Two taxis for British High Commission.' At least Butler could have organised decent diplomatic cars for the ten-minute drive to this damned reception, thought Simon bitterly.

Just one remarkable hour later, Carslake's mood was transformed. The reception was a sumptuous affair. The chilled champagne seemed unlimited, and plates and plates of cleverly created canapes were joyous. But the really important change was in Joe Kumpa's manner.

Although the British High Commissioner was formally host for the evening, Joe Kumpa took charge. But that was the only similarity with the Kumpa of earlier in the day.

Looming at the door, spectacularly clad in purple and yellow robes, Joe beamed at the English party as they arrived. Maggie was there too, also in traditional Yora dress. Once she was sure the guests had had at least two glasses of champagne each, she signalled to Joe, and handed him a microphone. Joe stood in the middle of the floor and welcomed the English guests.

He started by recounting a story about how as a thirteen-year-old boy he had listened to BBC World Service on a crackling old radio in his father's house. It was the World Cup Final, and Joe confided in his audience how happy his father had been – an old soldier of the Empire in the Second World War – that England had beaten the 'Jerries'.

Joe apologised for his lack of diplomatic language, but he was of a generation that had always seen Britain as his natural homeland in the Commonwealth, he said. He couldn't help seeing her historic enemies as his own. There was deep applause around the room from the Africans, and quizzical looks were exchanged among the High Commissioner's team.

Joe continued, remembering how this old World Cup broadcast had also played a major part in developing his passion for 'the beautiful game', and how the spirit of fair play invented by the English was such an influence on the conduct of his life. He tearfully concluded by thanking his 'charming host, Mr High Commissioner Butler,' for honouring African football with this reception, and sincerely hoping that he and his African colleagues would be permitted to work closely with 'that great nobleman Sir Albert Lewis, who is like a brother to me' and 'Simon Carslake, the cleverest young man in world football,' to achieve the 'right result' for the 2003 World Cup hosts.

As Joe raised his glass to toast the English party, Simon's head was spinning. Had he seriously misjudged the day's events? Had his lack of experience in African affairs led him to completely misread Kumpa's true intentions?

But Carslake had little time to think, because Joe was suddenly at his side, taking him by the arm, and pulling him towards the open French windows and out into the compound.

'So, Simon,' said Joe, still clutching Carslake's arm as he walked him across the stretch of dry grass and dust that passed for the High Commission's lawn. 'Quite a day uh?' Joe laughed heartily.

'Well yes Mr Kumpa... Joe...' Simon faltered, 'It's been a wonderful opportunity to meet you...'.

'No, no my friend. The pleasure is all mine.' Joe paused and looked around him to make sure they were alone. 'I just wanted to have a few words with you in private, Simon, because I think it will be difficult to have this conversation in front of... everyone tomorrow.'

Simon waited expectantly.

'I know I really should be talking to Albert about these things. Of course, I must always obey protocol in our official communications and I have great respect for Sir Albert.' He paused. 'But you see it's important that you and me have a VERY special relationship.' He paused again and looked carefully into Simon's eyes.

'I hope I'm not insulting you if I say that you are the man who will decide England's fate in this very difficult competition. Nobody else.' He fixed Simon with a look that was half genial and half menacing. 'But I think you understand what I'm saying.'

Simon did understand. He understood very well. Simon was tingling with pleasure that this leader of world football recognised that it was he, Simon Carslake, who was the most powerful man in the English EFO and represented the only hope of winning the 2003 World Cup bid. If he was feeling devastated by the earlier events of the day, he was now invigorated by the words of Joe Kumpa. Simon knew how good he was at his job. He wouldn't fail to meet this challenge, whatever it took.

Joe didn't wait for a response from Simon. He could see that his message had struck home. 'Good,' Joe said. 'Now we must get back to the party, Simon.' He laughed loudly and squeezed Simon's upper arm in his big fist. 'People will talk.'

Joe's concerns about Albert Lewis being sensitive to breaches of protocol were completely unnecessary, however – at least for that evening.

Albert had never enjoyed the heat, and as soon as he realised that, as EFO Chairman, he would be the official leader of the campaign bid team's trip to Yora, he had simply dreaded the thought of the visit.

After getting off the plane that morning with a persistent headache, the bumpy Toyota ride had only made him feel more queasy. By the time he was in Joe's office, Albert had feared he might throw up at any moment. He had recovered a little after a doze in his hotel room in the early evening, but he hadn't expected to enjoy the reception, and as soon as he arrived at the High Commission building, he had found himself a comfortable chair in a quiet corner under a ceiling fan, and let his eyes close at their will as Kumpa's words washed over him.

After an hour or so, he was woken suddenly by a little man in dark glasses, dressed in a light grey business suit with too-long trousers that bagged over his pale grey shoes. The little man was holding his hand out to Albert in friendship. 'Ah, Mister Albert, uh? So you are great friend of Joe Kumpa...'

With a supreme effort, Albert rose to his feet and shook the man's hand. He was too polite to do anything else, and he was too modest to allow the man's compliment to go unchallenged.

'Oh well, I serve on the same committee as Mr Kumpa, you know, that's all. It's very kind of him to say that I'm a great friend... but I don't think...'

The little man peered at Albert carefully and touched his nose. 'Ha!'

Albert wasn't sure how to respond to this gesture, but the man leaned towards him confidingly.

'I understand, Mr Albert. You wouldn't want too many questions asked.' He touched his nose again. Albert was now completely confused. A wave of nausea was once again encompassing him, and all he could think about was how to get rid of this friend of Kumpa's. But the man was persistent and leaned even closer.

'Oh yes... I'm sure you will be a VERY good friend... helping Mr Kumpa grow his assets,' the man whispered. 'It's not so easy to get round all these bank regulations these days, is it Mister Albert? But of course, as you know, Mr Kumpa has – shall we say – a very good arrangement with the National Bank here. It makes moving money so easy, doesn't it.'

'I'm sorry,' Albert said, struggling to keep a friendly tone. 'I don't understand what you're saying. I don't deal with any money. We have people to do that.'

The little man giggled. 'Oh Mr Albert, you English play such games don't you. But you can't tease me. As Mr Kumpa's friend, you're always making sure he gets his 10%...'

He left the comment hanging, long enough. Through his tiredness and queasiness, Albert began to understand what the man was saying. As realisation dawned, his head began to clear, and the implications grew more and more shocking.

Albert's instinct was to deny this scurrilous claim, to walk away from the stranger, and to forget what he had heard. Here he was in a strange country. Albert had heard about all these tribal rivalries. This man could be spreading lies about Kumpa for all kinds of reasons that he could never grasp.

And yet... The man in the grey suit had talked about details, banking transactions, percentages... Most important of all, he seemed to think that Albert knew all about Kumpa's alleged business practices and was himself complicit.

Albert knew he had to find out more. But how – without indignantly declaring his innocence and ignorance, and frightening off the little man? He had no experience or appetite for detective work, but he just knew there was only one way he could learn more from this man and establish the truth about Joe Kumpa: he had to play along with the man's idea of him as Kumpa's collaborator in financial dealings.

'10%... oh yes,' Albert said, with an assurance that surprised him. 'That's to say... Mister Kumpa always gets 10% of any funds coming to... the Yora Football Organisation.'

The little man was convulsed by laughter.

'The Yora Football Organisation? Oh but Mr Kumpa represents the whole of Africa, not just this little country, Mister Albert. You know that. Every little payment that goes to GFO members in Africa... Mister Kumpa always takes his tax!'

'Oh yes, of course,' said Albert. 'I just wanted to see that we were... that we understand each other. There are some... enemies... who might wish to do harm to Mr Kumpa.'

Albert wasn't sure how he had managed to invent this bit of sophistry, but it clearly convinced the little man.

'Ahhh, how well I know this,' the man said. 'I think we are on the same side, Mister Albert.'

Albert made no comment. His mind was too busy grappling with the information he was hearing. Joe Kumpa! A fellow member of the GFO Board! The top man in African football! A close friend of President Larsen! What did they call it... embezzling money? A criminal!

He realised the man was still talking to him in a lowered voice. 'I just want to say, Mr Albert,' he said, looking around him to check nobody else in the room was listening, 'that maybe you and me can do some good business in your country too.'

He handed Albert a card. 'Vincent Torda', Albert read, 'Managing Director, Aerospace Importing International, Senghore Drive, Mboge.'

'I come to London for my business,' the man said. 'Perhaps you can open some doors.'

He smiled at Albert and shook his hand. He started to walk away, but suddenly returned with an afterthought. 'Hey, Mister Albert, I hope you aren't a 10% man.' He giggled and winked, and walked quickly towards a group of Yoran men, also dressed in business suits.

A waiter offered Albert a silver tray of champagne glasses. 'Have you any beer please,' Albert asked. 'Oh yes sir. I get you beer. You want Yoran beer or European beer?'

'European beer please,' said Albert, and he slumped back into his chair.

Chapter 16

Contemplation

Boarding the plane at Mboge International Airport gave a sense of relief to every member of the EFO campaign team. It wasn't just getting out of the heat and the sun; it was also release from the constant pressure they all felt to say the right thing to Joe Kumpa, and from being forced to listen to his raging and changing views on both the English bid and those of the opposition. The dark Yora beer had also set its particular challenges to some of their digestive systems.

Each member of the team had his or her own personal thoughts about the visit. Had it gone well? How had they performed? What was Kumpa saying about the team to his GFO colleagues? He had constantly stressed that he was speaking honestly as a critical friend, but was this all a carefully crafted act put on for the visitors? How much was he giving them genuine advice, and how far was he leading them down a blind alley?

The young campaign team had all found the initial meeting in Kumpa's offices a real shock, unlike any other experience in their careers. The Foreign Office dossier prepared by Stephen Green had forewarned them to an extent. It had indicated that Kumpa was very much a wheeler dealer, using his African influence to advance his career in GFO and his wider business interests.

They had also attended a short introductory welcome from the British High Commissioner when they arrived two days before. He had presented his research on Kumpa and described his experience of the man at a couple of meetings since his posting to Yora four years before. Philip Butler had emphasised that while his own dealings with Kumpa had been fairly straightforward, the gossip about him in the business community was often rather negative. But these briefings had not prepared them at all for Kumpa's explosive manner and style.

As they took their seats in business class on the BA flight back to London, none of the team was more deeply in thought than Simon Carslake. He gladly gulped the gin and tonic supplied by the stewardess as he peered out of the window through the shimmering air above the aircraft wing to the dried out savanna fields beside the runway.

This was the vast African continent, a new experience that both thrilled and scared him. He thought for a moment about the days of empire building. How Victorian adventurers must have struggled to understand this land and its people.

Fastening seat belts for take-off brought him back to the present. As he had done a hundred times in the last twenty-four hours, Carslake thought about his conversation with Joe Kumpa at the High Commissioner's party two nights ago. He thought too about the phone call Kumpa had made to his hotel room the following day.

Again, in that call Joe had emphasised the importance of Simon's role in the bidding competition, crowning the moment by requesting – Joe Kumpa requesting! – a one-to-one meeting with Simon in London. As if to allay any doubt in Simon's mind, he said he would stay in his usual suite at Claridges for a long weekend. His secretary Maggie would agree dates with Simon's secretary, Stephanie.

Simon remembered that Kumpa had made it clear he did not need to meet Sir Albert, but if Simon thought that this would cause offence, he was happy to call briefly on his GFO colleague 'to pay my respects'.

Carslake felt unalloyed pride and pleasure that this giant of a man – physically and in global influence – had identified him as an important collaborator. By accepting the meeting, Simon knew he would be playing a game outside his EFO role and playing with men of real power to an extent he had never done in his career before.

He also had no illusions that this would be a highly dangerous and risky relationship. He had no doubt that Kumpa's friendship was entirely motivated by Kumpa's own interests. Carslake knew he was only of interest to the African if he could deliver what Kumpa desired.

None of this phased Carslake. Perhaps this was the opportunity he had been waiting for all his life. Perhaps this was the moment he would leave the ranks of mediocre men at the EFO and join the winners of the world. Carslake was thrilled at the thought of meeting Kumpa in some dingy bar in London to hear his plans for Simon's future.

But Simon Carslake wasn't completely clueless about the kind of work Joe Kumpa had in mind for him. It was now four months since Simon had met the man called Gerald who offered to sell him four votes for the EFO bid to host the 2003 World Cup – one sixth of the total votes to be made – if he could raise $8 million.

Hardly a day had gone by since that meeting when the proposition hadn't preyed on his mind. His thoughts had been wildly confused during that time. He had worked out quickly that it would be an almighty challenge to raise this amount legitimately.

He could hardly go to the government asking for those kinds of funds without a detailed description of the campaign activities the money was to support.

In an uncharacteristic moment of black humour, he had on one occasion smiled at the thought of a meeting with the Chancellor. The government's budget holder was of course a busy man, famous for not always listening carefully to detail. Simon imagined his pitch for ten million pounds to 'significantly enhance England's chances of winning the 2003 World Cup bid'. Not even his presentational skills would be up to that task, he thought ruefully.

The EFO itself could probably afford the money, but he couldn't let any of the campaign team into his confidence about its purpose, least of all the Chairman. Simon well knew he would be horrified.

Then of course there was the British Media. Even if he could find the money, he would never be able to keep the matter quiet. He laughed to himself as he imagined the front-page tabloid headlines. There were plenty of countries where bid teams could raise this sort of money. Countries where nobody would find out, and where investigative journalism was unheard of or forbidden by force. Hardly a level playing field for my team, he thought gloomily.

But he was stirred now by Kumpa's interest in him and his future career. It was no longer good enough to worry about the problems. The $8m project was a serious test of Simon Carslake's capabilities.

Maybe it was time to start believing in himself, just as Kumpa seemed to believe in him. If he wanted to play with the big boys, then he had to think big, take big chances, and not look down.

Maybe, just maybe, it *would* be possible to raise those funds, he thought to himself as he drained his glass. Simon had plenty of contacts, many of them in the City, some of them the kind of people who enjoyed a gamble. As the cabin lights came back on and the plane levelled its altitude over the South Atlantic Ocean, he ordered his second gin and tonic.

Yes! He would go for it; he would show Kumpa what he could do.

In the row of seats behind him, Albert Lewis was also deep in thought. To be more precise he was on BA's classical music channel, conducting Vivald's *Four Seasons* at the Royal Albert Hall. Eyes shut, right hand gently coaxing the first violins. It was his way of putting the visit to Kumpa's land to the back of his mind.

He hadn't spoken to anyone about what he had heard from the Yoran businessman in the grey suit forty-eight hours earlier. He had hardly taken in any of the tour of boys' clubs and training pitches that Kumpa had treated his English visitors to with relish. When Kumpa tried to talk to him, Albert averted his eyes. If what he had heard was true, he was ashamed to know this man. But was it true? Should he be listening to the gossip of a stranger, and use it in his mind to accuse a colleague?

When he got home, he would discuss the whole situation with Monica. She would know what to do next. Albert realised there was a huge responsibility resting on his shoulders. This wasn't what he wanted at all.

But he didn't want to think about it now. It was time for the next movement.

Chapter 17

Chasing the money

'Simon. Really. That was the deal, remember? You missed Melissa's concert when you were in bloody wherever you were. You promised her you'd take her to school when you got back.'

Anna was so furious she couldn't bear to look at her husband, so she busied herself with the breakfast dishes. She knew enough about these foreign trips to have little sympathy for Simon's excuses. For God's sake, she'd been on her own for the past four days and nights, running around after the children while he was swanning it up with some wealthy African potentate. Pissed on champagne every night no doubt while she collapsed into bed knackered.

And here he was on the first day back, telling her he had to get into the office to sort out some stupid problem instead of waiting for an hour and driving Melissa to school in Hammersmith. It wasn't bloody fair, thought Anna, as tears of rage and self-pity filled her eyes.

Simon did not believe in arguing with his family. He knew it would solve nothing. If he'd started, he would have found himself reminding his wife that if it wasn't for his EFO position they wouldn't now be living in a four-bedroomed house in Barnes, sending their children to private schools and planning their next holiday in the Maldives.

But he knew when to keep his counsel. Without a word he finished his coffee, put his mug in the dishwasher, lightly stroked Anna's shoulder, thought about kissing her cheek but thought better of it, picked up his briefcase by the front door, and left the house. Tony opened the passenger door of the Jaguar. 'Going straight to the office, sir?'

Simon had slept little the night before. He had used the taxi home from Heathrow to sift through his contact book. After waking Anna when he arrived, he worked in his study downstairs for an hour, checking all the relevant information he could find.

Networking had always been one of his skills, and his personal filing system at home was a crucial business tool. Before he went to bed, he wrote out four names on a sheaf of pages in his Filofax, together with telephone numbers, a contact history, and an estimate of the potential help each might provide.

He read his notes again at his desk in the EFO before picking up the phone to speak to his secretary. 'Steph, no interruptions from anyone please. No – certainly not the Chairman. I'll be in and out of the office all day. No, it's ok, I'll be having lunch in the City. No don't worry about booking a car, I'll take a taxi. No Steph it's fine. I will get a taxi on the street. Yes really – you don't need to do anything... thanks.'

By midday, Simon had made three arrangements for lunch in the coming week. And he'd fixed a meeting with Sir Richard Newlands for a brief drink at a discreet wine bar near London Wall in an hour's time. The banker's diary was busy.

Newlands wasn't Carslake's best prospect for funds, but that suited him. He could try out his arguments with the irascible ex-Guards officer and try to learn from the rejection he expected.

'Two million?' Newlands had spluttered, grinning irritatingly across the small round table in the corner of the bar. 'Where am I going to get that sort of money? And anyway, why the hell are you coming to me? The EFO's got plenty of dosh.' He drew on his small cigar.

'Yes,' said Simon, 'but what I'm needing is a bit of speculation. And the EFO isn't the kind of organisation...'

'Speculation?' Newlands guffawed. 'Well, what do you take me for, Carslake, a ruddy bookie? I run a bank, remember, and we're not famous for risk-taking you know.'

Simon tried to pour him more wine from the bottle, but Newlands put his hand over his glass. 'No, I've got to go soon.' He paused. 'I'll have some fizzy water.'

When Simon returned from the bar, he clinked glasses, and leaned in closer.

'Come on, Dick, the bank may be risk averse, but that's not true of all your companies is it? What about Malden Vinster? Took a bit of a chance on satellite TV I hear. And Prendergasts... they're backing some pretty whacky baseball takeover plans in the States.'

Newlands stubbed out his cigar. 'I don't know who you've been talking to Simon, but we do due diligence thirty times over on any investment one of my companies makes. Our corporate lawyers crawl over every detail until we're certain every penny of our money is safe for our shareholders.' He fixed Simon with a long stare.

'Now I've got to get back to the office in two minutes,' he said at last. 'You've told me nothing about what you want this money for. Convince me in 120 seconds that if I lend you £2m you will guarantee me its return... plus,' he pulled his jacket from the back of the chair behind him and began to put it on. 'Plus... a return of 10% a year. Then maybe we've got something to talk about.'

Simon said nothing. He swallowed the rest of his wine slowly. Newlands looked at him for a moment before shaking his head contemptuously, pulling up the collar of his coat, and proffering his hand. 'Thanks for the drink, Simon. Good luck.'

Simon took the underground to Waterloo. He didn't want to go back to the office, and he was in no hurry to get home. Maybe the others would be easier. But his confidence was rocked.

Chapter 18

Mr Wei and Mr Chan

The two delegates from the Alliance of Asian Football Organisations looked around nervously. There was not much to see. The former US military base that was now Bala International Airport only accommodated three arrivals a day. The flight from Kuala Lumpur that morning was less than half full, and as regular visitors to the tiny island of Eastern Kanoa, the two men recognised many of the business and government people now being met by local contacts or heading for the taxi line.

The two football men were always nervous when summoned by Lelei Fiso, their AAFO President and so were most of Fiso's guests, whatever the nature of their business with him. Some meetings with Fiso simply never happened, apparently, because people failed to arrive. It was sometimes said that these people were never seen again. As a close friend of Fiso's, the Eastern Kanoa police chief had not authorised any enquiries into these scandalous stories. And if he had, nobody expected any evidence or witnesses to be found.

None of these stories involved the disappearance of football men to AAFO's knowledge. But mud – and blood – sticks. Everyone knew that Lelei Fiso's business career had been buttressed by impulsive violence, and the two delegates at the airport that morning were survivors in a dangerous world. Fearing Fiso, and watching their backs, were prerequisites.

For Mr Wei and Mr Chan, however, fear was much more intense that day than at any time in the past. There were two good reasons. First, they were not in Eastern Kanoa because they had been invited by Fiso to visit their AAFO President; they had broken a golden rule by requesting a meeting themselves. Secondly, their purpose – as the two most senior delegates of the AAFO – was to deliver a devastating blow to the President's global ambitions.

The President had of course sent one of his five black Mercedes cars to collect them regardless, with a uniformed driver and armed passenger beside him in the front seats. The two men's 'request' to meet him was certainly deeply insubordinate, but maintaining his public image was always important to Fiso. So was his safety. Nobody entered the gates of his sixteen-acre estate except in one of Fiso's security tested limousines unless it was the Head of State (and even *his* car had to be parked a hundred metres from the house).

Wei and Chan were silent on the eight-mile journey. They had meticulously prepared what they would say to Fiso when they got to his estate and were lost in thoughts about the importance of the day. The car took them through the main gate, past the four-storey office block designed and built two years earlier to legitimise 'the business', and on to *The Ranch* as Fiso called his house (he loved the American West, its drama, and its lawless heroes). The two men glanced at each other. They had never before been allowed into Fiso's personal quarters.

The guard got out of the passenger seat and slung his automatic weapon over his shoulder as he opened the back door of the car to let out the two visitors. He spoke into a walkie talkie, told the two men 'stay here', got back in the car, and ordered the chauffeur to drive back to the gate, leaving Wei and Chan standing together with their brief cases in front of a large oak door.

Both men briefly wondered if the next sound they would hear would be gunshots. But there was no escape. All they could do was to wait and feel their business suits getting clammier.

They heard a window open on a floor above them. Chan realised he had been holding his breath for many minutes and let out an involuntary snort of relief. Wei waved respectfully towards the window.

'Mr President, we are so sorry to disturb you...' His voice trailed away. All their preparations for this meeting had proved worthless. Chan looked at Wei, and both men stared at their feet in a mix of embarrassment at their inadequacy, and a sense of doom for their mission.

Fiso's large head appeared at the window. He was a man of fifty-four, with black curly hair and angry eyes. 'I'm busy,' he shouted. 'You have ten minutes.' As Wei moved towards the door, Fiso shouted again. 'No... you can tell me what you need to from there.'

When they returned to Kuala Lumpur on the 6:00 pm flight, Wei and Chan immediately called their most trusted secretary, and took a taxi to meet her at the AAFO office. They had agreed between themselves to dictate a full report of their ten-minute meeting through an open window while it was still fresh in their minds.

They made no attempt to change the facts about how they had been treated, and how their carefully laid plan had been foiled. There was no point. All the other delegates knew Fiso well enough. Of course he would undermine the ultimatum they had tried to deliver. Forced to withdraw from the GFO Presidency, of course he wouldn't go quietly.

Recording the actual discussion between the three men required rather more creativity, but Wei and Chan were up to that task, too. Before the report was finished in the early hours of the morning, they had carefully and diplomatically presented the main thrust without risk of legal redress: mission accomplished. Their words were typed and ready for a press release to be drafted later that day:

'The AAFO Board has regretfully agreed with Mr Fiso that in view of his expanding business interests he will be unable to commit sufficient time to the GFO Presidency. He is therefore, with great sadness, withdrawing his candidacy from the 1996

election. He and AAFO thank all our many friends in GFO
who have expressed their intended support for Mr Fiso, and we
hope the election will deliver great leadership for the future of
our wonderful world of football.'

As the two weary men drank their final cup of coffee at 4:30 am, they smiled weakly to each other as they recalled a different version of events, peppered by the chilling rant of their President:

'OK you bastards. You in league with Larsen or what? These charges don't mean a fucking thing. Anyway, if it comes to court, what fucking judge is going to convict me? You think I can't pay off some judge? Everyone's got their price. Hear what I'm saying?

'I been in this game too long to let some Yankee cops take me down I tell you. Maybe I should help them get a case together against Larsen... Yeah why not? I can't stand the bastard. I bet he makes more in a week than I make with my medicine farms in a year...'

'Yeah, maybe I bring that bastard down. Why not? I got people who'll finish him. Why not? Yeah, take him out. Why not? Yeah... you look worried now, you bastards. I don't know what I'll do but I'll finish him. Maybe I help some other bastard be President. What do you say? All we Asian guys back a good candidate. Tell them bastards on the Board that's what we're doing.

'Talk to the Europeans. Italy, fucking Egypt, I don't care. Find another candidate and we'll vote for him. Anyone but Larsen. Yeah – what about one of them dagoes in America. Yeah – you tell those AAFO bastards to find another candidate and spend some money on him. Tell them if Larsen gets in, they're kissing goodbye to their pensions.'

None of this would ever be publicly reported, but the notes Wei and Chan had made on the plane were clear enough for their AAFO colleagues to understand.

Chapter 19

Brief encounter

The Chronicle's most widely read reporter was preparing to leave the office one Friday evening when the phone rang. *The Whistleblower* was used to receiving offers of stories about scandals and closet skeletons in the world of football. Often these people were timewasters, with no information of any interest, or worse, blatant liars. Sometimes they were people who wanted to make money from scraps of information.

'Hello?'

'Hello – can I speak to the journalist who calls himself *The Whistleblower*?'

The journalist delayed for a moment. It was 7pm on Friday night for heaven's sake. It had been a long week. The lads were going to the pub. Could *The Whistleblower* be bothered? It was easy to make an excuse.

'Yes – you're through to *The Whistleblower*.'

'Oh, you're *The Whistleblower*, but...' The line went quiet for a moment.

'Never mind. I just thought... Never mind. I think I can help you. We can be useful to each other.'

'How?'

There was silence again. *The Whistleblower* waited.

'Well, I can't tell you over the phone.'

'Why not?'

More silence.

'Because I can't afford to risk it. I'm... quite senior in the Organisation.'

'What organisation?'

'I think you know what I'm talking about. But I can't speak now. I'll call you tomorrow.'

He hung up.

The Whistleblower had been involved with enough newspaper investigations to know that informers didn't trust telephones. Often their first call would be to listen for the click of a recording device or for an echo on the line. *The Whistleblower* was careful to use no device on the office phone.

When the caller rang again on Monday morning, he sounded more relaxed. He asked for a face-to-face meeting. He wanted to meet when *The Whistleblower* was next in Brussels. He described a layby on the A4.

The Whistleblower had developed something of a nose for contacts who were genuine. There were two features of this man's call that presented a whiff of authenticity: firstly, the caller was clearly based in Brussels, where the GFO had its headquarters, so at least he was close to the centre of world football's powerbase; secondly, he was in no hurry to meet *The Whistleblower*. In the journalist's experience, time wasters and mercenaries usually wanted their conversations to be over quickly – before they were found out.

The Whistleblower had plans to visit the GFO the following week for an interview with a potential new Presidential candidate. The meeting with the informant was agreed for May 18th –at a picnic area near Wavre. *The Whistleblower* usually used taxis in Brussels but had to hire a Fiat Panda for the afternoon to meet the man, which was annoying.

There was only one car in the layby when *The Whistleblower* arrived: a big NSU estate. As *The Whistleblower* parked behind him, a tall man got out and walked towards the Fiat. He was dressed in a long waxed coat with a high turned-up collar. He wore a wide-brimmed bush hat pulled down over his face. *The Whistleblower* guessed from what could be seen of his face, that he was in his late forties or early fifties.

The Whistleblower could hardly avoid smiling at the man's exaggerated security measures. But once in the passenger seat, the man's expression showed that his purpose was deadly serious.

The Whistleblower was usually successful at detecting accents, but this one was difficult. Was it Irish? The man spoke softly and refused to give his name. He explained that although he was not employed by the GFO, he worked in the Brussels office 'in a special capacity'.

He told *The Whistleblower* that he had information that would 'blow the lid off' the organisation. And that if there was any whisper that he had provided it, he would 'definitely be a dead man'.

The Whistleblower had been involved in a number of investigations into terrorist activities in the previous ten years, and the man's words, spoken with a faint Belfast accent, sounded chilling. When *The Whistleblower* asked him why he had made contact, the man quickly became silent and stared ahead through the windscreen.

The Whistleblower was becoming irritated by his mannerisms, and then sceptical. Asked what he had to tell *The Whistleblower*, the man stared unblinkingly ahead for a few moments and then reached inside his poacher's pocket for a folded sheaf of papers.

The Whistleblower looked blankly at the rows of numbers, and then noticed a column of names.

'Do you know what this is?' the man said. 'They're a record of payments. Names. Dates. Amounts... big amounts.'

The Whistleblower traced a finger down the first column. The names looked Russian. The dates were all within the previous six months. The amounts varied between $10,000 and $90,000.

'I don't understand. What are these payments? Where are they from? Who are they for?'

Pause

'And for what purpose?'

The man looked carefully at *The Whistleblower* and shook his head slowly.

'No, No... I can't do this. It's too dangerous. I've got to go.'

The Whistleblower was taken by complete surprise. Suddenly the man had grabbed the file of papers, wrenched open the Fiat passenger door, run to his own car and accelerated onto the highway towards Brussels. Lighting a cigarette, *The Whistleblower* cursed, and punched the Fiat's steering wheel in anger:

'Shit! Why the fuck didn't I take down his registration number?'

Chapter 20

Panic stations

June 1996

The EFO seemed to have struck gold with Danny Creighton. When the campaign team visited Far East Asia in the first week of June, just two weeks after his contract with the EFO was signed, Creighton was better known amongst the dignitaries than Albert or Simon had dared to hope. In Jakarta, the lobby of the Grand Met Hotel was so crammed with local Liverpool fans that the EFO campaign team could only get to the reception desk to register if Creighton detached himself from the group to sign autographs.

At forty-two, he was an attractive asset. His lingering fame as a footballer was sustained by a trained athlete's body. Nature had also been kind. He had a finely shaped head, which he emphasised with a closely razored haircut. His natural swarthiness was topped up regularly on sunbeds and beaches, and set off by expensively gleaming dental work and the crisply ironed white shirts he favoured.

Danny wasn't often required to speak, except to fans. If local Press wanted interviews, Steve Monroe kept close control. Danny could talk about his career, about current matches (as he often did at home as a radio and TV pundit), and about his talented son Daniel. But questions about the EFO campaign were quickly diverted by the Press Officer.

The women on the campaign team joked a little snobbishly about his strongly scented aftershave, but in many parts of the world he visited with the EFO team, it was no more intrusive than the fragrances splashed on by local VIPs. The EFO women also talked amongst themselves about not wanting to be in a lift alone with Danny, but there was no actual evidence on which to base these fears.

Simon thought that Danny probably fancied two or three of the women in the team, but he had reminded Danny firmly from the start that he was being well paid in his ambassador role and that his responsibilities were serious. He emphasised that Danny was also enhancing his profile all over the world, and a decent award was also likely through the Queen's Honours. 'Keep it in your pants, Danny, if you don't want to put all that at risk,' were Simon's wise words.

But what was most reassuring to Simon was the presence on every EFO visit of Chrissy Creighton. She seemed, as Albert had suggested, to be a major asset wherever she and Danny went.

Chrissy was not like many of the footballers' wives of Danny's generation whom Simon had encountered. Privately educated, she was a former GP who met Danny through his club's medical adviser. She had been married to a wealthy hedge-fund manager at the time, and although her professional colleagues were astounded that she had left him, none of them could accuse her of gold digging.

She took to her World Cup campaign role with effortless charm. One evening in Kuala Lumpur, after the Creightons had gone to their room, Simon and Albert were relaxing with a beer when Simon made a point of congratulating the Chairman for finding her...and Danny.

'She's terrific isn't she?' said Simon. 'I have to hand it to you, Albert, choosing the Creightons was a master stroke. Danny may be the ambassador but we're getting more from Chrissy than we could imagine.'

Albert reddened. He usually did when complimented, but he was particularly taken aback by Simon's warmth. 'Well... maybe you just ought to listen to me a bit more often, Simon...' he chuckled quietly. 'She's got so much energy that girl.'

May and June were hectic months for Danny's international lobbying role. He wasn't contracted in time for the Yora trip, but after the Far East Asia visit, he and the team spent a week in South America and flew home via Australia.

It was in Australia at the end of June that Albert's words first began to haunt Simon. It was an important visit. The Australian Football Organisation was proud to have delivered a brilliant World Cup in 1995, and its influence in the GFO was growing. It was an occasion when Chrissy's energy and charm were likely to be a positive asset, and Simon was looking forward to a successful meeting of minds with the Australians.

The first indication of a problem was when Danny came back alone to the hotel from the centrepiece dinner in the Opera House soon after 10pm. Steve Monroe was also back early, taking a scheduled call from a London newspaper. He noticed Danny striding purposefully to the lift.

'Alright Dan?'

'Bloody woman,' was all Danny blurted out without looking at the Press Officer.

Steve went to the reception desk, cupped his hand over his mouth, and called Simon's mobile phone. Simon searched the Opera House private dining room with his eyes as he listened. There were plenty of stragglers sitting at the tables or moving between them. It didn't take long to check out the women who were still in the room.

'No she's not here. Shit. I saw her talking to Ross Bennett, that guy from Canberra for a long time over dinner. Shit. Stupid, stupid...'

He beckoned to Sara Thurlow, a trusted lieutenant.

'Seen Chrissy anywhere?'

'No, she was at dinner.'

'Yes, I know that,' Simon spat out. 'But where is she now? Go and check all the ladies rest rooms will you, Sara. Just a minute.

D'you know anything about that guy Ross Bennett she was next to at dinner?'

'Yes, remember in the briefing document, Simon. He's on his fourth wife. Obviously a bit of a womaniser. We warned the team to be careful about him. Come to bed eyes apparently. Oh,' she paused. 'And he keeps a yacht moored in Sydney Harbour in case he gets lucky... Why?'

'Fuck,' said Simon. 'Did anyone warn Chrissy?'

Simon took a taxi straight back to the hotel and was still sitting in the lobby with Steve at 4:30 the next morning. They had been over all the scenarios and clung on to a wild hope that nobody at the reception other than Danny had noticed that Chrissy and Bennett had slipped away. They were dozing uneasily when they heard the night porter walk past them as a taxi drew up. Both men got to their feet to meet Chrissy Creighton at the grand glass doors.

She smiled wanly at them, thought about saying something but thought again, kicked off her heels and grabbed a handful of ball gown as she headed for the lift.

The night porter looked doubtfully at her, but she waved her key towards him, and he touched his cap in response.

Simon went to bed for two hours, but didn't sleep, then called Albert on his room number. He gave the Chairman a full rundown of the evening's events.

'Of course, you're jumping to conclusions a bit here, Simon.'

Simon said nothing, but silently screamed.

'No, I s'pose you must be right,' said Albert on reflection. 'She must have taken a fancy to him. Are you saying she had it off with him?'

Simon could take Albert's naïve questioning no longer. 'Yes probably Albert, but you know that hardly matters. The point is she left her husband here in the hotel and spent hours with another man, probably alone on his yacht. It's what people are going to think. It's what the Press might find out. And...' he thought about it for a moment, 'it could mean Danny walking out on her.'

'Oh good lord, yes I see.'

'So I'm going to see them both this morning to find out what their reaction is to all this, so we know what our options are.'

Simon knocked hesitantly on the Creightons' hotel suite at 10:30. His biggest fear was that Danny would be packing and demanding that he or both of them were to be flown home immediately. To his surprise, he found the two of them at their breakfast table in hotel dressing gowns, behaving as if nothing at all had happened. Chrissy had removed all last night's make-up, and looked as if she had slept well and easily.

'Are we late for the taxi, Simon?' Chrissy asked with her customary winning smile. 'We'll be down in ten minutes.'

'Is everything... alright?' Simon ventured.

'Yeah mate, we're good,' said Danny through a mouthful of toast, without looking up from his copy of the *Sydney Morning Herald*.

Despite searching glances from almost every member of the campaign team, Simon said nothing to anybody for the rest of that day – until he moved to the seat beside Albert on the return flight to Heathrow.

Albert had his eyes closed, but he was aware of Simon's presence immediately. Albert didn't like sitting next to people on long-haul flights. It only encouraged long and deep discussions and made him feel trapped. The campaign team always booked an extra seat next to him for that reason.

Simon tolerated this indulgence. In fact it was useful. He didn't really want to involve Albert in team discussions. Parking him on his own kept him out of the way. But on this occasion, he needed to talk, and he needed Albert's advice. He had been completely thrown by the Creightons' behaviour in the last twenty-four hours, and he simply didn't know what to do. Albert knew these people. He had suggested them. He could damn well help sort out the problem.

The problem... thought Simon. What *was* the problem?

The reason he was thrown by the Creightons' behaviour was that they didn't seem to act as if there *was* a problem – when he met them in the morning, or here on the plane. He could see them now, ten rows in front. Chrissy was reading; Danny was listening to his headphones. They were behaving as if nothing of any importance had happened between them.

'Albert, I'm sorry, we've got to talk.'

Albert smiled grimly. 'Yes of course...' He put his copy of *World Soccer* into the seat flap in front of him. 'Creightons?'

'I don't know what the hell's going on. Danny doesn't seem to give a damn where Chrissy was last night. Chrissy doesn't seem at all ashamed. It's almost like some perverted game they've got going...'

Albert thought for a moment. 'Just supposing,' he said slowly, 'nothing did happen. Supposing she went off with that Australian bloke to some party or other. I don't know. Maybe they were both invited and Danny didn't want to go. We've agreed she's got so much energy. Maybe she wanted to dance the night away. Have fun, without any... you know. Surely she wouldn't risk her reputation so easily...'

Simon looked at Albert carefully as he spoke. He didn't deal in maybes.

'Albert, you need to talk to her.'

'Me?'

'Yes, rather like a father figure. I know she's great value for our campaign, but we've got to avoid this happening again – whatever it is. I don't know if there's any PR damage yet. We might have got away with it, but we can't have Chrissy deciding to party late – with or without Danny. I've already made clear to Danny about how he must behave. Please Albert, be firm with her...'

Simon got up from the seat. He felt a lot better now. He was confident that Albert would get the message across. 'God, this wasn't in the plan,' he thought.

Albert waited until he saw Chrissy get out of her seat. He knew that to reach the nearest toilet she would have to pass him.

'Chrissy – er Mrs Creighton,' he whispered at her as she walked up to his seat. She smiled.

'Er, would you mind... could I have a little word. After you've um... after you've um been...'

Chrissy's smile broadened and she nodded. 'Yes, of course you can, Sir Albert. But I think I'd better... you know... first...'

Albert blushed slightly. Minutes later, he felt a touch on his shoulder. 'I'd better tell Danny I've come to talk to you Sir Albert. He gets terribly jealous you know...' She winked at him and smiled warmly. She was teasing him, thought Albert, but with practised charm and respect for the older man.

'So,' she said as she slid into the seat beside him, 'I expect you're wanting an apology for last night.' She was looking straight at the Chairman, and her eyes betrayed no hint of shame. 'Well absolutely, Sir Albert. I do hope my behaviour hasn't had any repercussions for the campaign. It's just sometimes... well, I'm a woman Sir Albert and I can't help myself.' To Albert's great relief, she paused and looked out of the window, as if waiting for his response.

He was speechless. Never in his life had he been in this position. What was he to say to her? He was desperately thinking how he could end the whole conversation without looking more foolish and out of his depth when she spoke again.

'Well, when that Australian bloke "Ross whatever" invited me and a couple of his Aussie mates and their sheilas to go back to his yacht, I just couldn't resist. Oh, I knew damn well what Ross wanted,' she said. 'But that's where I get a bit naughty sometimes.'

She paused and turned again to the Chairman. As Chrissie's confession was unfolding, Albert felt paralysed. He didn't dare to look away from her gaze for fear of showing his hopeless embarrassment. His mind was blank. He knew he had no words to respond to what Chrissie was saying. He also knew he didn't want to hear any more.

Chrissie continued. 'You see Danny knows what I'm like. I try to play the footballer's wife, and you know most of the time it works. But just now and again I seem to remember I have a brain, and I can't let these idiots get away with their total crap.'

She looked at the older man carefully, and continued, seeming to confuse the look of panic on his face with one of disapproval.

'Yes, I am sorry Sir Albert, I know they're your friends.' She squeezed his hand gently.

'But some of these GFO guys at my end of the table were just so out of order. They obviously thought I was a dumb bimbo, married to Danny for his money and fame. So I thought I'd go to Ross's boat, and I'd just be the worst pick-up he'd ever had.

'You know he even had the nerve to say to me: "Don't worry honey, the only reason I'm in football is the tax-free benefits and the birds." What a waste of space.'

Albert suddenly felt a strange sense of relief. The words he was hearing now were not fitting the story he had expected to be listening to. Confused, but much more comfortable, he engaged more closely with what Chrissie wanted to say to him.

Chrissie seemed to take his more intense attention as a reproach however.

'Well I lost it, Sir Albert, at that point. Told him I wasn't a "bird". Told him how long I'd trained at medical school. And I also told him that if he had a heart attack on his yacht that night after drinking himself senseless and probably failing to shag some other "bird" he'd lined up, I wouldn't come running to save his life.'

She shook her head, seeming remorseful at last.

'Oh dear, that's a terrible thing to say isn't it. But it's just that some of these blokes are really awful. They're like men from another age. Have they never heard of women's equality?'

She looked at Albert nervously.

'And it didn't stop with Ross I'm afraid. No, there was some awful git from Indonesia there as well. Slobbering all over this poor little girl he'd brought with him onto Ross's yacht from her patch on the harbour. When I finished lecturing him, I gave her two hundred Aussie dollars to get the hell out of there.'

Albert suddenly heard himself talking.

'Well... it might not be very helpful for our bid Chrissie.'

They both sat in silence. Chrissie waited for more.

'But I think we can just forget all about it.'

She sighed deeply, smiled with relief, and kissed him lightly on the cheek.

'You know,' he said, partly to deflect his discomfort, 'some people thought you might have been having an affair or something.'

His voice trailed off. He hadn't wanted to confront this lovely woman with such an accusation, but he felt a surge of superiority to Simon and wanted to show he was not one of those people with such a sordid imagination.

Chrissie held his arm tightly and giggled to herself.

'Affair? With one of those idiots? God no! Can you imagine?'

'But somebody said to me Danny was furious when you didn't come home. Did he um... didn't he think...'

'What Danny? Nooooooo. Danny knows I don't stray. He does get bloody angry when I go off on one with stupid people like last night, but he knows how strongly I feel about these sexist bastards. Oh, don't worry, Sir Albert; he knew what he was getting when he married me. He could have had any number of bimbos.'

She thought for a moment and leant in closely to confide with him.

'Oh I know Danny's not perfect Sir Albert. Of course he's never going to be faithful to me. His appetites are so much greater than mine, you see. It must be all that fitness training gives him a hunger. But I know one thing for sure: he'll never leave me. He'd never survive without me.'

Her eyes sparkled as she smiled sweetly. She started to get up from the airline seat to move back to sit next to her husband, but Albert signalled he had more to say.

'Oh, just one thing. Don't say anything to Simon about this please Chrissie. He'll be worried about the effect on our campaign of course. He'll also think the worst of you, but I'm sure you don't care.'

'No I don't,' said Chrissie quickly. 'I care what you think, Sir Albert. And I care what Danny thinks.'

Chapter 21

Money worries

July 1996

Simon Carslake's mood changes became increasingly evident at work and at home after returning from Australia. The secretaries talked about it between themselves. Always a cold fish, now he hardly seemed to notice the junior staff in the office at all. At least the silly old farts on the Council had time to stop and tease them when passing their desks, they thought. By contrast, 'Snotty Simon' was up his own arse.

Even his own World Cup campaign team, some of whom had developed respect for his efficiency and quick mind, were finding it increasingly difficult to engage with him and get him to make decisions. They knew he was under a lot of stress. The Chrissy Creighton incident had worried them all, but it was Simon who bore the responsibility.

When he was in London, he was out of the office more and more, often leaving no contact number. Sara Thurlow, who was now effectively Simon's deputy on the team, had even had to remind him about that day's Board meeting. It was a critical event for the campaign: a proposal for a major global development project for African football was to be discussed. But Simon's reaction to Sara was furious. He would have to miss a really important lunch engagement to attend it, he said.

Anna Carslake was becoming seriously worried about her husband's behaviour. She was used to Simon's absences. She knew his job required him to meet all kinds of people at all times of day and night. But when he had to be late home, there was usually the reassuring sound of an EFO car pulling up outside, with the driver giving Simon a cheery 'night Mr Carslake'. Why was Simon using taxis so often if he was out on EFO business? Why did he say he'd walked back from Barnes Bridge station two evenings ago?

Simon had never given her cause to question his fidelity. In fact, Anna had sometimes wondered how much he was interested in sex, and was certain that his ego was his main erogenous zone. But she was quite sure that if some exotic creature did choose to flatter and seduce him with promises of career or social advance, he wouldn't find it difficult to desert his family.

Of course, she had thought bitterly, the chances of any other woman wanting to seduce her husband were pretty slim unless there *was* an extraordinary motive. Anna had never forgotten the words of her oldest friend Tina, who passed judgement on Simon's fanciability before realising Anna was actually dating him: 'God, can you imagine it? It would be like shagging a robot!' If only she'd listened, she thought often nowadays.

As Simon took his seat in the oak-panelled committee room for the two o'clock Board meeting, he made no attempt to join the cheery exchanges as members came in.

'You been chewing nettles, Simon?' Michael Sutton, the EFO Deputy Chairman grinned as he smacked Carslake hard on the back, before hailing a colleague at the other side of the room.

Simon grunted. Despite what Sara Thurslow thought, he knew exactly how important the development budget was for the World Cup campaign. Of course. It was a demand from Joe Kumpa, a requisite for his support of the EFO bid. But Carslake had never doubted that the Board would back the proposal. One million pounds over three years didn't challenge the EFO's spending limits. It could easily be spread between the campaign's contingency, overseas, and access budgets. And a third world development programme was distinctly on message for the British Government and would be well received by the broadsheet Press.

No, he wasn't worried about the development proposal. Carslake's pressing concern that day, just as it had been for the three weeks since meeting Joe Kumpa in Yora, was how he could raise money to make the English bid a winner.

The African had shown huge faith in Simon's ability that evening at the British High Commissioner's residence in Mboge. He had underlined that commitment with a private call to Carslake's hotel room later. He had convinced Simon that Kumpa really believed that the EFO's campaign could succeed, as long as more money was raised to ease its path.

A meeting with Kumpa in London would be arranged in August, Joe had promised. That would be Simon's golden opportunity to strengthen both the EFO's case and his own career prospects. But first he faced a massive test of his credentials. Four crucial votes supporting bids to host the World Cup 2003 could only be acquired if he could raise $8 million.

Simon just knew he could do it. He had the contacts. He had respect in the commercial world. And he had the unique lure of football – the razzle dazzle that turned dour business men into small boys, pursuing their childhood dreams as enthusiastically as once they pursued their club heroes for autographs.

He had known it was a major challenge, but it was the kind of challenge he loved. And the fact that he could share his plans with nobody else only intensified his sense of personal thrill.

Indeed, from the first rejection he had met from the banker, Sir Richard Newlands, three weeks before, he had only felt his excitement rising. Spurred on by the thought of pitting his wits against some of the sharpest and toughest money men in Britain.

After he had been rejected by the first four men on his list, he revisited his contact book and analysed the next four best options. After that he found another three. He had now met bankers, hedge-fund managers, corporate finance chiefs, venture capitalists, and private speculators at some of London's finest restaurants.

Carslake wasn't used to failing, but it looked as though he would fail in this task. This dawning realisation was a shock, and it made him sink deep into himself. He was admitting to himself that he had no other ideas for finding the money he needed. He was in despair. The campaign bid he was managing was now also doomed, he was convinced, and the dreams of his future were dashed.

As Simon sat beside the Chairman at the meeting, half listening to the discussion around the table, he became aware that his opinion was sought. He steeled himself.

'Sorry Mr Chairman, what was that? Ah yes, I completely agree with your assessment of our visit to Africa. It is vitally important for our bid's prospects – and of course for the wellbeing of global football in the poorest areas of the world – that we adopt an innovative and generous development programme.'

Simon's response was automatic and professional, but he was in torment.

Chapter 22

Farmer Wilf

Wilf Smith knew he would live to regret agreeing to run for the GFO Presidency in September.

Christian Larsen had a big reputation and Smith knew that anyone challenging him was likely to lose. He knew that a President with a firm grip on power would take some shifting. The GFO machinery was all geared to support Larsen. He understood that despite his outward bonhomie and age, Larsen was a ruthless politician who would stop at nothing to win re-election a third time.

Wilf Smith was not particularly ambitious. Successful in his own orbit yes, but not because of a burning desire to be top dog. Life had just been very kind to Wilf Smith. He'd been born into a rich family of New Zealand sheep farmers, and while maintaining a high level of involvement in the family's farming and related businesses, he had time and money for other pursuits. One of those was football – a legacy perhaps of his grandfather Pat who had played for Bohemians in the 1920s.

Wilf had been Chairman of the New Zealand Football Organisation for just over ten years. He devoted as much time to the job as he could, balancing his other principal interest as a prominent benefactor of both the theatre and music. This combination of interests was, by GFO standards, unusual.

Despite his reservations about taking on Larsen, Smith did feel some kind of public duty was involved. He didn't like some of the stories he heard about the way the GFO was run, and he felt that football – particularly in Australasia and the Far East – deserved better. So he was quite sympathetic to the plight of the Alliance of Asian Football Organisations when they found themselves without a candidate after Lelei Fiso withdrew. Then Alliance representatives had come to see Smith offering Asian support for him if he would put himself forward. Flattered by their approach, he didn't take much persuading.

Although Smith was an unassuming man, he was not to be underestimated. He certainly wasn't charismatic and would probably struggle with Larsen in any charm offensive. Quietly spoken and a little too serious for some people's tastes, he was known to be a straight and decent man. Certainly he was not likely to be caught with his fingers in the till.

While that reputation helped him with some of the two hundred or so members who would elect the President, others questioned whether he would be able to cope with the rough and tumble of the football world, with external demands from governments, broadcasters, and sponsors. Still others, who had been personally advantaged during Larsen's two terms of office so far, were extremely concerned at the prospects of regime change at the GFO.

Once decided on a course of action, however, Wilf Smith took his role very seriously. In the run-up to the 1996 Presidential election, Smith had done a fair bit of canvassing through personal visits and telephone calls to countries in all parts of the GFO empire.

But if he was in any doubt before throwing his hat in the ring, these contacts with members made him realise the extent of his task.

Despite all the challenges presented by his opponent, by July, just a few months before the 1996 GFO Congress in Tokyo where the Presidential election was to be held, Wilf Smith had become a reasonably well-established name in football circles. That alone mattered enormously in an organisation famous for uncertain voting patterns and untrustworthy promises of support. His candidacy for GFO President was certainly being taken seriously by President Larsen. He was not expected to win, but he had some acknowledged support – from parts of Europe where Larsen was never popular, and from a significant number of countries in Asia. But he knew that in Africa and the Americas, particularly, Larsen was extremely popular.

So Smith knew he was up against it. He realised he wasn't going to win but he was keen to put up a credible performance and that was the best he could hope for.

Chapter 23

Opening the books

The Chronicle was one of the few newspapers left in London that still employed messengers. They weren't paid much and their job was to deliver memos around the office, and haul parcels and letters up from the mail room. But in the archaic world of British newspapers in the late 20th Century, more than a few bright young men and women had used the messenger service as a golden opportunity to progress careers as junior reporters.

The Whistleblower was expecting the parcel delivered that morning. It was from the man in the waxed coat who had requested a meeting in a Brussels layby a couple of months earlier. There had been three more phone conversations with him. *The Whistleblower* had been intrigued by the accounts data the man possessed, but had put him under no pressure to send it to the paper's office. That was simply an investigative reporter's instinct: this man had a major story to tell, and he would tell it in the end in the way that he wanted to.

At their second face-to-face meeting in a Brussels bar last month the man had explained his role, and how he had obtained the kind of detailed financial information he had first shown *The Whistleblower* in the car. This was his story. The informant was a former accountant, who had run his own financial advisory business in Brussels for years. The company had failed a year ago, and after a week or so without work, he'd been contracted for twelve months to the GFO finance department.

He told *The Whistleblower* that for the first few months of his contract, his work was uneventful and was well within his comfort zone. He had performed his role well, and the previous November he had been seconded to the President's office. The President had his own financial manager, and *The Whistleblower*'s informant was initially required only to follow simple bank-chequing procedures overseen by the manager.

But the President's finance manager was taken ill in early December, and the informant was asked to take over the manager's responsibilities. Nobody seemed to care that the informant had no long-term experience within the GFO. He simply had a reputation for competence, speed, and – as a contractor – a willingness to ask no questions.

His new responsibilities appeared to be exclusively for what was known in the office as the President's 'special projects' account. The informant quickly learned that transactions for the ledger were almost entirely inward payments of significant amounts – sometimes more than a hundred-thousand dollars.

He was not a keen football fan, but he knew that Russia was bidding for the lucrative role of host for the 2003 GFO World Cup. The last thing he wanted was to cause difficulties with his employer and risk his own livelihood, but the number of Russian names and the sums of money appearing on the President's financial reports unsettled him.

He told *The Whistleblower* that he probably wouldn't have made contact if the issue was simply about financial reports. But something else had happened. Soon after he took over special projects, he became aware of a man known only by his initials LM, described by GFO colleagues as the President's personal assistant. LM was often in the President's office before anyone else, checking financial information line-by-line, and making sure that deposits were made to the correct account headings. He never spoke about anything else, and he never smiled

What the informant found out was that LM was not a GFO employee but appeared to command all the personal authority of a Board member. He used a privileged all-security pass to access anywhere in the GFO building, and he followed the President around the world. Any enquiries to colleagues in the President's office about his background or his role were swiftly rebuffed. LM seemed to inspire more fear than respect amongst the small group of GFO people who had any contact with him.

LM's menacing presence convinced the informant that there was something seriously wrong in the President's office. But it was also fear of LM that had made the informant pull back when he first met *The Whistleblower*.

The Whistleblower's decision to give the man time to grow in confidence proved to be correct. In recent months the informant had found that the sums of money from Russian sources had grown in frequency and had added significantly to the overall funds deposited in the President's special projects accounts.

The final straw was a realisation that new entries in the accounts, often involving the largest sums of money, usually coincided with short periods when LM was out of the office – clearly not on tour with the President, but on some mission of his own.

He had finally summoned up his courage and printed eight reports from the President's office computer. Each report included some of the highest sums of money he had seen, logged alongside some of the most common source names. Those reports were in the carefully sealed and packaged folder that *The Whistleblower* had received that day.

Chapter 24

London calling

August 1996

Within days of the English campaign team's return from Yora in May, Joe Kumpa was in contact. His official correspondence went via email to Sir Albert, congratulating the EFO Chairman on the quality of the English bid. He said he had greatly enjoyed the EFO's visit and was honoured that the English had chosen to visit Yora first on its campaigning tour.

Separately that day, Kumpa also sent a confidential email to Simon Carslake, repeating the personal plaudits and veiled promises he had made to him in Yora. The President of the Alliance of African Football Organisations reminded Simon that he was keen to visit London. He wanted to come soon, but his diary was 'full of shit'. August was the best time.

He made clear that although football was the main purpose of his visit, and Kumpa always enjoyed English club matches, he wanted to discuss 'other matters' privately. Of course he must 'pay his respects' to Sir Albert, he said as an afterthought.

It was also clear to Simon that Kumpa expected all his expenses to be met to, from, and during his stay in London. Those expenses would include costs incurred by Maggie, his assistant, who apparently was coming with him. He indicated he would like to stay in the beautiful art-deco Brook Penthouse at Claridges, a suite of rooms he had used before. There was no mention of a separate room for Maggie. At least, Simon thought, he hadn't asked for the more expensive Royal Suite.

'Steph, I think it would be best if you could personally deal with the hotel and travel arrangements for this particular visit. I'll be giving Mr Kumpa quite a bit of my own time while he's here and I want things to go smoothly. I'll also sign off on the costs. You needn't trouble Sir Albert with the details. I'll tell him what's happening.'

'That's fine,' Steph replied. This was nothing unusual. Simon often asked her to attend to his arrangements confidentially. She had no interest in the reasons why, and that's what Simon expected.

'Leave it with me. Will you be taking Mr Kumpa to a match?' She looked at the wall calendar above her desk. 'Arsenal are playing Chelsea while he's in London the week after the season starts – it's on the Sunday, the day after he arrives. Ideal.'

Simon sighed quietly. Yes of course he would have to take Joe Kumpa to a football match. Joe would expect it, and he would have to give his usual imitation of enthusiasm at the game.

'Check with Maggie, his assistant. Her details are at the bottom of Joe's email. You could try phoning her, but I wouldn't trust the Yora telephone system. If she says yes, ring the Arsenal people and get them to set aside Directors' box seats. Oh,' he had a brain wave. 'And I'll find out whether the Chairman is free.'

That could be a brilliant solution to his protocol problem, Simon thought. He and Lewis could meet Kumpa at Highbury and they could talk football to their hearts' content. And then dinner out with Maggie. He needn't tell the Chairman he was seeing Kumpa later on Sunday evening on his own.

On a cool early September morning, Simon was sitting nervously in the VIP arrival lounge at Heathrow Airport, waiting for flight YA7243. He had decided to meet Kumpa straight off the plane. Kumpa would appreciate that kind of attention. Simon wanted everything to go right for this weekend. The stakes were high.

He let his mind wander to the problems that formed the backdrop to Kumpa's visit. Simon hadn't been able to raise the money to pay for votes he had been offered to support the English

World Cup bid, and he knew that the future career he had mapped out for himself depended on it.

Kumpa rated him highly, Simon was convinced of that. He was also convinced he would be invited to work for the great and powerful man if he could prove his ability to tap into sources of big money. Raising $8m to pay for four bid campaign votes was a critical test that he was currently failing. Simon feared he would quickly drop out of favour if Kumpa found out. He knew that mustn't happen while the African was in London that weekend.

'There you go, Maggie,' Kumpa grinned as they came down the airplane steps. 'The centre of the empire. And boy wonder says he's giving us the full VIP treatment!' As soon as their feet touched the ground, the doors of a Daimler limousine clicked open, and they were on the short journey to the lounge where Simon greeted them with as much of a grin as he could muster.

Joe and Maggie were dressed in colourful African robes. Simon hadn't expected it, but he was carefully professional and avoided any mention of the spectacle they created.

'Welcome to London Joe... Maggie. It's so good to see you again.' He talked quickly, as he usually did when concentrating on delivering faultless organisational plans. 'Now, this gentleman will take your passports for checking, and we just need confirmation that your bags are safely in the back of the car, then we'll be on our way.'

Joe Kumpa's greeting was unrestrained. He clutched Simon in a tight embrace. 'Very impressive, Simon my friend. I was just saying to Maggie. We Africans know how to have fun but you Europeans are best at organising it for us!' Kumpa roared with laughter, and brought Maggie into a three-way hug. The officer waiting to check passports looked fearful he might be included as well.

Simon was reminded how it felt to be the butt of Kumpa's mockery. He wasn't good at banter, so he simply smiled. Kumpa could say what he liked; Simon couldn't. Hopefully, this uncomfortable relationship would one day be worthwhile.

Simon offered Joe and Maggie juice, coffee and croissants from the bar, and spoke to Maggie directly about their flight and her previous experience of London. At one point, he noticed Kumpa staring at him intently. God, does he think I'm chatting up his woman? Simon thought. He turned his attention to Joe, just in case.

A blue-suited airline official arrived and whispered in Simon's ear. Within minutes they were in the car, heading for central London with a police escort.

Simon turned round from the front seat to talk to Kumpa, but stopped when he saw him noisily kissing Maggie. Before he could turn back, he caught Kumpa's eye. 'You mustn't be embarrassed by Maggie, Simon. How could anyone resist this girl.' Maggie slapped his face as he squeezed one of her large breasts, but she was joining in Joe's laughter. Simon wasn't sure what to say. 'Only special VIPs get the police,' he said weakly. It was what he had turned round to point out, but it felt wrong now.

'Well, I feel suitably honoured Simon. I like it. I like it a lot,' said Joe, in a serious voice, reaching forward to pat him heartily on the shoulder.

Simon felt more confident.

'It's the least I... we... can do Joe. It is very good of you to come to London. I've been looking forward to our private discussions. I will value - so much - any advice you can offer me.'

'Sure I'll give you plenty of advice,' Kumpa replied. 'There are things I want you to understand.'

Simon was intrigued, but waited for him to continue.

'Anyway,' Joe winked at Maggie, 'we need a restful afternoon today, and tomorrow Maggie wants to do some shopping while we go to the Arsenal game. You know, I've never been to Highbury. Big part of that famous old English football history that your Chairman never stops talking about.'

He leaned forward. 'In Yora a lot of kids support Manchester United and Liverpool. All those cup wins you see. But they've heard of Arsenal too. Our kids know everything about the English clubs and their players. One day I hope our Yoran teams will be just as famous all over the world.'

'I hope so Joe,' Carslake said warmly. 'Our teams are known everywhere. I sometimes think we're the most international of all the football countries. In parts of Asia, they know us so well they bet on our results! But things will change. African football is the future.'

Maggie was staring out of the window. It was only her second visit to London and she was keen to enjoy the sights. She made a mental note to be sure Joe kept enough time for the two of them to switch off the football stuff at some point so they could be tourists.

In advance of the visit, Maggie had indicated her priorities. She would concentrate on shopping while Joe was at the football, focusing on Knightsbridge and Harrods.

'When you have had enough' Simon said 'just ask Malcolm to drop you back at the hotel. You will be able to have a rest while we enjoy the post-match chatter at Highbury.'

'That's very considerate of you,' Maggie said.' On Monday. Joe, we have a private tour of central London sights arranged by Simon's office, including that visit to the London Eye you are so keen on.'

'Excellent, excellent,' Joe grinned. 'Very impressive, so far Simon.'

'Well,' said Simon, 'enjoy your stay at this lovely hotel.'

'I am sure we will,' Joe enthused, 'and tomorrow Simon, after dinner you and I can explore that malt bar in the basement. Forsyth's I think it's called.'

Next day, the Arsenal Chairman welcomed Kumpa and Simon on arrival at Highbury, and took them to the board room to introduce the club's other directors and a few well-known former Arsenal players. Albert Lewis had already arrived, and was standing by himself, self-consciously sipping a light ale as he looked at portraits of the club's past managers.

Albert usually loved these occasions. He could talk for hours to directors about the state of the game, gossiping happily about the prospects of rival teams. He could indulge in nostalgia with former players he usually remembered well from their playing days, sharing memories of great games he had seen or read about. It was usually the perfect preparation for the main event. Ninety minutes of a glorious game of football played by some of the most talented young men on the planet. Ninety minutes that could be relied on – almost without fail in his long experience – to give him the most uncomplicated, sheer pleasure of his life.

Today was different though. Today he would be in the company of a man he suspected of cheating his own people of their money... some of the poorest people in the world. He was haunted by the accusation, delivered with chilling nonchalance by a business friend of Kumpa's in Yora, that Kumpa took a 10% cut of all money transacted with his Alliance of African Football Organisations. The business friend's word wasn't good enough for any public court, as Albert's wife Monica had warned him. But Albert instinctively believed the charge, and that was sufficient to make Kumpa's presence completely repugnant to him.

When Simon Carslake had told him that Kumpa was visiting London, Albert's first reaction had been mild irritation that the proposal hadn't been directed to him, the Chairman of the EFO. But his hurt pride didn't last long. Yes, he would represent the EFO at the Arsenal match, and have dinner with Kumpa and his fancy woman. But he didn't want any more to do with Kumpa on this trip. He didn't want to be responsible for him. And he didn't want to have to sign off all the freeloading. That was a job for Simon.

Joe Kumpa appeared to show no wariness towards the EFO Chairman when he spied him across the Highbury board room. He beamed widely and caused a few people in the room to jump when he bellowed: 'Albert!' Before Albert could compose himself, Kumpa had launched into a GFO hug, dislodging Albert's glasses in the process. 'Ohhhh so sorry my friend.' Kumpa reached down, picked up the glasses, and handed them to Albert. 'So great to see you again!' Albert managed a weak smile of greeting. He wasn't good at public displays of anger or resentment.

The match that followed was a free-flowing spectacle, ending in a 3-2 victory to Arsenal. Sitting next to Albert, Joe talked endlessly about the game, occasionally standing and cheering a great move, or howling his contempt for the referee, before sitting again with a loud belly laugh and calling the waiter for another beer.

At first Albert was worried that Joe's antics would be an embarrassment to the others in the Arsenal directors' box. But Joe's personality was contagious. Albert noticed a number of men behind them reached forward and clapped Joe on the back, laughing heartily with him. Joe flashed his winning smile at anyone who looked in his direction, and blew kisses at the elderly wife of Arsenal's longest-serving director.

My God, thought an exasperated Lewis, everyone loves this man. Don't they realise what a monster he is? But when the ex-Arsenal-and-England right back Sam Cutler nudged him and said: 'Bloody hell Albert, I didn't know these GFO blokes were so much fun,' Albert couldn't help nodding his agreement.

Two seats away from Joe and Albert, Simon was also enjoying Kumpa's performance. Attending these matches was always a duty rather than a pleasure for him. Being able to observe his potential mentor in relaxed mood was an unexpected bonus.

The game passed in no time, and when those who stayed behind after the final whistle regrouped in the board room, Kumpa was right at the centre of debate about the match.

By the time the three men got away from Highbury, and into the car for dinner, it was clear to Simon that Kumpa was more than happy with his London trip. Maggie was already sitting in the back seat, with six big shopping bags at her feet, all of which bore prestigious brand names. She thumped Kumpa cheerily on his arm as he nearly fell on top of her. 'Joe Kumpa,' she scolded. 'How much have you had to drink?'

The dinner passed happily enough too. Kumpa was on one side of Albert, and Maggie was on the other. Kumpa continued drinking, teasing Maggie when the conversation drifted, drowning her protests with loud laughs that caused a few of the other diners to turn their heads. But he also listened respectfully and quietly as Albert described at length his plans for investing in the lower tiers of the English game, and he spoke of his wish to encourage the GFO to create new coaching qualifications across the world.

After three or four large glasses of red wine, Albert was undoubtedly feeling warmth towards his African colleague. Somewhere in the back of his mind he sensed a dark cloud, but he couldn't remember what it was.

At the end of the meal, Albert resisted Joe's invitation to visit the hotel's malt bar. He was feeling a little woozie, and thought that malt whiskey would not help him at all. He also refused Simon's suggestion that the limousine should drive him to his hotel in Park Lane, preferring instead to take the night air for the short walk through Mayfair.

Kumpa winked at Simon when Albert had left. He said he would settle Maggie into their suite and join Simon in the bar. Simon went down to the basement bar, found a corner seat and ordered a blended malt. Forty minutes later, he was feeling anxious. Had Kumpa decided to 'settle' Maggie into bed a little too enthusiastically? Had the extraordinary number of beers, whiskeys, and glasses of wine caused the kind of 'hippo snoring' that Maggie had said she was worried about? Much more important, was Kumpa standing Simon up – deliberately or accidentally?

Twenty minutes later, the big man reappeared. He had changed from the smart western suit he had worn all day into a pair of pale blue slacks and a navy-blue polo neck sweater. He had clearly showered and dowsed himself in sweet smelling eau de cologne. As he sat down, Simon couldn't help noticing that Joe's thighs were so big he didn't even attempt to cross his legs.

Kumpa really was a marvel, thought Simon. There was no sign that he had drunk alcohol endlessly for the past nine hours. He showed no tiredness, and no desire to call off this meeting. He accepted Simon's suggestion of a malt he would enjoy and pulled his chair close to Simon's. He wasted no time in small talk.

'So... Simon. When will you have the money?'

'Soon. Very soon Joe,' Simon spluttered an automatic reply. He swallowed more whiskey than he intended to, in sheer surprise.

There was silence between them as Simon waited for Kumpa's response. Simon looked down at his glass but felt the big man's eyes drilling into his mind. He noticed that Joe's own glass was untouched on the table. Simon wanted desperately to break the silence, but he knew that whatever he said would have no credibility.

'Don't shit me, Carslake,' hissed Joe. Simon was so startled by the change of expression in Kumpa's voice that he looked straight at him. Kumpa's fixed stare hadn't changed.

Simon gathered control over himself. It wasn't the first time in his life he had been caught out with an untruthful response. It had almost cost him his job once, when a perceptive director questioned his report on sales for the fashion outlets for which he was responsible. Then, flustered but with no straight answer to give, he had invited the director to identify the claimed errors in his figures. He had learned an important lesson. Simon's indignant challenge was enough to silence the man because he had no concrete evidence for his suspicions. Simon had used that bold and risky strategy to counter opposition many times since. He slipped into it automatically in the face of Kumpa's challenge.

'The thing is, Joe, it's taking a bit longer than I expected. I've got plenty of interested parties. Plenty of friends in the city that can lend me the money, but they've got to be careful...' His voice trailed away. He knew he wasn't fooling Joe Kumpa.

'Yeah yeah,' said the African, shaking his head. He moved his mouth closer to Simon's ear.

'You English with all your governance and your due diligence and your regulation and your accountability and your safeguards against so-called fraud. Well let me tell you, Carslake, one of the things you got to understand is that bidding for the World Cup ain't about all that shit. It's about those countries prepared to pay a lot of dosh to come out on top.'

He took a large Cuban cigar from his pocket and lit it with the biggest gold lighter that Carslake had ever seen.

'You call it corruption, but it's how most people in the world do business,' Kumpa continued. 'Understand me? So you just tell Albert and all those other old boys in the EFO. You tell your city friends and your politicians. If they want the World Cup, they're going to have to get their hands dirty.'

He looked carefully at Simon, whose face was expressionless

'Dirty. And clever. And generous. They got to do things they don't want to do. They gotta make some nice contributions. They gotta up their game when it comes to football development – and make sure the money gets paid in the right places.'

His eyes suddenly opened wide with fury. 'Why the fuck did the EFO money for Africa not get sent to me. Eh? That wasn't smart Simon. If you want friends in high places, you fucking got to keep those friends happy.'

And then suddenly, the anger seemed to clear.

Kumpa leaned forward, and lowering his voice, put a hand on Simon's right arm.

'My friend, let me be frank with you. It's the big money will win the bid. Not your million pounds to Africa. Big money will make things happen, get voters on your side. So just you find that money you need to get the votes. You understand?'

Joe swallowed the contents of his glass.

'Now I'm going to say something else to you Simon. Because I like you. I think you understand this world. You're the only guy from EFO who does. And you need to know this: however much money England raises, you're never going to win this bid.'

Simon stayed silent, listening.

'A lot of people in the football world don't like England. Some people think you're arrogant. You haven't forgotten bossing people around even though the empire is long dead. And you haven't got used to the idea there are many better teams on the pitch and better candidates for hosting the tournaments too.

'Well, Simon. You got a nice little deal going with our friend Gerald. Those votes might be a big help to England. But,' he paused. 'I don't think you're gonna win in the end.'

'Tell me Simon,' his voice fell to a whisper. 'How much you care if England wins the World Cup bid?'

Simon breathed heavily. He said nothing to Kumpa, but he knew inside what the answer was.

'Because the thing is, you ain't gonna get rich from that deal. Oh yes, there's a nice little 10 per cent for you and me, Simon... but after you've paid out to your money men, is that enough for you Simon?'

He smiled and paused.

'How much you like to make real money... with big Joe by your side?'

Simon was still silent.

'It's there Simon. Bags of gold. Just waiting for you and me to grab it. Like the old colonials did with Yora minerals!'

Joe Kumpa threw his head back. Simon waited for his laughter to subside. Then Joe continued.

'See. I've got a proposition for you, my friend. Something to make us real money.'

Kumpa stared deep into Simon's eyes.

'Get that eight million dollars for the four votes,' he said slowly, 'and I promise you we'll sell them four votes to another bid campaign for fifteen million straight away.'

'You get it? Abracadabra! One minute those four votes go to England for eight million dollars. Then suddenly, those Board members change their minds who to vote for overnight... with a little help from more bags of gold!'

'And you Simon? Your stake in the deal nearly doubles. And old Joe gets his cut too. What d'you say to that Simon?'

Simon's head was spinning. He called a waiter to refill their glasses to give him time to think about what Kumpa was saying.

'OK... I'm not sure I quite understand, Joe...' Simon said at last, as coolly as he could. 'If there's more money on the table from another bid team, how come Gerald isn't selling these votes to someone else right now? Why would Gerald give me those votes for eight million dollars if he knows he can sell them for fifteen straight away?'

Joe Kumpa smiled indulgently.

'You see – our friend Gerald is a broker. He's told these Board members their votes are worth eight million if they sell them to you. And why would they question him? They make a lot of money from your deal.

'But he's also been talking to other bidders. Telling them they can buy the same votes for fifteen million.

'You understand markets, Simon. Them four votes were only worth eight million when Gerald came to see you early this year. But as the months go by, and the bidding steps up, them Board votes are like gold dust. By next year the value of them four votes will double again. It's always the same.

'So now Gerald goes back to the Board members and says: I've got a better price for your votes. He says: you got money already from England, now switch support to another bidder and you make the same money all over again! You get two bites at the cherry, he says to the bastards. And why should they complain? They get even more money from two deals... and maybe more before next year. Everyone's happy!'

'Yeah sure, these Board men could have waited 'til now to sell their votes. But they know damn well that they can make more money by selling two or three times as the market develops. And keep your money too! And Gerald helps them do it.'

Simon thought carefully as Kumpa spoke.

'And I guess nobody expects the English to complain that they've been stuffed to the tune of eight million dollars, when we don't get the votes we thought we'd paid for.'

Joe Kumpa threw his head back as he laughed at the absurdity of the question.

'Complain? What you guys going to say? It's not fair! We bought these votes for eight million dollars so we can cheat in the bidding game? We going to take Gerald and the Board guys to the International Court! You can't do this to us! It's our sense of fair play...! We're English!'

Joe's laughter slowly subsided. He moved his head closer to Simon and softened his voice.

'So think about it. And ask yourself this. Why should I care if you get shafted?'

He grinned, and grabbed Simon's arm

'Simon,' he said. 'I like you. I'm telling you all this because we can do great things together. You just gotta prove it to me by getting eight million bucks. And I prove it to you with a big slice of profit from not one – but two sexy deals.'

He pushed Simon's arm away playfully.

'Just get the eight million, and you'll be a wealthy man I promise you. I'll send you the bank account details. Then as soon as the money is paid in, you'll know the deals will be done. And don't worry. Once you got the money you can leave all the business to me and Gerald. You see we are straight with each other in GFO,' he chuckled.

'Cheers,' he said as got to his feet. 'And now I'm going to join that beautiful creature in my bed.'

Simon did not leave the bar. He ordered himself a MacAllan malt. It had been a long and stressful day and his body was begging him to head home. But the conversation he had just had with Joe

Kumpa had been so momentous that he knew he had to think about its consequences. And he had to do it right now. Alone. There was only one other couple left in the bar, and they were too caught up in each other to notice him.

He sipped the whiskey for a moment, deep in thought, then took out a pen from his jacket pocket. He found a notebook in his briefcase. Carefully, he went over Kumpa's proposition in his mind and made notes in a scribble that nobody else would ever understand.

The more he thought about it, the more he began to smile. So this offer from Gerald to buy Board members' votes was no longer just about helping England to win its World Cup bid. It was now Simon's opportunity to be a major player in international deal making. It was the kind of role he craved. No more pandering to the deadbeats in the EFO. He would be playing with the big boys. Generating respect and even fear wherever he went.

His smile widened. Of course, it was also the solution to the problem he had encountered in trying to raise eight-million dollars from the money men. Now he could guarantee a return for his investors, based on selling those four votes onto another campaign team. And all he had to do was work with Gerald to make it happen. 'Yessss', he hissed aloud. The couple didn't notice.

And so what if selling on those votes meant that England would lose its chance to win its precious World Cup bid? Kumpa had read him well, he thought. The only reason he wanted to win the bid was to boost his reputation inside and outside the EFO. He didn't care if England lost the bid as long as his own future with Kumpa and his team was to be even brighter. In fact, it would give him a strange pleasure if the EFO were to lose.

He drained his glass, closed his suitcase, and left the bar with a skip in his step.

Chapter 25

Taking control

Helmut Schneider was a Munich man born and bred. He hated Berlin. He hated Berliners' sense of superiority and their pretended 'liberal' tastes. Schneider came from a long line of Bavarian bankers. He never felt comfortable amongst the Media and advertising types he met in the Hotel Adlon bar when he had to be in the city.

As his taxi headed down the A100 from Tegel Airport towards the capital, he felt his mood worsening by the minute. 'Ugly buildings,' he muttered to himself, 'ugly people.'

It was a shame. He normally enjoyed his meetings with the Sports Minister when Frau Möller came to visit his Munich office. Melina was a tall, handsome woman, who didn't interfere much with the workings of the Deutscher Fußball-Organisation. The DFO had after all delivered considerable success on the field over many years, boosting Germany's global reputation and the profits of its sponsors.

Schneider wasn't entirely sure why he and the DFO President Dieter Bauer had been summoned to her Berlin office, but he guessed that the Sports Department, or even its parent Federal Ministry of the Interior, was worried about his bidding strategy for the 2003 World Cup. Fr Möller's letter to the President had been terse.

Ich möchte Sie und Herr Schneider sofort in meinem Büro sehen. Bitte vereinbaren Sie einen Termin mit meinem Sekretär.

Sitting in the front passenger seat, Schneider caught a glimpse of Dieter Bauer's expressionless face in the driver's mirror as the car turned into Wilhelmstrasse. There wouldn't be any support from

Bauer in that afternoon's meeting, he well knew. The President was a politician first and foremost. If Schneider had no answers to the Minister's questions, his head would be on the line... alone.

Schneider was a reckless man. He enjoyed the career risks he took on behalf of the DFO. But he was not a man who could be discarded without consequences. He smiled to himself as the car pulled up outside the hotel.

Bauer... du dummer Bastard... if you think I'm going down without you, think again!

The two men said nothing to each other as they took their cases from the driver and Schneider paid the bill. They stayed silent until they had finished checking in, when Bauer said: 'Lunch at 12:30?'

'No – I want to prepare for the meeting in my room,' Schneider replied.

Dieter Bauer looked unsure for a moment. He didn't want to involve himself in Schneider's plans for the meeting. Too much involvement meant too much liability in his view. Fleetingly, however, he wondered whether this meeting was being called because Schneider had overstepped the mark in some way. Perhaps the Minister would expect him to take direct responsibility for the Chief Executive's behaviour on this occasion. Should he demand that Schneider brief him?

He quickly reassured himself. His role as President was a sinecure. He had no executive responsibility for Schneider, or the way Schneider operated. Besides, Schneider was *ein einsamer Wolf* - and that was a good thing. The DFO would not have been so successful if its Chief Executive had been shackled with accountability. The Minister knew that as well as he did. Besides, Bauer had powerful friends in the Bundestag. He had little to fear from Fr Möller.

'OK,' he said coldly to Schneider. 'Let's meet here at two. Plenty of time to cross the bridge.'

The Minister's office was on the second floor of the Federal Ministry of the Interior. Schneider and Bauer sipped their coffees in silence as they sat in the ante room waiting to be summoned. Bauer looked at his watch and sighed extravagantly. Schneider was expressionless, flicking through an A4 notebook.

Voices from Fr Möller's office indicated a meeting had concluded. The Minister and two men emerged. Schneider recognised the second as a senior official in the Deutscher Olympischer Sportbund. Nods were exchanged as he passed. Bauer frowned... he hadn't been recognised by the Olympics man.

Fr Möller waved in the direction of Schneider and Bauer, but before they could get up, she said: 'Sorry. Just give us five minutes.' She ushered the second man back into her office. He was young, dressed in a sharp black suit. Schneider had seen his photograph before. He was a political adviser in the Ministry of the Interior, responsible for liaison between Government departments.

Fifteen minutes later, Schneider and Bauer were sitting on one side of the Minister's table facing Fr Möller. Seidel, her adviser, was sitting beside her.

'Herr Schneider,' said the Minister after brief introductions to Seidel, 'you should know we are worried.'

It dawned on Schneider that he was being formally addressed because of Seidel's presence. Why? Aaah that was it. It was the Federal Foreign Office that was really worried, and Seidel was representing their interests.

Schneider knew immediately why they were likely to be concerned. Schneider and Baskin's joint strategy for the 2003 World Cup bidding process was always going to raise questions with both Governments. He knew he would have to explain himself to the Sports Minister at one time or another, but he hadn't thought too much about the consequences for German foreign policy. He felt a frisson of excitement. He really was stirring things up. He smiled to himself.

'Oh,' said Schneider. 'I am sorry to hear you are worried, Minister. What's the problem?'

Fr Möller did not reply at first. She looked at Schneider without expression. She knew him well. She liked him, a very clever operator. She wanted him on her side.

'Helmut.' Her voice was softer, and warmer. '

Fr Möller glanced at Seidel as if to explain her change of approach.

'Helmut, we need to understand why you seem to be conspiring with the Russians over the 2003 World Cup bid.' She paused but held up her hand to indicate she had not yet finished.

'The Foreign Minister is asking... demanding to know... why you're doing this. His policy... our Government policy... is not to create bilateral forms of cooperation with Russia in international affairs. You know very well, Helmut, that you represent the German Government in your dealings with the GFO. You cannot – MUST not – adopt your own foreign policy!'

Schneider sensed Bauer shifting uncomfortably beside him as the Minister continued more formally.

'Helmut, I have to tell you that unless Herr Seidel is able to assure the Minister that this collaboration will cease immediately... I will have to remove you from your position.'

Dieter Bauer began to speak: 'On behalf of the Deutscher Fußball-Organisation, Minister, I can assure you and Herr Seidel that...'

Schneider interrupted him.

'Fr Möller, I completely accept the misunderstanding.'

Seidel jumped in.

'It's not a question of misunderstanding Herr Schneider. Do you deny that you have been collaborating with the Russians?'

Schneider smiled.

'May I finish?'

Fr Möller nodded.

'It is entirely my fault that I have not yet explained the DFO's plans in more detail to you, Minister. But please let me assure you that, based on my experience of these matters, I didn't feel that the moment for a candid discussion between us had quite arrived.'

Both Seidel and Bauer looked as though they were about to speak, but Schneider's flow was difficult to stem.

'I think you will agree, Minister, that on all international football matters – just as soon as the emerging picture becomes clear – I always brief you personally and immediately. However, I hope you will also accept that I've never given you information that I'm not completely confident about.'

'So... what is your briefing, Herr Schneider?' spluttered Seidel. 'We need to know.'

Schneider looked coolly at Seidel but addressed his response to Fr Möller.

'Minister,' he said slowly. 'I've always given you a personal and confidential briefing about these matters. No other Minister, and certainly no adviser, has been present at our discussions...'

Seidel reddened at the implied insult.

'Preparations for bidding to host World Cup 2003 are at a very delicate stage... it could be disastrous for Germany if the information I have for you is to be... leaked in any form.'

'Surely...' Seidel began, but Fr Möller signalled him to be quiet.

The room remained silent, and the Minister got up from the table and stood by the window. She turned to face the three men.

'Herr Seidel, will you please leave. I will talk to the Foreign Minister this evening. Herr Bauer, I'm sure Herr Schneider will brief you separately. Thank you both, gentlemen.'

Schneider looked carefully down at his papers. He sensed Bauer moving quickly towards the door. Still time for the old dog to meet his mistress in Unter Den Linden, Schneider thought. Seidel appeared to be mouthing soundlessly to the Minister before leaving the room and closing the door firmly behind him.

'So Helmut. What have you got to say to me that is so confidential that I'm risking my relationship with my Government colleagues?'

Her words were firm, but Schneider knew his relationship with her was secure. He had taken a risk that she would not accept a one-to-one briefing if she was under pressure from the Foreign Minister, but it had been worth it. He had won. As for the two men who had left the room, Bauer was never a threat and Schneider always enjoyed diminishing the President's reputation. He didn't know whether or not Seidel was a dangerous adversary. That was a question... and another challenge... for the future.

'As I have said Minister, the reason that I've not briefed you before is not carelessness or forgetfulness on my part.'

His face betrayed a hint of disgust at the very thought that he should ever be guilty of such human frailties. The Minister nodded her understanding.

'No Frau Möller... Melina... the fact is that I was expecting to meet you in two weeks' time. My secretary was even seeking dates in your diary. But of course, I understand that the rhythm of your political world sometimes demands a different beat.'

'I know you understand the political world, Helmut. And I in my turn understand the complexities of the GFO and its bidding processes. So, what can you tell me now – to help me reassure my Foreign Office colleagues?'

Schneider's face broke into a grin.

'The situation is quite simple, Melina. So simple in fact that it can be very easily misinterpreted and shared in the wrong quarters unless it's explained to other Government Ministers with the kind of extraordinary insight and knowledge that you can apply.'

The Minister knew Schneider's flattery techniques of old, but they never failed to delight her. It was always pleasing for an ambitious politician to be admired by a man whose reputation for ruthlessness and achievement soared in global sporting politics.

'You see, Minister, it's perfectly true that I've developed a very close working relationship with the Russian delegate at the GFO.

It's also perfectly true that as recent hosts of the World Cup, it seems extremely unlikely that Germany will be invited to host the 2003 World Cup. It's also true that there's an attractive case for sharing our influence with the Russians for mutual gain: for Russia perhaps to be awarded the World Cup if we can't win it, and for us to secure the 2005 Euro Championships.'

'To the outside observer, it might seem that your GFO delegate was indeed participating in a desperate collaboration, where Germany's interests are apparently being traded – perhaps at a low price. Well Minister, as a brilliant politician, you will know well that allowing that impression to prevail could be extremely valuable to our cause.'

'However,' he concluded, 'I can assure you, in total confidence, that I have no intention of relinquishing any opportunities for Germany to succeed in any area where I can influence affairs. May I?'

Schneider reached across to a jug in the centre of the table, and poured them both a glass of water.

'Before you go on Helmut,' the Minister said, 'the Foreign Office says it has intelligence that your Russian colleague says exactly the same thing to his Government.'

'Well, this is where my message is so simple, Minister, and requires your interpretation. The thing is... Melina, my simple message to you, and to you only, is that you can trust me to deliver what I say. And we both know that you alone can make the Foreign Office believe what we both know to be true...'

Schneider smiled.

'We can and will win the World Cup bid.'

Chapter 26

Gods and goddesses

September 1996

'Now we all know how important the GFO inspection is to our bid. We've called this particular project "gods and goddesses" – for the simple reason we have to treat the inspectors like gods and goddesses! Hopefully it will be a constant reminder of the standards we need to reach.'

Clare was chairing the meeting. A top-class administrator, she had been seconded from the MOD to the 2003 World Cup bid team for two years. In her short civil service career, she had gained a high reputation for organisation, and Simon Carslake had given her lead responsibility for the visit by six GFO Board members. It was a big appointment, because those men would evaluate England's facilities and ability to host the world's biggest football event, as well as assess how jolly a time they might expect at the EFO's expense. A Crystal Palace fanatic since the age of eight, Clare was thrilled to be involved.

'We're asking everyone in the team to contribute to the planning, over and above your daily responsibilities on the campaign,' she continued confidently. 'In fact we're going to need everyone working very long hours during the inspection itself.'

All sixteen members of the campaign team were squashed into the open-plan office the EFO had allocated for the duration of the bidding process. Everyone from marketing to Press Officers to diplomats to the events team had to be there. Some had grabbed a seat but others were standing at the back, and a few were sitting on the floor. There was an air of excitement in the room.

The campaign had been proceeding for more than eight months. In that time, visits had been made to ten countries and four continents to present the EFO case.

The inspection visit was the first chance for the EFO team to show off England to the most important people in the bidding process. This was more than just a marketing opportunity, getting it right was imperative.

'So let's start with the visit to Wembley,' Clare said. She turned to Billy Pitchers, a seasoned tabloid hack who had been at the EFO's Public Affairs department for four years before he joined the campaign team. 'Where have we got to?'

'Well,' said Billy. 'I think most of you know we plan to arrive by helicopter... three in fact.... We thought we could recreate the scene from *Apocalypse Now* – remember... when the American soldiers arrive by helicopter to music blaring away.... Wagner's *Ride of the Valkyries*. Steve and I thought we could take the helicopters' side panels out so the inspectors can dangle their legs. One or two of them might fall out, but that wouldn't matter that much as there are too many of them anyway.'

A few members of the campaign team laughed. A few others looked somewhat baffled. Stephen Green, sitting near the back of the room, shook his head despairingly at the infantile behaviour he too often encountered at the EFO.

'Don't worry,' said Steve Monroe, Billy's colleague, catching a glimpse of Simon's unsmiling face. 'We're only kidding.'

'But we *are* planning to bring the inspection team to Wembley by helicopters, coming from Battersea heliport, across central London, and landing on the pitch. It'll be an unforgettable way to see the capital. As they descend into the stadium the individual names of the inspection team will appear on the Wembley big screens. That should satisfy a few egos.'

'Yeah,' said Billy, 'and as part of their visit we'll invite each of them to take penalties on the pitch.'

'Dear God,' muttered Stephen Green to himself.

'But when we did that with the visitors from China, didn't one of them fall over on his ankle?' said Susie, one of the event organisers working for Clare.

'Yes, that's true,' Billy said. 'But afterwards the guy who was hurt said his ankle would eventually get better, while the memory of scoring at Wembley would stay with him for ever.'

The campaign team tittered.

'No, Billy's quite right,' said Susie. 'He did!'

'That's the great thing,' said Charlie Mason, who as Head of Press and an older ex-journalist, felt it was his role to give the team the benefit of his vast experience in considering the campaign's publicity plans and its likely impact with the Media. 'Everybody wants to go to Wembley, and they all love going on the pitch especially if they can score a goal.'

'I have a friend who used to work at Wembley, and he scored,' Billy muttered to Steve. 'He and his girlfriend did it in one of the goalmouths after everyone had gone home. He said it was pretty exciting except he was worried someone might come back to work and put the floodlights on...' Steve smirked quietly.

'Ok,' said Clare. 'Let's have one meeting please. Can we move on to hotel arrangements? Then we'll discuss transport. Laura, where have we got to?'

Laura Denning also worked for Clare. She had a reputation for being frighteningly efficient when she joined EFO from the events team of a major bank. Difficulties were mere challenges to be overcome according to her strictly 'can do' philosophy, and she always got the job done without a word of complaint. Her bosses loved her. One had said she was the perfect example of why he always employed people who were better at certain jobs than he was. But colleagues who preferred to deal with problems in a more considered way found her uncompromising nature difficult to deal with.

Laura opened a ring file folder before she spoke.

'The six members of the inspection team will all be staying at Claridge's. The hotel looked after our guests well for the Malaysian visit and we've sorted out one or two minor problems with the house manager. It's not cheap, but the standards are very high indeed. The chairman of the inspection team will have the Presidential Suite, the one that Larsen had when he was last here.

'I'm also dealing with transport,' Laura said without pause. 'This is more complicated but it's all fine. I've had extensive meetings with the Home Office and of course the Metropolitan Police. From the moment the inspection team arrives at Heathrow, the six of them will be treated like royalty. They'll be taken initially to the special VIP Lounge reserved for distinguished government guests. After a few introductions, including Sir Albert and the Sports Minister representing the PM, the visitors will be taken in chauffeur-driven limousines to Claridge's.

'The Met will provide a full motorcycle escort with all traffic lights set on green for the whole journey. This escort will be available for the whole of the inspection visit. For the rest of their visit, the inspection team will travel in EFO World Cup 2003 liveried London taxis. Everywhere they go the lights will be on green – which will give a slightly false sense of London traffic flow, but never mind. They'll love it. I must say the Met guys on the bikes are really supportive, and one or two are absolutely gorgeous!'

'Oooooh, show me, show me,' came Anthony's voice from a corner of the room. 'You must share Laura, you must share!' The tension in the room evaporated as the team began to giggle. Nobody minded Anthony. His camp persona was reserved purely for the team's private pleasure.

As the room grew quiet, Clare called Anthony forward

'Come on then, you naughty man. How are the key events going?'

'Well, apart from that Laura trying to steal all the good-looking men, everything is fitting into place quite nicely.' Anthony grimaced at the people who were starting to laugh again. 'Now,

now, Clare will get very cross.' He slipped firmly into professional mode.

'The dinner at the Tower of London will be spectacular, specially with the fireworks and the Grenadier Guards band at the end. When the Tower is closed to visitors, and you're the only ones there for a private function, the atmosphere is incredible. You get a tremendous sense of history and all the famous things that have happened there. I think our visitors will get blown away by it.

'They will also be getting a private viewing of the crown jewels, although of course the GFO has a bit of a reputation, and I will be smacking the mitts of anyone who tries to touch! It's a good job President Larsen isn't coming. He might fancy one of the Crowns for his coronation after he gets re-elected in September.'

'Sorry Clare... I'm being silly again.'

'Anyway, the curator at the Tower will give them a short chat about the jewels and answer their questions. Should be good. We're not sure yet which Cabinet Minister is hosting the Tower of London dinner yet. We're awaiting word from Number 10, but Stephen has stressed it must be someone who knows about football. And of course they will need to make all the right noises about how much the nation wants the World Cup tournament in 2003.'

Stephen Green put his hand up to speak, and caught Anthony's eye.

'Yes, I should say that Number 10 is being very strong on this. The PM is putting a lot of pressure on the Chancellor. He may not be the greatest orator, but he's a warm character, loves football, and obviously he's a global name.' There was murmured approval.

'Thanks Stephen. That's great news.' Anthony continued.

'There is then the dinner on the Friday night back at Claridge's. We're trying to get Elton John. This is going to be a rather exclusive occasion, but if you're nice to me one of you boys might get chosen as a doorman for the evening.

'We've got a good turnout of football 'names', including some notable internationals. Our very own Danny Creighton and Chrissy will be our figurehead schmoozers of course. We've also got some big foreign stars from the Premier League, who will talk about what a great thing it is playing in England. It promises to be an evening to remember.

'And last but hardly least, there's the visit to Number 10 to meet the PM in the Cabinet Room. This is a key moment in the week. The PM will really emphasise how much the Government is backing the bid. And how important he feels sporting development is, and how much we've pitched into Africa. He'll also stress the public's enthusiasm. Oh, and word is that he may even offer some additional support from the Foreign Aid budget, but I guess that's under wraps, Simon.'

Simon nodded. 'Yes that could be very sensitive obviously,' he said. 'The Foreign Aid budget is political dynamite anyway as far as the right is concerned. Any suggestion that it's being used to support our bid could be catastrophic to the Government and to us.'

If only I could get hold of just a little of that money that's being so carelessly discussed here... Simon thought to himself. Perhaps his face was betraying the thought. 'Carry on Anthony,' he said.

'Then finally there's the meeting at St James's Palace to see Charlie boy. Similar messages to the PM. Of course, HRH will have already had the inspection team and wives to Highgrove a few days earlier so he's certainly doing his bit, especially as he's not known to be a footy fan.'

'That all sounds very good,' Clare said as she got to her feet again. 'I just want us to run through the ground visits now. Obviously, these are supposed to be the core part of the inspection – regardless of the PM, Elton John and Prince Charles. Laura?'

'I can give you an overview, yes,' said Laura. 'The good news is that we've just had permission to use the Queen's Flight for the trips to Manchester and Newcastle. That's rather special to say the least and will make the inspection team feel very important. The plane takes off from RAF Northolt, and basically it goes whenever we're ready.

'We're finalising the itinerary, but we'll certainly visit Old Trafford. In fact we'll be able to take them to United's midweek home fixture against West Ham. Also in the North, we'll definitely visit Newcastle, Liverpool and Sunderland and a bit further south, Sheffield Wednesday. In the Midlands we'll go to Villa Park as well as the new Derby County stadium. Basically there's only time to visit some of the likely venues. We will of course include several London ones while they're staying here.

'I know that a few members of the EFO Council are trying to make the case for other grounds, but we're not including Barnsley for example, are we Simon?' The team laughed lightly again, but Simon shook his head firmly.

'There's an interesting situation in the West Country,' Laura continued. 'At the moment no suitable ground exists but Bristol City have ambitious plans for a new stadium, and we must refer to this or the West will not have any involvement.'

'Thank you, Laura,' said Clare. 'As soon as the itinerary has been agreed, we will circulate it to all of you. Remember, every detail matters.

'One last thing for everybody... uniforms. We've had you all measured so I hope you haven't put on weight in the last few weeks. Don't forget to collect your suits, skirts and so on from Maisie in the cloakroom downstairs. We want you all looking ultrasmart when inspection time comes.'

Chapter 27

A right royal do

The heir to the throne looked out longingly across his Highgrove estate. His eye was particularly drawn to the arcade of sweet peas leading to the vegetable garden. It was one of his favourite features at Highgrove, and he gave it his undivided attention whenever he could.

Sadly, today was not going to be one of his 'gardening' days. Rather it was to be devoted to 'hospitality', something which on the whole he disliked. They tended to be occasions when the estate was invaded by people he would not choose to entertain, and he was invariably glad when the last visitor had exited.

As his Royal Highness beckoned his private secretary, the grimace on his face made it perfectly obvious that he was far from happy.

'When on earth did I agree to entertain a bunch of footballers? I hope they don't think they can start kicking a ball about and making a mess.'

'I think that's unlikely sir,' said Sir William. 'I understand they're not actual players. They're administrators – people who organise the game worldwide. And some are getting on a bit, and fairly unfit, so I don't think they'll be attempting to play the game while they're here.'

Sir William paused 'At least I certainly hope not.'

'Remind me, this is the round-ball football not the oval one? And football is the game we started here and exported around the empire along with a load of louts?'

'Well sort of, your Royal Highness. The first-ever meeting to organise the game of football did indeed take place in a pub in London 1863, and the first international was between England and Scotland nine years later.'

'My,' said the Prince. 'When did you become a walking encyclopaedia of football?'

'I try to keep up with the briefing papers for your engagements sir.'

'Yes, fair enough, I get your point. Well it might be an old English tradition, but I have to say that I think my dear mother has done the right thing by avoiding football as much as possible all these years. I think I'm right that she hasn't been to a match since the 1966 World Cup final at Wembley.

'She said it was very boring and spent most of it seeing how many Derby winners she could remember in her head. She did enjoy watching the Germans lose, however. Apparently it was good fun pretending to commiserate with them afterwards at the post match reception.'

'I see,' said Sir William without a smile. 'Well there's a German and a Russian on the list today. Both countries are bidding to stage the World Cup apparently.'

'Good God,' said Prince Charles. 'I didn't know I was expected to help nation speak unto nation. What are the briefing notes like?'

'Oh they seem to be fine, sir. Plenty of useful information about our new all-seater stadia, and the atmosphere engendered in them. But I think you're probably better suited to discussing the broader benefits of Britain. Our wonderful traditions, and buildings, and rich history.'

'Ok then,' the Prince said with a yawn. 'It all sounds rather tiresome. Well, I'll stay here in the garden to digest these notes and have a quick look at the morning papers. Then I'll be in my room. When you need me to greet our guests give me five minutes notice and I'll come down.'

Just one hour later, Sir William's call alerted His Royal Highness that the first guests were imminent. Prince Charles took up position on the steps at the back of the house leading into the garden. It was a practised manoeuvre, allowing the guests to catch a glimpse of life inside the house before meeting the Prince personally at the back.

It was a beautiful spring morning. The six GFO visitors were accompanied by their wives, all of whom were anxious to size up the Prince. The party also included Sir Albert Lewis and Simon Carslake from the EFO, and the Sports Minister, Matthew Foulkes.

Sir William noted with a little distaste that neither EFO men was dressed as well as the overseas guests. Lewis's suit looked worn and cheap, while Simon Carslake's was too light a grey in colour and too tight.

Glasses of champagne in hand, the guests were invited to wander through the gardens. Along the route a string quartet entertained them, while a gardener was ready to answer their horticultural questions.

Once the tour was underway, Prince Charles began to relax. The group became more chatty, and one or two of the women were attractive, he decided. There was only lunch to be negotiated, and they would be gone by 2pm. Perhaps he would get a bit of time to himself after all.

Highgrove's Head of Hospitality had agreed with Clare at the EFO that a single banquet table in the Orangery would be most suitable.

He was pleased to find he was seated next to one of the most appealing looking of the women he had noticed in the group. She was clearly South American, and the Prince expected to find her broken English attractive as she settled into her chair. If her English wasn't good, he could at least enjoy listening to his own voice. However, the woman had obviously practised for this moment.

'Your highness Right Royal. I must introduce me for your pleasure.'

'Yes, how charming to meet you. Have you come far,' he tried the standby opener.

'No,' said the woman, to make clear that her introduction was not yet complete.

'My name is Valentina Sofia Isabella Luciana Gonzalez, and this is my husband Alejandro Diego Armando Maradona Nicolas Gonzalez, President of GFO in South America and senior Vice President of GFO Worldwide. My husband speaks English only a little so I will speak for him.'

She thought for a moment. 'Yes I have come far,' for further clarity.

'Ahhh,' said Prince Charles, struggling to take in all the information. Then it dawned on him that the woman on his left was speaking on behalf of her husband who was sitting opposite, and who was now beaming supportively at them both.

'Your very highness we are deeply honoured to be with you here in your beautiful home of Highgrove,' the woman continued, as if remembering a script. 'We understand that England would like our support to stage the World Cup in 2003.'

'We are very like to do that,' Señora Gonzales said without a pause, looking very seriously at Prince Charles. 'But we would like to be honoured by your country.'

Honoured, thought the Prince. What are they expecting, an earldom?

'We would like to be honoured by a future Royal grandchild being named after my husband or me,' Señora Gonzales explained.

'In the case of a girl, you have four beautiful names. My husband says these names are as beautiful as his dear wife. That is me, Prince,' she explained.

'While in the case of a boy, my husband offers the choice of Alejandro, or Nicolas, or of course the wonderful names of the greatest footballer there has ever been, Diego Maradona. His names were added to my husband's first names out of respect, you see.'

The Prince had no inkling who this Diego chap was, but convinced that the husband and wife were certifiably mad, he made a little gesture to Sir William who was standing by the door. Sir William recognised the sign immediately but pretended to miss it. There was no getting out of this quite so early for the Prince.

Charles suddenly realised Señora Gonzales had stopped talking as he'd been waving frantically in his private secretary's direction.

'So sorry, I thought a fly was about to land on you...' he said weakly.

Señora Gonzales looked as though she was desperately searching for meaning in the Prince's words. Her husband's smiling expression was unchanged. In the moment of silence between them, Charles saw his chance to turn to the woman on his other side. Unfortunately, she was talking animatedly to the Sports Minister, and before he could engage in their conversation, the Prince heard Señora Gonzales addressing him once more.

'We like your home very much, Prince,' she said. 'We also have a home... very bigger.'

Charles thought for a second that he might feign deafness, but the woman's voice was too loud for that to be credible. He gave Sir William another pleading look as he turned slowly back towards her.

'Yeeees,' he said carefully. 'The gardens are quite beautiful at this time of year...'

'One day you will come to live with me... and Alejandro...' she replied. 'We are more beautiful in Buenos Aires.'

The Prince of Wales stared at her in disbelief. He gulped from his glass of spring water. Then suddenly he rose from the table and headed for the house.

A few minutes later, Sir William was leaning his head towards Señora Gonzales. 'I'm so sorry, His Royal Highness has asked me to apologise. He has had to leave our lunch because he has a terribly bad migraine. He wanted me to say how very much he enjoyed meeting you and your husband, and wishes you a happy time throughout the rest of your visit to Great Britain.'

Chapter 28

Down and dirty

'There were 10 German bombers in the air ...There were 10 German bombers in the air'

Charlie Mason was singing quietly to himself and picking his nose when Billy Pitchers and Steve Monroe came into the Press Office. Looking up from his cuttings file, Charlie greeted his team members cheerily:

'Hi lads! How've you got on?'

'Fine,' said Billy as he took off his donkey jacket and draped it over a spare desk. 'Milbank's got everything we need. It's go go go for the Press conference on Thursday. All hail the England bid. What a brilliant performance by our good selves – totally nailed those GFO Board members...'

'Good... excellent,' said Charlie, absently, as his eye was caught by a piece from yesterday's back pages. *'There were no more German bombers in the air...* I bloody love that song.'

'You do realise it's a wartime kids' song, Charlie,' said Steve.

''bout my level really,' Charlie said.

'Oh, come on you wazzock, Steve' said Billy. 'It's a great song. Even the Germans seem to like it. I went to England against West Germany at Wembley last year – and both sets of fans sang it on the train. We had a right laugh.'

'Your old man might have been hofficer class, Steve,' Charlie added. 'But mine was a squaddie. Like him, I don't believe in going soft on the Germans. We beat them in two world wars and they still give us aggravation. They shouldn't be allowed to host the World Cup.'

'Yeah, let's ban them,' Billy chuckled.

Steve shook his head in wonder as he turned on his PC.

'I bloody would,' said Charlie. 'Honestly I would. They're nothing but trouble-makers. Always have been. Look at all that fuss in '66. The bloody ball went over the line, but oh no, the Germans want to pick a fight.'

'Well, we're gonna give them a hard time from now on,' said Billy. 'Charlie and I had a bit of a sesh in *The Flowers* last night, Steve. We've formed a little sabotage department. We're developing a 'bash the Germans' campaign. Probably do us more good than the inspection visit! We'll get Charlie the ammunition, and he'll find one of his old street of shame pals to fire the bullets.'

'Good analogy,' mumbled Steve.

'Good what?' Charlie said.

'Analogy,' Steve repeated. 'You know, wartime... ammunition... bullets... never mind.'

'I know you had a posh education, Steve,' Charlie said, looking over his glasses. 'But don't get all clever with me. I'm just a simple reporter, remember?'

'Yes,' said Billy with a grin. 'Real old school. Boozy lunches, fat expense accounts, a few pints, then invent some good stories.'

Billy and Steve laughed.

'Cheeky bugger,' said Charlie. 'You two could learn a lot from my generation. It was cut-throat in them days. No prisoners taken. If I didn't get a page lead every week at least, I'd get keelhauled by the Sports Editor. Not like your namby-pamby broadsheets.'

Steve spent a couple of seconds trying to disentangle Charlie's taunt.

'But seriously, Charlie,' said Steve. 'Is this anti-German propaganda thing for real? Hadn't you better check with Simon? Bit of a dangerous game, isn't it?'

'Bollocks,' Billy sneered. 'Don't you think the Germans will be doing the same damn thing? Anyway, much better if Simon and S'ralbert don't know what we're doing. They can deny it all.'

'Yeah, and we'll all get the fuckin' rap,' murmured Charlie. 'Anyway, we're only talking about using real stories, and spoon-feeding them to a few lazy hacks... let them pretend they've suddenly dug up a lump of gold instead of the usual crap. And don't keep calling our great Chairman S'ralbert, Billy. It's SIR ALBERT to you. You've got to be careful. The EFO takes its pomposity very seriously.'

'So anyway... we're doing it,' said Charlie. 'And our little bit of covert operations starts right now,' he continued as he shuffled through the side drawer of his desk. 'I've got a great story here I want to give to Dave Stanley. It's about the Germans building a new stadium in Berlin – on the site of Hitler's arena for the 1936 Olympics. Fucking fantastic! Lots of happy memories of swastikas and Nazi salutes!'

He threw a manila folder across Billy's desk.

'Here's some stuff about it. Photographs from the Olympics are dynamite of course. Dave's Picture Editor will love 'em. See if you can dig up some other stuff on the Germans' new stadium plans, Billy. I'm having a drink with Dave tomorrow night.'

He paused. 'But if fighting Germans makes you a bit queasy Steve, there's something else I need you to work on. It doesn't involve the Geneva Convention.

'Will in the campaign team – with the help of some of Stephen Green's diplomatic mates – has got some interesting stories about GFO Board members... including a few being investigated by journalists in their own countries.

'We need to go through the files carefully and decide which of them would enjoy a bit of attention from one or two of our brighter British journalists – your broadsheet Oxford pals probably, Steve. But we've obviously got to do our homework right first.

'Some of these GFO guys are up to their necks in dodgy dealing. Look at this one,'

Charlie pulled a memo out of a folder in his drawer and began reading: '*When grants are made to a local organisation from central*

GFO funds, in a number of cases it seems that the local Board member arranges for the grant to be paid via his personal bank account.' Charlie grinned at Steve. 'The rest of the report says that what comes out of the account is often smaller than what went in.'

'Brilliant,' said Steve, as he scribbled notes on his pad. 'Proper investigative reporting!'

'But be very careful, Steve. These GFO guys mustn't be able to point a finger at us. And Stephen Green is apparently shitting bricks in case his Foreign Office people get nailed. And let's keep Lewis out of this. He'd never believe any fraud allegations anyway. Probably apologise on the English nation's behalf to all the accused. OK lads, I think that's it.'

Billy and Steve both picked up their phones to call journalists who had left messages while they were out. But Charlie raised a hand.

'Oh, sorry there is one more thing. It seems there are a few unhelpful journos wanting to explore our bid budget in fine detail. So Steve, draft a defensive briefing for Simon and the Chairman before you go home. Do it as a Q and A to make it simple for Sir Albert... poor old boy gets a bit confused by numbers. And we don't need to be too bashful. If we spend ten to fifteen million, it will still be miniscule compared with the price of a top player.

'All I hope is, we don't spend too much time justifying ourselves to the fucking British Press who you'd like to think would support having the World Cup in this country.'

'Anyway, time for a quick pint?' concluded Charlie. 'Then I want to get home to watch the match. Onwards and upwards.'

October 1996
The Whistleblower writes...The President is dead...
long live the President...

Key names are gathering in Tokyo this weekend for the 25th annual Global Football Organisation Congress.

Anyone who is anybody in football politics – and some besides –will be found loitering in the corridors of power at Shigeru Yoshida Congress Centre in the Japanese capital's smartest district.

And there is much to discuss. Top of the agenda is the Presidential election, with the incumbent Christian Larsen seeking a consecutive third term in office. First elected in 1989, Larsen cuts a more controversial figure these days and is by no means certain to win, although he remains the favourite.

One tricky issue for Larsen is his age. By the end of a third term in office Larsen will be seventy-eight. Sport of course is used to septuagenarians at the helm, and anyone who questions him on his age gets brushed aside pretty damn quick. Certainly Larsen, a keen fitness fanatic, looks in good shape, and claims to have been 'overwhelmed' by those GFO members urging him to stand again.

Larsen has worked hard to woo support around the globe, but some of the bigger footballing nations complain he spends too much time with the smaller countries. Cynics point out that this is time well spent, because in the Presidential election every country, small or large has one vote. Keeping Barbados or Brunei happy is a lot easier than dealing with the complex egos of the Europeans or top South Americans.

So President Larsen is garnering votes by the bucket load from his friends in the smaller countries, many of whom have received so-called 'development' grants from the GFO – invariably presented in person by President Larsen.

Of more concern to Larsen's henchmen will be mutterings about GFO finances. There are growing rumours of some sizeable amounts of money unaccounted for. The President might just manage to sweep those stories under the carpet in this election, but signs are that a third term will be a lot more problematic for one of the most powerful men in sport than anything he has experienced to date.

Whistleblower is on the case.

Chapter 29

An honourable man

October 1996

Albert climbed stiffly into the back of the big Nissan and handed the driver a piece of fax paper with his hotel details. The driver nodded his head briefly in acknowledgement. Lewis knew he wasn't being rude. Taxi drivers in Japan much preferred to see an address on paper than hear a foreigner attempt to speak their language.

The driver grunted as he handed back the fax paper with a white gloved hand: 'Football!'

Albert smiled. 'Yes. GFO – big world meeting. You like football?'

The driver chuckled, and so did Albert. He knew the driver hadn't understood a word he said. It was a moment of welcome amusement for the EFO Chairman during the hour-long car ride between Narita Airport and downtown Tokyo.

He always felt tense when being driven in foreign taxis. Just as he felt uncomfortable when flying, unless he heard the pilot's voice belonged to a British, American or Australian man. (Monica had got used to flying in recent years and teased him now about his 'little Englander' mentality, but he couldn't help it.)

But today, *en route* to his hotel and then to the 25th annual GFO Congress, Albert had cause for anxiety beyond his travel phobia. For a start, he had been unable to dismiss from his mind the extraordinary story he had heard in Yora about senior GFO man Joe Kumpa and his alleged corruption. How had Kumpa's business associate described Kumpa... Mr 10%?

Although he had seen Kumpa in London only two months before, he had not had the nerve to voice his concerns at the time.

But even if he had had the nerve to tackle Kumpa in London with the businessman's story, he also lacked the conviction. Lewis generally thought the best of people and had told himself that powerful men like Kumpa always had enemies. It was easy to make up stories about Joe. He was larger than life, and a bit scary too, Lewis thought – remembering the uncomfortable meeting with Kumpa in his Yora office. But that didn't mean he was a law breaker.

Albert was loyal to his football colleagues, and he had served on the GFO Board with Kumpa for nearly two years. Surely in that time he would have heard other bad things about Joe. No, Albert reflected, why should he let this 'business associate' in Yora turn him into a cynic. He wished he could believe his own instinct.

But there was another reason for Albert's anxiety. He had told nobody else, but he remembered perfectly well that at his first ever GFO meeting in Paris last year – as a new Board member, desperate to impress and please, and with his thought processes a little loosened by alcohol – he had promised... PROMISED... the Russian and German Board members that England would not bid for the 2003 World Cup.

What had he been thinking by doing that? Committing his own organisation to stay out of the contest for the biggest prize in world football? And just as mortifying for Albert, what had he been thinking when he sat through the EFO meetings that decided England *would* bid, without mentioning the promise he had made!?

Not a day had passed since the EFO's decision when Albert had not expected a call from Schneider or Baskin, the Board members to whom he had made his commitment. At every EFO campaign meeting, at every business-as-usual internal PR meeting, he expected a Press cutting to be waved in his face backed by astonished voices around the table... 'What the hell... Albert, it says here... Albert, we have to deny this...'

Albert was an honourable man, and he was deeply upset that he had behaved dishonourably both to GFO colleagues and to his own EFO. But he was also a proud man, delighted by his late career rise, chosen to join the GFO Board, and now Chairman of the EFO. In his darkest moments, Albert confessed to himself that the most worrying aspect of that 1995 Paris commitment was that news of it would jeopardise all his achievements and his legacy, and shame him in the eyes of his family, and particularly his greatest supporter, Monica.

When his car reached the Hotel Niwa, and the driver had delivered his bags to the reception desk, Albert Lewis was delighted to be fast-tracked through registration and quickly shown to his room. He would have to meet GFO members soon, and the chances were high that he would bump into Schneider and Baskin during the next few days. But for now, he was glad to rest in his room alone, and think about what he would say if the subject was ever raised.

Little did Albert realise that his commitment was seemingly the last thing on the minds of either Helmut Schneider or Alexei Baskin in Tokyo that day. Helmut was in the bar, talking animatedly to GFO members from the Americas. His wife Giselle was in the hotel pool, with Alexei.

Chapter 30

Crossed purposes

Albert spent a difficult evening in the hotel dining room. He didn't enjoy Japanese food. There seemed to be too many flavours that offended his taste buds. He found the Hotel Niwa's traditional Kaiseki dining style a particular challenge.

In the dining room, he met two men from smaller European nations who he knew quite well. They seemed more enthusiastic about local food, and therefore (it seemed to Albert) were able to help him disguise his pickiness. At the end of the meal, he made a point of ordering drinks at the table three times, so that his colleagues were persuaded to avoid the bar and the German and Russian members he didn't wish to meet.

Albert hadn't noticed the effects of the three double whiskies he had drunk in quick succession until the other men said they planned to turn in for the night. It was nearly midnight, and they wanted to read Congress papers in time for the next day. After all, this was an important Congress, at which the next President was to be elected. As he got up from the table, Albert stumbled slightly, and three glasses crashed noisily to the floor.

He was quickly aware that the restaurant was silent for a moment. He mumbled an apology to the waiter, and a number of GFO men at other tables raised their glasses to him with sympathetic grins. They all knew the effects of too much alcohol at Congress.

As he made his way uncertainly out of the restaurant, Albert was suddenly conscious of a big, heavy arm around his shoulder, impeding his progress. He recognised the deep and powerful voice immediately.

Joe Kumpa had been crossing the lobby in conversation with a Japanese colleague when the sudden silence in the restaurant caught his attention. Without a word to the other man, he had turned nimbly on his heels to join Albert.

Albert's head cleared quickly, but this sudden physical contact with Kumpa had sent his mind spinning. At first, he thought that Kumpa was trying to help him, holding him upright.

'I'm alright Joe,' he slurred. 'I just had a l'il accident. I'm going to my... my... room.'

He felt Kumpa's grip tighten as he tried to walk away.

'Of course, my old friend,' Kumpa said as he steered Albert towards the bar. 'Joe just wants a little word.'

'Joe, I need to go a bed,' Albert said. '... don't want drink now. Just bed.'

'Of course, and I just want a little word,' said Kumpa, setting him at a small table in the corner of the bar by the window. Joe waved away a waiter.

'So...my old friend,' Kumpa said slowly as he sat down beside Albert on a small bench seat. Albert found Joe's aftershave almost gaggingly strong. 'I think we made a very happy agreement when we met in Yora. do you remember?'

'I'm not sure I can remember an agreement, Joe,' said Albert as carefully as he could. And then he recalled the discussion about Africa's need for new football pitches and equipment, and to pay for coaches. With great relief, Albert grinned back at Joe.

'Joe, we've got a million pounds sterling to help African football. We've just had it agreed with the Government. It's over three years I'm afraid, but I think we can do a lot with that kind of funding, don't you? Think how many pitches we can turf. Think how many footballs that will buy...'

Joe brought his face up close to Albert's, and spoke in a whispering growl that was clear enough for Albert to hear:

'Why you tell me this now. Why you not just send a cheque to me. Maggie can tell you which bank account. It's so simple, even for you English. Where's my money Albert?'

Albert didn't know whether to be unnerved by Kumpa's tone, or whether Kumpa was simply naïve about how British development budgets were channelled. It was understandable perhaps that Kumpa assumed all the funding would come direct to his Alliance of African Football Organisations.

Perhaps it was Albert's fault for not making things clear to Joe when the EFO Council had supported the development fund, he wondered. But he needed the International Development Department's approval, and with the usual pace of Whitehall, that had only just happened.

'I should explain, Joe,' Albert said, with sincerity and a note of apology in his voice as he began to sober up. 'We can't just release the money direct to your African organisation. It's not the way we do things. We have governance rules, you know. We've got to make sure every penny is accounted for. We will need you to be involved of course, identifying which countries have greatest needs, and recommending suppliers and that kind of thing...'

Albert broke off. Joe's face had contorted into fury. Beads of sweat trickled down his big cheeks.

'And THAT's not the way I do things,' he said slowly. 'I recommend you go back to London and make that payment very soon. If you don't...' he paused and brought his face to within an inch of Albert's. 'If you don't pay that money to me by next Monday, you can kiss that old World Cup goodbye.'

Joe Kumpa got up and walked to the bar, slapping the back of a GFO man that Albert didn't recognise and roaring with laughter, as if nothing had happened.

Albert went to bed but was not conscious of any form of sleep throughout the night. All he could think about was Kumpa's demand and threat to the English bid. Was it possible? Was it possible that Kumpa was just as corrupt as his business partner had suggested after all? Did Kumpa have so much power that if he didn't get his way, he could end the hopes and dreams of the great English football nation?

As dawn broke over the city, Albert's incredulity began to turn to anger. He had devoted his life to the greatest game ever known. He was now committed to the global football family. He believed in the potential for promoting peace and love between nations through football. If there was one bad apple in the GFO, it had to be removed.

This was a major burden on his shoulders. He was convinced that nobody else in the GFO was aware of Kumpa's financial dealings, and he had to overcome his natural reticence and confront the problem head-on.

As he dressed, he felt the effects of alcohol, stress and sleeplessness in the form of a headache. But he was not going to be side-lined today.

He sat in the lobby from 8:00am, rejecting a waiter's proffered tray of green tea. He had seen President Larsen arrive at breakfast at 8:15, and he waited nervously for him to appear by the lift doors. As ever, the President used breakfast as an opportunity to meet GFO members in an informal environment. And today, the day before the Presidential election vote, this was a crucial glad-handing occasion.

It was easy for the President. Nobody wanted to talk for long and let breakfast go cold. If anyone did want to talk, Larsen would quickly spy another man at another table. In thirty minutes, he could greet twenty or more people.

At a minute before 9:00 Larsen came to the lift doors. He was alone. 'Albert!' the President smiled as he saw the Englishman and pressed the up button. 'How is your bid? Going well, I hope?'

'Mr Larsen...'

'Christian, please.'

'Christian...I've got something very serious to say to you. Corruption is at the heart of this whole organisation. Do you realise? I'm sorry but I can't say it any other way.' Despite his determination to address the issue, Albert couldn't help being a little in awe of the President. He had rehearsed his words carefully, but now he said them, they seemed to lack the kind of drama to make Larsen stop in his tracks.

'My dear Albert,' said Larsen looking at him closely. 'This does sound serious. Now I have to be on stage in twenty minutes so now is not a good time. Why don't you speak to my secretary and we'll see if we can fit you in sometime later?'

With that, the lift door opened, and President Larsen stepped in. Albert could never remember moving so fast in his life. He was in the lift, just as the doors were closing.

'Albert, please, this is irregular.'

'I'm sorry... Christian,' said Albert as the lift began to move. Larsen's face pulsed with fury as the two men travelled in silence until the lift arrived on the 14th floor, the only access point for the President's Suite. Quite how Albert found the button to prevent the door opening he never knew. But he stood with his thumb firmly pressed against it for five minutes as he recounted the story about Joe Kumpa.

The President stared at him throughout with a steely expression. The voices outside were gathering force, and Albert and Larsen could hear talk of fetching lift engineers.

'I have to ask you... Mr Larsen... what will you do about this?'

Albert was expecting the President to doubt his word. That was understandable. He expected him to be furious for holding him prisoner in the lift. What he wasn't expecting was Larsen's silky response.

'Albert, why are you wasting my time with this tittle tattle? Perhaps I would be a little more sympathetic to your story about Joe Kumpa if I hadn't heard that your English Football Organisation is planning to buy four votes to support your World Cup bid.'

Albert was in a trance of confusion.

'Oh, come on Albert, you must have helped him find the eight million dollars?' Larsen looked at him coldly and spoke slowly. 'Why is Joe Kumpa any worse than your Simon Carslake?'

'And another thing... I understand that our Audit Committee is worried about some of the expenses that the EFO, and you and your lovely wife Monica I'm sad to say, have incurred in supporting your bid. It would be a terribly shameful thing for Monica if you were to be suspended from the GFO while your financial affairs are investigated...'

The lift doors opened. President Larsen was taken by the arm, and two security men pulled Albert out behind him. 'No, no, no,' said Larsen. 'Please don't be rough. It's not the GFO way we do things is it, Albert. Sir Albert is a little upset at the moment, and I think he probably needs to rest.'

Chapter 31

All the President's men

Larsen was sitting quietly in the salon of his Hotel Niwa suite. It had been a long day, marked by an unexpected encounter with the Chairman of England's Football Organisation.

But Larsen didn't allow difficult incidents to unnerve him. Albert Lewis had angered more than upset him. He felt more affronted by being kept prisoner in the hotel lift than alarmed by anything Albert had said.

The accusations about Joe Kumpa revealed nothing more than that the Englishman was a naïve and ignorant player in the global football game. Larsen had had little difficulty in rebuffing him with a counter challenge of EFO involvement in a massive bribery project. He had taken pleasure in implicating Lewis in Simon Carslake's vote-buying project. He knew full well that a clear sign of the Englishman's weakness was his inability to control his own Chief Executive or understand Simon Carslake's more realistic approach to winning the World Cup bid next year.

Larsen did regret, slightly, making fictitious threats about Albert and Albert's wife's expenses. He knew enough about the couple to realise that personal excess was highly unlikely for Sir Albert and Lady Lewis.

Besides, Christian Larsen had old fashioned manners. He loved and respected women – an attitude that had repaid him many times when wives of doubting GFO members convinced their men that the charming President was simply incapable of the kind of behaviour he was sometimes accused of. Larsen hoped that mentioning Monica as he taunted Albert hadn't destroyed a card which might one day prove to be a winner for him.

So it was with some satisfaction that he found that the lift incident after breakfast had had no effect on his 'state of the game' Presidential speech to Congress in the afternoon. Not a universal standing ovation from the floor this time, maybe, but a very warm reception, nonetheless.

That was a clear enough signal that tomorrow would become his Presidential re-election day. He knew the maths. There were 204 potential votes to be cast, one for each country affiliated to the GFO. To win outright on the first ballot he needed 136 votes, representing two thirds of the membership. But if he failed to win the first ballot, he was absolutely certain he would win the second by a simple majority.

As he ruminated over the next day's vote however, he began to frown. For this, his third Presidential election, Larsen wanted more than a simple majority of the votes. He wanted to win well. He wanted desperately to win on the first ballot, to demonstrate his unmatchable supremacy – today in 1996, and for the next (and last) four years of his Presidency.

He frowned because he wasn't feeling confident about winning on the first ballot. There was no obvious reason for his concern. His only Presidential rival was Wilf Smith, known to be a decent man but hardly a candidate with a dynamic reputation. As a late entrant, following the withdrawal of the much more menacing Lelei Fiso, Smith had had little time to generate a convincing campaign. And as a New Zealander, his natural sphere of influence was narrow.

But still, President Larsen was troubled by Smith. He never underestimated his opponents, and it was the very fact that Smith was such an unlikely and unfancied candidate that put him on his guard. Larsen had never doubted that he would have beaten Fiso, no matter how well his campaign was financed or how strong his support base. Ultimately, Fiso was a crook, and the world's Press knew it. GFO members outside those supporters with a vested interest would have recognised that Fiso's record would make his Presidency unsustainable, and their own futures uncertain with him at the helm.

Larsen's opponents in his two previous Presidential elections had certainly been tough, with impressive levels of support and no criminal records between them. But those candidates in 1988 and 1992 had proved no match for Larsen, the campaign king, with his unique understanding of his global electorate's needs and demands. So why worry about Smith?

When Larsen's team had first revealed that Wilf Smith was standing as President, their mood was understandably triumphant. They saw nothing in this genial New Zealand farmer to worry them. Larsen shared their view to begin with, but the more he thought about the election, the more he was troubled by uncharacteristic doubts.

After two terms in office, and despite relentless efforts to maintain his popularity, it was inevitable that some disquiet over his leadership would emerge amongst the football nations of the world. He was now a man in his seventies: fit and alert, with a keen awareness of the issues of the day, but still a generation apart from many of the members who had joined the GFO in recent years.

And there was something else, which his own Communications Director had dismissed but which still troubled Larsen: he sensed there was a new negative view of his Presidency in the air. The change wasn't obvious. GFO members themselves seemed loyal enough in public, and in person. But he sensed that rumours were growing, that a critical Press commentary was beginning to accompany every public announcement and event.

The most irritating critic was an anonymous British diarist called *The Whistleblower*. But there were others too, mainly in Europe, but also amongst the big Australian newspapers who were following the New Zealander's electoral progress with great interest.

There was usually nothing of substance in any of the pieces, but Christian Larsen knew that *The Whistleblower* in particular was sometimes uncomfortably close to the truth. Even mainstream football journalists – often long-term friends of his – were starting to ask sharper questions at Press conferences than at any other time in his Presidency.

The slanderous attacks Albert Lewis had made that day meant nothing on their own, Larsen knew. But supposing Albert was talking to colleagues? Supposing men who had been unquestioning Larsen supporters were now beginning to feel undermined by the rumours and fearful of their own futures? Supposing members' political masters at home were raising their own concerns about association with the Larsen regime?

Was this the kind of bow wave that often presaged a sea storm? Enough perhaps to prompt a change of regime with a new man, Farmer Smith, promising a breath of fresh country air and a stable GFO for the years ahead...?

President Larsen cracked his knuckles. When he heard a knock on the door, he realised he had been lost in thought for many minutes, staring unblinkingly at the plush green carpet under his feet. He quickly recovered as he let in the Laundryman.

'So, what's the latest?'

'Evening sir.'

The Laundryman sat in the armchair he'd been directed to and opened his briefcase.

'Well... just like last time, boss, my spies say you've got a significant group of Europeans against you.' The Laundryman spoke quickly as Larsen poured him a scotch. 'As we know, that's cos they don't like the attention you give minor countries. They want you eating out of their hands instead.'

'Yes, I know all that. It's always the same,' said Larsen irritably. 'What about the rest?'

'Smith obviously has solid support in Australasia, but it seems you're doing reasonably well among the Asians, and you've got lots of support in the Americas.'

'Lots? Lots? What does that fucking mean?' said the President, his eyes now blazing. 'How many times have I told you "lots" is not a number? How many times? And "reasonably well"?' he sneered. 'That's meaningless crap too. I don't pay you to give me shit like this.'

He slammed the bottle of whiskey on the table.

'Dear God,' the Laundryman thought, 'he's in a foul mood tonight'. This was the monstrous side of Larsen.

The Laundryman looked at him coolly. He wasn't used to being talked to like this, by the President or anyone else, but he resisted responding. One day maybe Larsen wouldn't be his boss – but right now he was, and it was a lucrative arrangement for them both. He passed a sheaf of graph paper to the President. There were figures in one column, names in another, countries in the third, and neat handwritten notes alongside each row.

The two men sat in silence as Larsen looked at the papers. The Laundryman noticed the President's breathing had slowed as he took in the figures, but there was no sign of reconciliation.

When Joe Kumpa entered the room ten minutes later, he sensed tension straight away.

'How's it going?' Joe said

Larsen looked at him, without expression.

'We've just had these figures from the team. I don't like it, Joe. Too close.'

'Close? Shit.'

'No, we'll win. Of course, we'll win. But I want to win good. This is my last term, Joe. I don't want to be a lame duck. I want it to be the best time ever. I don't want to fuck around through a second ballot and have the world's Press ask why I'm not as popular these days.'

Joe nodded, and then his face burst into a wide smile.

'Well maybe old Joe Kumpa's got just the right news for you, Christian. The Germans want to talk to you tonight. I think they have a proposition which might just sort things out. I think they're gonna offer to deliver votes for you tomorrow in exchange for support for their World Cup bid.'

Kumpa had expected his statement to cheer the President, but quickly realised his miscalculation.

The Laundryman started to say something, but Larsen's cold stare silenced him. The old man got to his feet, waving the papers in front of his face.

'What the fuck is going on here?' shouted Larsen. 'I thought Schneider and Baskin had done a deal? Why wasn't I told the Germans are now going alone?'

The Laundryman held Larsen's stare. 'News to me,' he said quietly.

'News to you?' hissed Larsen. 'I don't pay you to tell me what you don't fucking know. Listen, both of you. I'm out to dry here. We've always believed Russia are favourites. Shit they've paid their dues, haven't they?'

He pointed directly at the Laundryman. 'You should remember. You went to collect it. Nearly lost the lot. Remember?'

Again, the Laundryman started to speak but thought better of it.

'And now fucking Schneider wants to hold me to ransom, expects the President's support can just be swung his way...'

Larsen sat down and shook his head in disgust. He swallowed the remains of his drink.

'Look, Christian,' said Kumpa, 'you know Helmut. He might be fucking about. He might be joking about the World Cup. Don't forget, Christian, he's offering to help you win your election in the first ballot. Why don't we hear what he's got to say? If you don't like the offer, we can tell him to piss off.'

Larsen looked at Kumpa and nodded.

'Ok,' he said, in a softer voice. 'Ok Joe, you're right, we'll see him. We'll hear what he's got to say. But I don't trust those bastards. Never have.' He paused and continued quietly. 'Maybe you wouldn't if they'd done to your country what they did to Denmark...'

Larsen and the Laundryman sat together in silence for the fifteen minutes before Joe returned to announce 'our good friend' Helmut Schneider at the door.

'Come in, come in, Helmut,' beamed Larsen as he hugged the German as warmly as was required for an old colleague. He turned to the Laundryman. 'Will you do the honours? Thank you so much. Helmut – scotch? Water? Excellent.'

Larsen waited for the Laundryman to fill four tumblers and ushered all three men to pull their armchairs close to the coffee table.

'Well, Helmut, Joe says you would like a word, but he didn't really know what it was about.'

Schneider's eyes showed his amusement. He was quite accustomed to the Larsen way. It didn't faze him. He took a sip from the glass.

'Well,' said Schneider , 'it's getting late, gentlemen, so I will get to the point. I would like you to take a look at this, Christian.'

Schneider got out of his chair and handed the President two folded sheets of A4 paper. Larsen unfolded them and began reading a list of names.

A cool breeze crossed the room from the open window.

'Let me explain...' Schneider began, but Larsen interrupted.

'There's no need,' he said brusquely. 'I can see what this is. It's a list of countries and members here at the Congress under German influence. You will be dictating how they vote tomorrow.'

'I would hardly say dictating...' Schneider began.

'Well, what would you say?'

'Well... encouraging... perhaps. We wouldn't want people to think the GFO is an anti-democratic organisation now surely.' As Schneider smiled, Larsen's face grew darker.

'Anyway,' Schneider continued quickly, 'yes, these are all nations where Germany enjoys a particular relationship. Apart from the obvious places that have colonial or other historic links with Germany, there are countries on this list where we have strong business interests, or where we've been investing in football development over many years. There are thirty-eight countries altogether, Christian, nearly a fifth of tomorrow's electorate.'

The President was in no mood to play games or extend this discussion more than was necessary.

'No doubt you're about to tell me your thirty-eight votes will make all the difference for me tomorrow.'

'Christian, Christian...' Schneider replied. 'We've known each other a long time, and you know I'm a loyal and devoted supporter. We both know you're going to win tomorrow. But we also know how crucial it is that you win on the first ballot. That you make a loud and clear statement of your authority. Yes, these votes will be the difference for you President Larsen. They will deliver victory on the first ballot.' Schneider sat back in his chair and grinned as he raised his glass to the other men in salutation.

Larsen allowed himself a faint smile, but his voice was cold.

'Well, Helmut, this is most generous. I can hardly refuse your offer. Now gentlemen, it's been a long day...'

Schneider chuckled.

'Aaaaah,' he said, 'that's a very great pleasure. But Christian, there's a small favour I would like in return.'

He paused and steadied himself for battle.

'Christian, I want your endorsement for our German World Cup bid.' He watched the stony faces around the table.

He wasn't surprised that the response was silence. He allowed his statement to sink in.

Larsen spoke at last, his faint smile still lingering on his lips.

'Well...' he said, without emotion. He peered at Schneider. He was gathering his thoughts. He wanted to unnerve this self-assured man.

'Well, Helmut,' he said at last, 'maybe I'm confused, my friend, but I seem to remember you and Alexei Baskin visiting me in Brussels last year. Am I mistaken? Was there not some kind of agreement between your two organisations to support a Russian bid?

'I remember being rather impressed. You were full of talk about being 'thoughtful' towards other nations as I recall.'

Schneider refused to be intimidated by the older man's mockery. He laughed out loud.

'Well, Christian, did you really believe me? Give way to the Russians? I'm a German for God's sake!'

Nobody joined him in the joke. He stopped laughing.

'OK, yes, it was a very convenient arrangement – for us all. Our Russian friends have helped me with a great deal of... support in the last year. And... you have been helped by them as well, Christian... as we always promised you would be.'

'And Alexei is aware of this change to your agreement?" said Larsen.

'No, he is not,' Schneider said firmly, 'and I intend it will stay that way.'

His eyes engaged with each man in turn.

'But if you're worried that my news will mean the end of Russia's financial support to you or to me, Christian... well, you needn't. Nobody else knows my intentions apart from those in this room. Russia's bid will remain on the table. My relationship with Alexei is unchanged.'

He took a cigar from his inside jacket pocket.

'And I'm certainly not expecting anything that would embarrass you in front of our Russian friends, Christian.'

He lit the cigar.

'All I would like is that you make sure that your subtle influence with our Board member colleagues will help me to win. There are several men who always take their lead from you, Christian, and you're very good at helping them to make the best decisions.'

He narrowed his eyes.

'Of course, there's one slight obstacle in my way.' He exhaled.

'Some Board members are a little confused about whether Germany should be allowed to host the 2003 World Cup because we hosted it in Europe the last time. Christian, it would be extremely good to hear you explain in private – and in public – that there's no GFO rule that forbids this from happening. As I say, just a little favour to ask in return for my thirty-eight votes.'

Larsen thought for a moment about what Schneider had said.

'When Alexei does eventually find out you've been deceiving him all along, how do you think he will take it? I imagine he will be a little disappointed,' he said.

'That's probably an understatement,' smiled Schneider.

'You're a hard man Schneider. You really are.'

'That's a bit rich coming from you. Alexei will get over it.'

The two men eyed each other like fighting dogs for a moment, but Schneider found it easy to move from their exchange of words back to the deal under discussion.

'So... the only question now is: do you want Germany's support in tomorrow's Presidential vote, Christian? and if so, we will instruct our friends on the list accordingly.'

He paused.

'Oh... and of course there is the other matter of a million dollars, which we'll need tonight.'

'A million dollars?' Larsen spat out the words.

'You know as well as I do that many of our colleagues need a little financial incentive to help them fill out their ballot papers correctly,' said Schneider, 'and it seems only fair that you should bear this cost.'

He smiled engagingly.

'We'll happily distribute the incentive for you. I'm sure you would prefer it that way. Any cash left over can serve as our facility fee. We are, after all, doing you a pretty big service.'

'I need to talk privately with my colleagues,' said Larsen curtly. 'We'll come by your room later. ''

Schneider got to his feet, but added: 'One final thing, Christian. I know that you're a very honourable man, so I'm not asking for any kind of guarantee for your future support of Germany's bid. But if we find it doesn't happen, and Germany fails to win, then my career will be over... and you can be sure I won't go quietly. This conversation will no longer be private.'

Larsen's face displayed no emotion.

'Frankly my friend, you're getting on my nerves,' he told Schneider. 'Goodnight.'

The door closed behind Schneider, and Larsen, Kumpa and the Laundryman sat in silence.

'Bastard. Total bastard,' said Larsen eventually. 'The fucking Germans think they can order me around.'

He looked angrily at his colleagues, desperate for explanation. He got up from his armchair and paced the room to stretch his long limbs. Then he turned suddenly towards them and began to laugh.

'You know it's completely fucking predictable. I knew it! Right from the moment Schneider and Baskin came to see me, I just knew it was unbelievable that Schneider would let the Russians have access to his network of supporters across the organisation. Far too risky to let them fall into the pay of another big European nation. He wouldn't have done it with France or Italy or Spain. Why the hell would he do it for Russia?'

Larsen sat down and indicated to the Laundryman that he wanted his glass refilled. He shook his head in disgust.

The room fell silent again as the three men were alone with their thoughts. Joe Kumpa spoke next.

'Yeah, but Christian, he's taking a hell of a risk getting on the wrong side of these Russian business guys. When they find out he's reneged on his deal with Baskin, he's gonna be a marked man, surely...'

'But that's where Schneider's been so clever,' Larsen replied. 'They never will find out. If Russia loses, it's that poor bastard Baskin who'll get the blame. The Russians will just think he's fucked up. And Schneider won't care what happens to Alexei.'

He looked at Kumpa and answered the question he knew would be next on Kumpa's lips.

'And don't worry about us, Joe. Schneider's right. There's no exposure. All I've got to do in private is sound a bit more positive about the Germans. It won't take much to shift Schneider's old friends back in his direction, and nobody will know that I've helped him.

'And as for answering questions in public about whether Germany can host the World Cup yet again... well why not? I'm the President. I'm only answering honestly a point about the rules. It's true enough. There's no regulation against it. I'll choose my words carefully when Schneider sets up some German reporter to ask me about it.'

The other two men nodded.

'What's the list like?' Larsen asked the Laundryman. He picked up his copy of Schneider's papers once again.

'Looks accurate,' the Laundryman said. 'No surprises. I think you need their support to win the first ballot.'

'Yes ok,' said Larsen quickly. He gave a big yawn.

'You'd better go and sort out the money with Schneider.'

The Laundryman left Larsen's suite. Larsen looked at Kumpa.

'I won't forget this, Joe. Nobody issues ultimatums to the President without paying a price, and Schneider will pay.'

Kumpa nodded sympathetically.

'Well, what do you want to do Christian? We'll win the Presidency even without the Germans' support. That's for sure.

We don't have to play Schneider's game. D'you want me to stop The Laundryman... tell Schneider there's no deal?'

'No – I need to win big. Can you imagine what the next four years will be like if the jackals are snapping at my heels.'

Larsen continued to peer at Kumpa, as he turned over thoughts in his mind. But Joe wasn't good at long silences. His face brightened.

'I tell you what, Christian. They say that Schneider will go for the Presidency next time round. Well, we can make that very difficult for him... and expensive too.'

Larsen's face broke into a smile. He rose from his chair to shake Kumpa's hand.

'Thank you, Joe, for being such a good friend.' He looked at his watch. 10:15.

Larsen caught his reflexion in a long mirror. He looked himself up and down for a moment, composing his features, willing his face into the charmingly beneficent pose that was so reassuring for his GFO members. His customary smile returned to his lips.

'And now, I think it's time for us to walk the floor and press some flesh, Joe. There are people down there in the lobby who want to meet their President. Stay close and make a note of my promises. And keep an eye on the opposition. I want to know what they're saying.'

The two men left the Presidential Suite and took the lift to the hotel lobby as though the excitement of the previous hour had never happened. As the President stepped out there was a buzz of excitement, and he was greeted immediately with warm handshakes.

The lobby was crammed with GFO members, and those keen to take a close look at the President or even have a personal word pushed themselves forward.

Larsen was an expert at focusing on the individual with sincere eye contact. He never looked over the shoulder of the person he was talking to as he engaged him in conversation. His knowledge of world football was encyclopaedic. He could name the top officials in most of the organisations around the world and would recall with pleasure the last time he had visited each country.

He could also remember details of international matches relevant to each member, goal-scorers, and moments of controversy.

Now on the eve of his election, Larsen was at the top of his game, shaking every hand presented to him, bending his head forward to ensure he didn't miss a word that was said to him confidentially. He would respond if possible, but never sounding as if he was following a politician's routine. He believed in physical contact, sometimes putting a hand on a shoulder to acknowledge a request for help and repeating it so that Joe could note the details. This always reassured that the request was taken seriously.

Larsen worked the lobby for nearly two hours. Then the Laundryman appeared at the lift, and he said good night to the well-wishing stragglers.

Alone in his room Larsen was feeling more confident about the next day. He started pouring himself a whiskey and soda but stopped when the phone rang.

'Hello, my friend how are things?'

Larsen listened intently saying 'good' 'good' several times. Later he added: 'thank you my friend, thank you. This will not be forgotten, I promise you.'

Then he went back to pouring his drink.

'Tomorrow,' he said to himself, 'promises to be a good day.... a really good day.'

He selected a CD from a shelf above the room's sophisticated music player. He undid the buttons of his shirt and relaxed in an armchair listening to the second movement of his beloved Beethoven's *Emperor* piano concerto.

Minutes later there was a soft knock on the door, and Giselle Schneider stepped inside the Presidential suite.

After glancing both ways down the hallway, Larsen shut the door carefully behind her. Giselle poured herself a gin and red martini and smiled sweetly.

'Tomorrow will be very tiring,' she said. 'You need to be at your best. Tonight, I'm going to give you the most relaxing massage you've ever had, and tomorrow night, when you are re-elected President, you will make passionate love to me. Do we have a deal, Christian?'

Larsen smiled his acquiescence. 'Assuming of course I can wait that long,' he said.

As he spoke, he ran his hands down the back of her silk dress, and softly kissed her neck and shoulders.

'You look stunning, darling,' he said. 'Absolutely stunning.'

Chapter 32

Putting on the style

Helmut Schneider didn't look like a man who had had no sleep. Having shaved and showered, he was immaculate in his charcoal suit from Hugo Boss, and he felt ready for the long day ahead.

He had agreed to have breakfast downstairs with the other members of the German delegation to Congress. Yes, that was a bit tedious, he thought, but it was important to keep the team sweet. His plans and his vision for Germany, and for Helmut Schneider himself, depended on their unstinting support. He had failed to spend sufficient time with his colleagues at Congress on one occasion, and it had taken great time and effort to recover his authority.

As he stood in front of the faux-Japanese antique wall-mirror, he straightened his Deutscher Fußball-Organisation tie, and gave his GFO cufflinks a final and unnecessary polish. Then he left his room and made his way to the lift.

Meanwhile, on the twelfth floor, President Larsen was also preparing for the day ahead. After Giselle had returned to her room next to her husband's at about 3am, Larsen had drifted in and out of sleep for two hours. It didn't worry him. The President knew from past experience that this was a day when adrenalin would carry him through. The tension of the election would keep him fully occupied until lunchtime, and the afternoon would be spent thanking supporters both formally from the platform and informally in the lobby.

There would of course be a Press conference following the result. The GFO Media Centre had already briefed him on the arrangements for his audience with some 150 journalists from around the world, and for a series of 'one-to-one' interviews with selected influencers afterwards. This was a world he was well used to, and he was widely recognised as a class-act communicator. He knew it and so did the Media. He had one or two difficulties with the written Press, but he was a master of the television broadcast where he could deploy directly his natural skills and charm.

Like Helmut Schneider, Larsen was also elegantly dressed for the day ahead. His pride in his appearance was as fundamental to his operating strategy as everything else. His GFO colleagues expected nothing less from the man in authority. As he ate his breakfast and drank the Turkish coffee delivered to his suite ten minutes earlier, he allowed himself a moment to think about his achievements.

His mother and father would have been very proud of him, no doubt. His father had taken young Christian to watch the village football team in the 1930s but would never have imagined his son's success in the game. Both parents had died when Larsen was still working as a clerk in the local mayor's office before the war. It was on days like this in Tokyo, he thought sadly, that he wished they had seen their son on the world stage.

Half an hour later, there was a knock on the President's door and two GFO officials came to collect him for the walk to the Congress Centre. Larsen never walked alone to formal GFO events. He didn't want to be lobbied by members or Press at those times. Glad-handing had its place in his schedule. Now he had his own priorities, and the GFO staffers were there to make sure he kept to them.

One of the officials was a woman in her forties. She had worked for the GFO for nearly twenty years, and the President knew her quite well. She often attended GFO committees and subcommittees to take minutes. It was a role to which the President attached great importance.

Minutes could be all-powerful, and sometimes after meetings the woman would speak to the President about how to word or interpret a decision the committee had made. He always checked draft minutes with particular care when tricky or controversial subjects were discussed. He knew from experience he could catch out opponents by ensuring that the record of a meeting coincided with his own interpretation.

'Good morning, Chloe,' he said.

The other official was a man, considerably younger, probably in his mid-twenties, and the President didn't really know him. No doubt he hadn't yet attended one of the President's staff drinks parties. These were held on the last Friday of the month and were an opportunity for staff from different levels to get to know each other informally. They gave the President a chance to make even the most junior GFO official feel personally connected to him.

There were obviously risks in this informality. Larsen remembered one occasion when a young secretary from finance had had more to drink than was good for her. Midway through the evening, she had staggered towards the President, put her arm around his waist and told him she loved him. Before he could call over a manager to help, the girl was violently sick over the President's shirt front.

Larsen did not recall ever seeing the secretary again.

'Step inside a moment,' Larsen said to the two officials. 'I'll be with you shortly.' He disappeared into his bedroom, and took one more look at himself in the mirror. Then he picked up the papers he needed for the Congress and returned to the waiting officials.

Addressing Chloe again he asked: 'How do I look?'

Chloe knew what to say. 'Perfect,' she smiled, and Larsen beamed as he had done during this routine many times before.

'Well, let's go,' he said.

The three walked in silence to the lift and down to the busy hotel lobby. Larsen could feel the eyes of many of the delegates on his back as he moved briskly towards the main Congress Hall.

Members of the GFO Board were gathering as a group by the door, as they always did.

'Just one minute,' Larsen said to the officials, 'I need a word with these two.'

Larsen had spotted Helmut Schneider and Alexei Baskin deep in conversation, and he strode across to speak with them. The two men turned to greet him, and both embraced him with bear hugs and enthusiastic pats on the back.

'Mr President,' Alexei spoke first. He didn't know Larsen as well as the German did, and his sycophantic manner betrayed his nerves. 'Are you looking forward to your re-election? The mood is very good. I'm sure it's going to be a very good day. We've just been discussing how positive the delegates seem to be about your candidacy.'

'That's very heartening to hear,' Larsen responded with a broad smile. 'I've complete trust in your judgement, gentlemen, both of you.'

He looked around for a moment and lowered his voice.

'By the way, I've also heard some very positive comments about your plans for the 2003 World Cup. If I'll be celebrating later today, I think next year it'll be your turn in Russia to celebrate. Do you agree, Helmut?'

He looked straight into Schneider's eyes.

'Are you also picking up a positive response to World Cup Russia?"

'Yes, I am,' said Schneider without a moment's pause. He held the President's gaze. 'Alexei here is a great worrier, you know.'

He squeezed the Russian's arm, affectionately. 'And I've just been reassuring him.'

Larsen gave Baskin a broad smile.

'Oh, it will all be fine, Alexei. I'm sure it will. But first things first. I have a little matter to deal with today. Let me get re-elected and then we can turn to other matters.'

'Good luck, Mr President,' Alexei said, his voice more confident now.

'Yes, good luck,' said Schneider. 'Here's to a two-thirds majority.'

Larsen turned swiftly around. Re-joining the two waiting officials, he strode purposefully towards the hall.

Chapter 33

Four more years

Congress was due to start at 10 o'clock. Larsen had decided to make his entry a quarter hour later when the hall would be full, and the delegates settled. As the incumbent Larsen awarded himself certain privileges. While his opponent slipped into his seat virtually unnoticed, the President waited at the back of the hall for his entry at exactly 10:15.

There was nothing low-key about his arrival on stage. A voice announced: *Ladies and gentlemen... GFO delegates and Media representatives from across the world... please welcome GFO President Christian Larsen.*

The announcement had hardly finished before a tumultuous fanfare of trumpets heralded the President's long walk to the front of the hall, waving and smiling as he went.

Soon after his first election eight years ago, one of the GFO's major corporate sponsors made their global advertising agency available to Larsen to help develop his personal communications skills. It wasn't necessary. The account director had to admit to his corporate client that the agency was stumped as to how they could offer any advice; even their top award-winning team couldn't improve on this man's natural gifts.

'Organised spontaneity' was how Larsen described his approach to presentation. This meant briefing key supporters to stand-up and applaud the moment the President entered the Congress Hall.

And that's exactly what happened at 10:15 as the President walked down the central aisle between the delegates. Those who didn't stand immediately quickly followed the others. By the time he had reached the platform, the hall was a cacophony of cheering. Larsen responded with a broad smile and a calming hand gesture, seemingly overwhelmed by this unexpected show of support.

Joe Kumpa and the Laundryman stood at the back of the hall. 'How moving,' Joe chuckled. 'He'll be wiping a tear from his eye anytime soon.'

The Congress audience slowly quietened to listen to the General Secretary making more routine announcements. There were other items on the agenda for later in the day, but most delegates in the hall were only interested in the main event: the Presidential election

The format for the election was the same as on previous occasions. Each candidate would be invited to make a short speech of no more than thirty minutes. Then an elected representative of each country affiliated to GFO would step forward to receive a ballot paper from a bank of GFO officials, and one-by-one they would mark the paper and place it in the ballot box on the platform.

Larsen had ensured that the Presidential seat had a particularly good view of the voters, so he could catch their eye as they cast their vote. The President couldn't see exactly who each person was voting for, but the person marking the ballot paper could not be sure.

The whole election process, including speeches, would take little more than two hours, finishing in good time for lunch.

Once the General Secretary had completed his housekeeping notices, the Chairman of the morning session introduced the key business of the day.

Wilf Smith was invited to speak first. Clearly nervous, the New Zealander stuck carefully to his script to avoid mistakes. It was a competent speech. He carefully set out interesting ideas for GFO reform, without being seen to attack Larsen and his Board colleagues. He emphasised his credibility as representative of a small footballing nation, and committed to ensuring that the balance of power would move away from the big European nations if the GFO was under his command.

Joe Kumpa was not impressed.

'Where in hell did they find this guy?' he said to the Laundryman. 'He isn't in Larsen's league. When Fiso was running at least we had a serious enemy to deal with. Pity he pulled out. It would have been entertaining.'

'Not sure you would have found it very entertaining if he'd won,' the Laundryman said under his breath. 'We would both have been top of Fiso's list for elimination.'

Kumpa laughed heartily and nodded his big head vigorously.

Larsen's performance was very different. He appealed to the hearts as well as the minds of the GFO delegates. He began by thanking the men who had persuaded him to run again, despite his anxiety that people would have had enough of him. He talked about the great honour they had bestowed upon him.

He contrasted his friends' generosity with their enemies outside, who did nothing to further the cause of the greatest game in the world but criticised the men of action in the hall. Without mentioning them by name, everyone knew he was talking about certain journalists. It was a popular theme at Congress.

Larsen reviewed his eight years as President, reminding delegates how the game had grown and how he personally had focused on increasing revenues, especially from sponsors. He stressed that he had always tried to make sure that improved finances had been used to help a lot of the smaller developing football nations.

'Eating out of his hands,' Joe commented.

As if to underline Joe's point, Larsen's final statement pulled once more at Congress's heart strings.

'We are the football family,' he said, shielding his eyes from the spotlights in order to peruse every corner of the hall. 'As with every family, we must stand together to rebuff those people who are jealous of our success and seek to damage us and spoil the great work we're doing. We must stand united against them. We must defend the people's game.

'Gentlemen, if you decide today to re-elect me as your President, that is exactly what we will do in the next four years. Defend the people's game.'

As Christian Larsen sat down, the delegates rose to their feet, generating a crescendo of applause, and chanting 'the people's game, the people's game'. They then repeated his name over and over again.

Larsen graciously acknowledged his reception and stood once again, nodding and mouthing 'thank you, thank you' in every direction – first in English, then in seven other languages before taking his seat once more.

Even the Laundryman allowed himself a smile of satisfaction and joined in the applause. Laughing back at him, Joe Kumpa shouted above the clamour: 'Four more years...'

Congress delegates then began the slow process of casting votes. Each country was called out in alphabetical order, and a representative from that nation stepped forward. Although everyone knew that Larsen would win, there was still a palpable air of excitement. Delegates had travelled from across the world to help choose the GFO President, and they didn't want to miss a thing.

When the final nation had voted, GFO officials removed the ballot box to an ante room for the papers to be counted. Each candidate was allowed to have two representatives present at the count, and they followed the officials.

Shortly before one o'clock, the General Secretary rose to his feet to announce the result. Wilf Smith had received forty-eight votes, but Christian Larsen had polled 152 votes. There were four abstentions, he added, but nobody could hear him above the noise in the hall.

The Whistleblower writes... Is all as it seems in the GFO?

So, there you have it. A landslide victory for the incumbent President Christian Larsen. But even on this happy day, Whistleblower has to admit his organisation still has an unpleasant aroma about it.

Yesterday, as his re-election was announced from the podium at the 25th Annual GFO Congress in Tokyo, there was no mistaking that the man who not long ago declared the end of his Presidency was enjoying every minute of his new term in office.

Always the showman, Larsen thanked the delegates effortlessly in eight different languages. And in case you're thinking these were well-rehearsed one liners, easy to learn even for a seventy-four-year-old, think again. No, this is a man at the height of his powers, demonstrating genuine linguistic skills, and charming an audience which honoured him like Augustus.

And this was indeed an impressive result for Larsen. His 152 votes swept him past the two thirds majority required for victory on the first ballot, leaving opponent Wilf Smith from New Zealand trailing way behind with 48 votes after four abstentions.

This decisive victory probably surprised even Larsen. It certainly shocked a lot of pundits who thought he would win but not by much.

Rumours are rife about how Larsen achieved this scale of victory. There is no doubt for instance that somewhere in the mix will be the question of who hosts the 2003 World Cup, which will be decided next year.

Larsen might well get seduced by Germany or Russia, the European 'big beasts' as they like to be known. If so, Russia looks more likely – not least because they have never hosted the tournament.

Not always popular across the world, the Germans can still boast a significant list of 'friends'. Perhaps Larsen benefited from this German generosity, but at what price?

More disturbing still are rumours that money was changing hands in the early hours of today's vote. It's often rumoured that certain delegates require an 'incentive' in order to vote the right way. But quite where this money came from, and how much was involved, is a mystery. As Whistleblower knows only too well, the GFO hierarchy is never keen to discuss such matters. Indeed, their reaction is always incredulity that accusations could possibly be made.

But in case the third estate gets a bit cocky about the ways of the football world, the Whistleblower was intrigued to overhear English and German journalists weeping in their beers at the prospect of their individual nations hosting the World Cup. The reason? They would have more fun with their expense accounts in foreign climes than they ever could at home, they openly lamented.

All right for them of course. They can go wherever the tournament is held. A bit of sympathy for local fans and a hint of patriotic support for their home nation's bid would not go amiss. Not all journos are like this I'm sure...

Chapter 34

Seeking solace

When he arrived at Heathrow Airport, Albert was beginning to recover a little from his ordeal in Tokyo. He had actually managed to sleep for much of the flight, inevitably perhaps after the three wide-awake nights he had endured since his distressing meeting with President Larsen.

There was a limit to how many hours he could devote to replaying the events in his mind, however painful and memorable they were, and his body had succumbed to the drone of the engines.

It was probably the inflight rest that made him feel stronger and better able to recover from his nightmare. Although the dreadful stories he had learned about Joe Kumpa and Simon Carslake were still real, and the threats to the honour of Albert and his wife over his expenses were still chilling, Albert's emotions were starting to change from sheer helpless disbelief to a conscious searching for some kind of plan to deal with the situation.

Perhaps it was that singlemindedness that made him change his routine for the day as he exited the Arrivals terminal doors. After overseas trips – even to far flung parts of the world – Albert usually called in at the EFO office if he got home during working hours. He always felt hugely privileged to be travelling to so many countries and experiencing the world's best hospitality. Even though he enjoyed it all rather less than others seemed to, he knew that his life must seem amazingly exotic to the secretaries and junior staff at the EFO, and he wanted to show them his serious commitment to their day-to-day tasks.

Today, however, he wouldn't go into the office. There were two reasons. First, with the rumours he had heard, he couldn't bear bumping into Simon Carslake at present. Second, when Albert was holding information that he didn't know how to handle, there was only one person who he could confide in: Monica, his wife of nearly forty years.

Tony waved to him from the line of cars outside the terminal, and Albert gathered his thoughts as he walked to the EFO Jaguar.

'Hello sir, good flight?'

'Yes, yes, very good Tony. Thanks.... Oh Tony,' he waited before getting into the back of the Jaguar, as Tony held the door. 'I'm not going to the office today. I'm feeling a little queasy. Too much sake.' He knew Tony wouldn't question that excuse. Tony enjoyed a drink when not on driving duties, and Albert's weak digestive system was widely known in the office.

'Very good, Sir Albert,' said Tony as he closed the door behind the Chairman and got into the driver's seat. 'So where to?'

'I'm going home. Can you take me to Paddington?'

'Would you like me to drive you to Cornwall sir?'

Albert thought for a moment how much he would have liked to accept the offer, but a ten-hour round trip in an EFO car was unacceptable, he decided, even though he knew many of his Council colleagues would have taken the offer without question.

'No, I'm fine on the train, thank you. But could you please ring Eleanor to say I'm not coming to the office, and after that could you get Lady Lewis on the phone.'

Monica knew better than to question Albert's decision when she spoke to him, but she guessed he had uncovered something uncomfortable at the GFO, and that her naïve husband was in a state of shock. She wasn't surprised he was coming home.

It was early evening when Albert got out of the train at Bodmin. He had always liked the station. It was a throwback to an earlier, more relaxed age of travel, he felt. Monica could park safely and legally close to the platform, and except during July and August, the London train was usually empty by that time, making it easy to keep his case on the seat beside him in the carriage rather than risk his back muscles by heaving it into the luggage rack above, and he could disembark without any stress.

Albert had had plenty of time to consider his story, and he went over and over the events at Tokyo with Monica from the moment he got into the car, throughout dinner, until Monica put the kettle on at 11 o'clock that evening.

It was a long story, and it was all new to her. He hadn't shared with her the rumour he'd heard about Joe Kumpa when in Yora last year – because he wasn't certain about its veracity. He did now though, utterly convinced that Kumpa's business partner had been telling the truth. Then he related the events of the last few days, sparing none of the accusations he had heard in Tokyo.

Monica said almost nothing, as usual when Albert was unloading his worries.

As they sipped their tea, they sat in silence. Albert was waiting for his wife's opinion, her sympathy, and most of all, he wanted her practical advice on what he should do with the secrets he held. He could wait no longer. His eyes pleaded with her as he said in a shaking voice: 'Well, what should we do Monica?'

Monica pulled her chair closer to Albert's and gently rested his head on her shoulder.

'Well dear, I have to tell you. None of it surprises me. I'm sorry if you think I'm wise after the event. But when we've laughed at these people in the past – you know 'Fatty Kumpa' and 'Slimy Simon' – I've always thought there's much more going on than you would ever think.

'And I'm quite sure I'm not the only one who's looked at old Larsen and his grand lifestyle and his entourage all around him the whole time and said to themselves: something's not right here. I'm sorry, my love, if you think I should have shared these worries of mine with you, but that's all they were at the time. And now it seems I was right. Just call it womanly instinct.'

She smiled warmly at Albert and squeezed his wrist.

'But, let me ask *you* the question. What are *you* going to do, Albert? Tell the world that you've found corruption in a big global organisation? And how are you going to do it? Call a Press conference? And can you prove it, Albert? Where's the evidence? Imagine what a fool you'll make of yourself without it, my love! Think what the GFO's lawyers would do to you.

'And just think about this, Albert. If Simon Carslake really is up to his armpits in dirty deals, what does it say about you? You're his Chairman. Can it be true that you didn't know what your own Chief Executive was up to? And if you didn't know, what kind of a leader are you?

'So, at the end of it all, once you've been beaten in court, where will you be? Out of the GFO that's for sure. And England's World Cup bid will be a sad joke for the rest of the world. Albert, it will be the end for you.'

Monica looked at him hard and long and kissed him on the cheek. She filled a hot water bottle from the kettle.

'Come on love, up to bed,' she said.

Chapter 35

Playing for time

January 1997

Making the phone call was something Simon Carslake had been putting off for days. His fundraising efforts had not been going well, despite all the determined efforts inspired by Joe Kumpa's visit to London in August. This was not a call to report progress to the mysterious man who was offering him four crucial votes for England's World Cup campaign. This was a call to play for more time.

He would have to lie. The very thought of talking to Gerald in any circumstances sent shivers down his spine. To try and play games with a man who managed illegal trades involving millions of dollars was simply terrifying.

Simon knew he had to steel himself. He had to sound convincing.

He was now dialling Gerald's number a third time. The first two times he had cancelled the call so he could once more rehearse what he would say. This time he swallowed hard and let it ring.

'Gerald, it's Simon Carslake here.' Simon's office was a steady cool temperature, but he felt perspiration on his temples as he waited for Gerald to respond. The response was abrupt.

'You have information?'

'Well, things have been busy,' Simon replied. Now the dialogue was starting, Simon began to feel more confident. He was used to dissembling, and he began to slip into a familiar pattern.

'I'm glad to hear it. So, you have the money.'

'I need a bit more time to tie up loose ends,' said Simon. He took a deep breath. 'But I want guarantees for the four votes.'

The phone was silent. Simon struggled to retain his composure.

'Look,' he said, surprising himself at his courage. 'This is a big risk for me and my people. I can't just hand over eight million dollars without certainty you can deliver.'

There was still silence.

'I don't even know who the hell you are.'

Gerald sighed at last.

'I told you. There are other players in this game. If you think you can get these four votes some other way, go ahead. I'll put the phone down now.'

Simon heard his heart thumping. Shit, he thought, am I losing this? He just had to stay in the 'game' as the man described it, or he would lose the biggest opportunity of his life.

There was another pause, and Simon felt a huge relief as Gerald spoke again.

'I can't hold the door open for you guys for long. And no, I won't tell you whose votes we're talking about. Not until money has changed hands.'

He paused again, and Simon sensed he had something more to say.

'But I can tell you this little deal has approval from on high. More than that Craslake. If you get the money and I don't deliver those votes... I'm a dead man.'

Simon clenched his fists. This man was vulnerable to failure too.

'OK, OK,' Simon replied. 'Give me a month to finalise things.'

'Two weeks maximum before I need the first million to show your intent. Don't bother arguing. I haven't the time. I'll ring you in two weeks.'

Gerald was gone. Simon put the phone down with a mixture of relief and foreboding. He had bought himself more time. But not much.

Chapter 36

The Blue Lagoon

February 1997

'Hey Danny, have you seen the punkah wallah?' Billy Pitchers said.

'The punkah what?' Danny Creighton didn't like to show his ignorance to these smart-arse Press Officers, but he didn't have a clue what Billy was on about.

'The punkah wallah, over here behind the screen. He's limbering up for our dinner. It's alright, I didn't have a fucking clue either mate! One of the ambassador's staff told me all about it. A punkah is a cloth fan for keeping people cool during dinner. It's suspended from the ceiling. Look! He's starting it up again!'

Billy and Danny watched wide-eyed like two little boys as the carpet like contraption began to whoosh backwards and forward.

'All the posh bastards who used to run the British empire had them,' Billy added. 'They found it too hot so they had a punkah like this one. Fucking impressive I reckon. Feel it keeping the room cool. The guy pulling it backwards and forward is the punkah wallah. Hey, you know what, Danny? Apparently, they're usually deaf people who become punkah wallahs. Guess why?'

'Don't be such a clever bastard Billy... Why?'

'Well,' said Billy with a satisfied grin. 'It's obvious mate. A lot of the conversation taking place over dinner was highly confidential. They didn't want the natives listening. But if the punkah wallah was deaf... no problem. The nobs could chat away and the locals were none the wiser.'

'I wonder if the guy pulling ever pretended to be deaf so as to infiltrate like,' Danny said.

'I hadn't thought of that,' Billy replied, looking thoughtful. 'But you're right mate. I bet he did.'

'Are we eating here in the Embassy, Billy?' asked Danny. 'I was hoping we might be going out on the town. Looks a bit dull here.'

'Yeah, I know, shame isn't it.' Billy said. 'It's because we've got the Minister here. The Ambassador is hosting a dinner in his honour, and we're invited. Can't really refuse I s'pose! But we might get a bit of time after dinner, and maybe we can take a look at the nightlife then.'

He paused, and grinned. 'Oh of course I'll have to come with you, Danny. Make sure you don't get into trouble.'

'What, keep me on the straight and narrow? That's fine with me as long as you've got the EFO credit cards.'

Later that evening, the guests assembled in the British Embassy gardens for drinks before dinner. Her Majesty's Ambassador to Thailand, Daniel Thompson, was a genial host who clearly loved his role. His wife, Jessica was also warm and spent a lot of time with the English visitors advising on where they might get a suit made the following day.

'Oh, you can get measured up in no time,' she assured them, 'and you can have a high-quality suit made by the end of the day. They will deliver it to you here. It's really not a problem.'

'Bet that's sweat shop labour,' Billy muttered to Clare, his campaign team colleague. 'Exploiting the locals.'

'Yes, probably,' Clare smiled. 'But I don't think now is the time to raise that issue, Bill.'

Billy chuckled. 'I can see the Daily Mail headline now – *"EFO gaffe insults the Thais"* – nah, you're right... best not.'

Two of the Embassy staff continued to pour champagne. It was a warm evening, and the conversation flowed with the alcohol.

'I'm covered in Deet, but I don't care,' Billy said suddenly to Clare as he downed his third glass. 'Don't fancy malaria much!'

'Yes, I could smell you as you arrived,' Clare said. 'But better Deet than body odour I always say, Billy.'

Just then the Ambassador's First Secretary, Hugo Morris, appeared in the doorway leading into the garden. He was accompanied by the Sports Minister Matthew Foulkes and his private secretary, Francesca. They had been sightseeing in Bangkok before calling on the Thai Prime Minister. This was a very pleasant public duty for Foulkes: he and the Thai Prime Minister had been contemporaries at Oxford. Hugo Morris introduced the Minister to the Ambassador.

'How very civilised, Ambassador,' Foulkes said, as he cast his eye around the garden, lit by Chinese lanterns. 'And what a gorgeous embassy building,' he purred. 'We do have some remarkable places dotted about the world, don't we?'

'Yes, we certainly do,' said the Ambassador, 'We completed this beautiful building in 1876 so we've been here for well over a century. But not for much longer, I fear. I think the Government will probably sell the site in the near future. Oh well, needs must.'

'Indeed?' Matthew Foulkes smiled. 'Can't justify it to the taxpayer these days of course. Good to see we're enjoying it while we can!'

The Ambassador took the opportunity to call his guests in for dinner. The Minister was guest of honour, but Daniel Thompson was quick to establish Danny Creighton's seniority within the visiting EFO party. He was 'delighted' to have the Minister present, but 'extended a warm welcome to the great England footballer, Mr Danny Creighton' as well.

'Blimey,' Billy said to Clare as they found their places at dinner. 'Simon will be sorry missing out on this.'

Clare was to sit next to the Minister, while Billy was further down the table, opposite Danny.

'I'm sure you're right, Billy. And Sara not here too. But we'll make adequate deputies won't we. Just enjoy it. But don't get pissed.' She lowered her voice. 'And keep your eye on Danny. Remember, Chrissie's not here, and you're his minder.'

As the first course was served, the punkah wallah got to work, and Billy winked at Danny. The Minister was especially grateful for the punkah breeze, and so were the guests sitting nearest to him.

'Very effective that chappie behind the screen,' the Minister grinned to the Ambassador who was beside him. 'I think the PM would like a bit of that don't you, when cabinet meetings get a bit overheated?'

The two men laughed.

He turned towards Clare on his other side.

'By the way, Clare, talking of Prime Ministers, I need to brief you about my meeting with Thailand's PM this afternoon. He's an old Oxford chum of mine, and I have to say I think our friendship has really helped you lot out. He seems very keen to support your bid.'

Clare winced at the Minister's claim. His arrogance was widely known in the civil service ranks she had left to join the EFO campaign team on secondment. She smiled her encouragement.

'Anyway, to cut a long story short, I told him we'd be delighted to play an international fixture against Thailand. He's very excited about it. He's going to announce it at some Media event here tomorrow.'

Clare's face froze. She didn't know quite how to respond. She cursed Simon for his absence. 'Preparing for the AGM,' he had said. What the hell was more important to the EFO bid than dealing with the Sports Minister's decision to make up his own campaign strategy.

Foulkes was waiting for her compliments.

'That sounds great,' she managed to blurt out. 'Has anyone spoken to the manager?'

'The manager?' Matthew Foulkes looked puzzled. 'The manager of what?'

'The manager of the England team, Dick Stone,' Clare said, desperately trying to hide her frustration with a man who seemed to her incredibly stupid.

The Minister clearly had no idea how much angst went into finalising England fixtures. Not only was there constant pressure from the league clubs not to have too many 'friendly' international matches outside European and World Cup qualifying games – matches that risked their players' fitness. There was also a steady trickle of 'public relations' requests from sponsors to be scheduled.

The campaign team was meticulous in avoiding upsetting the England team management. It had been agreed at the start of the campaign two years earlier that any wish to involve the England team in a strategic friendly had to be stringently assessed for its benefits to the bid before it was approved by Simon Carslake himself. He would then take it on to be discussed with the England team manager directly. In fact, no plans for 'friendlies' had been approved yet by Simon.

Clare excused herself and whispered to Billy the news she had just heard from the Minister.

'Holy shit! What a fool,' Billy said.

'Yes, I know,' said Clare, as calmly as she could. 'But where is Dick now?'

'He's on holiday,' Billy said. 'Getting a break before the Euro Cup. California, I think. I'll have to check.'

'Well, get hold of him wherever he is,' Foulkes said irritably when Clare relayed Billy's information. 'And tell him what we're doing. As I say the Thai Prime Minister is an old friend of mine. He's a good egg, keen to help. Says the game will secure the Thai vote. So don't stand any nonsense from this manager bloke.'

'Yes, thank you,' Clare spoke through gritted teeth.

'After dinner I'll call the office in London. Simon Carslake will have to talk to Dick Stone.'

'Carslake?' repeated Foulkes, as if he had just remembered the name, but wasn't sure whether to be impressed. 'Remind me of his position?'

'He is our Chief Executive,' Clare replied, struggling to keep her exasperation out of her voice. 'You've met him at several international matches, Minister.'

'Well, I daresay I have,' Foulkes said grumpily. 'I've met so many people since I started, especially at matches of one sort or another. Anyway – whoever he is – will he be able to sort your manager chappie out? If not, you'd better get your Chairman on the blower. Failing that I'll get No. 10 on to it.'

'There's no need to do that,' Clare said quickly. That would be the last thing Simon would want, she thought to herself. 'I'm sure Simon will talk to everyone concerned.'

'Good,' the Minister said. He started to turn back towards the Ambassador but remembered something else.

'Oh, by the way, I should have said it's two games not one. One match at Wembley, the other over here. The Prime Minister is going to come up with some kind of trophy for the two teams to fight over. Great commitment from him.'

He didn't wait for Clare's reaction.

Clare sat glumly, toying with her meal. Suddenly a warning bell sounded in her head. Oh Christ, she remembered, the Minister had said that the announcement would be made in Thailand tomorrow! Supposing the first that Dick Stone heard about this friendly was from some newspaper ringing him up on holiday.

Dinner was followed by coffee in the lounge. But Clare had already excused herself. She eventually found a telephone with the help of Hugo Morris.

London was seven hours behind. Luckily Simon was at his desk when Clare got through.

She told him bluntly that they had a problem.

'Don't tell me Danny is screwing the Ambassador's wife,' Simon chuckled nervously.

'No Creighton is fine,' Clare replied, glad to have a moment to calm herself down. 'He gave a tremendous coaching session today with a bunch of local kids. It got some great coverage here. Not sure if it got picked up by any British papers.

'However,' Clare began, but then paused. She was not enjoying this very much.

'The Minister has caused a bit of a problem this afternoon. Did you know he's a personal friend of the Thai Prime Minister? Apparently, they were big mates at Oxford. It's not in our briefing papers as far as I can see. Anyway, while Billy and I went out to the coaching session, the Minister went off to see his old pal. It wasn't until halfway through dinner tonight he casually announces that he had said we would be very happy to play Thailand in an international fixture... not once but twice!'

'It gets even worse, Simon. He told me that the Thais are very excited by the idea, and their PM wants to announce it at some Media event tomorrow. Simon, what the hell is Dick Stone going to say?'

She swallowed. The line was silent.

'Hello? Simon, on a scale of one to ten, with ten being mad as hell, how furious are you?'

Simon ignored the question, and Clare felt faintly embarrassed at her flippancy.

'Presumably,' Simon said at last, 'you want me to call Dick? He's in California on holiday. The tabloids have already caught up with him. He's been photographed by the pool with a couple of girls just a bit on the young side for a fifty-year-old man. Getting him out of bed with this news will go down a treat.'

'I'm sorry, Simon,' said Clare. 'I'm not sure there's much I could have done about it. The Minister's just gone off piste. And he thinks he's done us a great favour.'

Simon laughed loudly.

'It's ok. Leave it with me. I'll get hold of Stone and ring you back so don't go to bed. It could be a long night.'

Simon didn't take long to get hold of the plush Californian hotel where Dick Stone was trying to relax. His bedside phone rang at precisely 3:54 am.

'Fuck off,' Stone said before Simon could complete his opening sentence.

'Dick, it's Simon Carslake here. I'm sorry to disturb you.'

'I don't care if you're the Queen of England, just fuck off. I'm asleep.'

Dick Stone slammed the phone down, rolled over and put his head under the pillow. He felt the other side of the bed and remembered. She'd left just after midnight.

Simon thought hard what to do next. He had no other options. After ten minutes he made the call again. In California Dick Stone did his best to ignore the ringing but eventually picked up the phone.

'This had better be important Mr Carslake, it really had. I'm trying to have a holiday and you're not on my party list. What the fuck is the problem?'

Simon stumbled through Clare's story as best he could. Stone listened in disbelief.

'There's no way we are going to play Thailand. I'm the fucking manager and I decide the games we play.'

Simon was extremely skilled at dealing with difficult people. In fact, he enjoyed the challenge of using his persuasive skills to win debates in the most hostile circumstances. He sometimes imagined his talents would be ideal in a hostage situation or talking down a suicide.

'Dick,' he appealed in his most conciliatory tone. 'Please believe me, this isn't easy for any of us. As you know, I've been absolutely rigorous in minimising our campaign's effects on your brilliant work. But you want us to host international tournaments, don't you? Fans love it. Your players love it. You've told me that, Dick, it gives them extra pride.'

He waited for a moment, but Stone was still listening.

'Well, I do my very best to keep you and the team out of all this. But occasionally things get out of our hands, and we have to do things differently to the way we would like. I'm afraid this is what happened tonight. We had no idea until tonight that the Sports Minister was going to invite Thailand to play us, but he's done it now.'

'Well, perhaps he'd like to do the team selection too, would he? For Christ's sake who is the fucking Sports Minister anyway. I've not even met him.'

It was part of Simon's skill to sense a change in his adversary's manner and turn it to his advantage. He was quick to pounce.

'His name is Matthew Foulkes. Jesus Dick, I had no idea you hadn't met him. That's my fault entirely. I'll put that right. I'll arrange for you to talk to him when he's back from this trip. He's relatively new to his job. Nice enough but not really a football man.'

'Well, that's a statement of the bleeding obvious.' said Stone. Simon said nothing. He sensed a change.

'I'm still fucking mad about this, Simon. How many times is this going to happen? It's your job to stop people interfering not helping them do it.'

There was a pause in the conversation.

'Well, I'm not going to do it. And if you tell me I've got to, I'll fucking resign tomorrow.'

Simon cursed quietly to himself. He'd thought he was winning. But this was getting worse. He went into automatic response.

'No, no, no! Look Dick, I'll play for time. I'll say I'm having trouble getting hold of you. But I'll ring you again in an hour. Meantime, please think about it. I really need your help on this one, Dick.'

As Simon put the phone down, he had a moment of inspiration. He looked up a telephone number in his Filofax, and dialled Sir Albert Lewis.

Back in Bangkok, Clare and Billy had found a quiet area in the Embassy garden to discuss what was happening. Clare had given up smoking two years earlier but had accepted three of Billy's cigarettes in the half hour they had been together. She had done most of the talking, while Billy – usually difficult to repress – sat glumly swigging from a bottle of lager.

Eventually, Clare too fell silent. There was nothing they could do or say that would change anything.

Billy could sit still no longer and went back into the Embassy lounge. The Ambassador, Hugo Morris, and the Sports Minister were in deep conversation on the other side of the room. As he approached them, he realised they were discussing the politics of South East Asia. Turning away from the group as quickly as he could, Billy suddenly noticed that Danny wasn't in the room. He went behind Hugo's armchair, to avoid interrupting the discussion, and whispered in his ear.

'Has Danny gone to bed?'

It was Hugo's job to be sober and to be completely aware of who the notable people were in the EFO party.

'No, I think he's gone out,' said Hugo. 'Mentioned something about seeing the nightlife.'

Billy felt slightly sick. 'Oh god,' said Billy. 'Why didn't someone tell me?' he mumbled to himself, before remembering that minding the ex-England footballer was his responsibility.

'Oh God,' he said to Clare when he found her again in the garden. 'We can't let Danny loose on his own. Not in a place like Bangkok, not at this time of night.'

Clare closed her eyes and stared at the starry sky above them.

'This trip isn't going too well,' she said and reached for another of Billy's cigarettes.

Hugo Morris came out to the garden.

'I gather from our man at the gate that Danny took a taxi to Patpong. I'm sorry guys, it's mostly bars and dancing down there, pretty seedy and plenty of "girls".' He indicated quote marks with his fingers.

Clare found a hidden depth of leadership, despite everything.

'Look, I have to stay here to speak to Simon when he rings back. But Hugo, could you take Billy to try and retrieve Danny?'

Hugo paused before answering. This wasn't really a task for a First Secretary, but he enjoyed a bit of drama, and had few excuses to visit Patpong.

'Ok,' he said. 'I suggest we get out of our monkey suits. I'll see you on the drive in ten minutes Billy. I've got a pretty good idea where Danny will be.'

Clare smiled her thanks to Hugo. It was gone midnight and the Embassy party was thinning quickly. The Minister had had a long day and slipped off to bed, oblivious to the problems the EFO was having with Dick Stone or of Danny's venture out on the town.

Meanwhile in London, Simon had got through to the Chairman. Sir Albert Lewis knew Dick Stone well. He had seen his club and international career develop as a player and supported his appointment as manager of the England team last year, even though he had a patchy club management record. After realising that he'd failed to persuade Stone, and that the England manager was even threatening to resign, Simon reluctantly recognised that Albert was his last chance.

As he listened to Simon's drawling account of the Minister's actions, Albert quite enjoyed hearing the Chief Executive's obvious discomfort. He was also pleased that Simon was asking for his help, apparently conceding that the Chairman and his knowledge of the game did have some value after all. He got Dick Stone's telephone number in California and rang him.

Over the phone to California, Albert told Dick Stone how much he agreed about those 'bloomin' politicians' sticking their noses in. He didn't find it difficult to back up Dick's belief that Simon Carslake should have been stopping this kind of thing happening. When the manager called Simon a 'snake in the grass', Albert decided that it wasn't the time to admonish him and even allowed himself an encouraging chuckle. Eventually, the matter was settled satisfactorily, but only 'as a personal favour' to Sir Albert.

As that problem was being resolved, Billy and Hugo were making their slow way between neon-lit night clubs, with their driver hooting frequently to avoid scantily clothed young people crossing in front of the car.

'If Danny just asked for a nightclub, his taxi will have probably suggested either *The Blue Lagoon* or *Pussy Galore*,' Hugo said.

They reached *Pussy Galore* first. It was full of young bodies, and Hugo and Billy could barely breathe as they fought through the crowd for a sight of Danny. Then they made the short walk to the *Blue Lagoon*.

There was a crush in the doorway, but once inside they could see across the dance floor to the bar on the other side. Billy suddenly shouted to Hugo above the noise.

'There he is! There's Danny with that little crowd of glamour girls at the end of the bar.'

There was a lot of giggling in the group, and it looked as though Danny was the clear focus of their attention. Then, as a new number started on the dance floor, one of the girls grabbed Danny's arm and tugged him away to dance. Hugo and Billy could hardly see Danny's face amidst their writhing embrace.

'Lady boys,' shouted Hugo. 'I wonder if Danny knows.'

'Jesus,' said Billy. 'I shouldn't think so. How can you tell.'

He did a double take as he saw a strange grin appearing on Hugo's face.

'Trust me,' said Hugo. 'I have a well-trained eye for these things.'

Billy didn't want to hear any more.

'Best get him out of here,' he said.

Billy and Hugo timed their arrival at the bar as Danny and his dance partner returned from the floor. The two men could see Danny's dilated pupils under the strobe lights. He had had a great deal to drink and had possibly taken other stimulants too. By the bottles lined up on the bar, it also looked as if he was the main source of drinks for the party.

'Hi Billy,' shouted Danny when he saw the EFO man. 'It's great here. Come and have a fucking drink. We're having a great time.' He then shouted even louder above the bass and drum music, but he seemed to have a memory problem as he tried to introduce his new friends to Hugo and Billy.

'Oh, it must be our lucky night,' purred one of Danny's party. 'Three lovely Englishmen all to ourselves!'

Billy leaned in close to Danny and shouted in his ear.

'Sorry mate, but you're needed back at the Embassy. We've come to give you a lift back.'

Danny gave Billy a shove backwards.

'But I haven't been here long,' Danny slurred. 'It's fucking boring at the Embassy, man. I'm having a great time here with these girls.'

Billy was losing his patience.

'Yeah well, the thing is Danny, Chrissy has been on the phone wanting to speak to you. D'you want me to tell her you're too busy entertaining lady boys.'

'What? Fuck!' said Danny, his eyes trying to focus on Billy. 'What'dya mean ladyboys? You mean like drag girls...?'

'Fraid so, my friend. That's what this little group are. Now I don't think Chrissie would be too pleased to hear about that. And not too good for your image with sponsors either.'

Danny waved towards the group without looking at them.

'Got to go. Got to go," he announced. His new friends pouted at each other. 'So sorry,' he said as he walked towards the entrance ahead of Hugo and Billy, muttering under his breath, 'lady boys... fuck!'

Outside, Hugo Morris grabbed a tuk-tuk. 'British Embassy please,' he said.

May 1997
The Whistleblower writes... GFO men are up for the Cup... and the Royal Box...

Whatever they say about the EFO Cup losing some of its appeal to the big English clubs, it still seems to attract plenty of international interest. No fewer than ten of the GFO's most important members are guests of EFO Chairman Sir Albert Lewis at Wembley this weekend for the Tottenham v Liverpool Final.

Apart from the appeal of the beautiful game, of course a lot of them rather like sitting in the Royal Box at Wembley, Whistleblower understands. 'All part of our great charm offensive' for the World Cup Bid, one EFO insider explains to me.

Good to know the GFO's decision on who hosts the 2003 World Cup will be decided on the basis of who can offer voters the most attractive away days.

Chapter 37

Making friends

May 1997

Albert stood looking down Wembley Way. He loved Cup Final day. He had adored everything about it since he was a small boy. He knew that the air of excitement he felt waking up on Cup Final morning was shared by thousands of football fans all over the country. As he watched Liverpool and Tottenham supporters slowly making their way towards the majestic old stadium, he felt a real sense of privilege.

He looked up at the magnificent twin towers. He couldn't help but feel a little sad. Like many other football fans the sight of the towers brought a lump to his throat. He knew it was very likely the old towers would have no place in the new Wembley. Some supporters held out hope by organising petitions, writing to the Prime Minister and even the Queen. Lewis had received many letters on the issue. He had his own views but as Chairman he kept those to himself.

'I'm Chairman of all this,' Albert smiled to himself. 'And it'll be me down on the pitch later shaking the players' hands.'

He felt a grip on his shoulder. It was Greg Turner, the GFO Board member for the Americas.

'Ahhh a great sight, Albert.' Turner said. 'Looks like you're reminiscing.'

Goodness, Albert thought. He was so lost in his memories that he had completely forgotten his guests. Greg Turner was a genial companion. Albert liked his soft Canadian accent. He seemed to understand Albert's emotional connection with one of the most important events in the global football calendar – and in Albert's life.

Albert smiled at Greg and took his elbow as he directed him towards the Wembley VIP facilities.

'So sorry, Greg,' he said. 'I was remembering the 1953 Cup Final, the one that became known as the Matthews Final. I was lucky enough to get a ticket from an old boy in Truro. I don't know how. You know, a year or so ago I met Stanley Matthews at Number 10 here in London with the PM. What a lovely man. So modest. I'm talking about Matthews not the Prime Minister!'

They both laughed.

'I was also looking at these Spurs fans and thinking back to when they did the double in 1961. Great team that was, Greg, great team. Beat Leicester City here two nil. Smith and Dyson got the goals. I can still name the double winning side.'

'You have a real passion for the game, Albert,' said Turner, wheezing slightly as he climbed the stone steps that were so much a part of the Wembley experience – no matter how important the visitor. He held out a hand to stop them both on a landing.

'It just made me want to say something to you. You know Albert, I've been sensing your mood at meetings in the last few months – particularly since Congress last year. You're not too happy with things, Albert, I can tell.'

Albert thought for a moment about what Turner had said. It was true. The Tokyo Congress in October last year had changed fundamentally his feelings about the GFO. What he had heard from the President and Joe Kumpa, one of his most senior GFO colleagues, had shocked him. And what Greg Turner had observed was right. At the three committee meetings he had attended since the 1996 Congress, Albert had made no effort to disguise his disenchantment with the GFO.

He didn't know much about Turner, but he had no reason to accuse him of any wrongdoing. He felt he needed to explain himself.

'You see, Greg, to me football isn't about VIPs sitting in posh boxes doing deals with each other. It isn't about money, money, money. And it certainly shouldn't be run by a bunch of crooks, fattening up their own bank accounts.'

He looked at Turner carefully. He would be frank with him, he decided.

'You know as well as I do, some of our GFO colleagues have come to Wembley today not because they particularly want to watch the Cup Final. Not because they care who wins. They just want to be the fat cats in charge, staying at Claridges, meeting the Royals, poncing about the place. They're not fans, Greg. The fans are the poor sods outside, travelling down from Liverpool to get here, somehow getting enough money together to buy tickets and the coach fare. Singing their hearts out for the love of their club and the game.'

Turner appeared to be listening intently, nodding encouragingly.

'What's so shocking to me,' Albert continued, ushering his guest to a corner of the concrete stair landing, and speaking more quietly, 'is how unaccountable the whole set up is. The fans don't know the half of it. Of course, they should ask more questions, but why should they? Why can't all these clever buggers running world football just appreciate how lucky they are and behave themselves? Greg, don't you think that too many of our colleagues have got their hands in the till?'

Turner smiled, and Albert Lewis felt compelled to continue.

'Look at these World Cup bids, Greg. I've seen it with my own eyes. All the campaigners sucking up to the Board members and their wives. Whipping them off first class all around the world. Staying at the finest hotels. Introducing them to royalty and world leaders – I know, Greg, because England did it ourselves last year at Highgrove. And how many Board members take cash handouts?'

'Can you prove that?' Greg asked quickly. Albert was impressed by his interest.

'It's not easy. I'd like to, but I'm not a ruddy detective,' he replied.

'Be very careful Albert,' Turner whispered. 'You're dealing with some very powerful men. Don't underestimate Larsen. Behind that charming exterior is a heart of steel. If you make an enemy of him, he 'll feed you to the wolves without a second thought. He's ruthless, believe me.'

'I know that, Greg,' Albert said, beginning to feel a real affinity with the Canadian. 'I know, he controls everything. And I know Joe Kumpa is his right-hand man. He seems to have his own rackets going.'

Greg Turner laughed without humour in his voice. 'Yeeees, but Albert you have to be very careful with Kumpa too.'

'And why is that, Greg?' said Albert quickly. 'I know he's a big man with a lot of influence. But the bigger they are the harder they fall.'

Turner looked at Lewis carefully.

'Albert, you know very well about your man Simon Carslake?'

Albert was on his guard immediately. Yes, he knew from the President himself that Simon had been offered some votes to support the England World Cup bid. And yes, perhaps he should have tackled Simon immediately after hearing Larsen's accusation. But he had let the matter go, and nine months had now passed.

Albert had been mortified to hear at the Congress in Tokyo last year that his colleague might have even contemplated bribing GFO Board members, of course, but he had no proof that what he'd been told was true. Challenging his Chief Executive on such a serious charge was a major step – and he was reluctant to take it without proof.

It would poison forever an already difficult relationship, and if Albert was wrong, he knew that Simon would use the mistake to undermine his authority. Simon might even try to oust Albert from the EFO. Albert would have been happy to take that risk if he had real evidence to back his challenge, but as Monica constantly reminded him, gossip between GFO members was not enough.

Albert had made careful enquiries and found that no money from the EFO campaign budgets had been used for any other purpose. He had even asked the EFO's Finance Head to let him know of any significant withdrawals from other budgets in the last 12 months, but nothing was reported.

As the months passed, Albert began to wonder whether President Larsen's claims about Simon's scheme were huge lies. Larsen had threatened to expose Albert with a ridiculous accusation about his own expenses after all. Who was to say that his story about vote buying wasn't also concocted by Larsen and his cronies to sabotage the English World Cup bid, and to ruin the reputation of the EFO?

Albert was flustered now to hear that Greg Turner knew about the Simon Carslake rumours. He had told nobody other than Monica. He felt exposed.

'Now Greg, I've heard those claims obviously,' he said. 'But I can assure you there's nothing in them at all.'

'If any money had gone astray from EFO budgets I would know.'

Greg Turner held up a hand to interrupt Lewis.

'Albert, Albert, Albert. You do know that Joe Kumpa is working very closely with your man Carslake.'

He paused to let passing spectators go by before continuing.

'You know they're both taking a cut from the deal. Word I've heard is that Carslake is raising the money in the City of London, well away from the EFO. Be careful, Albert, big Joe is very close to your man. They say Carslake might have a good future in the GFO one day.'

Albert stared at Turner, unable to speak. Great God – could THIS be true?

Turner left him with his thoughts and stepped up the final staircase to the Royal Box overlooking the halfway line of the Wembley pitch.

Following in a trance, Albert could hardly hear the chants from the rival supporters as he reached the door to the executive box. He let in Greg Turner without a look in his direction.

None of the other Board members had arrived yet. Simon and two other members of the campaign team were at the bar, pouring from a champagne bottle. Greg Turner took a glass, nodded at Simon and reached inside his jacket for his mobile phone. He went to the back of the room for some privacy. He scrolled down his contacts, pressed a number, and waited for a reply. It wasn't long before a familiar voice responded.

'Hello Greg, what can I do for you?'

It was the Laundryman.

'I think we've got a problem.'

The Laundryman's voice displayed no emotion. 'What sort of problem?'

'It's our friend Albert Lewis. I'm at Wembley, and I've just been having an interesting little chat with him. He's been a real pain in the arse around the Board recently. Not one of the guys at all. Joe asked me to educate him about the real world of bidding. So, I told him a bit more about Carslake, and how close Carslake now is to Joe. We thought it might be enough to make him resign, but I'm not so sure.

'I think he's a tougher bastard inside than he looks. Just want to say, he could still be dangerous if he's clever enough. Maybe we need to prepare some ammunition to fire back if he sounds off.'

'OK Greg, I'll tell the boss. Let me know if there are developments.'

Greg pocketed his mobile again and went to speak to the campaign team. That Sara, he thought, pretty little girl...

Albert walked deliberately to the front of the box and stared down at the Wembley pitch. Two military bands were parading their impeccable routines. But of their music, he was conscious only of a drumming rhythm. It seemed to echo in his aching head.

His Deputy Chairman Michael Sutton gave him a half-hearted wave but left him alone.

Albert's mind was a blur. He was going on holiday the next day, and that was all he wanted to think about. He yearned to see his family again and go for walks along the Cornish coastal path. He had planned to talk to Simon today to discuss arrangements in case he was urgently needed. But now he decided he wouldn't. He couldn't.

He thought about Simon yet again. He recalled what Greg Turner had told him, but did that really change anything? All he was hearing was rumours. The only effect they had on him was to focus his feelings of growing contempt for the GFO. The whole damn lot of them. He was starting to think he could never again bear to attend a GFO Board meeting. He would have to resign as EFO Chairman, of course. He would be letting down the EFO and its World Cup bid.

It was an extraordinary thought for a man who had achieved the highest position in English football he could have imagined. But in his despondent mood, he was increasingly convinced that that was the right thing to do – for the EFO, for him and his family, and maybe even for world football itself. It was a business he no longer understood, and no longer believed he could work in.

Had Albert been looking for Simon in the box at that moment, he would not have found him. Simon had encouraged his campaign team to take champagne bottles around the room personally, looking for opportunities to talk to the eight GFO Board members who had accepted the EFO's invitation.

He then left the EFO suite and walked along the concrete corridor that linked the Wembley VIP boxes.

Once outside, Simon put on a baseball cap in case he met anyone he knew, and quickly found the private box where he had arranged to meet the Arthurs brothers. Both were keen Spurs fans, and to Simon's irritation, were unwilling to talk to him until after the national anthem had been sung and the teams' pre-match preparations were complete.

'So, Simon,' said Eddie, the younger brother, eventually, motioning Simon to a plush seat beside him. 'Bit pissed-off we can't come and meet the royals with you.'

He winked at his brother Tommy. Simon wasn't sure if Eddie was joking or not. These were guys with a lot of influence. He wouldn't have been in the least surprised if they had expected him to introduce them to the Duke. But then Eddie flashed him an easy grin.

Sitting behind the brothers, Simon could see a number of faces he recognised from soap operas and reality shows. He wondered how the two brothers knew these people.

He didn't feel comfortable with the two men. They had lived pretty violent lives it seemed, even if you compensated for the tabloids' sense of drama, and he was never sure how far he was accepted by them.

The minor celebrities were obviously there to impress anyone who noticed, or cared, but they weren't expected to have any kind of business relationship with the Arthurs.

Simon had no celebrity cache. He knew very well that his only value to them was the business opportunity he presented.

Unlike the mainstream financial contacts that Simon had approached for funds, the Arthurs had no shareholders to worry about. If the deal looked good, they were happy.

They didn't worry too much about security either. They knew that Simon was not operating within a gangland syndicate. His life was their guarantee.

They didn't take long to make decisions. When Simon suggested the return they could expect on their two-million-dollar investment in his project, they haggled a bit, but accepted quickly. They even suggested there might be more funds available.

When he had first been introduced to the Arthurs by a city trader friend who had grown up with them, Simon had been simply petrified.

But it quickly became clear that it was worth him overcoming his fears. The introduction had been just in time. When Simon talked to Gerald in Paris as he'd agreed on his New Year phone call, his ability to absolutely confirm that the eight million dollars was secure gave him a new sense of invulnerability.

This was the world of his future, Simon thought, with a thrill as he noticed Tommy's wife smiling at him.

As the second half of the match unfolded, the smiles on the faces of the Arthurs' party were being replicated by Tottenham fans around the stadium. Following a lack lustre performance in the first half Spurs, the favourites to win the EFO Cup, were 2-0 down at half-time.

The manager's team-talk in the interval must have been impressive however as Tottenham emerged for the second half a transformed side. They were awarded a penalty for a Liverpool handball offence straight from the kick-off – a piece of drama missed by many of the VIPs sitting in the Royal box who were still enjoying their half-time hospitality. Now back in the game, Tottenham pressed hard for an equaliser, and were rewarded by a superb goal from captain Georgie Miller's freekick from just outside the goal area with just ten minutes to go to the final whistle.

The game looked as though it was heading for extra time when in the eighty-eighth minute Spurs achieved the ultimate comeback. Their Spanish international striker Alvaro finished off a goalmouth scramble by scoring the winner. Passions were running high even in the Royal box now as Liverpool desperately raided the Spurs goal in the final minutes. This was as exciting as football ever gets, and even the GFO guests seemed to be gripped by the occasion as the referee blew his final whistle.

Albert was certainly enjoying himself. 'Without doubt one of the best Cup Finals we've seen,' he whispered to a smiling Duke of Kent, the Queen's representative for the day, as the gleaming trophy was placed in front of the two men with the blue and white ribbons of Tottenham Hotspur.

After the presentations and the departure of the royal party, Greg Turner led a chorus of congratulations from the GFO guests. 'Quite unforgettable experience Albert,' he said, clapping Lewis firmly on the shoulder. 'I knew you guys could put on a good show but I didn't know you could control the spectacle on the pitch!'

Albert could hardly control his pleasure. In this moment, it wasn't difficult to forget his contempt for certain members of the GFO. Today, he was the proud head of English football, entertaining football men from all over the world.

'Well, gentlemen, I'm glad you enjoyed the Wembley experience,' he said, his voice breaking with emotion. 'This evening we'll celebrate! We'll take you back to Claridge's for a short rest before we go on to the Houses of Parliament for drinks on the terrace overlooking the river Thames, and dinner hosted by Matthew Foulkes our Sports Minister.'

June 1997

*The Whistleblower writes... The English Disease threatens
World Cup hopes for 2003...*

*English football hooligans have been back in force this week on the
streets of Marseilles, venue for England's first game in the group
stages of the European Football Championships, Euro Cup 97.*

*Damage to shops and restaurants has spelt disaster for
England's reputation. Euro insiders say that if the trouble
continues, serious consideration will be given to whether the
England team can stay in the tournament.*

*But Whistleblower is able to reveal that there are also
implications for the bidding process for the football GFO World
Cup 2003. A plot has been hatched by some of England's
opponents to stop England, and it's all to do with timing. The
story goes like this...*

*Whistleblower has seen the minutes of the GFO Board
which originally determined to vote on the GFO World Cup
2003 venue at its March meeting earlier this year. Before Euro
Cup 97 in other words. Then following a recommendation
from the GFO President, citing too heavy an agenda, the
Board decided to postpone the World Cup decision until later
this year. After Euro Cup 97 that is!*

*Insiders have told Whistleblower that opponents always
thought Euro Cup 97 would be a problem for England with
every chance of serious fan violence in France. If the World
Cup vote was pushed back it would mean that damage to bars
and shop fronts could also wreck England's GFO World Cup
bidding prospects.*

*As one senior GFO Exec member said to Whistleblower
yesterday: 'Who in their right mind would reward
troublemakers by inviting their country to host the GFO
World Cup?'*

So those plotting against England seem to have won an early victory, courtesy of the yobs, with a little help from the GFO's senior Board members.

It's a sad reflection on some members of GFO (an organisation that claims to foster the football family worldwide), who tonight are rejoicing in the misfortunes of a fellow member. Machiavelli would have felt very much at home.

Chapter 38

Here we go!

July 1997

Simon Carslake got to his office early. The International Sub-committee had agreed to meet at 9:00 in order to discuss Euro Cup 97 hooliganism, and he didn't want to be late. Things were going well for Simon's financial plans, and he didn't want to raise any suspicions at the EFO that he was anything other than totally committed to managing the GFO World Cup bid.

As he began to remind himself about the troublemakers' activities by reading the Press Office's digest, his phone rang.

'It's Number 10,' said Steph, his secretary. 'I'm putting them through.'

For a moment he envisaged the Prime Minister at the end of the line, but of course it was one of the special advisers – young and ambitious men and women under the command of chief fixer, Rob Marshall.

The voice belonged to Di Edgcombe, Number 10's expert on sports matters. Simon knew her well. They'd had lunch together a couple of times and spoken recently in preparation for Euro Cup 97. The PM was planning to go to at least one of the England games and the arrangements had been planned meticulously.

'Morning Di,' Simon said cheerily. 'Are you well?'

'Fine, fine,' Di responded. 'I only wish I could say the same for the Prime Minister. He's like a bear with a sore head. What a pathetic performance that was the other night. Number 10's mixed team could have done better than that.'

'Yes, I hear it wasn't very good,' Simon replied laconically. 'As you know, I'm not the best person to ask, Di. But my guys still think we can win the group,' he said.

'God, Simon,' said Di. 'I can't believe the EFO actually has a Chief Executive for a World Cup campaign who doesn't like football.'

'Now that's not fair,' he said. 'I quite like it; I just don't know anything about it.'

Di laughed.

'However. Serious voice,' Di continued. 'It's matters off the pitch that I'm ringing about. I gather you have a top-level meeting, and Rob is anxious we speak to you beforehand. By the way the Sports Minister might show up at the EFO. Rob has told him that it might be a good idea in case he needs to make the PM's position clear to all your colleagues. So don't be surprised if he shows.'

'Thanks for the warning,' replied Simon. A seemingly routine EFO meeting was beginning to sound tricky. Simon remembered with horror the last time the Sports Minister had been involved in England's World Cup campaign. His promise to the Thai Prime Minister that England would play two friendly matches against Thailand had seriously damaged his relationship with the team manager.

'Anyway,' Di continued, 'it looks now like the yobbos have destroyed whatever chance we had with the World Cup bid. It's therefore our view that pulling out gracefully is preferable to soldiering on and being badly beaten and publicly humiliated.'

Simon was stunned. He could hardly believe what he was hearing. He knew that the behaviour of England fans in France had been bad. He knew that there were serious worries about its effects on England's bid for the 2003 GFO World Cup. But it hadn't for a moment occurred to him that it might mean withdrawing from the contest.

He processed the news from Di in seconds. He had two million dollars sitting in a bank account in Panama. He had been promised more money by the Arthurs brothers, with a recommendation to talk to a bank in Iceland that could help him raise yet more money to reach his eight-million dollars target. Shit, he thought, he had confirmed with his contact, Gerald that he was confident of getting the money, ready to trigger an amazing financial deal that would transform his career. He had even called Joe Kumpa to tell him...

Holy shit! He suddenly remembered something else. That Panama account was in Joe Kumpa's name. If the England bid was to be withdrawn, he would have to get the money from Kumpa to pay back the Arthurs. The full extent of what Di was saying was clear – and catastrophic.

He swallowed hard before replying.

'Yes, Di, that would be pretty tragic after all the work we've put in... and... I wonder whether that's the right decision.'

Di was puzzled. She liked to hear Simon's left-of-field views, but when the PM had made a decision...

Simon chanced his arm.

'Of course, some people will argue that by pulling out the government will hand victory to the louts. We'll have to see what my colleagues say. I suspect opinion will be divided. I think the Chairman will believe we should stay in the race regardless.'

Di said nothing. Simon was clutching at straws.

'Also, Di, some of our bods don't like being told what to do by politicians.'

'Yes, let me see,' Di said at last, a good deal more coldly. 'They would be the ones who like coming to Downing Street parties, sipping government champagne and want these GFO types to get five-star government treatment. Oh yes, they also expect members of the Royal family and the Cabinet to run around meeting and greeting the GFO lot. Oh, and they also expect a good wad of public money to pay for it all.'

Simon breathed heavily, anxious to behave as he would have been expected to. He managed a little laugh.

'Yes, point taken, but then you know my views. The EFO is still in the dark ages and there's no sign of radical reform any time soon. Certainly not before nine o'clock this morning.'

'Hmmm, well let me know how it goes anyway. Let's talk later,' Di said.

Simon put the phone down just as Steph placed a large cup of coffee on his desk. He looked glumly into its depths. I think I'm going to die, he said under his breath.

He had fifteen minutes to spare before the meeting. He flicked through some meeting papers which Steph had left on his desk. He noticed a letter from EFO council member Cyril Townsend, one of the Chairman's keen supporters. Townsend was also a member of the EFO's international subcommittee, so would be attending this morning's discussion about the future of the bid.

Scanning the letter quickly, Simon saw that Townsend was still concerned about toilet facilities at Wembley. He would probably raise the matter that morning, Simon thought to himself. It was quite possible that Townsend had also written to Number 10 about the toilets at Wembley and would add another voice to the 'withdraw' camp. What an irony if Simon's glittering future was to be unravelled by Cyril Townsend's bladder failings, he thought bitterly.

Perhaps it was the bizarre idea that the failed old guard of the EFO might be his nemesis that enabled Simon to rediscover his powers. But in a moment he had rallied. 'Come on,' he thought, 'this will be the biggest test of your life... You're Simon Carslake. You're a winner. You can do this.'

He gathered up his bid papers for the meeting. He didn't want to be late, but nor did he want to get involved in the chit-chat beforehand.

Albert was already in the conference room as Chairman, at the head of the long table. He didn't look up as Simon entered the room. The fact that Albert ignored Simon as he sat beside him was no surprise. Simon had seen their relationship deteriorating as the campaign wore on, and Albert had become increasingly detached from the campaign's activities.

He had also heard from friends in the GFO that Albert was less and less involved in the global organisation's operations outside World Cup matters. None of this worried Simon. He had always believed that Albert would have no effect on England's chances of winning the bid.

And now, whether or not England won the bid was immaterial for Simon; the only thing that mattered was that England kept in the bidding game, so that he could buy four Board members' votes at the price agreed and then sell them on to another bid team at a higher price. Everything was in place. The Arthurs would make their money, Simon and Kumpa would make their money, and Simon's financial future would be assured. But if England was to withdraw its bid... he couldn't think about that.

Albert nodded a good morning to the eighteen people in the room while the EFO Deputy Chairman, Michael Sutton, slipped into an empty seat, mouthing apologies for lateness, which Albert acknowledged, if a little impatiently. Simon thought to himself: I bet you'd be glad to see the end of this adventure, Sutton... now you can get back to your quiet life.

'Right, let's be clear about the purpose of this meeting,' Albert began. 'We're here to discuss the behaviour of some so-called English football fans in France at Euro 97. And we want to look at how it will affect our bid. I suggest we start with an assessment from Mr Green regarding the Foreign Office view.'

Only the Chairman ever addressed Stephen Green as 'Mr' but Stephen liked it. Working on the bid for the last two years, he had been part of a team in which everyone was younger than him and certainly a lot more informal. It made a pleasant change to work with Albert's ways.

'Mr Chairman, we've all seen the Media coverage of England fans in France. There have undoubtedly been problems in Marseille both before and after England's first game.

'French police have informed us that thirty-five arrests were made, mostly outside the ground after the game. The behaviour of England fans seems to have deterred tourists and other countries' supporters from entering the popular areas of Marseille. There was a certain amount of fighting with French football fans, but most of the problem was the drunken misbehaviour of the English, causing damage to bars, restaurants, and shops. It's difficult to predict what will happen next, but the authorities are expecting further trouble when England play their second game in Lyon.

'Now, Mr Chairman, as you say, for this particular meeting the important question is how this will affect our World Cup bid. Well, Foreign Office posts are reporting widespread negative coverage in the Media in many countries. The overall impression reminds people about the hooligan problems England was famous for not so many years ago.'

'A question please, Chairman.' Cyril Townsend had put his arm in the air. 'Just for information, what are these posts you are referring to?'

'My apologies,' Stephen replied patiently. 'Posts is a term we use to describe our diplomats around the globe. They keep us up to date on developments in the world and also report on perceptions of the UK, telling us how UK activities and policies are seen by others. In this case they've been giving us feedback on the extent of the coverage, and an assessment of how much harm has been done to our reputation. Shall I continue, Mr Chairman.'

Albert nodded.

'The overall picture is pretty bleak, I'm afraid. Pictures of English troublemakers are everywhere leading to widespread condemnation. In countries where there are GFO Board members, the posts are primed to pick up any comments and views relating to the bid, and several have reported definite reputational damage likely to affect England's capacity to attract votes in support of our bid. I will circulate later today a compilation for you all to see.'

'Thank you, Mr Green,' Sir Albert said, sadly. 'That was both informative and of course rather depressing. Colleagues may have specific questions for you in a moment, but I'm going to ask our Chief Executive to comment next.'

He paused as Eleanor, his secretary, whispered in his ear. 'Oh, but just a minute. It seems the Sports Minister is about to arrive, so I suggest we wait a few moments for him.'

The subcommittee didn't need to wait long before the conference room door opened, and Eleanor appeared alongside the portly frame of The Right Honourable Matthew Foulkes MP.

The Minister was looking flustered and breathless after running up the two flights of stairs to the meeting. His ruddy complexion was evidence of a heavy meeting the night before. Most people on the committee knew Matthew Foulkes's reputation for enjoying his food and fine wines.

'So very sorry to be late,' the Minister drawled.

'Not at all, Minister. We've heard from Mr Green on the Foreign Office's reports,' Sir Albert replied as Foulkes settled in the vacant seat on the other side of the Chairman and pulled an untidy bundle of papers from his bag. 'But I think you've already seen the official reports.'

'Yes, indeed I have,' Matthew Foulkes said, surveying the room as he perched his reading glasses on the edge of his nose. 'And appalling reading they make too. What is it about football that attracts these mindless individuals. They're a disgrace to our country. An absolute disgrace! You don't get this sort of nonsense in rugby do you? I can tell you the Prime Minister is spitting blood. As you know, the PM is very keen on football, but we simply won't tolerate this sort of behaviour either at home or overseas. And there's no question it does great harm to our reputation.'

'God,' whispered Sara Thurlow to a colleague beside her. 'He sounds as though he's blaming us for the hooligans!'

The Minister continued, and his voice became angrier.

'I don't mind telling you,' he said, 'football has to get its house in order. If these louts can't behave themselves the moment they see a pint of lager, then they've got to be banned. Stopped from leaving the country.'

Albert was becoming increasingly irritated by the Minister's manner. He thought that the old blame game over fan behaviour had got past this point years ago. Most observers of football violence, which had tainted the English game off and on since the 1970s, now recognised that there was no single cause. Football was just a meeting point for young people's disenchantment. The clubs and the EFO could do their bit, but good governments saw it all as a wider problem. Hooliganism needed the attention of all kinds of organisations.

'I hope you would agree, Minister, that in England things have improved a lot because of all-seater stadiums,' he said, barely disguising his annoyance. 'These days we get nothing like the trouble we used to in this country.'

'Not much of a help when England yobbos behave like this though, is it,' the Sports Minister growled. 'And here we are spending all this money bidding to host the World Cup, and these people are destroying our chances every time they start a fight.'

Albert was tempted to argue on, but he called the meeting to order. The Minister was an idiot, he decided. 'Simon? What have you to report?'

Simon breathed deeply. He was determined to make the most positive case he could, no matter how much of a challenge it was, and even if it wasn't based on much reality.

'Well, Chairman. I have to say I beg to differ with some of Stephen's reports.'

Stephen Green flushed slightly.

'The reaction has certainly been pretty mixed. The Gulf countries for example have responded very badly, but that is to be expected given their culture.'

'Yes,' interrupted Cyril Townsend. 'Well, there's no way the Saudis would tolerate this type of nonsense. Lock them up and throw away the key - that's what they would do and quite right too. Oh, and I'm quite sure the Arabs wouldn't tolerate the toilet situation at Wembley either. You know, Chairman, this is an issue I'm very concerned about and it's not going to go away.'

The Minister looked bemused. 'Forgive me,' he said, 'how did we get onto toilets?'

Albert smiled at his old friend. 'Look Cyril, we can't discuss facilities at Wembley now. Simon would you please finish what you were saying about the voting situation.'

'Well, Chairman,' Simon continued, 'it's quite interesting. You see, although in parts of the world there's a strong reaction to England fans' behaviour... on the other hand, my – *football* contacts...' he smiled at Stephen, 'seem to suggest that the opposition is surprisingly low key.

'Other members of the Asian confederation have been much more positive, notably the South Koreans and the Japanese. They seem to understand that we'll bear down on this problem before 2003. And our best friends in Europe have at least remained quiet publicly.

'There's a similar picture in Africa. Joe Kumpa, President of the Alliance of African Football Organisations and a very influential voice in the decision-making process as your campaign team knows very well, has actually been saying how sorry he is to see England's reputation damaged, but he believes it will not have an adverse effect on our vote.'

Albert couldn't resist a snort of contempt. 'Yes... crocodile tears,' he muttered.

The Minister didn't like to be left out. 'I'm sorry,' he said. 'What d'you mean by that?'

'Well Minister, Mr Kumpa seems to have an inconsistent record on support for our bid. He's said to be one of those behind changing the date when the GFO decides on the World Cup bids. Originally it was to be in March, but two years ago President Larsen proposed the decision should be taken later.

'We think that those behind this move – and Mr Kumpa is very close to the President – wanted a new date after Euro 97 in the full expectation that English fans would behave badly and dramatically damage our chances of success. Both the Germans and the Russians supported this change and used their influence to get it passed.'

'Stitched up like a kipper,' volunteered Reg Smart.

'Yes Reg, that's one way of putting it. And their plan seems to have worked.'

Simon cursed his carelessness. He remembered now the frenzied discussions in the campaign team about the changed date of the GFO Board meeting in Brussels. Everyone just assumed it was designed to make England's chances of winning more difficult – not that it would cause questions about continuing with the bid. What an irony, Simon thought, if Joe Kumpa – his mentor in world football – was to be the architect of his downfall.

But now was not the time for regrets. Simon was fighting for his future.

'Well, I'm not sure we should be too negative, Chairman,' he said in his most reasonable voice. 'We're not perfectly positioned, certainly, but I don't believe the damage to our reputation is all that bad. I see real evidence amongst the worldwide football community that this is NOT such a serious matter as some seem to think. Football people know that our newspapers hugely exaggerate everything about English football, on and off the pitch. They know that we have a strong and effective police force that will keep perfect control. They've seen it before. They also know what a stable country we are, and that counts for a great deal.

'And there's another vitally important consideration.' He paused to look around the table.

'My own view is that as the head of football in England, we simply must not allow ourselves to be at the mercy of the minority of football supporters who can't behave themselves. As you know better than most, Chairman, ninety-nine per cent of football fans have no interest at all in violence.'

He paused again, before launching his final compelling statement.

'In fact, I would go so far as to say we owe it to the vast majority of football people in this country, who devote so much of their lives and their emotions to the game, to make damn sure we win this bid – just to show the troublemakers. Or at least to do our very best to win, not cave in at the first setback.'

Simon was pleased with himself. He looked around the table. The senior members of his campaign team smiled their support. There was a murmur of agreement from a number of Council members.

Albert nodded his acceptance of Simon's position without comment.

'Right, now I intend to go round the room and give everybody a chance to state their view. This is a very important decision.'

Views around the table were varied. Simon's rallying cry was recognised and admired, but there were also negative voices. Michael Sutton muttered something about how the EFO mustn't damage its reputation by pursuing a hopeless cause and incurring more cost.

Finally, the Minister made his view clear. 'It is of course ultimately your decision,' he said. And then after a pause: 'but if you insist on going ahead with your bid, you will do so without government support.'

The meeting went quiet. The subcommittee looked at the Minister in shock. There was a strong feeling of betrayal in the room. The discussion had been pointless. Simon thought for a moment he was about to be sick.

'Well,' said the Chairman. 'I suppose that makes things clear enough. We'd better prepare for a Press conference this evening. Simon, we'll need to write to President Larsen.'

The Minister spoke loudly to draw attention to his final words as the subcommittee members started to get up from their chairs.

'Just a minute... um...' the Minister hesitated. Sometimes he had trouble remembering the names of people he had met.

'It's Sir Albert,' said Albert helpfully.

'Yes, sorry. Just a minute Sir Albert. Send a draft of your letter to the GFO and your Press statement to No 10 before it goes public will you. We don't want the government blamed for any of this...'

Chapter 39

Off to Rio

Helmut and Giselle Schneider had spent twenty-four hours in London and were now taking a taxi to Heathrow airport.

They arrived with plenty of time to spare. With a twelve-hour flight ahead of them they decided to stay on their feet for a while and do a bit of shopping. There seemed no limit to the children's capacity for receiving presents.

Shopping over, they were soon being directed to their first-class seats on a British Airways 747. While Giselle chose fresh orange juice, Schneider began the day in customary fashion with a glass of chilled champagne.

Neither of the Schneiders particularly liked flying. Giselle invariably felt a slight sense of unease. She would try to concentrate on the instructions for an emergency but always felt it was all rather futile. She had a particular liking for British Airways. She thought if anyone would be of use in a crisis the British Airways staff seemed like a pretty good bet. The captain would usually sound reassuring and the cabin staff, particularly the slightly older ones, gave the impression at least, that they knew what they were doing.

Schneider tried, if he could, to fly with the German national airline, Lufthansa. He knew the Chairman of the airline well and thought it was important as a leading representative of German football that he should fly the flag for his country whenever possible.

While he didn't particularly like flying he did it so often on GFO business that he had stopped worrying about it and concentrated on other things, particularly at take-off and landing. He always travelled first class of course and this was a considerable compensation, making the journey bearable. He couldn't remember the last time he had sat in an economy seat.

'Rather ironic to be travelling to Brazil with British Airways don't you think?' Schneider said to his wife. 'They're a sponsor of England's bid.'

'Well, if it was up to me, darling,' said Giselle. 'England would win. I simply love London. It's such an exciting city. The shops are fantastic, the hotels superb, and the restaurants are so good nowadays.'

'Yes, well that's as may be,' Schneider said with a smile. 'But you be careful what you say and who you say it to. I don't want to see those comments in the papers.'

'Oh Helmut, give me some credit,' Giselle replied. 'How long have I been playing these little games with you.'

She pecked his cheek. An elderly lady sitting in the row behind smiled at the sweet moment. She knew no German words, and assumed the middle-aged pair were teasing each other lovingly.

'Well, just remember,' Schneider said without looking up from his briefing documents. 'Some of these Media types are out to get you to say something embarrassing. They target wives. Best to avoid them if you can.'

'Tell me, Helmut,' Giselle said. 'Out of interest, what chance does England have?'

'Out of interest and as a matter of fact... they have no chance. What little chance they did have went out of the window with all that fighting at the Euro Cup in France. They signed their own death warrant. The word is that their own government are making them pull out as a result. It might already have happened for all I know.'

'God, how terrible,' said Giselle, flicking through a copy of Vogue left in her First Class seat package. 'So it's us or the Russians?'

'That's about it.' Schneider tried to look at Giselle's reaction without her noticing. Mindful of his wife's liking for his Russian colleague Alexei Baskin, he was wary of too much elaboration.

It had been raining for days in Europe, and Giselle was looking forward to sunshine in Rio. While Schneider went about his football business, which would include a two-day visit to Bolivia, Giselle had plans to lie by the pool and do some sightseeing. Helmut had arranged a personal guide through his football connections. She hoped he would be bronzed and witty but not too young. These boys looking out for attractive middle-aged women were very boring.

Schneider had serious issues on his mind. He needed to find out exactly where the South Americans stood on the World Cup bids. Alejandro, an old friend on the South American Board, had briefed him thoroughly but Helmut needed to eyeball them.

He knew that Alexei and his Russian colleagues were also having trouble working out what the four South American Board members were planning to do. But Schneider wasn't phased by this mystery. It was invariably the case with the South Americans that whenever an important GFO decision had to be made, they would go to ground, only to reappear as a significant influence on the final decision.

Nobody was sure how good Schneider's language skills were. Some colleagues believed that his Spanish was much better than he pretended, and that even his Portuguese was adequate. Whatever the truth, he liked to use an interpreter for important discussions in South America, in order to pick up on the nuances in conversation.

After take-off, the Schneiders settled down to lunch. Giselle then managed to sleep for several hours while Schneider played on his laptop with various permutations for the 2003 bids. Working out what votes each country might get in the early rounds preoccupied him.

It was an uneventful flight and on arrival, mid-evening, they were taken through VIP arrivals where a private limousine was waiting to take them straight to the Cobacabana Palace Hotel.

The Schneiders' room booking had been made by his South American colleagues, and Schneider was naturally given the Presidential Suite. Giselle momentarily felt a little uncomfortable: she had stayed in this room before, but not with Schneider. Attending a GFO football tournament in Rio twelve months ago she had spent the night with Christian Larsen in the same bed she was now going to share with her husband.

Her guilt didn't last. She was tired and wanted to lie down. Besides she had long ago stopped fretting about Schneider. He was so preoccupied with football and the GFO she felt quite justified playing around a little and having a good time. She enjoyed male company and the flirting that went with it, and yes, she had to admit she still enjoyed sex while Schneider, these days, showed no interest whatsoever.

Next day Helmut had an early start for a four-hour flight to La Paz, the headquarters of South American football. Giselle was still half-asleep when he left for what would be an overnight visit to Bolivia. She decided to have a light breakfast served in the suite, giving herself plenty of time before the arrival of her guide at 11 o'clock. Right on time she took a call from the desk and walked down two flights to meet him.

The concierge led Giselle across the lobby to where a man in his late 30s was standing, looking out of the window. He was wearing an elegant cream suit. He turned around as the concierge approached and extended his hand to Giselle, smiled and said: 'Welcome to Carnival city, Frau Schneider. I am delighted to meet you.' Giselle shook his hand and smiled back. She wasn't disappointed with her escort.

'I've been looking forward to today and tomorrow very much indeed,' she said

'I'm under strict instructions to cater for your every need... whatever that may be,' he replied in perfect German.

'I hope,' Giselle said coyly, 'I won't be too demanding. Please call me Giselle.'

'That will be my pleasure. And you must call me Gerald.'

Schneider's journey was thankfully uneventful. But it was another four hours of flying, and he was finding the whole trip tiring.

Schneider had been to the South American headquarters once before on the occasion of the official opening. Guests from all over the world had been invited in a no-expense-spared event hosted by the Bolivian President. There had been a light show and some impressive fireworks, and Schneider remembered how the modern, predominantly glass building had looked rather fine bathed in all the very colourful flashing lights.

Now in the bright midday sunshine, the headquarters looked just as impressive as Helmut's limousine drew up at the main entrance. As he stepped from the car he was met by his old friend Juan Gutierrez, President of the Alliance of South American Football Organisations, who walked forward from the doorway with a broad smile on his face.

'Welcome my friend.' Juan said as he hugged Schneider. 'It's good of you to come all this way to see us. Now come upstairs to the Boardroom where my colleagues are waiting to meet you. Let me lead the way.'

Juan introduced Schneider to his five South American colleagues, and an interpreter.

'We thought we might find an interpreter helpful for your presentation, Helmut. But first let us show you round the building, and then we will have coffee.'

Schneider found these ritual displays in the third world intensely tedious. He never bothered to show guests round the sparkling steel and glass Deutscher Fußball-Organisation building in Munich. He took German engineering and construction quality for granted and believed that visitors should too.

He was expected to admire endless display cabinets full of trophies, together with countless wall-mounted photographs of Juan and his colleagues meeting South American politicians, the majority of whom looked crooked to Schneider's eye.

The one face Schneider did quickly recognise was that of GFO President Christian Larsen who seemed to appear quite frequently in the photographs. At one point Juan drew Helmut's attention to an empty space in a cabinet.

He was laughing loudly. 'We had the English here a few weeks ago,' he explained. 'I told them this space is for my knighthood which I look forward to receiving!'

After the tour they gathered again in the Boardroom, and after seemingly interminable conversation over coffee, Juan invited Schneider to make his presentation.

Schneider realised he should not speak for too long. No sooner had he started than one of the Bolivian Vice Presidents dozed off. After a while he started to snore. Schneider pressed on regardless and was grateful when the other Bolivian Vice President managed to kick his colleague hard under the table.

At the end of his talk, the South Americans asked a few polite questions but it felt to Schneider that they were going through a familiar practice with any overseas visitor. A long way to come for so little, he thought.

It was not until later in the day that Schneider began to feel that his plans were coming to fruition. Juan and Schneider had agreed beforehand that they would have dinner together. At last, here was the chance for crucial discussions to take place about financial support from Germany for South American football countries.

'When you go back to Rio,' Juan said, 'we need you to have a discussion with the man who negotiates all our development finance arrangements. Indeed, he is also the person we asked to entertain your wife while you were with us. He is called Gerald. I know – a European name, but he was born and brought up in Rio and knows the city really well. He's expecting to see you on your return.'

Juan's warm manner didn't change as he provided Schneider with the information he was seeking.

'We would expect you to come to a lucrative development deal if you want us to support you,' he smiled.

It was just as well Schneider had chosen to stay the night in La Paz. Gerald had indeed been looking after Giselle in Rio. He had shown her a perfect view of the city from the Sugar Loaf. Then they had travelled by the single-track train to the statue of Christ the Redeemer. A late lunch on the Copacabana beachfront completed a happy day.

After a rest, Giselle insisted she was ready to sample the Rio nightlife.

'It's not my husband's type of thing,' she explained to Gerald over an early evening cocktail 'But I am sure it's yours Gerald,' she smiled.

Giselle was right, and after a wonderful evening together, Gerald brought her back to the hotel by taxi.

'We might as well put the Presidential Suite to good use,' she said. 'I hate to see luxury wasted.'

Chapter 40

A desperate man

Simon had never felt so powerless as in the days following withdrawal of the EFO World Cup bid. Disregarding the Sports Minister's instruction to let No 10 approve the official withdrawal statement before contacting the GFO, he telephoned Joe Kumpa's office in Brussels that evening. He didn't even bother to wait until his own office was empty. He had to act fast.

Kumpa listened carefully to Simon, who was trying his damnedest to disguise the panic in his voice. Simon was careful to explain that it was the Government that had made the decision for the EFO, and that Simon had argued brilliantly in an effort to counter their view, but that – sadly of course – the decision to move the vote until after Euro Cup 97 was a problem that even he couldn't deal with.

In the silence that followed, he reminded Joe Kumpa in as reasonable voice as he could manage, that of course Simon's investors had already paid out a large sum of money to fund four votes in support of the bid, and, as demanded by Joe, that money was now in a bank account in Panama.

Of course, Simon continued, if Joe wanted the deal to simply transfer to another bidder, and he could guarantee a similar return for Simon's investors, he would do all he could to keep them involved in the deal...

'Oh dear, Simon,' said Joe Kumpa at last. 'This is very sad news. For you.'

The blood drained from Simon's face. He didn't notice through the glass partition of his office as two of his campaign team politely signaled they were leaving for the evening. He struggled to control his voice and his thoughts.

'I'm sure it will all be fine, Joe. If I can just tell my people that nothing has changed despite England pulling out, they can still get their profit and keep my deal going... we can still contribute to Gerald's long-term plan. Nobody will notice the difference, and everyone will make money.'

Kumpa was silent. Simon was desperate and he knew his voice was showing it.

'Or... Joe I hate to admit defeat but... well if we can't use the money for my deal... I will need to return it to my money men.'

He paused, pleading silently for a response. He heard his voice weakening.

'Joe, these are very dangerous men. They'll hear tomorrow that the England bid is over. They'll expect me to return their money immediately... or... or... offer them another deal... a better deal... or at least the same. Please. Please Joe.'

Simon could feel his body shaking as he held the receiver.

'You have a saying in England I quite like,' said Joe Kumpa at last. 'You live by the sword... You know what I mean Simon? Oh my friend, you can't believe how much I would like to help you. But you see everything HAS changed. You and England are no longer in the team. Gerald likes to keep things nice and simple, and I agree with him. We can't have outsiders involved in our business, Simon. As long as you were running the EFO campaign, I could trust you as a colleague. But now? You've gone rogue Simon. Like an old elephant.'

'But the money... can I get the money back, Joe?' Simon managed to burst out.

'That's just not possible Simon. It's already been distributed you see. Didn't Gerald say: we don't have a returns policy – not like in your retail days.'

Simon could hear Kumpa's grin at the end of the phone. He said nothing. He barely registered that Kumpa had bothered to research his former career.

'And of course, you didn't have any kind of contract for the deal, Simon. I'm sure your friends with the money will understand how these things work.'

Kumpa let his points sink in.

'Oh and remember Simon, this conversation never took place.'

The phone line went dead.

Simon sat in his office, staring at the phone, alone with his scrambled thoughts. Why had he been so stupid? How had he got mixed up with people like this? What would the Arthurs do to him? How could he escape? Even...should he end it all now?

But that question was alien to Simon's personality, however bad his troubles. Simon was a survivor. He had always been a fighter. He knew he had to buy time. He had to find some way of putting pressure on Kumpa. He had to make the Arthurs brothers believe that their money was safe. He had to find a way out. But how? HOW...?

Chapter 41

On the run

Simon held his nerve. He played his role perfectly at the EFO Press conference announcing the bid withdrawal. He was careful to show no evidence that the Government's hand was behind the decision. He indicated suitable disgust for the behaviour of some England supporters at Euro 97, without providing the tabloids with too many headlines. On behalf of the bid team, he thanked the GFO for its support, he thanked the Government for its support, he thanked the Chairman and the EFO Council for their support.

As agreed, there were no questions after the statements were made. There was a hazy promise of one-to-one briefings after the dust had settled.

Nobody was surprised that Simon chose to absent himself from the office that day. It had been a tense time for everyone, and the strain was expected to be worst for him. Simon was not a heavy drinker, but he needed somewhere to be alone. There was a drinking club in the City he had heard about from one of his banking contacts. He got there at 11:30, and ordered a bottle of Chateau Lafitte. It was a wine that he had heard a GFO man order at the Ritz. At 1pm, he ordered a second bottle.

His mobile phone buzzed from time to time but he didn't look at the number.

He left the club at 4:00pm. His walk to the tube station was unsteady, and he realised he had eaten nothing all day. He found a steak house, and after thirty minutes he was feeling better. He chose to walk to Waterloo, to clear his head and have more time to think. It was nearly seven o'clock when he walked onto his platform to wait for the Barnes Bridge train.

Anna was in the kitchen, packing the children's lunch boxes for the next day. She looked at him with little affection.

'God you look awful, Simon. Are you alright? I heard the announcement. So it's all over.'

She began to spread children's clothes around the Aga.

'Oh, by the way, you've had God knows how many calls. Didn't you have your mobile with you? Honestly these football blokes are awful. Real gorblimey East-Ender bloke must have rung seventeen times. Said he'd see you later. Are you going out again Simon...? You might have told me, I've made fish pie...'

Simon went into the dining room. The bay windows looked out on the street. He had thought he had noticed something unusual as he came in. He turned off the lights and pulled the curtains aside an inch. There was a transit van parked outside. Simon could see two men in the cab. Both were wearing baseball caps.

'Yes, I've got to go out again,' he said. 'Where's my overnight bag? I've got a meeting in... Birmingham...'

Ten minutes later, Simon was opening the driver's door of his BMW. Starting the engine, he could see the two men in the van peering through the windscreen. They were too late. He lost them in traffic on the East Sheen Road.

Chapter 42

Facing the music

August 1997

Charlie Mason had warned Albert that the Press conference might be a bit lively. On the face of it, the event was quite straightforward: publicising an EFO initiative to encourage more girls in school to play football. It was a good news story. Money was being committed to support the training of school-based coaches, and centres of women's football excellence were being established all over the country.

The trouble was that this was the first appearance by the EFO Chairman since the announcement that England was pulling out of the bid to host the World Cup.

Charlie had discussed with Albert whether the EFO should put in a different man to chair the Press conference. But that wasn't easy. Simon Carslake, the Chief Executive, was just as involved in the withdrawal from the bid as Albert had been – even more so perhaps. He was also very hard to locate currently. He hadn't been seen in the office since the Press announcement about the bid, and rumours suggested he was being lined up for a major management role in another high-profile public-sector organisation.

As for the other Council members, Charlie was even more reluctant to risk them as the voice of the EFO on women's football than Albert. At least Albert had some experience with football journalists, and a number of them liked him personally.

Charlie had booked a conference room at the Grosvenor Hotel, big enough for the fifty or so football Press corps from newspapers, radio and television expected to attend. What he hadn't bargained for were the dozens of general news reporters. Twenty minutes before the 11:00 planned start, he was appalled to see that all the seats were occupied, and people wrestling with notebooks and cameras were squeezed against the walls on three sides of the room,

Albert was due to come onto the platform from an area behind the conference room, and Charlie whispered to him nervously: 'It's jam packed, I'm sorry. Not just football types. It's news people too. I'm afraid they're going to dwell on the yobbo fans thing. Some are going to ask whether we're a bunch of wimps for giving in to them...'

Albert didn't appear to be listening. In fact, since the EFO had pulled out of the World Cup bidding process, he didn't seem to care about much. That was fair enough. The Chairman and the EFO campaign team had put in a lot of effort to promote England's chances, and now it was all worthless. It was Charlie's job to manage EFO top brass in front of journalists whatever their mood. So if Albert didn't seem to care about the potential storm he faced as much as he should have done, the Press Chief was on his guard. That was fine.

But Charlie knew that his problem with Sir Albert ran much deeper. In fact, he had noticed a big change in Albert's behaviour many months before the recent decision to pull out of the bid. For a start, he had been surprised and disappointed that Albert had not come into the office after his flight back from the GFO Congress in Tokyo the previous year. It might have seemed trivial to some of Charlie's colleagues, but Charlie was always keen to get feedback from the Chairman after such a major event and had set aside an hour in the afternoon for that purpose.

When Albert's secretary, Eleanor, told Charlie that Albert was going home to Cornwall, he thought the decision very odd. He even asked Tony the driver what Albert had told him at the airport, but Tony had shrugged, muttered something about too much booze, but as always avoided saying too much to a PR man. Conversations with his passenger were confidential.

Charlie's antennae were twitching. He didn't like this at all. The Albert he was used to dealing with would have been seriously agitated by the presence of so many non-football journalists – and that's how Charlie would have preferred him.

He could then have offered to take the questions himself, spewed out the standard EFO line about why so-called fans' behaviour in Marseille gave the EFO no choice but to withdraw its bid, deny any interference from the government, and underscore the EFO's commitment to rooting out this evil that was bringing shame upon our great nation etc... and then let Albert talk about the girls football stuff.

But Albert showed no sign of panic, and certainly no willingness to let Charlie handle the difficult questions. He took to the stage and began to read the prepared brief about women's football. As Charlie had expected, within moments, there was a blaze of camera lights and a cacophony of voices from the room:

'Sir Albert, what's the latest on the World Cup bid?... Were you told to withdraw by Number 10?... Did the GFO order you to scrap the bid?... What do you say to the millions of football fans who accuse you of giving way to blackmail?... Sources in government say you were running out of money, is that true?... There are rumours in the city your Chief Executive was trying to raise millions to support your bid, is that right?... How much money has been spent on the bid?... Are you absolutely, definitely going to bid for the Euro Cup in 2005?... Why do you think that bid will be any more successful if England fans' behaviour is just as bad..?'

Albert was silent. Eventually the reporters realised that their shouted questions were achieving nothing. Then he spoke:

'Gentlemen,' he said. There were groans. 'Oh sorry, ladies... ladies and gentlemen.' More groans. 'We're not here today to go back over the history of the 2003 World Cup bid, and the reasons why we're withdrawing. We're here to talk about the future. The future of ladies playing football.' More groans, mainly from women journalists.

'*Women* playing football for God's sake, not *ladies*.' said one.

'Beg pardon?' said Albert, looking a little confused. Charlie whispered to him: 'You should call them women footballers not ladies.'

'Oh yes, women playing football. That's what we're here to talk about,' Albert said, his face reddening with a mix of embarrassment and irritation. 'And I suggest if you don't want to listen to what we've got to say on that, then you're wasting your time here, and the time of all the journalists who do want to hear about it.'

Sitting beside him, Charlie glanced nervously around the room. There were one or two shrill voices from the back: 'Come on Albert, you can't just talk about what you want...' Albert was silent. Gradually, a number of people began to look at their watches and leave. Charlie saw other EFO Press Officers handing them an information pack, but some of them made a big point of leaving it on a chair.

The next thing Charlie heard was a woman's voice. 'Susan Taylor, *Women's World*. Can you tell us how many girls are likely to benefit from your schools budgets?'

Albert looked down at his brief, and spotted the answer quickly. 'Yes, we think that our funds will support a full-time football coach dedicated to training girls in every local education authority... In addition, we're going to be running our own elite course for girls at the EFO Performance Centre in Cheshire...'

Over the next twenty minutes he took eight questions and answered them meticulously. Charlie had never seen him so calm and yet so enthusiastic for his subject. Thank God, he muttered to himself.

The questions began to tail off, and Charlie was about to wind up the Press conference, when he heard a confident voice from the back. He couldn't see the face, but he recognised with some dread the voice of Isla Payne, football correspondent from *The Chronicle*, one of the country's oldest newspapers.

'Is your policy on women's football the same as the GFO's?' she said.

There were confused looks amongst some of the journalists left in the room, particularly those with no interest in football politics. But Charlie spotted the danger straight away.

'Shall I explain what I mean?' Isla said. 'Last week a Board member of the Global Football Organisation – responsible for the development of football all over the world don't forget, and an organisation you're a member of – was recorded saying how much he liked women's football "as long as they wear tight kit".'

There were audible smirks amongst some of the male football journalists, while many of the women shook their heads in disgust. 'God...typical.' 'Really? That's appalling.'

Charlie leaned across Albert, offering to take the question for him, but Albert was in no mood for reticence. He cleared his throat.

'I do think that what we need to see is women's football attracting more men to go and watch it...' he began. Charlie closed his eyes in horror.

There was uproar from the floor. 'Oh well, you've said it all...' 'Did he really just say that?' 'Unbelievable...'

Then Isla's voice was clear again.

'So, what you're saying... what the EFO Chairman is saying is that all your investment in women's football is just to turn on men. Is that what you're saying? Women with tight tops attract male spectators, and that means more money for the EFO?'

Albert turned to Charlie, with a whisper: 'Who is that young lady?' Unfortunately, as Charlie recognised straight away, Albert's microphone was still turned on. Before Charlie could say anything, Isla was on her feet.

'This "young lady" - as you call me – has been covering football for three years now. You've seen me at most events in that time, but of course you wouldn't know me because I'm not one of your male CRONIES...'

'Now just a minute,' said Albert, raising his voice in a way that Charlie had never heard him before. He had a terrible sense that all Albert's good work was about to be undone. The Press conference was about to spiral into complete disaster.

'Maybe I didn't express myself very well. When I said that it's important that men need to start watching women's football I didn't mean for a moment that I want them to be titillated by what the ladies, the women, are wearing.

'No no no no no...' he said, his Cornish accent becoming more pronounced with every word. 'What do you take me for? I've got a daughter and three granddaughters. I don't want them ogled by men. EVER.

'What I meant was that everyone in this wonderful game of ours – women and men – need to give our women footballers every support we can. Our coaches need to give up their time to help girls in school learn their skills. We need all of you in the Media to sell women's football so we can see it on TV and hear about it on the radio. Above all else we need football spectators – and at the moment the truth is that most of those are MEN – to go along and watch, to fund the teams, to talk about incidents on the pitch, to help make women footballers our heroes...

'Now that's all I've got to say. Thank you for coming.'

As Albert left the stage, Charlie walked straight to where Isla was putting her notebook and pen in her briefcase.

'Was that alright, Isla? He does say things he doesn't mean to, sometimes,' Charlie began.

'Very interesting, Charlie, very interesting,' she smiled at him and left.

Chapter 43

Deadline for the Whistleblower

Frank Hedley, the News Editor of *The Chronicle,* was fed up with waiting for prima donna correspondents arriving late at his weekly news conference. The general reporters with significant news stories managed to get there on time; it was always the head-in-the-sky 'experts' who were a law unto themselves.

The Whistleblower was often the last to arrive. Hedley was particularly irritated this week because he was waiting for 500 words on the state of the EFO after pulling out of its World Cup bid. Left to himself he would have ignored the event completely. England were no longer bidding. Who cared if it was going to be Germany or Russia or Kazakhstan? Only a handful of world football watchers, and he didn't see many of them amongst readers of *The Whistleblower* column.

That column had started quite well, he admitted to himself. He liked the acid, cynical tone *The Whistleblower* adopted, and a number of other papers had picked up on its theme of immorality and gross vulgarity in the hallowed halls of world football, sometimes quoting *The Whistleblower* as a direct source. But since England had pulled out of the World Cup bid, it had definitely lost its appeal. It wasn't being quoted nearly as much, and readers' letters hardly mentioned it. The trouble was, as Frank knew only too well, his Editor was a big fan.

'Can we start, Frank, I've got a call booked for Three.'

'Just wait five minutes, Terry. Then we'll have to decide to lose the fucking column altogether this week.'

He heard his office door handle turning.

'Ah at last. I thought you'd forgotten all about us.'

Isla Payne took off her wet raincoat and hung it with her scarf behind the news Editor's door. 'Yes, sorry Frank, sorry everyone.'

Unlike most journalists covering football, Isla was in no way a fan of the game. She had become *The Whistleblower* by chance. Her Editor at *The Chronicle* liked the long tradition of diary pieces in national newspapers. He hated football, more even than any other game, and it appealed to him to appoint a brilliant young, female, investigative reporter who was also not a football fan, to seek out the kind of stories that average football reporters had no interest in or ability to uncover.

He hated big pompous institutions like the GFO and the EFO with too much money and power. He saw in Isla just the right kind of journalist to take them on.

Isla had successfully hidden *The Whistleblower*'s real identity for more than three years. Her cloak of anonymity had made her commentaries infuriating for the GFO. The Press Bureau couldn't guess where her information was coming from or where her stories might lead. Isla's growing reputation didn't cut much ice with her own newsroom however.

'Well, we needn't keep you long, love. Where's your piece?'

'I haven't actually finished it yet Frank. I've been working on it, but I just need to see someone to confirm a few things. Give me another twenty-four hours. Please.'

'Oh, for God's sake Isla. How many times? I need your copy now.'

'No you don't, Frank. You just need to know it's coming in time to put the paper to bed ... and it is. It'll be 1,500 words give or take. Now I've got to dash. I'll bring it to your desk later this afternoon, Frank.'

And with that, Isla grabbed her raincoat and scarf from the hook and exited Frank Hedley's office. She stopped at the last desk on the floor, which was unoccupied, and took out her Filofax. Then she dialled a number, and after a few moments, she spoke.

'Hello. Sir Albert? Nice to talk to you too. I just wondered if you'd be free for lunch tomorrow. Yes? Oh excellent. How about Le Gavroche. At one? I'll see you there. Oh no, I don't think you need a Press Officer with you, do you?'

Chapter 44

Cards on the lunch table

Albert took a taxi to Mayfair. He had never before lunched with a journalist without a Press Officer present. He wasn't sure why he had agreed to meet Isla today, but that was fine. Released from the pressures of England's World Cup bid campaign, he felt liberated – willing to do things and meet people he had never dared to before.

He was enjoying getting away from global football politics and back to grassroots issues in England. Talking yesterday about women's football and the need for coaches was a bit like the old days in Cornwall when he was arguing for scarce Council resources. That was a time when he truly felt he was changing things... helping the young... growing the game.

The Press conference yesterday had lifted his spirits. He was pleased he had braved the journalists on his own, without needing his Press Officer's help with difficult questions. He had meant everything he said about getting women and girls into football. And he was proud to explain his personal views as a dutiful father and grandfather: not the sexist old man everyone seemed to associate with football administrators.

Albert hadn't been aware of this journalist Isla Payne before yesterday. She was right to challenge him for that. She was a woman in a male football world, and Albert wouldn't have noticed her at other Press events. He would have assumed she wasn't important. A number two to a big-name newspaper man perhaps, learning the ropes.

He didn't know much about journalists, and what he did know made him wary. But he sensed that this girl was different from the hard-drinking, lazy old football hacks he had met over the years. It wasn't just that she was young; she seemed to be brave and honest and not likely to be beguiled or bought off by football's cynical PR games.

He liked the courage Isla had shown yesterday, taking him to task for talking clumsily. And when Albert had managed to explain to the journalists how much he really did care about spreading his love for the game across all genders and ages, he was almost certain he saw a little nod of her head and smile of approval. He liked that too.

But perhaps there was another reason why Albert Lewis accepted his lunch invitation.

Albert was still troubled by the awful rumours he had heard about global football and the GFO. He had shared with Monica the accusations. She was sympathetic but told him to be careful how he acted on them, and he had so far kept his counsel. Since the England World Cup bid was pulled, he had less reason now to be in contact with GFO members, so it was easier to distance himself from the likes of Larsen and Kumpa.

But he knew that in all conscience, he had to deal with these stories somehow, some day. He couldn't allow the game he loved to be disgraced by men who were abusing their power and raiding the resources that should be helping boys and girls in the poorest football nations of the world. And now he was free, what better time to act.

As the taxi grumbled up Park Lane, he wondered whether this would be an opportunity to share his secrets and suspicions, to talk to someone who knew the world of football, someone who might listen sympathetically to what still seemed to him extraordinary tales of vice. Someone who seemed to care for the truth, and was committed to pursuing it?

When Albert approached the young woman already seated at the table, his heart sank a little. He hardly recognised her. She seemed older than when she spoke out so bravely yesterday. She looked tired, and there was no warmth in her features. He noticed she was wearing a lot of makeup. That disturbed him. Did she think he was the kind of bloke who needed to be enticed? It made him doubt his judgement, uncertain how much he could trust her, and the first ten minutes at the table were awkward.

Isla Payne kept looking – as subtly as she could – at her watch. Ah, he thought, so she had much more on her mind than lunch with him. He immediately felt hurt and let down.

As the waitress collected his empty soup bowl, there was silence at the table. Albert suddenly put both hands flat on the table and addressed her loudly.

'Look here... is it Miss or Mrs Payne?'

Isla looked up, surprised by Albert's directness. 'Oh, um, Ms Payne I suppose or Miss if you like. Isla...'

'Well, the thing is, you seem to be in a bit of a hurry to get out of here, and if that's the case I won't delay you. Thank you very much, my starter was very nice.'

He began to get up from his chair. Isla was shocked. She didn't quite know what to say, but she understood immediately why he was cross.

'Oh please. Look, I'm so sorry. Please don't go.' She put her hand on his arm. Albert was surprised by the physical contact and sudden change in her manner.

'Look...' She shook her head in embarrassment. 'Look, let me be absolutely honest. Yes, I am against a deadline today. The thing is,' she paused to gather her words, 'the thing is I think I've got a very big story, and I was just kind of hoping you would help to confirm it.'

She paused again.

'But no, that isn't fair on you. My story is all about fraud in high places, and it's obviously got nothing to do with you, Sir Albert.'

She smiled at him with warmth, and Albert felt she was being genuinely contrite.

'Please,' she said. 'Have another glass of wine.'

Albert slowly sat down and let her fill his glass.

'Oh God, I should explain,' she said. 'The reason I invited you for lunch was actually because I was rather impressed with you at the Press conference yesterday. I'm sorry, that sounds very patronising – and not very believable with the way I've started.'

She ran her hand through her dark curls. She seemed younger again, thought Albert.

'Yes, I was impressed, Sir Albert, and I have to say I'm not easily impressed, and most of your EFO colleagues are not so... impressive.' She smiled again and offered him a cigarette.

Albert refused it, but he gave a modest little smile back.

'Well,' he began, 'I try to do my best. And so do all my colleagues Miss er... Isla. But it's not easy for some of us old chaps to change.' He broke off, not wanting to sound like a fuddy-duddy.

'Anyway.' He took a sip of his wine. 'That's very nice what you said about me. Very nice indeed.'

They sat in self-conscious silence for a few moments.

'But you didn't invite me just because you thought I was a decent bloke, surely?'

She gave a little laugh.

'No. Well the thing is... I *am* working on this story... and I'm sort of stuck... and my copy deadline is this afternoon... and I wondered yesterday if you could help me... and I kind of asked you on the off chance... I honestly didn't think you would accept... on your own... and now you're here... and I realise that you can't know anything about my story... so I've been a bit silly.'

She lit her cigarette as her voice trailed off. She inhaled hard before continuing more decisively.

'Anyway, Sir Albert,' she said brightly. 'Let's forget my deadline. And let's have a good lunch. I've got another piece I can do quickly this afternoon. It's quite good. I'll save my big story to next week – I know nobody else will touch it.' She smiled again. 'Why would anyone touch it? Most of my Press colleagues have got a vested interest in keeping the GFO gravy train on the tracks. Oh shit...'

Albert knew how secretive reporters were about their exclusive stories. Yet she had just told him the subject she was working on. The GFO. Was this fate?

'Well,' he said slowly. 'While we're here, why don't we see if I can confirm any of your story.'

And then as an afterthought, he said: 'Don't worry, I'm not going to blab about it to *The Whistleblower* or anyone.'

Isla spluttered, holding her hand to her mouth.

'Oh good God, Sir Albert, that's so funny. Of course there's no reason why you should know... I *am The Whistleblower.*'

'You... but I thought...'

'Yes, of course, everyone thinks *The Whistleblower* is a man,' she laughed. 'Isn't it amazing that I've got away with it?'

Albert was intrigued to see Isla relax in the pleasure of the moment.

'Oh there are plenty of GFO people know me as just a reporter at all the Press conferences,' she continued, 'and of course I file a lot of basic stories to put them off the scent. But none of them have got a clue that it's me writing *Whistleblower* stuff.

"D'you know – one of the guys in our office even told a PA sports reporter once but he couldn't believe it! Thought it was a wind up! Can you imagine – the very idea that a woman might report on football politics!' She giggled then composed herself and turned her face to Lewis.

'Look, please don't tell anyone. There aren't many advantages in being a woman journalist but having an element of surprise can be useful. Mind you, I bet Larsen and co would find it a lot easier to refute *Whistleblower* stories if the world knew they were written by a woman!'

She reddened slightly. 'Sorry, Sir Albert, I'm afraid I can be even more disrespectful about the GFO's top men than about your colleagues at the EFO.'

Albert was barely listening. His mind was racing. *The Whistleblower*! He remembered the odd *Whistleblower* diary pieces he had heard about from other people. Describing GFO gambling and womanising. Talking about Larsen's age and how he carefully won members' loyalty. Weren't there even bizarre accounts of 'buying' votes before the President's election?

Albert didn't read the newspapers that much and certainly not *The Chronicle*. It was a bit highbrow for him. The Press Office sent him cuttings, but he usually ignored them. Simon Carslake would mention anything affecting the EFO bid, and Charlie Mason in the press office would brief him if the story was important enough.

But he knew very well that other GFO Board members were worried about *The Whistleblower* diary. 'Who is this *Whistleblower* guy, Albert?' they would say. 'Surely your Press people have found him by now? Obviously someone with a grudge. Have you offended anyone Albert?'

So these *Whistleblower* pieces weren't the outpourings of an embittered, inebriated hack as everyone had assumed. They were painstakingly and intelligently gathered insights, researched and validated by a young woman reporter who had penetrated a highly secret GFO network of middle-aged men. And all the time she had been reflecting the very same malaise that stared him in the face from his privileged insider position, but he hadn't even noticed. Albert felt real shame at his ignorance and his indolence. His voice was a halting whisper, and his rheumy eyes glistened with emotion.

'I'm sorry... Isla. I didn't take your pieces seriously. I didn't understand how much you knew. You see...'

He paused and looked down at the tablecloth.

'I could have told you so many things. I know stories... information... accusations about the GFO. Awful things, Isla. About money. Big money. And cheating at votes. And people making a cut from development deals...'

Isla smiled weakly. She was never good at disguising her feelings.

'Thank you, Sir Albert,' she said. 'I'd love to hear your gossip one day. But let me be completely frank with you. I've spoken to so many GFO members who have stories they want to tell.

All interesting. Some of them for sale of course... but I can't use anything unless I've seen or heard the evidence directly, or unless I have a source who is prepared to go on the record. I'm afraid that puts an end to an awful lot of enthusiastic whistle blowers... Now, how about some dessert.'

'No,' Albert said firmly. 'This is important, Isla. Try me. You said you've got a hell of a story about the GFO. Let me see if I can confirm it.'

She looked wary, but there was a determination in Albert's eyes that she found hard to resist. She decided she had nothing to fear from this gentle man.

She described her story. A deal had been struck between Russia and Germany to ensure Russia would win the 2003 World Cup bid at the next GFO Board meeting. She understood that although Germany was behaving as if it was seeking to win, travelling the world to garner support, it was actually priming its supporters to switch to Russia when the voting took place.

Isla believed that Germany was doing this because the Deutscher Fußball-Organisation knew it couldn't win another bid so soon after hosting the World Cup eight years before, so a deal had been struck for Russia to have a clear field in winning the World Cup. And in return for Germany's help, Russia would help Germany win the vote for the 2005 Euro Cup.

Then she added something else. She said that the arrangement between Germany and Russia was not the 'big story'. Everyone knew that scheming between World Cup campaign teams and helping each other to win had happened many times before, even though it was officially forbidden by the GFO.

No. The real story, the story that she believed could be career-ending for a number of people, was this...

She looked at Albert carefully and stubbed out her cigarette.

Russia was spending millions of dollars to bribe the GFO's leaders to support its bid, she said quietly.

She looked into Albert's eyes before she went on. He held her gaze in silence.

In a hushed voice she said she had evidence that significant payments were being made into the President's private bank accounts by the Russians. She had seen facsimiles of cheques. She had seen a list of Russian names. She had researched those names. Interpol contacts had confirmed that many of them were criminals engaged in a range of serious activities all over the world.

There was no doubt in her mind that Christian Larsen was one of the most corrupt men ever to head a world organisation.

As a journalist, it was a red-hot story, she told Albert. As far as she knew, nobody else had access to the financial information she had been given, and nobody else was investigating Larsen's affairs to her level of detail. She was determined that her story should be told, but she knew – as ever – that a few photocopies of financial accounts were not enough to stand her story up. She needed endorsement from a leading GFO man before *The Chronicle* would publish it.

Albert listened intently as Isla talked. He was sure now he would tell her everything he knew. It wouldn't be easy.

Could he confirm the Germany and Russia 'agreement'? One of his nightmares was his apparent collusion with Germany and Russia in Helmut Schneider's hotel room at the Ritz Hotel in Paris two years ago. He was too ashamed of that discussion to explain the details to Isla, but he was in no mood to deny the truth.

He took a deep breath and acknowledged forcefully and convincingly to Isla that he had personal knowledge that the two organisations had been talking about a collaboration.

On the other hand, he couldn't confirm Isla's allegations about Larsen's money making, he said, but he told her he wasn't in the least surprised. He had heard many stories about the President's personal wealth, and he knew enough about the sort of money said to be washing around in world football circles that her story certainly rang true to him.

Albert then told her about the first time he had heard of Kumpa's financial dealings – from a local business crony in Yora nearly two years before, and about the threats he'd received from Kumpa himself in Tokyo if EFO development money for Africa was not paid directly into Kumpa's bank account.

He was reluctant at first to discuss Larsen's claims about his own Chief Executive because he didn't know whether to believe them himself. But Isla had trusted him with her information; surely he could trust her with his, however inaccurate it was.

So he described how Larsen had alleged that Simon Carslake was attempting to buy votes to secure the England World Cup bid. And he repeated Greg Turner's words at Wembley just a few months ago: how GFO rumours claimed that Simon was increasingly seen as helping Joe Kumpa with his financial schemes.

Albert then explained to Isla that he found these accusations implausible. He didn't pretend that he liked Simon personally, but he was a man who worked closely alongside him and led a committed young campaign team. Albert thought it highly unlikely that Simon would risk his reputation as a successful administrator by doing anything fraudulent. Besides, Albert said he believed the GFO's leadership was quite capable of falsely tarnishing his English organisation in order to scare him off their trail.

When he finished, Albert sat nervously for a moment, toying with his napkin. He had never before spoken these words aloud to anyone, and he wondered whether it all sounded like baseless gossip to Isla Payne.

'I hope to God none of it's true,' he said a little lamely.

Isla stared at him without saying a word. Albert heard her breathing heavily through trembling lips.

'What is it?' he said.

'Are you sure?' Isla whispered. 'Are you sure about what you remember?'

Albert Lewis looked puzzled, but before he had a chance to answer, Isla was explaining her question.

'I'm sorry. That's so rude of me. It's just that I have to be sure... absolutely sure. It's just that what you've told me makes me think that something else I heard – something that seemed to me too preposterous for words... even for the GFO... might actually be true.'

She waved away a waiter, hovering to take an order for dessert. Her quivering fingers reached into a pack on the table, and she lit another cigarette with difficulty.

'You see... you see I'd also heard that World Cup votes are up for sale. And yes, Sir Albert, I've also been told that Simon Carslake has been trying to raise funds to buy those votes. But it's worse even than that. I've also been told that sometimes votes get sold and resold for a profit throughout the bidding campaign. And I've heard that if Carslake had bought Board members' votes, Kumpa would have helped him sell them on to another campaign team at a hugely inflated price.'

She didn't look at Albert, but she sensed his shock.

'So Sir Albert, I'm afraid your rumour is probably true. Carslake is working with Kumpa. If you'd still been bidding, your Simon Carslake could have made millions for them both... by selling on votes to support another bid team!'

The two sat quietly. Isla was thinking, trying to calculate what all this meant for her and her newspaper.

Albert's mind was in turmoil. He was trying to come to terms with the truth he had never before been able to accept: Simon was a traitor to the EFO, to his own campaign team, and to his country. How could this be happening?

Isla spoke first.

'Sir Albert, all this... It's astounding. Nothing less. It could blow the Global Football Organisation apart...'

He nodded slowly and sadly.

'But you know... I can't use it,' she said quickly.

She waited for him to respond, but he was still deep in thought. She knew she had to make him understand the reality of the situation.

'Sir Albert... everything you have learned... where's the proof? Do you have recordings of any of these conversations... with your man in Yora, with Kumpa, or with Larsen? Is there evidence that Simon Carslake has siphoned off funds from the EFO to pay for these votes? Do you know any of his financial contacts? Anyone who would go on record as providing him with money?'

She answered her own question.

'No, of course you haven't. You see, we can't take on an organisation like the GFO unless we're completely waterproof. They're far too powerful. They'll scare the living daylights out of everyone – my Editor, the management, the owner. *The Chronicle* simply won't touch this story because the GFO will sue our balls off. At very least they'll get a gagging order to keep us quiet. And once the World Cup vote is decided next month, nobody's going to give a fuck about a dead story.'

She waved her hand briefly to excuse her language.

'That's the reality. I'm sorry,' she said hopelessly.

'I know,' said Albert. For a moment, Isla thought he hadn't been listening properly. But then he turned to her, with eyes blazing.

'I know. So there's only one thing to do. We're going to have to... I'm going to have to... confront the GFO Board with what we know. And it's going to have to happen in Brussels next month, Isla, before the vote happens. Will that be enough for you to write your story?'

Isla lit another cigarette. She couldn't bare this. It hurt her to tell this brave man there would be no immediate rewards.

'No Albert. It won't be enough for you to speak to the Board. It's a private meeting. How can I report something I'm not a part of.'

She looked at him carefully. He looked lost. Then she spoke again.

'There is another way. It could be enough if you let me interview you immediately after the meeting. Confirm everything you've said to them, and everything they've said in reply. On the record. If we put you at the centre of this story... a respected voice... a man who sits on the top committee of the GFO... a man with an impeccable personal reputation. It might just work.'

She paused.

'But I have to tell you. If you do this, your GFO career will be over. Maybe your EFO career. There will be all kinds of lies and recriminations against you... and your family. Your life will be hell, perhaps for years...'

Albert stretched his arms behind his head. His voice was firm.

'I will do what I have to do,' he said with no emotion.

Chapter 45

Lost in translation

September 1997

It was 8th September 1997, the evening before one of those GFO events when the world would stop still to watch and listen. The furious rounds of lobbying were finally coming to an end. Twenty-five members of the GFO's Board would tomorrow decide which country was going to host World Cup 2003.

The atmosphere around GFO Headquarters in Brussels was tense, even though everyone – from Board members and officials, to journalists and film crews, to observers from the world-wide football community – seemed convinced that the Russians were going to win. The Press came from all over the globe. No self-respecting football journalist would miss this occasion whether or not their own country was bidding. The journalists, the photographers and the radio and television reporters would all make sure they didn't miss a thing.

Media commentators had been arriving all day, and having sorted out their GFO accreditation many of them were relaxing in the bars and lounges of the conference hotel. In one corner of a bar, a few GFO staff were talking excitedly about what the next day would entail. In the brasserie restaurant a group of football writers reminisced about previous World Cups, telling stories that most of them had heard before, but which still generated a good deal of laughter.

Once the television reporters had done their pieces to camera and the print journalists had filed their stories, they settled down to discuss what each had said in their pre-event reports.

'I've been to more of these things than I care to remember,' announced a white haired French journalist, 'but I've never known so many firm predictions in favour of one candidate. Five candidates in play, but everyone thinks Russia is a banker of a bet.'

'Quite right *mon brave*,' slurred a British freelancer at the same table. 'Whenever I've got close on the football fixed odds, it's always the banker lets you down. Just as your carefully crafted accumulator is about to shell out the money then the top team loses at home to the fucking bottom one.'

'Too right, Dave,' said another man at the same table, 'but I'm pretty damn sure the Russians have got this sewn up. Schneider is playing a longer-term game. It's obviously in his personal interests to help the Russians. It'll help him get the Presidency when Larsen goes, no question.'

'Well maybe,' said the Frenchman, 'but it might make his Presidential election chances even better if his country is hosting the 2003 World Cup.'

The men at the table paused for thought.

'Then of course there's the little matter of this so-called gentleman's agreement,' he continued. 'Ironic title don't you think? Can't say the word gentleman is the first I think of when Messrs Baskin and Schneider are mentioned!' The men all laughed.

'Oh well, let's see what it all amounts to tomorrow,' came a voice from the end of the table. 'Same again all round?'

It wasn't just the journalists who were firmly predicting a Russian victory. Most people around the world who were professionally involved in football, or even interested outsiders, seemed to have assumed that Russia's victory was a formality.

However, all elections have the potential for upsets, and the GFO had a particularly good record for delivering the unexpected.

After all, the Russians had been firm favourites from the start of campaigning some two years earlier. To the casual onlooker that might have seemed surprising given the presence of Germany in the running. What was commonly believed amongst journalists however was that the leader of the Russian campaign, Alexei Baskin and the wily German campaign leader Helmut Schneider had done a deal. Russia would get Germany's support to host World Cup 2003 while Germany, too recently the host of the GFO World Cup competition to make its bid credible, would be supported by Russia to host Euro Cup 2005. This deal, while it had no official status, had become known as the gentleman's agreement.

The story passing between sports desks was that the two men saw themselves as big beasts in the GFO jungle, who could pretty much get their own way if they cooperated with each other. Schneider and Baskin were said to be irritated by England's decision to bid for World Cup 2003. There were rumours, which no journalist dared to submit for publication, that the English had reneged on an agreement with Germany and Russia to stay out of the bidding. Nobody could be found to confirm or deny this story.

Despite all these uncertainties, however, Russia was generally thought to be the nailed-on winner.

In fact, it was only the most assiduous students of GFO campaigning who could detect any weakness in that assumption. There were some who had expected Germany to withdraw from the contest in order to assure Russia of its good intent. There were even a few reporters who described deep discontent in the Bundestag at the suggestion that the Deutscher Fußball-Organisation would allow its bid to be trumped by the Russians.

Helmut Schneider was well aware that these murmurings were unsettling for his Russian ally. That evening, sitting together in Schneider's suite at the gloriously art-deco Hotel Leopold, Baskin was unable to disguise his nerves, and Schneider was doing his best to reassure him.

'Look,' Schneider said softly, 'we both know that the only serious question is what happens to the Brazilian vote when Brazil gets knocked out. You've been very generous to the South Americans, Alexei, so I don't see the problem. They've all said they'll back you after Brazil, and nobody expects Brazil to get beyond the second round. Here...' He handed the Russian a large glass of brandy.

'And Alexei, come on, we're doing all we can to make sure of the South Americans, aren't we? They would hardly have the nerve to join us this evening if they weren't backing Russia.'

Schneider smiled broadly and clinked his glass with Baskin's.

'OK, OK, I guess I just don't trust these dagos, Helmut, that's all,' sighed Baskin. 'They say one thing, they promise everything, and Christ knows what they're thinking. But you're right, I'll certainly be a lot happier once I've looked them in the eyes.'

Two hours later, Schneider took the hotel lift to the lobby, to meet the interpreter recommended to him by the Laundryman.

Schneider was anxious that the interpreter understood exactly what was expected of him at this evening's cocktail reception in Schneider's suite. He didn't know or care whether the interpreter was an academic linguist or had learned his skills in international trade of some kind. He simply needed to know that the man was competent, experienced, and discreet.

'We have a group of South Americans at this meeting,' he said to the interpreter. 'They only speak Spanish and Portuguese between them. My colleague at the meeting is Russian. He also speaks English but not a word of Spanish or Portuguese. I've explained to you what the meeting's for.'

He paused, waiting. 'Well, tell me. I need to know you understand.'

The interpreter nodded.

'I understand you will be asking the South American gentlemen to indicate their voting intentions tomorrow. And this is of... particular interest... to your Russian friend.'

Schneider stared at him with cold eyes.

'Yes, that's right. And remember, whatever the South Americans say in response – and I mean what*ever* they say – you will interpret it as support for the Russian bid. D'you understand?'

The man's nod was barely perceptible, but Schneider accepted it.

'And remember, I also speak Spanish and Portuguese. I will listen and alert you if I want you to stress something, or even correct what has been said, but I want my contribution to be minimal.'

The interpreter's face expressed no emotion.

'Good. And if you and I need to speak in confidence, I suggest we talk in Chinese. That is one of your languages, right? And it's one of mine too.'

He smiled. 'I'm pretty damn sure no one else in the meeting speaks a word of it. Is that all clear?'

'Yes, it is,' the interpreter said

'We talked about a thousand Euros for your fee. Well, if all goes well, I'll double that.'

Then Schneider led the man to the lift.

Chapter 46

Things change

The following morning, at ten past seven, Albert was trying to find a grey sock. He had another pair of black socks with him, but he liked the dark grey ones he'd been given by Monica's sister last Christmas. They had a bit of thickness to them, and they stopped his shoes rubbing his bunions too badly.

His choice of socks might have seemed trivial. But Albert knew that if he was going to be as brave as he wanted to be today, he would need all the help he could get. He certainly didn't want his feet to be troubling him.

He found the other grey one eventually. Monica must have put it with his underpants. He breathed a sigh of relief.

His mind went forward to the GFO Board meeting due to start in less than seven hours. He had spent a number of sleepless nights worrying about what he would say. He had once looked in his address book for Isla Payne's telephone number but was too ashamed at the thought of telling her he couldn't go through with their plan to expose the GFO.

He was so right to be doing this, Albert thought, but it wasn't going to be easy. His secrets struck at the heart of the beautiful game of football... the people's game... the game he had devoted his life to.

He was going to launch a devastating attack on football's global rulers. Revealing what he knew would end his career of course. He knew he would cause confusion and pain to football friends and closest family. But his was the responsibility, and his alone.

When he had declared to Isla just a few weeks ago his intention to 'confront the GFO Board' in Brussels that day, he hadn't formed a clear plan for what he would achieve.

He had carefully practised a few statements about the GFO, reflecting his own outrage at the iniquities he had heard from so many sources. He had convinced himself that once he had made other Board members aware of the appalling truth about their precious Organisation, there would be a general storm of protest at its leadership, and strong support for his own brave stance.

As a result, he imagined President Larsen would be embarrassed and helpless at the shock of his attack. Perhaps the President wouldn't be overthrown that very day, but surely there would be instant demands from GFO colleagues for an enquiry at least.

And the reactions of members would be enough for *The Chronicle* to present a detailed and cataclysmic story to the world – adding Isla's carefully researched evidence to his own account of today's events, provided to her as they had agreed immediately after he had launched the biggest thunderbolt ever to hit the world of football. The plan was hatched. Now all he had to do was activate it.

At five to two that afternoon, there were twenty-five members of the Board assembled in the GFO Council Chamber, including President Larsen who would chair the meeting.

There was an air of anticipation in the room as the men filled out their ballot papers for round one. After that, they just needed to wait patiently for the outcome. Joe Kumpa chuckled and nudged Greg Turner who was sitting next to him... 'and the 2003 World Cup is sold to the highest bidder which is....' but then he was silent with the rest of the Committee as the President was handed the result of the first ballot by the GFO staff member responsible for supervising the count.

Larsen stood at the podium on the horseshoe stage, and pitched his voice so it could be heard by the oldest men present:

'Gentlemen, I'm able to announce the outcome of the first round of voting for hosting the 2003 World Cup tournament.

'As we all know, shortly before the vote, England withdrew its candidacy, leaving five countries in the contest. Votes cast for these five candidates were as follows: China 2 Morocco 5 Germany 5 Brazil 5 Russia 7. There was one abstention.'

There were murmurs of interest, though not of great surprise. At this early point, the voting pattern gave few clues to the final outcome. What nobody was expecting was an intervention from the long table of members.

'Mr President!' The delegates looked puzzled. The GFO's meetings were orderly affairs. They all knew the rules.

'Mr President, can you not see, this voting is a sham,' Albert continued, his voice straining with tension. 'I...I...I have heard terrible things about how some campaign teams have tried to buy votes. And how Board members have been promised all kinds of benefits for their support. Mr President, this voting process...' he paused, more to draw nervous breath than to create drama '...is unfair. It is...CORRUPT.'

Albert looked nervously around him, waiting for those looks of surprise to become gasps of awe. But as more and more members recognised his voice, the mood of the room began to change. Some of those who knew him swapped glances. Some looked concerned, others grinned or winked at each other, while still others shook their heads in disgust.

'Oh, do shut up Lewis,' said one voice to his left. 'Just because England couldn't get its act together, don't wreck it for those who have.'

There were a few cheers and laughs at this, but most of the men remained silent, appalled by this hectoring exchange. The GFO's sense of its own decorum ran deep. Many of its members understood that this was a moment that required self-discipline. For Albert, however, the GFO's image was of no concern anymore.

He had to make Board members understand what he was saying, what he was feeling.

'Wreck it?!,' Albert responded as he got to his feet, his face reddening as he waved his papers towards the Board member who had taunted him. Members strained to catch a glimpse of the Englishman down the table, but nobody made a move towards him.

'How can I be wrecking something that's already worthless? How can YOU – WE all – continue to take part in this fraud? Do you not understand what's going on? In all our names? Do you not hear the lies? Or the promises made in return for your votes? Or see money changing hands? Do you think cheating is the only way for candidates to win in our great football game?'

If Albert was expecting these accusations to stir Board members, he was terribly wrong. A couple of men were sniggering. He heard a voice in American English: 'Oh for God's sake. Who you been listening to, you old fool? How many times have we heard this stuff. Get the hell outa here...'

Again, murmurs around the table indicated a confusion of opinions. Some members hated this undignified shouting, while one or two brayed their agreement with the American. But one thing was clear: there was no support for Albert. No sympathy. No interest in what he was saying. Albert knew it.

'Gentlemen. We should be ashamed.' His voice cracked, and he slumped back in his chair. 'We should be ashamed,' he said again, barely audibly.

There was silence. No protocol had been devised for such a challenge. Faces were turned towards Larsen. He got down from the podium and stood behind Albert's chair. Albert felt the overshadowing presence of the President.

'Gentlemen, I always felt it was unfortunate to hold this meeting after lunch...'

He waited for the laughter to die down.

'May I remind you,' President Larsen said more seriously. 'There is a system in place to report any wrong-doing. There's an appeals procedure.'

Then he paused, considering carefully and quickly his options for damage limitation. At present, Larsen thought to himself, Albert Lewis merely represents an irritation at the meeting, some embarrassment to Larsen's leadership in front of his GFO tribe, perhaps. And information that would find its way to the Press Room outside, he knew.

But this was an unruly outburst... probably caused by alcohol... This is not a major story. Not unless he failed to manage it.

In a moment, Larsen knew what he had to do. He must depersonalise this exchange with Albert. If it began to look like a spat between the GFO President and the Chairman of the EFO, British journalists would create havoc. All those criticisms of England's bid disaster, all those cartoons of the EFO 'dunderheads' mocked for caving in to hooligans and withdrawing from the campaign, would be quickly forgotten if the English nation was at war with the rest of the world.

Larsen chose his next words with deliberation.

'Gentlemen, my message is to everyone in this room. Your GFO is proud of its honesty and integrity. I know I can speak for every member of our Board when I say that. Perhaps it is naïve of us to assume that everyone in our organisation has the same degree of confidence. And perhaps it is time to remind ourselves that your GFO maintains the very strictest governance procedures to protect ourselves from any attempts to exploit our famous openness and trust.

'So, gentlemen, I say this without hesitation. If ANYONE believes they have evidence of malpractice of any kind in the dealings of the GFO, it is their duty to bring that evidence to me personally. And I can assure you that if I receive ANY information of this kind, I will not hesitate to act on it.'

There was spontaneous applause, and sporadic cheers. Larsen knew he had won the day.

Albert didn't move from his chair. He couldn't. His whole body ached with tension. He was paralysed with a sense of failure. The men beside him half raised themselves from their seats so he could get past them. Their faces were blank: no hatred, no contempt, but no compassion either. They just wanted him to leave and glanced at each other in confusion that he was still there.

Albert was on his own. The club was closing ranks.

He didn't know for sure how many Board members knew as much as he did. Four or five surely. Ten perhaps. More? But Larsen's shameless denial of his accusations, and confident invitation to any other critics of GFO to come forward, had somehow made things safe for everyone again. If Board members stuck together, Albert's little storm would pass and things would get back to normal. After all, there would be new bidding teams coming along in a very few years, and there would be new financial opportunities to enjoy... more luxury gifts, more free trips and five-star hotels.

Larsen was pleased with his handling of the affair. He had been calm under fire, as always. And he wasn't worried that Albert would give him any more problems. If Albert wanted to come to him with evidence of rule-breaking activities, Larsen would deal with it satisfactorily. Voting appeals processes always took time – many years perhaps. The GFO was very good at dealing with awkward issues. Wrap them up in bureaucracy, bury them in procedures... that was the answer. And Larsen had dealt with more difficult and clever men than Albert Lewis.

The man from the south-west of England would have to learn or he would have to go. Silly man, getting on the wrong side of the system. Larsen smiled imperceptibly and regained his control of the meeting.

'I have given you the result of the first round, and China with the lowest number of votes must now drop out, leaving Morocco,

Germany, Russia and Brazil to contest round two. I will ask GFO officials to distribute a new ballot paper.'

As the official reached Albert, he pushed the ballot paper away. 'I abstain,' he said to the official in a loud voice. 'Please record my abstention.' The GFO man nodded his understanding.

The sound of Albert's voice set a new buzz around the table. Greg Turner got up from his seat and stood beside Albert. Albert hardly noticed him.

'Albert, Albert, my friend!' Greg whispered. 'Come on, I think you should go. Take a time out. Why don't you go walk round the block? Make you feel better. Give me a call later. We'll have dinner ok?'

Albert felt Turner's arm almost lifting him out of his chair and through the door. Turner gave him an encouraging pat on the back, but as Albert turned to thank him for his sympathetic words, the Canadian had disappeared back into the Council Chamber.

A hush fell across the room as the last ballot paper was distributed, and the Board members once more got down to business. The President gave out his instructions. 'Please complete your ballot paper for round two by marking with a cross which of the four countries is your preferred choice for hosting the 2003 World Cup. When you've done this, fold your ballot paper and hand it to one of the GFO officials in the centre of the room.'

Greg Turner nudged Joe Kumpa and offered his expert advice. 'If you ask me, and I'm sure you're about to,' Turner said with a smile, 'Morocco will be the next to go. I imagine they've got your four African votes behind them, and at least one of the Arabs in the Asian confederation. I reckon Brazil can get at least one more than that, even if they've relied a bit too much on the old Brazil glamour.' He laughed aloud as he sambaed in his chair. 'The three South Americans are backing them anyway, and so are my two guys in central and North America.'

'Oh Greg... you're not a Brazil supporter?' enquired Kumpa, wide eyed.

'Come on Joe, give me a break,' laughed Turner. 'You know I like a bit of old-world European style – well, German style to be precise. My old friends from Germany have been very generous.'

Just then, two officials handed a folded sheet of paper to the President, who immediately addressed the men at the table.

'I'm now able to announce the outcome of the second round of voting. Votes were cast as follows: Morocco 5, Brazil 6, Germany 6, and Russia 7. There was one abstention. As Morocco was the country with the lowest number of votes, Morocco must now drop out of the contest, and we will move on to round three with Brazil, Germany and Russia still in contention. There will be a ten-minute adjournment for you to discuss amongst yourselves before we hand out the ballot paper for round three.'

Alexei Baskin rose from his seat and moved quietly across the room to compare notes with Helmut Schneider. 'So far so good,' Baskin said. 'I guess this is where we kiss goodbye to the Brazilians. Then we have the more delicate business of turning Brazilian supporters into Russian ones. But the South Americans seemed ok last night didn't they?'

'Yes,' Schneider said, hesitating slightly. 'Perhaps less so when I saw them over breakfast. It seems German corporate largesse may have turned their heads a little.'

'German largesse?' Alexei exclaimed. 'What about Russian largesse? They've had everything they wanted for months now.'

'I know, I know, but Alexei I can't control every German car, bank or technology company that wants to invest in South America,' Helmut replied.

He looked carefully at Alexei's face. His features were hardening perceptibly.

'Let's not panic, Alexei, let's speak to them again in the next break. Brazil will be out by then, so their own first preference candidate will have gone. I'm sure it'll be ok.'

Alexei replied: 'It had better be, Helmut, it had better be. I hope you're playing straight with me. This is not the time to fuck around.'

'It'll be fine, my friend,' Schneider said coolly. 'Let's get through the next round first.'

By now, the President was ready to distribute ballot paper number three. With fewer candidates remaining, the ballot was quickly concluded and the President gave the result.

'I'm now able to announce the outcome of the third round of voting. Votes were cast as follows: Brazil 6, Germany 8, Russia 10. There was one abstention. As Brazil is the country with the lowest total of votes, Brazil is eliminated and the fourth round will now take place between Germany and Russia. Once again, to enable a brief discussion amongst yourselves there will be a fifteen-minute adjournment before the ballot papers are handed out.'

This time Alexei Baskin went quickly across the room to where the South American Board members were sitting together. Their expressions did not betray their feelings.

'I'm sorry about Brazil,' Baskin said with as much sincerity as he could muster. 'But this is the final round now, and as we discussed, we're asking you to transfer your voting support to Russia.'

The men said nothing. Baskin looked from one face to the other. A bead of sweat ran down his temple. 'That's as we agreed when we came to see you in Buenos Aires,' he reminded them slowly. 'As you know, the Germans are quite content with this arrangement.' Baskin didn't know what else to say. He needed Schneider's language skills to confirm German acquiescence in the plan.

'Yes,' said Javier Sanchez, the senior GFO Board member amongst the group of South Americans, 'but... things change.'

Baskin's face was pale. 'But when we met last night...' he stuttered, '... you said everything was fine.' Deep at the back of his mind, he was stunned to hear the man talking English so well. Why had Helmut insisted on using an interpreter?

Sanchez looked at his colleagues as he answered Baskin.

'I think you'll find that *you* said everything was fine,' he said. 'We were not so sure, and we still aren't sure.' Before Baskin could answer, he added: 'You know it might be best if you left us alone so we can have a few minutes to ourselves.'

'No... no... this is not happening,' uttered Baskin under his breath.

'Hey, you shouldn't allow yourself to get too stressed, Alexei,' added Sanchez with a smile. 'It's only business.'

'Stressed?!' Baskin exploded. 'Where the hell is Helmut?' he almost screamed, and then realised he needed to control himself. 'Let me speak to him,' he said menacingly to himself. 'Where the fuck is he?!'

Baskin stormed off to find Schneider in deep conversation with GFO Board member for the USA Carl Lander and Angelo Mora from Costa Rica. 'Join us, do,' said Schneider with a smile.

Baskin looked at him carefully. He wanted to believe that Schneider was still a friend and co-conspirator, but he wasn't sure anymore. 'Helmut, something is badly wrong,' he said. 'This has all the makings of a complete farce.'

'I can't agree more,' said Carl Lander. 'Whoever told you the USA would vote for Russia...?'

'You did, you did,' screeched Alexei. 'You said the bloody cold war is over. And you said when we came to see you with Helmut there wouldn't be a problem supporting the Russian bid.'

'Ah well,' said Lander. 'Maybe we hadn't heard from the White House then. The President of the United States is not keen we support the Russians, pretty much down to your government and its Middle East policy I understand,' he said with a casual wave of his hand. 'I'm sorry, Alexei, but that's the way it is.'

'But why didn't anyone tell us this?' said Baskin. 'Helmut you knew all along, didn't you, didn't you?'

A GFO official raised his voice: 'Gentlemen, please go back to your seats.' The voice once more permeated the room. 'The final ballot paper is about to be distributed. Once you've cast your vote, please fold your paper and return it to one of the officials.'

Baskin sat down and looked across at the South Americans, hoping for a sign that they had decided what to do. But it wasn't there. Their expressions gave nothing away.

On Baskin's left was Andriy Kovalenko. He was the reliably pro-Russian Board member from the Ukraine. 'Problem?' Kovalenko asked. 'You look as though you were in trouble with the South Americans.'

Baskin turned to him with a grim smile. 'Americans,' he blurted out. 'South AND North Americans. We spoke to them all last night and everything was ok. Now suddenly things are not ok.'

'Never trust them,' replied Kovalenko impassively. 'You never know where you stand with them. Still, it will all be over shortly.'

And he was right. All the ballot papers had been handed in and soon the officials were returning, once more handing a folded results sheet to the President. He took the folded sheet without looking at it.

'I have here the result. After four rounds of voting, we now have the winner of the bidding contest to host the GFO 2003 World Cup.'

He beckoned to a small, stocky man standing close to the rostrum. He talked quietly to the man for a moment and handed him the sheet of paper. With practised dexterity, the man took an A5 envelope from his inside jacket pocket and slipped the folded paper inside it. He nodded to Larsen, who turned immediately to address his Board member colleagues.

'Gentlemen, in keeping with our traditions, I will announce the winner to the world at the same time as any of us know the result. I have here a sealed envelope, which has been prepared by our head of security.'

Larsen paused for effect, then slowly looked over his reading glasses, and smiled at his colleagues.

'I entirely trust Monsieur Kuttel. He alone has seen the result. And he is sworn to secrecy.'

The committee members could tell from his smile that the President was about to make one of his little jokes.

'Believe me, I have tried to persuade him to let me see it. But he insists on disobeying his President.'

Larsen let the chuckles subside.

'And so gentlemen, we should now make our way to the Media Centre, where the world's Press are waiting, and where I will announce the result. Seats have been reserved for Board members and the bid teams.'

Chapter 47

Where's Albert?

Isla felt an unfamiliar mix of emotions as she realised that Albert had failed in his purpose at the Board meeting.

Isla liked Albert and admired his courage in pledging to speak out against GFO fraud, understanding very well the storm that he would unleash, and how awful his experience would be. But she also had a professional stake in his adventure. She needed his evidence to stand up her own exclusive story – the best of her life, and one that her Editor agreed would be front page lead the next day as long as it was linked to Albert's claims at the Board meeting.

A plan had been hatched to meet the Editor's demands. Isla was to meet Albert outside the Conference Hall as soon as he could escape from the furore expected at the Board meeting. She would whisk him away in a taxi to a secret Brussels hotel location before any other journalist knew what was happening. She would confirm with him the exact information he had provided at the meeting and the verbatim response of Larsen and other Board members, and then phone her news desk to update the story she had already written.

Isla knew all the facts behind Albert's revelations – partly from her own research but mainly from information he had provided at lunch less than two weeks before. Long and frustrating meetings with her Editor, News Editor and the lawyers had concluded that the newspaper would not publish the story unless it was directly attributed to a GFO source.

There was no doubt that her Editor supported the idea of *The Chronicle* scooping the world's Media: 'I'd just love to see the look on Larsen's smug face when he realised this newspaper had brought him to his knees...' But Albert's testimony was critical to the story's validation.

When two hours of the meeting had passed, and Albert had still failed to appear outside the second-floor goods lift as agreed, Isla was irritated more than alarmed. He had probably been confused by the emotional experience, she reasoned. Anyway, she had plenty of time to find him before other Press people scented anything newsworthy.

She stayed calm, walked briskly around the outside of the Council chamber, and then downstairs to the lobby. Perhaps Albert wanted to put distance between him and his colleagues. Perhaps he wanted to make the getaway with Isla as fast and easy as possible.

But Albert wasn't at the reception desk, nor was he outside the building where the taxis were waiting. Isla broke into a run as she climbed six flights of stairs, pressing lift buttons on each floor in a desperate hope he would miraculously emerge. Gulping for breath, she ran down to reception on the ground floor to phone her office. The paper's switchboard girl told her there had been no calls left by anyone called Sir Albert Lewis.

'Oh, just a minute, there's a call for you,' the girl had said suddenly, and Isla heard her News Editor's voice: 'Isla, what the hell's happening. We were expecting you to tell us when you would be ready to file...'

'I'm on it,' she shouted. She put the phone down. She was breathing heavily as she made her way back to the Press Room outside the Conference Hall. She refused a cup of coffee offered by a waitress but took a glass of champagne from the tray and swallowed it all at once. 'Yes Albert,' she thought, 'what the hell IS happening? Where the hell ARE you?'

Although the Board meeting was held *in camera* as ever, members came out from time to time for comfort breaks, and most were rigorous about refusing to comment on voting progress as the GFO's strict rules required. One or two of them found being privy to the unfolding story too much pressure to bear of course. They couldn't resist the instant Press attention that a muttered comment or two bestowed on them. It would also mean a good lunch sometime in the future, that was for sure.

The journalists gathered in the Press Room were sceptical of off-the-cuff voting reports and winner predictions. GFO events were always shrouded in rumours... and very few were true. Nobody was filing a story until the President announced the winner.

What did seem intriguing, however, was some of the gossip that was gradually emerging about a Board member's behaviour. Rumours had quickly spread about an embarrassing outburst from an embittered and (probably) drunken Englishman. He had said nothing of any importance, it seemed, and he'd left the hall in shame. Nobody knew where he was. 'Poor old England,' laughed a photographer from Albania.

Isla heard them too, and while her colleagues were speculating and seeking more details of this weird story, she found a free phone, and contacted her News Editor.

'Frank,' she said, cupping the phone. 'It hasn't worked... Frank, there's no point in shouting at me.... Let me speak... he didn't do it... he didn't make any detailed claims about Larsen or Germany or Russia or the money changing hands. Seems like he was bullied out of saying anything much. I don't know why. I can't find him. Yes, I said I can't find him. Fuck knows. Listen, it's still a great story, Frank, but we can't run it tomorrow. You'll have to pull it Frank. Of course, I'll have to talk to the lawyers - again. Shit.'

Chapter 48

And the winner is...

The urge to hear the result was enough to get Board members pushing out of the Council Chamber and making their way quickly down a short corridor and into the much larger Media conference centre where the announcement of the winning country would take place.

The Council chamber had been intimate and rather intense. In the short gaps between each round of voting Board members had been able to leave their places and have private conversations with each other, either in some corner of the room, or outside on the patio that looked out over the lake and was well protected by trees.

Had anyone witnessed these comings and goings, it must have looked like an open theatre stage set, with actors appearing from every direction offstage to come and say their piece.

Now the Board members were in a very different environment. Camera lights flashed incessantly, and three hundred journalists created a constant loud buzz of excitement. As the Board members began to arrive, unable to quell their own eagerness, the volume was raised even further. Some members created extra uproar by seeking out their local correspondents, waving and shouting their recognition loudly in their own languages.

As ever, journalists were anxious to get the story first, even though the official announcement was only minutes away.

A microphone was thrust towards Greg Turner as he took his seat.

'Mr Turner, can you tell us who's won?' said a North American voice. Turner ignored the question and continued talking to his Egyptian colleague.

The Board members had pride of place in front of the stage, and as they took up their seats it became clear that two remained empty. A sharp-eyed journalist from *Le Figaro* quickly surveyed the rest of the group. Sir Albert Lewis was missing.

As well as Board members, seats had been allocated to the bid teams to the left and right of the committee. There were also small podiums placed at different points around the room, each allocated to the bidding countries. They were for bid teams to take questions after the announcement of the winner. The GFO believed in fair play. Even losers should be heard.

The President of the GFO was now standing in the wings with the two senior Media officials. They had a perfect view of the hall, but nobody could yet see them. Occasions like this were meat and drink to Larsen. He was the ultimate showman, he was anticipating the attention he knew he was about to get from millions of television viewers, and he would revel in it.

'We'll give them a few more minutes,' Larsen said to the officials. In his hand Larsen had the sealed envelope.

'I take it you two know the winning country,' Larsen said. The man and the woman looked at each other nervously. They had heard the President say in the Council chamber that the GFO Head of Security was the only person who knew the result.

'Yes sir, we do,' said the older man, taking a chance that Larsen wouldn't be shocked or angry. It was traditional for Media handlers to be present at the count for all GFO events, and Larsen was not surprised at their response.

'Don't tell me,' he said playfully. 'It will spoil the surprise!' Then, after another moment or two, he said quietly 'Ok, let's go.'

A door opened to the side of the stage, and a sonorous voice announced: 'Christian Larsen, the President of the Global Football Organisation.'

A smiling President strode purposefully to the microphone at the centre of the stage.

'Ladies and gentlemen,' he said. 'Welcome to the announcement of the host nation for the GFO 2003 World Cup.' He paused to wait for the room to become completely silent.

'After months of deliberation, the GFO Board has today conducted a ballot according to its rules to decide which country will host the tournament. I have here the result.'

The President held up the envelope and slowly presented it to all corners of the room. He then began to open it. Pulling out a sheet of pale blue paper, Larsen unfolded it, and looked at the name of the winning country, showing no reaction.

Then, with a broad smile for the cameras, he announced:

'The winner is... (long pause)... Germany.'

The hall was silent for a moment, as if everyone was absorbing the information, but then there was a general gasp of surprise. Nearly everyone had been anticipating a Russian victory.

Board members turned to each other, seeming to search for explanation in each other's eyes. 'Wow,' Greg Turner said to Joe Kumpa. 'You have to hand it to Helmut. I don't know how he does it, pulling off a result like that. Surely the odds were heavily stacked against him. Amazing!'

Kumpa said nothing but mused: he could think of one or two things Helmut Schneider might have done to people's bank accounts. He had no intention of sharing that thought, however, and smiled back at Turner.

'You know what they say, Greg: if you live by the sword you'll die by the sword. And in the case of Alexei Baskin you could say he lives by the secret deal and he dies by the secret deal.'

Kumpa was enjoying the analogy. He had no sympathy for the Russian campaign leader, it seemed. He continued with a grin. 'Baskin was quite prepared to plot with Schneider. He thought it would give him victory. And if it backfired on him, that's tough. Of course, he'll be hopping mad, but who can he blame?'

To their right, the German delegation had risen to its feet and was celebrating with bear hugs and loud whoops of joy. It wasn't a display that endeared them to many in the hall.

The President steadfastly stuck to his position on stage, smiling without warmth at the Germans' antics. Following GFO tradition, he now instructed all the bid teams to come forward to shake hands with the Board members standing beside him. This was always a potentially awkward moment.

In a few cases, where there was little cause for tension between bid-team members and the men who had determined their fate, handshakes were accompanied by brief, animated exchanges. But there were also painful expressionless encounters, where both sides were clearly anxious to get things over and done with before recriminations became inevitable. The South American Board members seemed particularly concerned to steer away from long conversations. They tended to avoid the eyes of those who shook their hands and were well practiced in looking vaguely into the middle distance.

While this ancient GFO ritual of peace and reconciliation was enacted in front of them, hundreds of journalists busied themselves exchanging information as they tried to fathom out what had actually happened in the voting process. Their failure to work out the story appeared to make one or two of them frustrated and prompted a number of shouted questions towards the front of the hall.

'What happened to the deal between Russia and Germany?' shouted a young Frenchman. 'Did the Germans betray their Russian friends?'

Untargeted towards any individuals, mainly because nobody knew who had the answers, the questions were easily ignored.

The handshaking ritual lasted another ten minutes. Then a hooter sounded the convening of individual national Press conferences. The two Press conferences attracting most journalists were those held by Russia and Germany.

As winners, the German campaign team occupied the hall, while the other teams spilled into ante-rooms outside. Four men from the German team congregated around the dais at the front of the hall. Above their heads a giant screen showed the result of the final round of voting: Germany 13, Russia 11.

DFO President Dieter Bauer took centre stage for his moment of glory in front of the world's Media, expressing his delight at Germany once again winning the contest to host the tournament. He beamed proudly for good reason. This personal exposure would help to bolster his authority back in Munich where his re-election was imminent.

Bauer quickly sensed that the journalists were not in the mood to indulge him for long, however, and he passed on the microphone to Helmut Schneider. Bauer didn't like Schneider, but knew he was a natural street fighter, much better equipped than he was to handle rowdy journalists.

Schneider was not going to miss his opportunity for public glory either of course. He would have to unleash the journalists to put their questions eventually, but he took plenty of time to make his rehearsed speech (aimed mainly at the German Press) and allow for photographs. He said he had always been confident of winning, but never complacent. He thanked his opponents for a fair fight and wished them good fortune in future bidding competitions. At last, with shouts from the floor becoming more and more persistent, Schneider gave way to questions.

The story about 'a deal' with the Russians was the basis of the first shouted questions. Schneider was expecting the accusation and was coolly prepared for rebutting it.

'Deal?' he said, frowning his confusion. 'That is not the way we do things at the GFO or in Germany. We don't believe in murky deals done in a smoke-filled backroom somewhere.'

He looked at the earnest faces in front of him. He sighed a little, as if he despaired of the cynicism of the people questioning him.

'Each country submitted its proposals for hosting the tournament, and Germany's has been fairly judged as the best,' he explained, like a schoolmaster dealing with rebellious students. 'We're proud of our bid. Why shouldn't we be? We have tremendous experience in staging tournaments, and we're confident that Germany 2003 will be the best World Cup ever held.'

He was not surprised that his statement had failed to quell the doubters, and the next accusation was more serious.

'Herr Schneider,' called an American voice. 'There are strong rumours that you promised to support the Russians to win this World Cup bid. And in exchange you were meant to host the European Championships in 2005. Whaddya say to that?'

If Schneider sensed a growing danger, he appeared to show no signs of nerves. Instead, he laughed out loud.

'Well, it's very funny to me that the *Chicago Post* seems to know about this agreement between Germany and Russia, but I didn't... after all I'm merely the Chief Executive representing one of the countries supposedly involved!'

Unabashed, the *Chicago Post* man was quick to come back, however.

'Why then do we hear rumours that the Russians have been betrayed? That last night promises were made by various Board members to support Russia, but in today's vote those people supported you. They voted for Germany.'

Schneider was undaunted.

'I think we must allow our Board members the right to change their minds about how they're going to vote, even in their beds. Indeed, in my experience of these matters people often make up their mind on the day itself.'

'So, Herr Schneider, are you denying that financial incentives made some Board members switch their allegiance?'

Schneider stared at the questioner for a second or two with a grave expression before he spoke. 'It's rather sad,' he said slowly, 'that just because the result of a vote is not as certain commentators would like, they immediately assume something improper has occurred.'

He turned his gaze away from the American in disgust. But if he believed that he had quelled these impertinent questions, he was about to be disabused.

A reporter with a blue-and-red Moscow television badge was next to speak: 'Herr Schneider, I believe that in June, just three months ago, you visited South American football representatives at their headquarters in La Paz. You said at the time that you went to present the German bid.'

Schneider was unsure whether to take on this line of questioning or to dismiss it as presumptuous. But he rarely flunked a challenge or a questioning of his careful planning. 'That's correct,' he said, with an eyebrow arched, expecting more explanation.

'But,' the reporter continued, 'a week ago you went to South America again, this time to Brazil and Argentina.'

Schneider allowed himself another chuckle. 'I hope we've not reached a situation where you gentlemen of the Press are going to question the motives of every meeting or journey we make as football representatives? I've always made it my business to visit colleagues around the world. Germany has a proud record in providing support for the development of the game in many different countries and we intend to continue this work in the months and years ahead.'

He held his breath for a moment, half expecting a more detailed forensic analysis of his South American relationships. He was relieved, but perhaps slightly disappointed, that the questioning was losing its sharpness. He continued to answer every question thrown at him competently and coolly. Unable to penetrate Schneider's defences, many of the journalists were becoming either increasingly agitated, if they were aware of rumours of a 'deal', or bored with the story if they were unaware.

At the back of the Press conference the Laundryman stood as a silent observer. Then he was joined by Greg Turner.

'I've been watching the disintegration of Alexei Baskin.' Turner whispered. 'It's dire. Poor guy is destroyed.'

The Laundryman gave no reaction. 'Well, here it's rather different, as you might expect,' he said at last without looking at Turner. 'Vintage Schneider. Not a single question to ruffle him. Virtuoso performance.' Turner wasn't sure, but he thought he heard the muttered words 'what a bastard'. Before Turner could respond however, he saw that the Laundryman was striding to the ante-room outside the hall, where the Russian Press conference was in full spate.

Stirred perhaps by the accusations levelled at the German team, journalists were now crowding into the room, and at the lectern Baskin looked like a broken man. To every question about a deal with the Germans, he was desperate to unload his sense of betrayal and anger. But he could concede nothing to the world's journalists about an arrangement that was forbidden by GFO World Cup bidding rules. He could say nothing about how Schneider had broken an agreement. And he could accuse nobody on the Board committee of choosing to vote for Germany because Schneider's financial incentives had trumped his own.

'We live to fight another day,' Baskin said weakly, as the journalists started to file out of the room. His voice was full of emotion, his hands were shaking, and sweat was pouring down his face.

The Laundryman gave a little derisive snort, as he left the Russian to his own thoughts. 'That man will not be fighting another campaign any time soon,' he thought to himself. 'Perhaps he never will.'

Chapter 49

Three's a crowd

'Well, Helmut,' said President Larsen as he ushered Schneider to an armchair beside him. 'I hope you're satisfied with that outcome? Close, but you got it.'

The President had invited Schneider to his suite for a celebratory glass of champagne at close to midnight. There weren't many people still up to see Schneider take the lift to the top floor.

Larsen's voice was as friendly as he could make it. His relationship with Schneider was functional. He had never liked the man, but Schneider was a useful ally when their interests coincided.

It was expected by everyone of course that the President would congratulate the winner of the World Cup bid but this meeting was more important than usual. Larsen owed much of his power in the GFO to a keen and forensic interest in the campaign battles that permeated the GFO's operations. He wanted to find out how the German campaign team had been successful: it was always important to him to understand how success was achieved in his organisation.

As he sat down, Schneider handed Larsen a Havana cigar. He smiled warmly at the President as he sucked slowly.

'Yes, we made it,' he said. 'And we owe you our deepest thanks, Christian. Your influence cannot be measured.'

Larsen waved his cigar dismissively.

'After this,' Larsen replied, with a touch of acid in his voice, 'you'll have to go a little more slowly. People will think Germany are getting greedy.'

'I know, I know,' Schneider smiled. He had no sense of the bitterness behind Larsen's comment.

'You're right of course, Christian. But at least everyone knows they will get a superbly organised tournament from us. German efficiency and all that!' He laughed loudly.

Larsen didn't laugh. He tired easily of German claims of superiority in any area. His childhood memories had left their mark. He changed the subject.

'How did Alexei take it?'

'I haven't seen him.' Schneider replied.

'It won't be easy for him,' said Larsen. 'He'll get a hard time in Russia. They expected him to win.'

Sympathy was not in Schneider's nature.

'I'm sure he will. But you know he didn't play the South Americans very well. I think Alexei took them for granted after we had our agreement. Just assumed their votes were in the bag. Quite easy for me to give them a nice little extra incentive after I visited them. Not difficult to persuade these Latins, Christian, as I'm sure you know.'

Larsen said nothing. He didn't like to hear idle talk about Schneider's dealings with GFO members.

'So...' Schneider continued with a satisfied air, 'it all fell into my hands. When Brazil went out with six votes, I reckon they split five to one in my favour.'

He laughed again as he remembered the meeting.

'Of course, your friend Albert Lewis took himself right out of the equation.'

Larsen made no comment.

Undaunted by the President's cold manner, Schneider continued.

'Well at least it didn't come down to your casting vote, Christian. That could have been a bit tricky. The Media get very excited about who votes for who, don't they, but half the time they haven't got a clue what's happening.'

'Yes,' Larsen said. 'There was a lot of guesswork going on at the Press conference, of course. There always is. One or two journalists thought they'd worked out the voting patterns but it doesn't matter.'

'And no difficult questions about... our financial arrangements,' Schneider said with relief.

'No. Everyone seemed more interested in the outcome. Of course, there may be more awkward questions in the coming days...' Larsen looked at the ceiling as he took a long draw on his cigar. 'There's an English journalist...calls himself the *Whistleblower*. He seems to have good sources of information. I'd like to find out who he is.'

'I wonder if there's someone in your office providing him with bits of information,' teased Schneider.

'No there isn't,' Larsen snapped. He continued unsmilingly. 'I hope all our finances are sorted out, Helmut?'

'Don't worry about all that, Christian. The Laundryman is serving your interests very well. He's never been off the phone to my finance guys in the last few months.'

Schneider stood up to stretch his legs. 'Shall we have another glass of champagne?'

As Schneider was pouring the drinks, there was a loud knock. Larsen looked puzzled as he crossed the room to open the door. Alexei Baskin immediately barged his way into the smoky room.

'Well, well, well.' he said. 'What a surprise to find you two together. Having a little celebration? What a pair of fucking bastards you are.'

Larsen and Schneider were unnerved by the Russian's appearance. He stood before them, drunk and dishevelled, barely able to stand upright. His normally carefully combed hair was ruffled. From the state of his suit, it looked as if he had fallen to the ground at some point in the evening.

Larsen felt for a pager in his jacket pocket. It was his direct link to the GFO Head of Security. He didn't want to use it. Any sudden activity on the top floor of the hotel was bound to alert some of the journalists who hadn't yet left for home.

Larsen was watchful. He was experienced enough to know there was nothing he could say at this moment that would pacify Baskin. Schneider on the other hand was tempted to respond aggressively to the Russian's challenge. But sitting with a glass of champagne in his hand beside Larsen, he felt caught in the very act of deceit that Baskin was accusing them of, and somehow this held him back. He didn't move, said nothing, and looked blankly at Baskin, waiting for more.

'How was I so naïve to have thought of you both as friends? Eh...?' Baskin shook his head violently, holding on to the door frame for support. 'Why did I think that after years of loyalty to you, Mr President, I might expect something in return? How stupid was I to believe anything either of you ever said? I've seen you both in action. I've seen what bastards you are. Why was I stupid enough to think you would treat me any differently from anyone else?'

Schneider saw Baskin reach inside his jacket. With difficulty he pulled out a brandy bottle and took a long swig. Schneider couldn't help himself any longer. He wasn't going to be harangued by a drunk. He moved towards him.

'Now look, Alexei...'

'Just shut up, Helmut!' Baskin shouted, swaying to one side with the force of his delivery. 'I'm sick of the sound of your voice.' He glared at Schneider... pointing with one outstretched arm, his eyes closing with emotion.

'I know everything about you,' he slurred. 'I know all about the games you played, the lies you told me about the South Americans. Some gentleman - some agreement.'

Schneider was silent again.

'Yes Helmut, I found out all about that little trick you played last night with the interpreter,' he sneered. 'Very clever. And I know about your secret visit to La Paz to buy support from the same guys you know fucking well I'd done a deal with.'

He stood over Schneider's armchair, breathing heavily, his face contorted with emotion.

'And this...' he said, motioning between the two seated men. 'This... pact with the Devil... How much money have you taken from Russia, Mr President? Tell me. Two million dollars. Three million dollars. Do you care about the agreement we all made?'

He shrugged.

'No. You just change your mind. You support Germany, and you quietly tell your Board member friends to do the same. Because Germany can bankroll you as well. So. Tell me. How much do you cost to buy, Mr President?'

There was silence in the room. Larsen watched Baskin carefully. His eyes were closing with the effect of the alcohol. What would the man do next?

'Well, you're both going to pay a very heavy price for what you've done to me,' Baskin said at last, very slowly. 'I have a gun in my room.'

He moved to the doorway and turned back to them.

'I promise you both. You'll regret what you've done.'

He slammed the door. Schneider and Larsen looked at each other and said nothing.

Schneider took another cigar from the breast pocket of his suit and toyed with it nervously for a moment. He smiled uneasily at Larsen.

'He does have a gun you know. Belonged to his father. He told me about it one day. He takes it with him everywhere, apparently.'

Chapter 50

Consequences

Nothing in his career as a football administrator had prepared Alexei Baskin for the confrontation he had just had with Helmut Schneider and Christian Larsen.

Throughout the campaign, he had always realised defeat was a possibility. He was a Russian. Gloom was in his nature. He had been raised to expect the worst.

But as time had passed, he grew more and more confident that the arrangements that he and Schneider had made, with Larsen's endorsement, were watertight. The logic for the deal with the Germans seemed unarguable. The money to secure support from Board members and, most preciously, from the President was never in doubt.

Russian government institutions, security agencies, and businesses were generous in their contributions – convinced by his entreaties that winning the bid would deliver fabulous riches and influence for all his supporters.

The nature of Schneider's deceit began to dawn on Baskin as his expectations of victory slowly unravelled in the Council Chamber. At first he refused to believe that his German colleague had been responsible. But as the Americans declared their support for Germany, he spied a look of triumphalism in Schneider's face for the first time. This was his doing.

When the scales finally fell from his eyes, it wasn't difficult to believe that Larsen had also betrayed him. As he left the Press conference five hours earlier, ignoring the angry Russian reporters thrusting microphones in his face, he felt a gentle pat on his back. It was Atid Mookjai, a young Board member from Thailand.

'So sorry, Alexei. Really great campaign. But we must vote the way our President likes...'

The scenes in the Council Chamber, in the Press Room, and now in the Presidential Suite seared into Baskin's mind. He was a broken man.

He didn't have far to go to reach his room from the Presidential Suite. Both Baskin and Schneider had suites on the same level as the President. He swayed down the corridor, leaning against each wall from time to time, to steady himself.

He remembered his room number, and when he entered, he knew through the haze of his mind that he had a pressing need. That was it. He negotiated his way across the bedroom to the wall safe. Miraculously, he recalled the number. Clumsily he opened it. His gun was where he had left it, the only object in the safe.

Sitting on the edge of the bed, Alexei Baskin began to cry. Just a few tears at first but then he began shaking uncontrollably as tears streamed down his face.

Something made him get up from the bed to stare at himself in the full length mirror behind the door. He could hardly believe his own state of self-destruction. It made him weep even more with a mixed sense of shame and injustice.

'How could they do that?' he asked his mirror image. He had never felt despair like this.

How different he had imagined this night would be. For months he had played in his mind the triumphant scenes that would accompany his victory. The congratulations from Schneider, and Larsen, and the other Board people who would have gained so much from Russia's support. The preening questions from the Russian news agencies and Media companies. He would be a national hero, bringing home the most prestigious world football event. Finally putting to bed the old suspicions about Russia and its people. He would be publicly honoured by Russia's President. It would be a climax to his career.

He thought about the reality. What would happen now? He would be criticised, ridiculed even, in his own organisation, in the Media, and in the Politburo. He had used vital assets and gambled on his success. And he had lost. He had lost even though Russia were favourites. He had lost to Germany, the enemy of the past, the nation that had no right to win because it had won too many times already.

Baskin felt his whole body surging with nausea. He could feel his heart beating loudly. He was sweating from every pore. Oh my God! My heart, he thought.

He became aware that someone else was in the room.

It was Giselle Schneider.

'Alexei, I came to see how you are. I knocked but the door was...' she began, and then looked at him with horror.

'Alexei, you look dreadful.'

'I feel... I think I'm dying...' he blurted between heavy involuntary breaths.

She put his hand in hers for a moment but withdrew it quickly. She stood up.

'Alexei, I'm going to get a doctor. I'll be as quick as I can. Just lie on the bed.'

She decided it was better to go to the front desk to explain the situation, rather than rely on the phone. She flew down two flights of stairs, found the concierge, and explained the situation as coolly as she could.

'I'll go back to Mr Baskin's room, now. Please bring a doctor there as soon as possible.'

'From what you say madam, I think maybe I call an ambulance. Yes?'

'Yes, yes do that. Just ask them to hurry.'

She took the lift to the second floor, but before returning to Baskin, she went to see if her husband was back in his room. She met him striding down the corridor. Before she could say a word, there was a loud bang. One look at each other confirmed the source of the shot.

'Oh my God.' Schneider said. 'Baskin has shot the President.'

Schneider and Giselle turned quickly together and ran towards the Presidential Suite. Helmut hammered on the door.

'Are you ok Christian? Christian!'

Larsen opened the door. His face was grey. His body was trembling.

Giselle said urgently: 'Is Alexei with you?'

Larsen said: 'No... no... he's not in here...'

Giselle stared at the two men. They were frozen in shock. She left them alone, kicked off her heels and ran to Baskin's room.

The door was open as she had left it. As the two men joined her in the doorway, tears poured down Giselle's face. She turned to Schneider and Larsen.

'You fucking bastards. Both of you. Look what you've done. Just look what you've done.'

Alexei Baskin was lying on the bed. Beside his head on the white linen bedspread was a massive pool of blood.

Chapter 51

Changing the story

When Isla got to her office on the day after her return from Brussels, she steeled herself to ignore both the banter from her newsroom colleagues and the speechless fury of Frank, her News Editor.

She had already filed the main story from the GFO. Readers of *The Chronicle* had been told that Germany would host the World Cup in 2003. She had written a soulless piece, she realised with a little professional shame, mainly regurgitating the GFO's official Press statement. She hadn't much enthusiasm for anything else.

Isla knew there was a much better story: the double dealings that enabled the Germans to secure such unexpected success against the favourites Russia and the involvement of the President and his henchman in securing that victory. As soon as she heard Larsen announce that Germany had won the majority vote to host the 2003 World Cup against all expectations, she had no doubt how the voters had been 'encouraged' to support Germany's campaign.

She was desperate to research this latest twist in the GFO saga that she had tracked for so long and add it to her chronicle of corruption. But at the moment she had no platform for her past revelations, and little appetite to find anything new.

Frank Hedley was still insisting that without an interview with EFO Chairman Albert Lewis – a man who was in the Council chamber as the votes were cast – *The Chronicle* could publish nothing about the GFO but the bare facts. The financial and reputational stakes were far too high for the paper.

Isla knew the prospects for her story were diminishing as the hours passed. Frank now viewed Albert Lewis as a discredited and unreliable source. He guessed that Albert really was as naïve as he had seemed at the Board meeting. He was a 'joke' according to GFO members who afterwards commented on his bizarre interruptions, and Frank accepted their judgement.

It was hard not to believe that Albert's motivation was directly connected to England's embarrassing withdrawal from the bidding competition, Frank thought. Any involvement with him over a GFO story now would be toxic for the paper. Isla had been stupid to get involved and he, Frank, had been stupid to go along with her plan.

Isla Payne had made no contact with Albert since their failure to meet in Brussels. Her first instinct as a journalist had of course been to call him. She wanted badly to know what had happened, why their plan had failed, and even whether she could get her story back on track with his support.

But Isla was still furious and felt personally and professionally let down by him. She had shared her best-ever story with Lewis, trusting him to help her publish it. And he had screwed up. She wasn't sure she could have a conversation with him now. She was hurt to the core.

He had also deeply embarrassed her with her colleagues... in her own office, and particularly amongst those rival male football reporters who had got a whiff of a major disclosure in the air, and who now sniggered that '*The Whistleblower* has dug her own grave' with a non-story. Albert had seriously damaged her career as an investigative journalist, she was convinced. Her reputation within her own newspaper was tarnished. Would her Editor, her News Editor and the paper's executives ever trust her again to break a major story?

At a human level, she couldn't help liking Albert, there was no doubt about that. But above all else Isla was a tough news reporter. Whatever he had to say to her now, however plausible and understandable his excuses, it would all be worthless to her.

As the morning wore on, she tried to concentrate on writing a *Whistleblower* piece about what failing to win the World Cup 2003 bid campaign would mean for Russia, but her heart wasn't in it. Normally she quickly became engrossed in her own work at her desk. 'Typical woman', some of her newsroom colleagues would mutter as they chatted about their own stories, last night's TV, Tracy in Accounts... anything that prevented them from getting down to work.

She gave up on the Russian piece and rifled through the bits and pieces of story leads that Frank had thrown on her desk. But all the Press releases and newswire snippets blurred under her gaze.

As she left her seat to get another coffee from the machine at the back of the office, she noticed through his glass office wall that Frank was looking at the ceiling, mouthing soundlessly as he chewed his pencil. She recognised the behaviour: it was Frank's familiar thinking mode, and it would usually end in a sharing of his thoughts... and a call to action. From time to time, he would glance in Isla's direction. It didn't surprise her when his door opened and he walked purposefully towards her.

'That's where your story is Isla,' he said triumphantly. She waited for illumination.

'Albert Lewis,' he said. 'You know all that shit he gave you about Larsen's bribery and so on. Well, that's an exclusive, love. Only you had all that stuff. You're our star witness. 'How I was nearly fooled by a madman fantasist...'

Isla began to protest as Frank's idea became clear to her, but he was ready to fight his corner. He wouldn't stand for any more of the young girl's nonsense.

'You've got all the evidence he's a loony, Isla. You could bring the old bugger down. The GFO would love that. All you've got to do is get him to admit he lied to you because he was pissed off with England's bid having to be withdrawn. You've got the rest of the story in your notes. Honestly love, it could be brilliant. Turn the whole thing round. I reckon you'd have Larsen and the rest of them eating out of your hand for the next three years... Wouldn't do you any harm here either. Go on – give him a ring now.'

Only twenty-four hours before, Isla would have been horrified at Frank's suggestion. Today, she had no appetite to resist.

Yes, why not, she thought. Talk to him. Find out what he had to say about the GFO meeting. If he wouldn't talk to her... or if he didn't have good reasons for his failure... well, why not stuff him? He'd let her down. He had it coming. And perhaps Frank was right. She could turn it into an amazing story. Nobody else had the lowdown on all Albert's accusations. And Larsen and the rest would sit up and take notice, that was for sure. Yes – maybe stuffing Lewis would be a brilliant move for her and the paper.

It was seven o'clock that evening when Isla finally reached Albert at home. She had tried his office number, and although the EFO switchboard and his secretary hadn't confirmed he was not in, Isla had recognised hesitation in their voices. So from three o'clock onwards she had phoned his home number every half hour.

'Yes, who is it?'

Isla was shaken to hear his voice.

'Albert?' she said, cursing herself for sounding too friendly. Damn.

'Oh Isla. Is that you? Oh thank you so much for ringing. I thought it might be you but I was worried you'd be cross.'

'Albert, I'm absolutely seething!'

She held the phone away from her mouth for a few seconds as she gathered her wits.

'Look... my career is in tatters. And... and... and even more important, those bastards are going to get away with everything. You do realise that? Fuck Albert, we were going to bring those guys down. Have you forgotten how important that was to you when we had lunch? Jesus Christ...'

She paused, hoping that he would make some kind of lame excuse so that she could continue to vent her anger. And yes, right then, she was ready to drill him for information about what happened when he addressed the Board. And if he'd made a fucking idiot of himself, yes she'd happily drag his name through the mud.

'Come on Albert,' she whispered to herself, 'try and defend yourself.' But there was no sound from the end of the line. God, if you've hung up on me...

Then suddenly she heard Albert's voice.

'Yes, I understand completely,' he said, his voice cracking with emotion. 'I've made a terrible mess for you, Isla, I'm so sorry. I don't think I'm cut out for espionage...'

Isla's whole body began to heave as she put the receiver down on her desk and cried silently. Jan at the next desk got up and stood behind her, unsure how or whether to comfort her. This wasn't common behaviour in the newsroom. Nobody had prepared her for this. Jan was relieved when Isla waved her away.

Through her sobs, Isla could hear Albert's voice faintly through the receiver lying on her desk. She put her finger firmly on the telephone button to disconnect it.

Chapter 52

Second opinion

Isla didn't have a partner. She had never been very good at establishing long-term relationships – or relationships of any kind. Some of the men in the office thought she was a lesbian, too embarrassed to admit it to her newspaper colleagues, although she wasn't. Anyway, if she had been, she would have enjoyed shocking them.

At the age of nearly thirty, Isla was disappointed she hadn't found a man to relax with. Part of the problem was she didn't get to meet many single men, and she found very few of those she met attractive. When she did manage to date someone she fancied, she usually scared them off quickly with her intense commitment to work. It wasn't just about her journalism career. She had had the same problem at Sussex University back in the late 80s. Isla always preferred work to play.

She had only fallen in love once in her life as far as she could tell. Three years ago, she was introduced in a pub to a television editor. He was middle-aged, overweight, and drank too much. But he was funny, and intelligent, and he had grey Irish eyes that she couldn't avoid. When the others in her group left the pub, he offered her another drink. He asked her really interesting questions, and he told her about all kinds of things she knew nothing about.

They slept together in hotel rooms on three occasions. Isla afterwards cursed herself for being so naïve, but it never occurred to her that he was married. She sometimes wondered whether she would have minded if she had known, but she didn't have a choice.

He called her at work one day to say that his wife suspected him and he didn't want to risk his marriage. So that was that.

What Isla had was a small group of close individual friends – all men. It was funny, she thought, although she was hopeless at keeping relationships with men, it was her male friends she needed when she was unhappy. Curiously, they were all men who had no direct involvement in her newspaper world. One or two of them had started as boyfriends; one was a cousin; one was a friend of her father's.

When she left *The Chronicle* office after her phone call with Albert, she couldn't face going back to her little flat in Streatham. She called Rob from her desk, and she was lucky. He had just got home to his place in Brixton. He hadn't thought about what to eat, so they agreed to meet at a pizza restaurant in Tulse Hill.

Rob was younger than Isla. They had met at a party, in the kitchen. He had quite fancied her and found her intriguing. They got chatting, and had a dance, but when he tried to kiss her he realised she wasn't interested. It would have been easy to walk away, but he had sensed they had some kind of connection. He admitted to her afterwards that he always found the whole chat-up thing incredibly stressful and was relieved they could talk normally to each other without any expectations of anything physical.

And that was how it was. They met every month or so. Often it was just to spend an evening together in the pub, chatting about nothing. But when Isla needed something more, Rob was a good and sensitive listener. And when he'd heard the problem, he could make insightful suggestions. Isla didn't always take his advice, but it usually helped her decide her own course of action.

She was already at the pizza restaurant when he arrived, and he saw from the full ashtray and the redness under her eyes that he needed to be on top form that evening.

He hugged her, awkwardly, as he always did, and grinned encouragingly. She smiled back weakly.

'Oh God, it's so sweet of you to come out like this Rob...'

He shrugged and started to answer, but when Isla needed to talk, he knew better than to stem her flow.

'The thing is I'm really worried I'm losing it. I don't think I'm up to my job any more Rob...'

For the next twenty minutes, Rob listened as Isla told him about how some elderly guy had prevented her getting an incredibly important exclusive story to Press. She told him that her News Editor had suggested 'shafting' the bloke using information that would still be a 'helluva' story, but that when she got to speak to the bloke that evening she found herself unable to force him to say anything incriminating. She had simply burst into tears. Now she had lost both her incredibly important story, and the 'helluva' story as well.

Rob's face usually carried a well-tried neutral expression when listening to Isla. But on two occasions as he listened that evening he had to take sips of red wine to avoid giving away his feelings. Isla was absorbed in her account, of course, but eventually couldn't help noticing his difficulty.

'Rob... are you smiling?' she asked, horrified.

There was no escape for him.

'Isla, I'm sorry. But is this for real? Are you actually worried that you're going soft?'

He couldn't help himself. His face broke into a broad smile. The surprise made Isla giggle a response.

'Whaaat! Why are you being so horrid?'

Rob grasped both her hands.

'Isla, how many times have we talked about how much you worry that you have NO feeling for the people you skewer in your articles. How many times have you told me you think you're some kind of psychopath?

'And now you're telling me you're worried about being unable to shaft some bloke? You're worried about being *too* nice?'

It was a moment of complete relief for Isla. She felt a sense of clarity and assurance about her life and livelihood that she'd never sensed before. She laughed aloud with Rob. It was the first time she had laughed for months, she thought.

They finished a bottle of claret and ordered two more large glasses after their plates had been cleared away. She hugged Rob goodnight with real emotion... for the first time.

When she opened the door of her flat it was 10:30. Could she? Should she?

She got her address book from a pocket in her shoulder bag and dialled the number. She worried for a moment that Albert's wife might answer. But the tired-sounding voice at the end of the phone was Albert's.

'Yes, who's this?'

'Albert, I'm sorry to ring you so late. It's Isla.'

'Isla?'

'Yes, Albert, I just wanted to say how very brave I think you were to go into that meeting and face all those men.'

The line was quiet. Then Albert spoke, so quietly that Isla had to hold the handset tightly to her ear.

'But it was pointless...'

She waited, but he said nothing more. Isla drew a deep breath.

'Albert... Albert, do you still believe everything you told me about the GFO?'

'Yes,' he said quickly, 'and you know I'm right, Isla.'

'I do,' said Isla. 'But Albert, my paper wants me to discredit you. Get you to say that everything you told me was a lie. To give us a story about you and the EFO.'

He was silent.

'Albert, I won't have anything to do with that. I know you haven't lied to me.'

'I don't know what to say,' Albert replied. 'I haven't lied to you. Would it help you if I said it was a lie? I don't care much anymore. My career is over. Perhaps I should stop being a nuisance – to the EFO, to English football, and to you Isla. Tell me what you want me to say.'

Isla felt tears welling in her eyes once again. This good man was now so broken by events that he didn't care anymore what was written about him.

'Albert, *no*. You and I both believe in the truth. It's not too late if we work together on this. We'll have to write it really carefully, but if you trust me to present your story... I ... I... I don't care what my paper says... I think we can do this.'

Chapter 53

Retribution

November 1997

'Did you hear me, Albert? I said I'm just popping out to see Marjorie. She's home now after her hip.'

'Oh, ok, love,' said Albert.

Monica turned back from the hall and put her head round the lounge door. 'Are you alright, Albert? You're not still thinking about Simon Carslake?'

'No, no love I'm fine. Off you go. Oh, you might need some petrol. Morrisons is on the way to Marjorie's. You'll get a good price there.'

Still thinking about Simon? Albert smiled to himself. Perhaps a few years ago he might have been worried about a young man with a young family without a job – and few prospects of finding one soon. He might have been horrified at the thought that he'd put him in that position. But not today. Albert had been through too much heartache himself to feel sympathy for a man he despised as much as anyone he had ever known.

Anyway, Simon would be fine. He'd made a pile. There would be plenty of opportunities in the future. Even after the EFO had set up its enquiry into why he had resigned so suddenly as Chief Executive and left the country. Even after the police had got hold of him to understand his involvement with a London crime family. People like Simon usually came up smelling of roses.

There was collateral damage that was much more important to Albert than the fate of Simon Carslake – or any of the other so-called football men whose careers his story might have affected.

Isla Payne his journalist friend, for a start. Isla had told him not to worry that she'd been forced to leave *The Chronicle*, but he did.

When he first agreed to work with Isla on the GFO story at lunch back in August, there was no doubt that *The Chronicle* would publish it. But after the debacle in Brussels and his failure to provide Isla with a clinching interview, the Editor and News Editor quickly lost interest. They had had enough of Albert. He'd messed them around too long, they told Isla. He was damaged goods.

When Albert had then agreed to go on the record with everything he knew, Isla had pleaded with them to change their minds. And when that did no good she berated her Editor for 'lacking the balls' to publish. *The Chronicle* Editor certainly had no sympathy for any football institution. That's why he'd been happy for Isla to use her *Whistleblower* diary to throw editorial brickbats at these preposterous rogues, he had reminded her indignantly. But providing a platform for a tirade of criminal charges was quite another thing for the paper.

The Editor liked Isla, however, and was stung by her taunt about his lack of courage. So he did what he usually did when confronted with a challenge: he passed the buck. He knew that if he consulted the paper's owner, he'd be instructed to get the views of the legal department. And that's what happened.

As the paper's lawyers had no other basis for forming their advice, they also passed the buck. They spoke directly to the GFO's legal department... and quickly heard back that if *The Chronicle* ran the kind of story proposed, the paper's future would be a short one. This certainly gave the Editor a decent defence for the potency of his *cojonas*, but it wasn't enough to prevent Isla's resignation.

Albert tried to persuade Isla not to leave the paper and forget all about the story if it would save her job. Isla was touched by his concern but there was no stopping her now. This could be the greatest moment of her career. She wouldn't give up this chance to launch an audacious investigation into global corruption, even if it meant walking out on her employer.

And she was determined that the story would indeed be a comprehensive scrutiny of one of the world's most powerful institutions. Isla had been conducting her own investigation into fraud at the GFO for nearly two years after all.

The information she had pieced together led almost inevitably to Germany's 'surprise' win at the September Board meeting vote. She was certain she knew how the committee had been 'encouraged' to support Germany's campaign.

Her gut feel for months was that Schneider's seemingly relaxed acceptance of a Russian win was deeply suspicious. She had heard many rumours about the German Chief Executive's special relationship with the GFO President and his associates. In any other major organisation that would have been viewed as a deeply unhealthy conflict of interests.

A year before, she had heard talk about the Germans helping Larsen win his Presidential bid by encouraging their GFO friends to support him – and intimated as much in her *Whistleblower* column at the time.

A disenchanted GFO Brussels secretary had also relayed local gossip about the 'closeness' between President Larsen and a German woman and Isla guessed from the clues that the woman was Giselle Schneider. If she was right, she knew there was a price to pay for such intimacy somewhere along the line.

Isla also knew something about a man who helped Larsen enforce his allegiances and collect earnings from around the world. She was told by a temporary driver employed by the GFO that this man often disappeared into Larsen's hotel suites at major GFO events. He looked tough, said the driver (after a few drinks had loosened his tongue), more a military man than a football executive.

It didn't take Isla long to link the driver's account with the story told by her informant in Larsen's own 'special projects' office, about a man known as LM. Her financial informant had given her data that showed millions of dollars of payments from mainly Russian sources. If Larsen was receiving big money from the Russians to back their bid, the Germans must have been trumping the deal impressively to encourage Larsen and his team to switch support to them!

But it wasn't just about President Larsen or the Germans; Isla had gathered bits and pieces about Joe Kumpa, too, and particularly how he controlled Africa's football operations and finances. Kumpa's African football colleagues were always happy to talk to a young woman like Isla late in the evening at some obscure restaurant.

Kumpa was known as Mr 10%, guffawed Tommy Mmoye, who had represented a big West African country's football organisation for many years. Nobody minded, he said, as long as the rest of the money was fairly distributed around the continent. 'Now how about coming back to my room...'

Added together, Isla's information presented a picture which alone was too patchy to use as the basis of a credible story. From the time she had lunched with him at *Le Gavroche*, weeks before the GFO World Cup meeting in Brussels, she had known that Albert's personal testimony as an insider was key to establishing the story. It would help her to stitch all her theories together. And Albert's own experience would of course add a powerful voice.

Together, their story was deadly, Isla believed.

When Isla left *The Chronicle* and began to hawk the article around London newspaper contacts, reaction was understandably cautious. Isla was respected amongst broadsheet editors as a highly competent journalist, but this story was sensitive. In the murky world of newspaper ethics, nobody seemed to want to risk a battle with *The Chronicle* if the paper claimed the story was rightfully theirs, let alone to risk a war with the GFO.

But eventually Isla got lucky. *The Morning Citizen* was a direct competitor of *The Chronicle*. The two newspapers had a long history of mutual contempt. *The Morning Citizen's* Editor, Michael Finnegan, couldn't resist the opportunity to spike his rival's guns. *The Morning Citizen* also had deep pockets, and a reputation for taking risks. After a two-hour meeting with Isla and Albert, Finnegan told his legal department he was going to take a chance and run the story. *The Morning Citizen's* owner was in the Caribbean. What the hell!

Once the story was sold, Albert resigned from the EFO. He knew he wouldn't be of use to them any longer. His performance at the GFO World Cup voting meeting had made him a laughing stock. His published accusations in tomorrow's *Citizen* would be fiercely contested by the GFO no doubt, and he would have no future as a member.

His disclosures would also point to his own organisation's fraudulent activities, and underline the fact that all Simon Carslake's misdeeds had occurred on his own watch as EFO Chairman and figurehead for the EFO's World Cup bid – just as his wife had warned him they would.

Albert had discussed with Monica whether to stay on at the EFO to face the inevitable barrage of Media questions, because he hated the idea of disappearing without defending himself and his innocent colleagues. But he and Monica had agreed that the sooner the EFO was able to heal its wounds the better, and that could only occur if he left immediately.

So a week before, just days after Isla had finished writing and submitted their story to *The Morning Citizen*, Albert sent his resignation letter to the EFO Board. He had packed his personal effects into an overnight bag, careful to leave behind – but with some sadness – many gifts from other footballing nations. He had taken a taxi to Paddington to catch the afternoon train to Bodmin.

He was sorry to leave so many friends at the EFO without saying goodbye, but there would be time for that later he hoped. He did phone Eleanor, his secretary, at her home each evening in the following weeks, to find out as much as he could about the fallout from his resignation.

It was Eleanor who told him that Sara Thurlow, the highly capable young woman from the World Cup campaign team, had been appointed CEO, at least on a temporary basis. 'Just the job,' Albert thought. 'Competence, charm, sensitivity. Perfect antidote to Carslake.' And George Pirrie from Newcastle was widely canvassed to follow Albert as Chairman. That was good too. George was younger than many of the Council members, but he was a listener, and a thinker before he said anything. Above all else, George was a football man through and through.

As he turned to the back pages of the *Daily Sentinel*, Albert's smile broadened. There was a double page spread, analysing in detail the likely outcomes of the big matches around Christmas time. Albert loved the football at this time as much as the festivities. Always had done. Soon be the draw for the Third Round of the EFO Cup, he thought. He took a sip from his coffee cup. Life was ok.

Chapter 54

Helping hands

There had been moments in the past few weeks when Christian Larsen had wondered whether his charmed life as President of the Global Football Organisation was about to end.

The death of Alexei Baskin had created a twenty-four-hour Media storm, with all kinds of rumours circulating about Russian intelligence involvement, and even unattributed tales from hotel staff about hearing a gunshot on the night he died. Eventually, the GFO's Press officers had regained control.

It was of course simply a tragic heart attack for a man who had striven effortlessly, but ultimately failed to win a major prize for his motherland. The GFO presented a number of medical experts who testified to how common a heart problem was for a middle-aged man who had encountered a major disappointment.

Larsen himself had released a number of indignant statements about the 'appalling cynicism displayed by some reporters' who appeared to show no respect for 'his relatives and members of his global football family, who are all deeply saddened by the loss of Alexei.'

Having managed the death of a close colleague so successfully, surely Albert Lewis's performance at the World Cup Board meeting should have caused the President very little or no concern? After all, Lewis's outburst had been widely mocked by those Board members in the room, and nobody outside the GFO had been present to hear the Englishman's words.

However, although claims of impropriety at the GFO were not unknown, the accusations Albert had made against Larsen and his closest GFO colleagues face-to-face were unusually intense. The episode certainly prompted some Board members to break their vows of confidentiality and allow a few titbits to leak out.

Fortunately, most of the Media pack in the hotel ante-rooms were too absorbed in the unexpected result of the World Cup bidding process to pay much attention to the rumours about Albert Lewis's behaviour on the day. But once the journalists had filed their stories about Germany's success and were gathered in the bar in the evening, a few recalled what they had heard earlier. As one Rome sports magazine reporter muttered to an Italian Press Bureau colleague: 'Nessun fumo senza fuoco...'

The GFO's Press Officers were quick to counter curious questions. They confirmed that Sir Albert had 'been taken ill...' during the meeting and had gone home. They couldn't be sure whether he'd been 'overdoing it' or was 'depressed that England had withdrawn its bid.' They certainly wouldn't comment on suggestions that Sir Albert had been drinking before the meeting. 'That is scandalous,' said Senior Press Officer Michel Horst, but he refused to deny it.

But it was two weeks after the meeting that Larsen's supreme self-confidence was fully tested by the Albert Lewis affair. GFO Communications Director Yannis Patsikas told him on the phone that an English journalist was said to be hawking around an 'exposé' of the GFO, written in collaboration with the English football Chairman. When Larsen sat opposite Patsikas at a hastily organised briefing lunch, Patsikas noted the beads of perspiration in the creases of the President's forehead. He had never seen that before.

After their lunch, Larsen took a taxi to *Le Chalet*. It was the bar where eighteen months before Schneider and Baskin had told him about their campaign plans for the 2003 World Cup. A long time ago, he thought. He ordered a beer as he passed the bar and found a table in a quiet corner to sit and think.

On the face of it, Albert Lewis was not the kind of man to unnerve him, he mused. He had met and worked with Albert's kind many times before. Committed football men, often a bit simple-minded, but usually so seduced by the fruits of world football administration that they quickly became loyal and trusted colleagues.

Albert's failure to show any evidence of avarice or philandering set him apart, however. Larsen's contacts confirmed that Albert's 1960s three-bedroomed house in Truro was his only property. And try as they might, nobody could uncover any infidelity in his marriage to Monica.

Albert was certainly different. Larsen couldn't imagine any other GFO man he had ever known confront football colleagues and the Organisation's leadership as brazenly as Albert had done at the Brussels meeting. Larsen prided himself on his skills in reading people, but Albert was a mystery. And if he couldn't understand Albert, he couldn't predict his behaviour.

Larsen was also unnerved because he didn't know what and how much the English EFO Chairman really knew about GFO operations. He remembered the conversation he had had with Albert in the lift in Tokyo. Albert had clearly known then about Joe Kumpa's earnings from overseas football aid to Africa. Much to his regret, Larsen himself – in a fit of anger at the man's naïvety – had told him about Simon Carslake's involvement in buying World Cup votes. He hoped to God that Albert wasn't clever enough to carry around a tape recorder.

So when Albert had told Board members at the Brussels meeting that the World Cup voting was a 'sham', what did that mean? Did he know about Schneider's discussions with Board member colleagues? And was it only World Cup voting irregularities that Albert had uncovered? Did he know about the help Larsen had received from the Germans to aid his election? Did he know how much money the Russians had made available to his office, in order to get Larsen's support for their bid? Larsen's eyes narrowed in frustration. How clever was Albert at making connections?

At lunch, Patsikas had shocked Larsen by telling him that the British journalist Albert was rumoured to be in league with was *The Whistleblower*. The name was increasingly familiar to the President and his closest colleagues. It was the pen name of a diarist on *The Chronicle* who had produced irritating commentaries on GFO events for the past few years that were uncomfortably close to the truth.

Fortunately, Patsikas had said that *The Whistleblower*'s newspaper had rejected the GFO story – with a little persuasion from the GFO's lawyers, but Larsen had plenty of experience of determined and intelligent reporters. Would this journalist help Albert piece together and publish – somewhere – anywhere – the kind of information that would condemn Larsen and his career?

A man came into the bar. Recognising the GFO President, he grinned and moved towards Larsen's table with his hand held out. Larsen deftly picked up his coat from the chair beside him and left.

Chapter 55

Off the hook

December 1997

Larsen smiled broadly to himself as his Lufthansa flight touched down at JFK Airport a week later. He was looking forward to dinner at *Osteria Morini* more than he could ever remember. He felt like a condemned man who had just been given a Royal Pardon. He felt his mouth creasing into a smile of pleasure as his taxi drew up outside his favourite hotel on Broadway.

He had time to soak in his deep bath before changing for dinner, and he took fifteen minutes to re-read the London *Morning Citizen* article that had appeared the day before. It was the fourth time he had read it, but he just wanted to be sure that he hadn't missed any vital details.

'EFO director tries to buy World Cup votes', screamed the headline. **'And $1m was for him!'**, was the bombshell in the line below.

The reporter's by-line was Isla Payne, 'international football expert', and the information source was 'EFO top man Albert Lewis'.

Larsen still couldn't quite believe his luck. The story presented EFO Chief Executive Simon Carslake as a scheming criminal whose purpose in leading England's bid to host the World Cup was to secure unimaginable riches for himself and position himself as a crooked international broker, trying to persuade GFO Board members to sell him votes for the contest to host the 2003 World Cup.

According to the story, Carslake had been unsuccessful in securing funds to buy the votes he wanted before hooliganism caused the EFO to withdraw its bid. A number of leading bankers confirmed his attempts to get their backing.

'When he asked me whether Lazarette would fund England's World Cup bid, I was very suspicious. I asked him why, but he didn't give me a straight answer. So I told him I wouldn't touch his scheme with a bargepole!'

Rumours of funding from gangland London were hinted at but unconfirmed. The *Citizen* promised its readers it would ask Simon Carslake himself when they could track him down. The Chief Executive was on the run apparently, believed to be 'on holiday' in Australia, leaving a wife and two children alone in south London.

What really pleased Larsen as he read the story for the fifth time were of course the omissions. He had seen the original article that the *Citizen* had been planning to run – and it met all his worst fears. It was dynamite for him and his closest confederates.

The original piece quoted Larsen himself, confirming to the 'EFO top man' that votes were indeed for sale. It quoted Joe Kumpa, describing how he wanted the EFO's African development budget to be paid into his personal bank account. It was peppered with unattributed quotes from GFO members, talking about the German team's questionable campaigning methods, how the German team reneged on a deal with the Russians, and how it helped to get President Larsen elected. It presented photocopies of photocopies of financial entries alongside various Russian companies.

The part of the original story that dealt with Simon Carslake was much as it appeared now, except that the original draft had been redacted to remove a suggestion that Simon had been offered four votes 'by a Larsen henchman' and that Kumpa had offered Simon a 'sell on' deal to another campaign team once he had bought them. In today's published version, Simon Carslake was a loan operator, prowling around apparently innocent GFO Board members for many months trying but failing to persuade them to sell their votes.

It was the GFO's Chief Attorney Jack Ames whom Larsen could thank for obtaining the original copy. Indeed, Larsen was (secretly) generous enough to credit Ames for saving his bacon. His senior lawyer had played a clever game, mused Larsen, as he got out of the bath and reached for a thick white towel.

When GFO Communications Director Yannis Patsikas got the word that *The Morning Citizen* was next day publishing the story that *The Chronicle* wouldn't touch, Ames's 9:00 phone call to the *Citizen* was friendly enough. He had known Pat Williams, head of *The Morning Citizen*'s legal department, at Oxford. Ames was a Rhodes scholar and prided himself on understanding the eccentric characteristics of the British establishment. He certainly read this situation well. Williams had been horrified to learn only the day before that *The Morning Citizen*'s Editor was publishing Isla Payne's story without any reference to him or his legal team. So when Ames rang, Williams steeled himself for heavy threats.

But, to Williams's great relief, Ames couldn't have been more sympathetic. After inquiring about Pat's family, he assured the London lawyer that he didn't want to make any difficulties with Pat's Editor. But he did suggest that Pat might send over a copy of the article 'in total confidence', just to make sure there wouldn't be any repercussions for *The Morning Citizen*. The last thing Ames wanted was to find himself in court with his old friend, he said soothingly.

Perhaps it was the GFO man's conciliatory tone, or perhaps it was Williams's sense that this was the only chance of saving his own reputation as well as the newspaper's, but he quickly decided to break a fundamental rule of his profession. He emailed the proposed article to Ames.

At 11:00 on the day before publication, Ames and Patsikas sat down with President Larsen to consider the situation. The Simon Carslake part of the story was pretty watertight according to

Ames. Simon was quoted directly, and since Simon had already disappeared in mysterious circumstances, he was hardly in a position to dispute the veracity of the details. Apart from mentions of a conversation with Joe Kumpa, which clearly had to go, Ames recommended no action on that section of the story.

As for the rest of the article, it didn't include one piece of concrete proof against any GFO member. There was spurious gossip, obtained from low-level GFO staff or unnamed members in unnamed restaurants. Larsen and Kumpa were 'quoted', but without any supporting evidence other than the word of this 'EFO top man' whose own organisation was mired in accusations against its own Chief Executive and who was widely suspected of being slightly mad. It was simple enough, Larsen and Patsikas decided: Ames had to tell the *Citizen* that if it published the article, the GFO would riddle it with legal gunfire.

Ames proposed a better solution. He would suggest a compromise to Williams. The GFO had no problem whatsoever with the story about Simon Carslake. It looked like a damn good story, actually, apart from in one or two details. But if the *Citizen* was to include all the specious references to GFO Board members, it would completely undermine the potency of the EFO scandal. So the paper would be left with no story at all. Which was a pity.

His very strong advice would be that Pat Williams should forcefully recommend to the Editor that the story should focus clearly and exclusively on the EFO scandal. And in case there was any doubt about the seriousness of this message, President Larsen would send an immediate email to Lord Perryman, the *Citizen*'s owner, repeating this advice.

Larsen had a good sense of what were workable solutions and immediately agreed to this course of action.

They couldn't of course be absolutely sure whether Pat Williams had followed the advice of his own volition, or whether Lord Perryman had supported him, but the three GFO men were pleased to receive a new version of the article that was proposed for publication by three in the afternoon. It contained no references to GFO individuals at all. Even vague mention of a shady meeting with a man offering to sell votes was carefully worded to make clear that he was not a GFO employee.

They agreed an email to state their support for the article, with a quote from Yannis Patsikas expressing the GFO's deep sadness at the behaviour of the EFO and its senior representatives.

'Noo York Noo York,' Larsen hummed as he donned his charcoal-grey, silk-woven suit and tightened his navy-blue, GFO tie.

Larsen didn't mind that he was the last to arrive at the restaurant table on this occasion. Joe Kumpa and the Laundryman had planned their timing in order to be there to welcome him.

'Christian!' Kumpa exclaimed, jumping up from his chair and half stumbling as he hugged Larsen. The President flinched under the weight of his colleague, but the grin on his face was unmovable. 'Hello my friends,' he said, nodding respectfully to the Laundryman. Only GFO colleagues received a bear hug.

Larsen could see from the almost empty jeroboam of champagne that Kumpa and the Laundryman were in high spirits. He caught Carlos's eye. The head waiter didn't need any more urging and arrived at the table with a fresh bottle in an instant.

Larsen had reported the events of the previous day to the Laundryman by phone and had no doubt that Kumpa would have had explained to him how clever Larsen's strategy towards this London newspaper had been.

'Christian!' Kumpa said again, too loudly for the Laundryman's liking. 'Nobody does it better. You know... like the song. *Nobody does it better!*' He reached out to squeeze Larsen's arm.

'Well,' said Larsen, retaining his grin, 'I think we have good reasons to be pleased.' He raised a glass high above his head.

'I don't believe we'll hear any more from Albert Lewis. He's resigned from the EFO. Yes, I believe that our friends in London are in a terrible mess. There's an arrest warrant out for Simon

Carslake, and the Metropolitan Police are interviewing all the English campaign team and inspecting all the EFO's documents.'

'They'll find nothing,' said the Laundryman. 'Only the three of us know anything about Gerald, and he of course said nothing to Carslake that incriminates anyone from the GFO. Carslake can say what he wants. Nobody will find Gerald.

'But... I can't really comment on anyone else's contacts with Carslake,' he continued slowly, swirling the champagne around his glass.

Kumpa gave a hearty laugh, which quickly turned to a growl as he realised what was being intimated.

'Don't you be so cocky,' he said. 'If you're talking about me... Joe Kumpa knows his business. I talk to these people – yes all the campaign team in Yora. And I make a deal for Carslake. He could have been veeeery useful to us, remember. But it's just talk.' He looked into the Laundryman's eyes. 'I *never* write nothing down. I *never* let them record nothing.

'Sure... I tell Lewis we need the eight million damn quick. And yeah... I tell him the bank account he's to pay the African development money.'

He turned to Larsen, and his voice was no longer strident.

'But listen, Christian. No evidence – right?'

Larsen could see that Joe had been unnerved by stories about him. He was quick to release the tension.

'Of course not, Joe. I have every confidence in you. And so should you!' his eyes flashed for a moment at the Laundryman. 'I don't want *any* finger pointing here. We are *strong* together.'

Larsen waited a moment for his words to strike home. Then he continued in a quieter voice.

'For us, reputation is all. Patsikas has briefed his Press team to deny any more claims from the English. The script is: would you believe people whose top bid campaign guy has been exposed as a fraud?'

Kumpa nodded his head violently. 'Yes... that's the answer. We have all the cards.'

He raised his glass and grinned at the Laundryman as if to make friends once again.

'And what of our business interests?' Larsen asked the Laundryman.

'All in order,' he responded. 'All the money is transferred from the Bundesbank. It will be in your accounts by Wednesday.' He paused as Carlos stood by the table, providing clean glasses for wine and water. But Larsen was quick to reassure him. 'Don't worry about Carlos,' Larsen said, tugging affectionately at the waiter's sleeve. 'I have no secrets from this man.'

Larsen, Kumpa and Carlos laughed, before the President indicated the Laundryman should continue.

'I have some more news from Germany,' he said, glancing at Larsen: 'I hear that the Schneiders have divorced.'

There was silence for a moment.

'Yes, I had heard this,' Larsen responded slowly.

The other two men said nothing.

The meeting quickly regained its bonhomie, and so it continued for two more hours until each man got unsteadily to his feet and made his way to the elevator and their taxis.

When they had left, Carlos told the other waiters he would clear the three men's table, in case there were any documents Mr Larsen would want to be returned directly. There were no documents, and Carlos was able to quickly collect the glasses and dishes and begin to wipe the table clean. Glancing around him, Carlos's last act was to reach inside the vase of freesias in the centre of the table and unhook a small device.

Later, as he got his coat from the staff cloakroom, Carlos took a padded envelope from his inside pocket. It was addressed to Margaret Parham, International Investigations Chief, FBI, 935, Pennsylvania Avenue, Northwest Washington, DC 20535-0001. He put the device in the envelope and sealed it carefully.

Foot notes

Alec McGivan

I was born and brought up in the blue and white part of Bristol. But when my Grandfather came to visit in 1959, and decided to take my older brother to his first football match, it was Bristol City not Bristol Rovers playing at home that day. In due course, I followed in my brother's footsteps to Ashton Gate. We've been devoted to the City ever since.

I was lucky in the first half of the sixties to watch the legendary John Atyeo, scorer of 350 League and Cup goals in 597 appearances for Bristol City. I was there in my usual position at the East End for the last two of these goals, scored in his final game against Ipswich in May 1966.

As a teenager, the covered East End was undoubtedly the place to be. No seats in those days of course. When there was a big crowd, it swayed back and forth amid the metal barriers, and the chanting and singing was deafening. In the Sixties, opposition supporters were often allowed under the same covered end roof as the home supporters, greatly heightening the tension between the two. Approaching the ground and hearing the noise of City's East End created an adrenaline rush like no other.

In my lifetime, Bristol City have enjoyed only four years in the top-flight (1976-80). A treasured moment was the opening game against the mighty Arsenal at Highbury. I remember how proud I felt as we came away with a 1-0 win.

Mention Coventry to any City fan around their mid-fifties and they will recall 19th May 1977, when the boys in red managed to keep their Division One status...just!

Sunderland, playing at Everton the same evening, were also in danger of relegation. It's a long story, one played out in front of nearly 37000 fans.

Suffice it to say that when Bristol City were 2-0 down early in the second half things did not look good. Somehow Gerry Gow, Norman Hunter, Chris Garland and co clawed their way back as we sang our hearts out.

There were other great occasions of course, like winning a Cup Final at Wembley even if it was only the Freight Rover Trophy. Then the game when former England striker Joe Royle scored four on his debut, and the match versus Hull when City keeper Ray Cashley with a huge clearance and a lively wind behind him managed with only one bounce to send the ball into the Hull net.

There were famous FA cup victories too against Leeds United in '74 and Liverpool in '94. I missed the second of these as my wife was about to give birth to our twin children. Much as I love Bristol City, I was not going to miss that!

I have been very lucky to have seen football all over the world, including the '98 World Cup Final and the '99 Champions League Final in Barcelona. Both these games I attended with the truly great Sir Bobby Charlton. That was a privilege I will never forget. But my heart is with Bristol City.

Always has been. Always will be.

Hugh Roderick

I got the football bug at eight years old. It wasn't particularly an age thing. My family had moved from South Wales to Wolverhampton, and the cultural shift from Welsh rugby was irresistible.

But the date was crucial. It was 1960. After eleven years of FA Cup wins, League titles, and European giant-killing, the howl of the Wolves echoed across every school playground in town.

My rugby-loving father finally took me to Molineux on March 10th 1962. I wore my 'old gold' and black silk rosette and looked enviously at the older boys with their noisy wooden rattles. Squeezed in the smoky enclosure (1s/3d for boys), I was hooked for life.

We beat Bolton Wanderers 5-1, but all wasn't well with the Wolves. Eighteenth out of twenty-two in the First Division that season was our worst for thirty years. Talisman skipper Billy Wright had retired, and although Broadbent, Clamp, Flowers, Murray and Slater remained from the fine teams of the 1950s, we only survived relegation with some panicky mid-season signings.

And then things got worse. The Board lost faith and sacked our manager and inspiration Stanley Cullis. I wrote angrily to the Express & Star, but to no avail. Two years later we were a Second Division club.

We got back of course. And in the following decades we found young gold like Peter Knowles and John Richards in our own ranks, and wisely bought Derek 'the Doog' Dougan, Frank Munro, and later Steve Bull. We had our moments to savour. Two League Cups, UEFA Cup finalists, and (joy of joys) wins in the Texaco Cup and Sherpa Van Trophy finals!

I had gone by then – that is to say, physically from Wolverhampton but never spiritually from the Wolves. Now Molineux is unrecognisable from my 1962 debut appearance. And I often wonder how Stan Cullis, creator of the long passing, speedy Wolves teams of my childhood would like the tricksy Portuguese Wolves of the last few years.

It doesn't matter. Because the truth is, whatever the results, whoever the owners, managers and players, I'm always Wolves. Wolves Ay We!

Printed in Great Britain
by Amazon